# THE
# CONSEQUENCE

## THE EVOLUTION OF SIN, #3

*USA TODAY & WSJ* **BESTSELLING AUTHOR**
giana darling

*To the French, who taught me the language of love.*

*"He used to think he wanted to be good, he wanted to be kind, he wanted to be brave and wise, but it was all pretty difficult. He wanted to be loved, too, if he could fit it in."*

—F. Scott Fitzgerald

*Sinclair*

*L*e cœur a ses raisons que la raison ne connaît point.
The heart has its reasons which reason knows nothing of.

Blaise Pascal was a fucking genius. Then again, he was French, and my countrymen knew a thing or two about being in love.

Therefore, it should stand to reason that I may have inherently known a thing or two about love as well, but the idea that love could outweigh logic had never occurred to me. It could have been because I couldn't remember much about my birth parents, my Roma mother and her French husband, who both died mere months apart when I was seven years old. Willa and Mortimer Percy had adopted me when

I was sixteen, but our family was one of deliberate choice and calculated divination. They loved me in their own way, I think, but it was a secondary emotion. A result of pride and cultivation, the way Frankenstein might have loved his monster.

Then there was the love of Elena Lombardi.

She loved me for the reasons I loved myself: my drive and work ethic, my reasonability and sophistication. I enjoyed her company and coveted her mind; the twisted turns it took to shortcut the obstacles in our road to success. She was dark beneath the veneer, hiding away the same inherent ruthlessness I had been born with, and even though we never spoke about the deep-seated ugliness that poverty had wrought on our souls, it was a comfort to both of us just knowing it existed.

The truth was, we saw in each other the ideal partner for our ideal selves, and for years, it was enough because it never occurred to me to ask for more, for the kind of love my kinsmen waxed poetic about...

... and then I saw her.

It wasn't love at first sight. That implies my response to her was subtle and warm, something easy and quintessentially human.

No, the moment I saw Giselle Moore sitting curled up and vulnerable with sickness and fear in the first-class cabin of that plane, my humanity—the class and refinery that I had cultivated for years—sloughed off me like molted skin and revealed the heart of the animal I secretly knew myself to be.

My heartbeat roared in my ears, and my groin tightened with a desire so fierce, I almost doubled over. Only one thought reverberated through my head like a fucking mantra.

Take her.

Take her.

*Own her.*

I felt the pulse of the words in my blood as it scorched through my body and ricocheted off the walls of my heart. I wanted her. It was primal and fiercer than anything I'd ever experienced before. It took every ounce of civilization I had left in me to approach her politely, to keep my twitching hands in my lap instead of spreading them all over her luminous pale skin.

At first, she was reserved with me, barely allowing her eyes to slide my way. I took the time to visually devour her, noting how the golden freckles across her shoulders and cheeks contrasted with the olive tint of her complexion, how her auburn hair glowed like copper under the dim cabin lights. And when she finally met my gaze, I stared hard into her eyes, wide and pure as silver dollars.

I found myself jealous of her smiles, wanting to own them for myself. When I leaned over her, the smell of her lavender and honey fragrance intoxicated me. The soft brush of her aroused breath against my skin nearly made me lose control.

Even as I left her behind on the plane, I knew that meeting her had changed my life, but I could never have guessed how much.

I wasn't a man who believed in fate, but when she showed up at The Westin in Los Cabos, I couldn't say I was surprised. It solidified the proposal that had waited poised on the tip of my tongue since I had first laid eyes on her—a weeklong affair to purge myself of this egregious need for her. Those torturous hours while I had waited for her answer were some of the longest of my life, and they set the precedent for the weeks of indecision that followed, horrific bouts of self-loathing peppered with moments of such clear, bright joy that they obliterated all memory of shame and hatred.

Now, here I was, rearranging everything I had always known and thought I wanted, to make space for my siren, my Elle. The mantra that had infiltrated my head like a siren's song from our first meeting had only intensified, sunk into my bones, and saturated my blood. I couldn't take a breath without feeling her in the previously unused muscles of my heart.

Look at me; she'd even turned me into a fucking poet, a true Frenchman when I'd forsaken my homeland years ago.

I was jeopardizing my reputation and therefore my career, and polarizing the only family that had ever really cared for me. Worst of all, I was forcing the love of my life to choose me over her sister.

Did you want to know the worst thing about this clusterfuck of a situation?

I didn't care.

Everything I had loved before Elle paled in comparison to my need for her. The thought of anything getting in the way of being with her both incensed me and perversely excited me because I knew I would eviscerate it.

It wasn't rational, and it was completely out of character, but as my compatriot Blaise Pascal said, "*the heart has its reasons which reason knows nothing of.*" And since the moment I met Giselle Moore, my heart had stopped being mine to reason with.

Which was how I found myself opening the door to my suite and temporary home at the St. Regis with a completely idiotic smile on my face—high on my courage, exhilarated for the first time in my life at the prospect of my future because a gorgeous redhead by the name of Giselle Moore had just promised to be in it indefinitely—only to find my ex-girlfriend at the door.

It was obvious that Elena had come directly from the airport by the large canvas bag she carried over one shoulder. She was still wearing one of her power suits, an inky black ensemble from head to toe that was meant to detract from her femininity. Instead, it high-lighted her delicate beauty like a neon pen. She looked polished and gorgeous, and not at all heartbroken.

"Daniel, we need to talk," Elena demanded. "I don't care if it's a bad time. I'm not leaving until you hear me out."

It was a bad time.

The worst.

It was fucking *awful* because I had just shared the most extraordinary night of my life with the woman I had finally convinced to be mine, and she was currently tucked away within hearing distance of this very conversation, wearing only a post-coital smile and the scent of our sex on her skin.

Anxiety pricked my skin like a thousand hot needles. I couldn't afford to lose her, not after tasting, however briefly, the possibility of a future with her.

Giselle Moore was mine. And I wasn't going to let anyone get in the way of that.

Not even her sister.

"I appreciate that we need to talk, Elena, but now isn't a good time," I said, widening my stance so that I blocked most of the doorway.

"Don't be ridiculous. It's eleven thirty at night. You can spare ten minutes to talk to the woman you devoted the past four years of your life to," she snapped.

I gritted my teeth against a brief flare of guilt as she brushed past me into the suite. She stopped in front of the couch, delicately placing her coat, bag, and Prada purse there before facing me again with her hands clasped before her. Even in her righteous indignation, Elena comported herself like a princess. She was heartrendingly beautiful, with a face like a Renaissance painting and a spine made of titanium steel. If I had never met Giselle, I knew I would have stayed with Elena for the rest of my life. It would have been so much simpler that way.

Yet the thought was singularly depressing.

Giselle brought my ordered black and white life into color with her passionate strokes and exceptional love. There was no going back from something like that.

I crossed my arms. "I leave for Paris early tomorrow morning."

"I just got back," she said as if that made it unacceptable for me to leave.

I didn't say anything.

"Fine, that just means it is even more imperative that we talk now."

Stuffing my hands in my pockets, I considered the wisdom of either just kicking her out or hashing it out with her. I was well aware that Giselle was in the bedroom listening to our every word. It might do her good to realize how serious I was about leaving Elena, to hear some of the things I needed to say. And a large part of me realized that Elena needed the opportunity to discuss her feelings with me. When I had ended things with her last week, she barely spoke, barely even moved. She just sat perched on the edge of the couch with her hands demurely held in her lap. I deserved a thorough tongue lashing at the very least and even a good hard slap or two across the face. It was, pathetically, the least I could do to ease her pain.

"Okay, take a seat. Can I get you some water?" I asked, moving forward toward the bar to pour myself a much-needed drink.

I had briefly tidied up the suite before answering the door, more out of habit than anything else, and I was intensely grateful for my compulsion now. Still, I cast my eyes about the room, spotting the neat pile of Giselle's clothes partially hidden under the coffee table on the other side from Elena.

*Fuck.*

I composed my features and carefully slid my gaze to her. Thankfully, taking her seat and smoothing the immaculate black pants over her thighs preoccupied her.

"A whiskey, please."

I nodded curtly, two cold glasses of liquor on the rocks already in my hands as I skirted the coffee table. I kicked Giselle's purple garter belt farther into the shadows as I moved past to sit on the chair adjacent to Elena.

She accepted the tumbler with a tight smile and a sincere thank you because her politeness wouldn't allow for anything else.

"What is it that you would like to say?" I asked, leaning back in my chair and crossing one leg over the other.

Elena's eyes flickered over the bare skin of my torso as my muscles contracted with movement. She had never been overly effusive about my looks, something I had always been thankful for, but I knew that the sight of me unclothed affected her. Strangely, perhaps, the knowledge did nothing for me.

I wished for Elle's sake that I was wearing a shirt.

"I want to better understand this early mid-life crisis you seem to be having. I've had time to think about it, and I can see that your company's expansion could be putting too much stress on our relationship." I opened my mouth to speak, but she held up her hand. "We both have one-hundred-hour workweeks, and even though our professions have always come first, we need to remember to take time for us."

I knew she must have taken the time to read articles and books about our situation: what-to-do-when-your-partner-leaves-you-unexpectedly and how-to-breathe-life-back-into-your-relationship psychology dissertations and magazine findings. When Elena was faced with a problem, she researched the hell out of it so that when the opportunity arose, she could beat it to death with thought and theory. I knew all of that because even though we weren't married, we had lived like husband and wife for the past four years. I knew all of the things that made Elena Lombardi frequently intolerable and constantly brilliant. I could see the despair she tried to hide in the lines around her pursed mouth and the helplessness she held tightly in her clasped hands. I was actively destroying her, and it was killing me.

It helped to remind myself that it was the least that I deserved.

She offered me a small, shaky smile.

*Putain.* I was such an asshole.

"It's too late for that, Elena."

"It doesn't have to be. There is no *deadline* on a relationship, no expiration date. We can work this out. A co-worker recommended an excellent couples counselor."

"Not interested."

"Don't be so closed-minded," she urged, her voice still pleasantly modulated even though her hands had unconsciously curled into fists.

"It's not a matter of obstinacy. Counseling wouldn't work for us."

"How can you know that?"

*Because I'm savagely in lust and irrevocably in love with your sister, who, coincidently, is lying naked about fifteen feet away from us in my bed.*

"Because we don't have any issues to work through. We've never been passionate with each other, which I always thought was a good thing," I tried to explain.

"It is," she agreed eagerly.

I scrubbed a hand over my face, caught the scent of Giselle's sex lingering on my fingers, and fought the urge to lick her off my skin. "It isn't a good thing for a couple. How can there be erotic love without passion?"

Elena's lips twisted, then went lax. "Are you saying that you aren't attracted to me anymore?"

*Yes.*

Instead, I said, "Have you ever heard the Greek term, *philia*? It describes the love between two warriors or best friends, a partnership based on unswerving loyalty and respect."

Elena blinked at me. "Are you kidding?"

I spread my hands and shrugged. "The Greeks actually valued it more highly than romantic love."

Her eyes, just shades darker than Giselle's, narrowed dangerously. I sounded callous and cruel, as I often did when discussing emotional issues. It was difficult for me to marry the empathy I felt with the logical methodology of my thoughts. Giselle was the only one who gave voice to my mute soul. I wished, irrationally and unfairly, that she was beside me.

"I..." Elena cleared her throat. "I thought we both valued those characteristics. You make our relationship sound so... unfeeling. Maybe I didn't do a great job of showing it, but you mean the world to me, Daniel."

Her words pressed around me like a cold iron fist. Was it possible to feel heartbroken even though I was the one ending things? I wanted, no, I *needed* to be with Giselle, but in doing so, I was effectively antagonizing my best friend. Elena and I had never been as perfect as we thought, but we were still a team. I was losing my right-hand man, and despite how unromantic that might have seemed, it was fucking devastating all the same.

"You mean the world to me too," I said.

But my love for your sister is bigger than the world.

Elena stared at me. She was still waiting for the punch line of a bad joke, for me to laugh and tell her it was all a ruse.

I sat taller in my chair.

It would be unkind to allow her to think she stood a fighting chance of winning me back, so even though doing it sickened me, I slaughtered the last of her hope.

"But I'm not in love with you, and I'm not going to change my mind about this. I want you to have the Gramercy apartment and the furniture. I've moved out the things I wanted to keep and had them put into storage. We never had shared bank accounts or any other permanent assets."

A choked sob escaped her lips like the whistle from a punctured balloon. She clapped a hand over her mouth, cleared her throat, and resumed her enforced dignity.

I had never wanted to hold her more than I did at that moment.

I cleared my throat too. "I am sorry, Elena. It makes no difference, I know, but I need to tell you that you are my dearest friend. Hopefully, after the dust has settled, we can find that again."

Elena stared at me impassively for a long time. It was utterly silent throughout the hotel suite, but I didn't allow myself to linger over thoughts of Giselle and what she thought of the entire conversation. That would come later. For now, I owed it to Elena to be present.

I tried to relax the muscles in my face, open my posture up so that she could see how much I was grieving, and even, if she was perceptive enough, how little I deserved her understanding.

"You're serious," she finally breathed.

I nodded.

She took in a deep, shuddering breath and let it out slowly through a mouth I had kissed a thousand times. It was indescribably strange to look at the woman I had thought myself in love with and feel so devoid of feeling. I was sure it made me a horrible person. I let myself drown in it for a minute.

"Okay." She stood swiftly and strode forward to offer me her hand.

I stared at it before clasping it within my own. She had long, lean fingers that stroked piano keys more passionately than they had ever stroked me. I rubbed the back of them with my thumb, and it felt absurdly *final*.

"I don't want to see you for a while, but I don't see why we can't be amicable about this. You've become a fixture with my family and friends"—I fought the urge to wince—"and I can accept that sometimes, people just grow apart."

"They do."

She nodded curtly and dropped my hand. I watched her pick up her bag, carefully cross her coat over one arm, and begin the slow walk to the door. It was the most surreal moment of my life to watch my former partner walk out of the same space she unwittingly shared with my new lover. If it hadn't been so fucked up, it might have been a little poetic.

So it took me a second too long to realize that Elena had tripped on something and was bending over to examine the purple scrap of lace caught on the sharp edge of her high heel. It then took me a half-second more than that to register the aberrant look of horror on her habitually placid features and the venomous bite of her words as she whispered, "You fucking cheating bastard."

# Chapter One

*Giselle*

$\mathcal{I}$ was the picture of a well-loved woman.

My skin was still flushed and naked beneath the plush hotel covers, my red hair a chaotic mass of just-fucked glory. I had just enjoyed the most glorious sex with the most glorious man I had ever laid eyes on, and in the morning, after what should have been a night of continued sex and very minimal sleep, I was set to travel to the most romantic city in the world with the love of my life.

But happily-ever-afters were for princesses with hearts of gold and white knights in shining armor, not disloyal Italian artists who got off on being spanked or the morally ambiguous men who introduced them to said fetishisms.

So, it shouldn't have surprised me that Elena had arrived at our door to remind me that this impure princess and tarnished knight did not deserve a happy ending, at least not that easily.

The moment I heard her perfectly enunciated English, I bit my lip so hard the skin broke, and the metallic taste of blood replaced the flavor of Sinclair on my tongue.

It felt too soon after our reunion to ask Sinclair to fight any battles for us. Despite our recent lovemaking and his continued declarations of love and devotion, it was hard not to doubt the man given the inception of our relationship and his initial unwillingness to end things with my sister and his girlfriend, Elena.

Despite my qualms, Sinclair handled the situation with the kind of aloof control that I had come to expect from him. He spoke bluntly, skirting the line between brutality and honesty. I could picture him reclined in a chair, a glass of whiskey dangling from two fingers as he regarded Elena, lazy but powerful like a crocodile waiting in the weeds.

It was harder to imagine Elena's reaction. I didn't know her as well as I should have, and when she responded to Sin's clear dismissal, it was with English words as smooth and emotionless as plastic.

I winced when he spoke about giving her the house, sank further beneath the covers in cringing sympathy when he declared their love platonic, but my empathy felt displaced because Elena didn't seemed perturbed by him. They conducted their breakup like the dissolution of a business agreement.

Like most things that seemed too good to be true at first glance, it all went to hell in a handbasket.

"You fucking cheating bastard." I heard Elena seethe after a long moment of silence.

My mind immediately flashed to my discarded clothes. Before I could consciously assimilate what her words meant, I was hopping up and out of bed. I hovered behind the partially closed door to the main room of the suite, my skin rippled with goose flesh. My body was aflame with the impulse to flee, but there was no place to go.

"Elena," Sinclair began.

"Shut up!" she hissed. "Don't open your lying mouth, Daniel Sinclair. What *the fuck* have you done?"

I heard movement in the other room and darted toward the bathroom. There was no place to hide in the palatial room, so I hurried back into the bedroom.

"Did you seriously cheat on me? Who the hell is she?" Elena was saying, her voice saturated with the sounds of Napoli.

There was no gap to wiggle under beneath the bed. My heart thumped in my ears, pumping so forcibly that my limbs shook with each beat. What would happen if she came into the bedroom and saw me?

"Is she still here?" Elena's voice was just outside the bedroom, high and hard with infuriated disgust.

The door began to swing open just as I dived through the door to the closet. Happily, the walk-in was filled with rows of Sinclair's clothes. I separated the lower level of button-up shirts so that I could nestle between the fabric and the wall. Pulling the hangers back together, I tried to slow my ragged breathing. I hugged my knees to my chest and tucked my chin into the space between my knees; reminded of the times I had hidden as a child back in Naples. I would have taken hiding from the Camorra over my sister any day.

The door to the closet cracked loudly against the wall as it was flung open, and Elena stormed into the room.

"She isn't here, Elena," Sinclair said calmly as Elena stared to rifle through the clothes on the other side of the closet from where I sat.

"Fuck you," she spat. "Like I would believe anything that comes out of your disgusting, deceitful mouth."

Sinclair's sigh echoed throughout the room. "She left just before you got here. I'm sorry you had to find out this way."

My sister snorted so hard, it sounded as if it hurt. "Because there is a good way to find out my fiancé is fucking a *puttana*."

"She isn't a whore, and I am not just *fucking* her."

There was a long pause.

I shifted slightly to peer between a gap in the hanging fabric, unable to curb my curiosity. Elena was in profile, her muscles wound tightly around her nuclear core. I could practically hear her jaw clenching. It was only a matter of time before she exploded.

So, of course, Sinclair lit the fuse.

"And we were never engaged."

My gasp was covered by the horrified, pained noise that those words forced from her. She whirled around to face Sinclair and shoved him so hard that he took a step back. I watched as she advanced on him, pressing him against the wall by the door with both fists clutching his shirt. When she spoke, her mouth was so close to his that for a moment, I thought they were kissing, and my stomach clenched.

"We are common law partners. We live together. We were going to adopt a *baby*. We were going to be a family, Daniel. Don't stand there and tell me we weren't engaged. We were partners in every way that matters."

Sinclair stared calmly down into her face, his hands coming up to cup her elbows gently. "We were *partners*, you are right. We made plans together, supported each other, and navigated our careers together. But we were never partners in the only way that matters." He paused. "I don't believe that we were ever in love with each other."

Elena's hands fell away from his rumpled shirt as she took a shocked step back. Even though it wasn't my nightmare that I was watching unfold, I was acutely aware that our roles could have been reversed. The combination of empathy and relief ran salty, wet tracks down my cheeks.

"Speak for yourself," she whispered.

"I know I'm being..." Sinclair searched for the words and went to tug at his hair in frustration only to realize he had cut it off at Elena's behest weeks ago. "Cruel. But if you will think about it for a while, I know that you will see the truth instead of the brutality."

"Just because I'm not demonstrative doesn't mean I don't love you," she said, her voice weak, fading like the last notes from a wind-up music box.

I wondered if it was because she believed him or if the shock and horror of it all was killing her.

"Tell me, Elena, do you think about me in the spaces between each thought? Do you feel me in your chest like a second beating heart? Do you need me more than your next breath?" Sinclair pounded his fist against his chest and spread his fingers out over his heart. "That is what it is to be *in* love."

"You are in love with the whore," Elena said, her voice once again monotone and without accent. "My God, you actually think you're in love with her."

Sinclair tilted his chin and stared at her coolly. "I am very much in love with her. That doesn't excuse my infidelity, and it doesn't make this any easier to do. But it's the truth."

Elena's pale lips trembled as she pressed both palms to her thighs and smoothed down her trousers. She did it carefully three or four times in a row, her gaze fixed on the movement of her hands over the cloth. Finally, she looked up at Sinclair and stepped forward once more.

"You are the worst kind of bastard, Daniel, because you pretend to be a gentleman. I want you to understand that I won't ever forgive you." She smiled thinly, her face sliced in half by the sharp edges of her mouth.

Sinclair nodded. "I can't expect you to."

"I don't want to speak with you again unless it is through a lawyer," she added.

I understood the spiteful game she was playing, throwing things at him to see how much he could take. I felt sorry for her because I knew he would accept every ounce of bitterness she doled out; no one felt more deserving of hatred than Sinclair.

She was only going to grow angrier when she realized it.

"I understand."

"And I want you to stay away from my family," she snarled, stepping forward to press a finger into his chest. "From now on, you no longer fish with Sebastian, you no longer eat at Mama's restaurant, and you sure as hell stop being friends with Cosima. If I see you with them again, I'll rip your fucking eyes out."

The mass of emotions clogging my throat made it hard to breathe, and I choked on them when I realized that she hadn't even bothered to put a moratorium on a relationship with me.

I knew by the way Sin's jaw hardened that he heard the slight too.

"I was friends with Cosima before I even knew you, Elena," he tried to reason.

"I was your partner before you even knew the whore you've been sleeping with, Daniel," she mocked. "Deal with it. She won't want to be friends with you anymore, regardless. I don't think this is too much to ask for."

For the first time all night, Sinclair softened, stepping forward to lift a tentative hand and place it on her shoulder. She stiffened under his touch but allowed it.

"I am so sorry for hurting you, Elena, and I will do anything to make this easier for you. But I can't promise to stay away from your family. They are my family now too."

A loud *crack* echoed through the room as Elena slapped him hard across the face. "Stop pretending to be reasonable, stop making me feel like the bad guy here. You *cheated* on me, Daniel! If you can't seem to get that through your head, I'll make sure everyone you know understands what a bastard you are so that you don't forget it."

I swallowed a sob, curling my knees into my chest and hugging them, as Elena stormed out of the room. The door to the suite slammed shut with an angry bang behind her.

Sin stood rooted to the spot, his head turned slightly from the impact of Elena's slap. I couldn't breathe without sobbing, so I swallowed convulsively and held my breath. After a long minute, he unfroze, rolling his shoulders back and swiveling on his heel so that he faced my hiding spot. He crossed the space in two huge strides and crouched before me, parting the clothes and lifting my curled form effortlessly into his arms. I was sobbing by the time my cheek hit the overheated skin of his chest.

"I love you, I'm sorry," he whispered, over and over again.

I tried to take comfort from his words, especially because I had yearned for them for so long, but they were only a drop in the ocean of my pain, and I knew I deserved to wallow in it.

# Chapter Two

*Giselle*

I woke up disorientated and disgusted. I remembered slowly that Sinclair had ushered me from the tainted suite and onto the private plane that would take us to Paris. The company plane was an extravagant yet practical purchase given how often he had to travel now that the business was becoming an international entity.

I had been delirious and dehydrated when he had gently buckled me into one of the deep cream-colored leather seats, and before we could take off, I'd fallen asleep.

Now, my body ached from the hours I had spent crying. My eyes felt like dried olives, and I knew my breath was disgusting by the gritty texture on my gums. Yet when I turned my head to look over at Sinclair, he was staring at me with uncharacteristic warmth over the pages of *The New York Times*.

"Hi," I said softly.

"Hi."

"Why are you smiling at me like that?"

"I'm not."

"You are too. It is all in the eyes with you."

He lowered the paper slightly to reveal his small grin, and I laughed quietly in delight.

"I was smiling because you are beautiful but mostly, because you are here with me. It reminds me of the first time I saw you, sick and scared on the plane to Los Cabos. The sight of you punched the breath from my lungs."

"I was barfing into a courtesy bag," I reminded him dryly.

He lifted one shoulder in a shrug. "Most women never look so alluring."

I laughed at him. He was being playful with me to make me feel better, to ease the pain of betrayal I felt like a stab wound in my chest. The agony was worse, I thought, because the wound was self-inflicted. Sin's good humor was like pressure on the damage, staunching the blood flow, but I knew the relief couldn't last forever and that there was a very real possibility that the pain would.

"Come here," he ordered softly.

Immediately, I was up and out of my chair. My legs were shaky as I stepped across the small space between us to where he sat on a leather sofa, but I wasn't sure if it was from my flight phobia or the way he ordered me around.

I knew it wasn't very feminist of me, but I loved my bossy Frenchman.

I folded myself in his lap and sighed heavily when his arms cradled me closer to his chest. We were silent for a few moments, luxuriating in our closeness.

"I want to get this out of the way before I move on to more entertaining ways to distract you." He inhaled deeply, steeling himself. "I have made you miserable these past few months, and I hate myself for it. You were always the right decision, the *only* decision. It is almost inexcusable that it took me so long to commit to it."

I made a noise of complaint, but he ignored me.

"Now that I have you, I don't plan to let you go. I mean it, Elle. In a sense, we barely know each other, we haven't even had the time to date yet, but I want you to know that the heavy things, the serious questions and answers that usually accompany a long-term relationship, are on the horizon for us. I'm not a patient man, and I meant what I said about tying myself to you in every conceivable way. I never want to wake up again like that morning in Mexico, knowing I had let you slip through my fingers."

The ragged edges fluttered and settled around my heart. I let out a heavy sigh and replaced the grief with the deep, pleasurable smell of Sin.

"We need this vacation," I murmured.

"We do. I will need to do some work, but I'm sure you will have people to catch up with, and I will make as much time as possible to be with you."

"Honestly? I didn't have many friends in Paris, only my university mentor, Odile Claremont and Brenna." My stomach clenched at the thought of my AWOL friend. I hadn't heard from her since I had returned from Mexico, and her lack of communication was alarming.

"Candy, Robert, Duncan, and Richard are already in the city, and Cage will be there in a few days."

I instantly brightened. "That's great. It will be like a little Mexico reunion!"

Sinclair smiled down at me tenderly. "I shouldn't have been surprised that you made such a good impression on them. By the time we left, you had them wrapped around your pinky finger almost as tightly as you did me."

I strained up to nip his chin between my teeth. "I thought it was a little weird that they were so accepting of our affair, given that they know Elena."

He sighed into my hair. "The only one who ever liked her was Margot, and even then I think it's because they are so similar."

"Sin?" I asked quietly, after a moment of silence.

"Yes, my siren?"

"I love you."

His arms constricted around me. "I will never tire of hearing you say that."

"I don't plan to stop anytime soon."

The plane chose that moment to dip and tremble, which wrenched an anxious whimper from me before I could help it.

"We touch down in under two hours," Sinclair said, his voice transitioning to its deeper, steelier tones. "Until then, I expect you to be naked."

Warmth sluiced through my veins as I immediately lifted my dress over my head. It turned me on to know that my body reacted to his words even before my mind could.

It was awkward to disrobe on his lap, so I slipped to the ground between his knees as I tossed the dress onto my abandoned chair and tugged off my underwear. When I looked up at him through my eyelashes, he was all I could see.

"I want to watch you take my cock down your throat."

I shivered, goose bumps rolling across my skin. My hands fumbled slightly as I undid his belt and tugged the zipper over the straining bulge in his pants. His eyes tracked every detail as I freed his erection, dragging my tongue from the base of him to the tip. His musky flavor exploded on my tongue.

I wrapped my hand firmly around the bottom of his shaft and squeezed, watching the veins pulse. My eyes stayed on his as I flicked my tongue on the underside of his crown and placed him in my mouth before taking him as slowly as I could to the back of my throat.

"You look so sexy like this," he practically growled as his hand slid through my hair before wrapping the strands in his fists. He didn't try to control my pace, but the firm tug was just enough to remind me who was in control.

"Are you wet, my siren?"

I was. My wetness leaked down the inside of my thighs. I groaned around his length, which made him groan too.

Before I could even process the change, Sinclair had switched places with me so that I was sprawled on the sofa. He quickly pushed my legs apart and secured them wide with the seat belts until I was spread open and immobile. I watched him beneath lowered lids as he stared at my exposed flesh, his expression tight with longing.

"You are so beautiful, Giselle," he breathed, leaning in to plant a kiss on each inner thigh.

I trembled when he dipped a finger into my wetness and placed it in his mouth.

"And you taste extraordinary."

I wanted to tell him to touch me harder, sink into me and take me hard, but as if he could read my mind, he shook his head and settled down more comfortably on his knees.

"I need to take my time with you right now. I want to paint your body with mine, map your breasts and thighs with my tongue and trace new paths across your hips and ass with my fingers. I want you incoherent with pleasure, so saturated in me and my love that my name is the only word in your mouth."

I gasped as he softly closed his lips over my clit and laved me with his tongue. From somewhere deep in my sleeping rational mind, I was astonished he could have such an effect on my body. I only had to feel him in the room with me to have my heart racing. A single touch of his skin against mine ignited a furious fire deep in the heart of me.

I watched his dark red head pressed between my thighs as he pleasured me with languid strokes. The sight of such a powerful man, still impossibly immaculate in a thousand-dollar suit, on his knees before me made me feel dizzy with power.

He worked me over masterfully, pausing whenever I grew too excited, licking along every erotic seam of my body until I shook with desire. I tried to press him closer, yanking his silky hair between my fists, but his warm chuckle only fueled me, and the gentle press of his nose against my clit aroused me but failed to satisfy. Curses fell from my lips in a mad torrent as I begged him to make me come.

He ignored me.

A little while later, my muscles had grown slack, and my head lolled on my neck as I murmured his name over and over again, incoherent with an overload of pleasure.

"My sweet siren wants to come, don't you?" he teased against the folds of my sex. "You want to come against my tongue?"

A soft groan was all I could manage.

I could feel his smile against my damp inner thigh. It was the sign he had been waiting for.

With a skillful twist of his fingers and a soft nip of his teeth over the hood of my clit, I exploded at the seams. It was a messy orgasm, my hoarse shouts primal and my body flailing against my restraints as every muscle in my body clenched and unclenched in a mind-blowing release.

Before I could get my bearings, Sin had gathered my bound legs up in his arms and was pushing inside me. A rattling groan escaped me as he slid across highly sensitive tissues. I was about to protest when he ground his hips against my clit and another orgasm was wrenched from me like a waxing strip, edged deeply with pain and all the more intense for it.

I gasped and shuddered as I held on to him, pushing my hips against his as he surged into me. His name was a mantra, a benediction on my lips. I wanted him to come inside me with a savagery that stole my breath away. My nails scoured down his back to hear his moan. I sunk my teeth deeply into that delicious ridge of muscle where his neck met his shoulder to feel him shudder against my tongue.

"I want to feel you come inside me," I begged.

"Fuck," he groaned. "Take all of me."

"More," I demanded, "I need more."

Sin pressed his damp forehead against mine. "Come with me."

"Yes," I hissed as his hips ground into me and my back arched off the couch.

His lips caught mine and muffled my shriek of ecstasy as I pulsed around him, undone again by this man. He breathed my name against my neck and followed me into blissfulness.

When he collapsed against me, and our sweat ruined his beautiful suit, I ran a limp hand through his hair and hugged him as tightly as my spent muscles would allow. Somehow, this gorgeous creature who had mastered my body from the start was now my partner, the love of my life. I could feel our hearts beat in tandem. I let the terror I had held at bay since I had first laid eyes on him in Mexico tear through me on a deep exhale.

"I've got you," my Frenchman murmured against my neck because he always knew the right things to say. "I've got you now, and I'm never giving you up."

I let the tears roll down my cheeks, and I wasn't sure if they were happy or sad, or maybe even a little bit afraid of the things our fragile new bond still had to face.

# Chapter Three

*Sinclair*

I loved Paris the way someone might love an eccentric, acerbic great-aunt who palmed them five-dollar bills and snuck vodka into their punch at family functions. The combination of her gorgeous excess, her calculated haughtiness and secret grim reminded me acutely of my reasons for loving Elena. It was wrong of me to compare my aloof admiration of the city to my feelings for the woman I had just spent the past four years of my life with, but as I rode silently through the beautiful streets of Paris, it was impossible not to think about my ex-girlfriend.

We had never been to Paris together before. Giselle was a large reason for Elena's reluctance to spend any time in the city, but we also disliked traveling together for business. The purpose of such a trip was to accomplish work, not dilute productivity with romantic dinners and afternoon visits to museums.

The irony of my desire to do just that with Giselle was not lost on me. How could two sisters be so incredibly different and more so, invoke such contrary emotions in one man?

I ran a hand through my hair, a nervous habit I had never kicked. I needed a haircut, but Giselle liked my hair long, and it was finally beginning to curl around my ears as it had in Mexico. I'd grow out my hair to the conceited length of Cage's if it meant Elle would fist it in her small hand while I worshiped every dip and curve of her luscious body.

She was quiet beside me, her anxieties lulled by multiple orgasms and the steadiness of my hand against the bare skin of her thigh. The trust she had in me was evident in my total influence over her body; she was warm, pliable wax under my careful touch, not only ready but willing to be molded into whatever shape and consistency I deemed best for her. No drug, adrenaline sport, or any other false ecstasy could come close to the feeling that power evoked in me.

I wanted this trip to be healing for her, but more than that, I needed it to fortify our bond. We belonged together—this I knew without a doubt—but any relationship, especially one as new as ours, could bow and break under the strain of so much hatred and so many lies. I needed to tie myself to her in as many ways as conceivably possible so that no amount of external conflict could pull us apart. My selfish desire to do this was so great, I was even contemplating a fucking tattoo of her name across my chest. Unreasonably, I wondered if she might consider the same thing.

My fingers clenched unconsciously around her thigh, bringing her bright gray eyes to mine. The serenity in her expression calmed me.

"You are very quiet," I noted.

Her lips twitched. "It's making you uncomfortable."

I raised my eyebrows at her, knowing it would make her laugh.

I wasn't disappointed.

When she was finished giggling, she leaned toward me to press a fragrant kiss to my jaw. "You are so much more volatile than anyone knows."

"Because I want to know every thought that runs through the gorgeous mind of yours? That's hardly unreasonable."

Her lips pursed in an expression of doubt that I was all too familiar with. Giselle wasn't a confident woman at the best of times, and I hadn't given her much reason to believe in me. She might have believed that I loved her, but she didn't trust that I wanted to love her. I'd been fighting it for so long that she obviously still felt like a burden to me.

God, I was fucking disgusting.

"Giselle," I said, tugging her hands so that she was forced to face me. I ran a hand through her copper-colored hair and let it rest on her cheek. "Have I spent too much time telling you that you are mine and not enough emphasizing that I am utterly yours?"

She smiled slightly, but in her reserved mood, I couldn't tell if it was sincere or meant to placate me. Before I could question her further about it, the car pulled up on the narrow street in Saint-Germain-des-Prés where we would be staying.

I watched with the eager anticipation of a child as Giselle laid eyes on the building. Her beautiful features shone with joy as she realized where we were.

"Sin, how did you know?" she crowed, spinning around to throw her arms around me.

I chuckled. "I may have done a little background check at some point. I was starved for information about you when we weren't talking," I explained with a deceptively casual shrug. She didn't need to know how I had spent countless hours poring over everything I could find about her. "I may have stumbled across your Pinterest account."

Her delighted laugh pealed like Parisian church bells through the Town Car, and the sound echoed throughout my body. I was utterly dazzled by her.

"I've always wanted to stay here. Did you know Oscar Wilde died here in 1900?" She pressed her nose to the glass, her hands spread wide against the pane.

I chuckled. "That would explain why our room is named after him."

She spun to face me, her petal-pink lips soft and dewy as they opened and closed in shock. I had to fight the urge to press them to my hardening cock.

"You are amazing," she breathed.

I sank my hand into the silky hair at the base of her neck and pulled her close until I spoke against those enticing lips. "Only for you."

She kissed me with smiling lips and then dove out of the car. I chuckled as I collected our luggage and followed her into the lobby. I found her standing in the small but ornate reception, her face tipped to the ceiling and glowing with joy. It took my breath away to see her like that, especially after months of causing her only pain.

I snagged her hand as I walked past to check in, but she remained blissed out on our setting and didn't clue in to my exchange until I said, "Yes, my girlfriend and I will need a car to pick us up at eight o'clock to take us to *Chez Dumonet*."

She stared at me as I accepted the old-fashioned key to our room, but I ignored her until we were safely enclosed in the elevator.

"Yes, siren?"

"I'm your girlfriend?"

I struggled not to smile, shrugging one shoulder instead. "A bit juvenile, I know."

"No," she whispered after a brief pause. "It's perfect."

"You can call yourself whatever you want, Elle, as long as it implies that you are mine."

She blushed beautifully.

I led her down the hallway to our famous Oscar Wilde room, opening the door for her so I could watch her expression of awe as she passed into it. Cage had an apartment in the city, my parents had a house just outside Paris in the countryside with enough room for us *and* a traveling circus, but I was glad I had decided on the hotel because it meant I got that look on her face.

"It's just how I imagined. Did you know he was a bit of a social pariah? He was cutting edge and sexually progressive for his age, not to mention very gay." She smiled wryly at me. "It's fitting we're staying here."

I raised an eyebrow. "If you're a homosexual, Elle, I'm afraid you should have told me sooner."

She laughed and skipped over to me, throwing her arms around my neck to pull me down for a loud, smacking kiss.

"Thank you for this."

"Mmm?"

"Thank you for taking me away. Thank you for bringing me here, to the second love of my life."

I smoothed a hand down her hair and collected the ends in my fist so I could tip her head back. "Just how thankful are you?"

Her eyes darkened as her pupils dilated, and her voice was breathy when she said, "Why don't you let me show you?"

My cock twitched when she gracefully sank to her knees before me. Her gorgeous red hair shimmered like flames trapped in a silk tapestry. I had to swallow the lump of longing that clogged my throat. I had her, she was right in front of me, begging for me to take her and own her in the exact way I longed to, but the residual panic of loss still haunted me, and it took me a moment to center myself.

I ran a hand down that crazy beautiful hair, pressing her face into my crotch as I did so. She breathed in deeply, moaning at my scent. My fingers flexed against her head.

"Open my pants and take my cock out."

A little shiver ran down her back as her quick fingers undid my trousers and wrapped around my painfully hard erection. There was a bright flush painted high on her cheeks, and her fingers shook slightly with the force of her arousal. It was enough to make any man feel like a fucking king. How could you not when you had a queen worshipping at your feet?

"Hands behind your back. I want you to use that pretty mouth on me."

I'd never enjoyed blow jobs before as much as I did with Elle. It had a lot to do with the sight of her pretty pink lips wrapped lewdly around the width of my shaft, how she strained to take the length of me down her throat, working past her gag reflex to slot me into that tight canal. Don't even get me started on the thrill I got from looking down into her eyes with my dick stuffed down her throat. But mostly, I loved that as soon as I pulled her off me so I could run my fingers, tongue, or cock through her pussy, it would be absolutely drenched with arousal.

My erection snapped back up to my stomach when she let go, but she was quick to run her tongue up the seam of my balls and the underside of my shaft before taking the entire thing in her mouth with one strong downward suck. She moaned loudly, and the sound vibrated through me, sending sparks up my spine.

"You want this, don't you, my siren? You love to take me straight down your throat."

She moaned loudly. Her lips were tight around my tip as she slowly took every inch of me into her mouth. She tipped her head carefully to look up at me, and there was pure, unadulterated rapture in her eyes. The sight was so erotic it made me see stars.

Before I couldn't, I pulled her off my cock, wincing at the intense pleasure of her lips sucking hard as she tried to keep me in her mouth.

"I have plans for tonight, though, and they do not include coming in your mouth."

She pouted then licked her slick, swollen lips greedily as though she couldn't stand the absence of my taste in her mouth.

Fuck, she was phenomenal.

Before she could react, I had lifted her into my arms and was depositing her on the bed.

"Close your eyes," I commanded softly, rewarding her with a kiss to each shut lid as she obeyed.

I got off the bed and went to retrieve the bag of toys I had brought from my suitcase by the front door. Quickly, I grabbed what I needed from the fully stocked bar and shucked my clothes. On quiet feet, I returned to see Giselle lying perfectly still and serene, just as I had left her.

"Good girl," I said as I moved around the bed to secure her hands and feet to the old-fashioned bedposts. "I've waited for ages to have you like this, and now that we have *time*, I will not waste it."

I got off the bed, smiling slightly at her moan of disappointment, and laid out the implements I would need so they were in easy reach on the bedside table.

"I'm going to touch every inch of your delicious body until your skin is singing and you are beyond begging, until you are shaking and mute with pleasure."

I watched a flush sweep over her body, my words like a brush inked with desire and brushed across all that creamy skin. I hadn't craved a paintbrush between my fingers in years, but the urge to paint her like that was nearly as strong as the urge to take her.

So I compromised.

She gasped as I drew the thick, plush head of a clean paintbrush from just behind her ear, down the elegant line of her neck, and into the hollow of her collarbone. Her skin pebbled under the soft, ticklish strokes, and when I passed circles over her tight nipples, her chest arched off the bed to increase the contact.

"I wish you could see all your gorgeous, creamy skin blush with the pleasure that I'm giving you," I said before groaning in the back of my throat. Her breathing stuttered in response as she sank further into subspace. "It is just a pale pink under this brush, but it will be reddened by the time I'm done with you."

I circled her navel, watching her belly flutter in anticipation, but I dipped the bristles in the divot there. She squirmed when I traced the tender intersection of her legs and groin.

"Be still," I ordered.

Immediately, she held herself taut, only her pulse still bouncing madly in her breasts and throat.

"Good girl," I soothed as I wet the end of the brush in the well of her arousal and swirled the dampened end teasingly over her clit.

Her hips shot off the bed.

"I told you to be still," I reminded her, my voice saturated with displeasure.

She shivered, fisting her hands in the sheets and biting her bottom lip in an attempt to control herself.

I passed the brush once more over her swollen button, round and round in progressively harder strokes until her mound glistened wetly in the low light. Leaning over the bed but careful not to touch her with anything other than the brush, I blew cool air across her sex. Her legs quivered in response. I dipped the brush in her dripping pussy once more before I brought it to her breasts. Her nipple pulled ever tighter as her juices cooled and dried on her skin. She moaned loudly when I followed the path of the brushstroke with my tongue and sucked a nipple into my mouth. I drew on it hard, curling my tongue around her peak.

"Ah," she exhaled a long, low gasp when I did the same thing to the other nipple.

"Your pussy tastes so fucking sweet, Elle. Rich and sweet like wild-flower honey. Here," I said, bringing the brush back to her sex for more of that sugary nectar. "Try it."

I coated her parted lips in her own wetness and watched as her tentative pink tongue poked out to steal a taste. She hummed once before her tongue completed a full sweep of those plump, pouting lips.

My cock throbbed, bobbing against my stomach and leaving a trail of sticky pre-cum there. Before my control slipped entirely, I traded out the paintbrush for a suede flogger. Carefully, I trailed the soft tendrils over her primed skin.

She shuddered.

"Do you know what this is, my siren?"

"No, sir."

"It's a flogger."

She shivered delicately because she knew what that was.

I trailed the falls teasingly over her entire form, lingering until she writhed.

"So eager. Do you need a little pain, siren?"

"Please."

I wondered if she deliberately forgot to address me as sir in order to be punished or if she was so consumed by anticipation that she really forgot. I decided it didn't matter.

My wrist flicked, bringing the soft tendrils down hard across her breasts. A long, low moan wrenched from her diaphragm.

"Please, what?"

I brought the tails down again, once on the tender underside of her left breast and then again on the right.

"Please, *sir*," she gasped.

"That first night I took you in Mexico, I wanted to do this," I explained, modulating my voice so that it was stripped of the furious arousal churning in my gut. "I wanted to beat your breasts red with a flogger and fuck them with my cock while they were still hot."

A strangled whimper escaped her parted lips. The euphoria that came with dominating a beautiful, strong woman, seducing her so completely that she was at the mercy of your darkest desires, thrummed through me like thunder.

"Would you like that, Elle? Would you like me to fuck you here?" I asked while I continued to strategically lay into her beautiful tits.

I wanted to clamp her rosy, taut nipples, but she wasn't ready for that even though the savage in me didn't really care.

"Yes, sir. Please," she said, the last word dragged out on a groan as the edges of the flogger wrapped around one of her nipples.

Her back came arching off the bed.

"Be still," I ordered.

Her body shook with the strain.

The color of her chest was a deep, ruddy pink when I finally set down the flogger. I reached for the glass I left on the bedside table and grabbed a fat ice cube between my fingers. She hissed as I ran it in light circles around her pain-warmed nipple.

The ice melted quickly against her skin. The next time, I reached for two cubes and held them tightly to each nipple until she murmured incoherently, the pain of the cold sharp against the background of pleasure. When those chips dissolved, I leaned forward to lick up the wetness with my tongue before sucking a nipple deep into my mouth.

She tasted fucking fantastic.

The beast inside me roared his approval.

Simultaneously, I took one nipple between my teeth in a firm grip and twisted the other sharply with my fingers.

"Ah," she moaned.

"Do you want me to fuck these gorgeous tits, Giselle?" I asked.

"Please, please, please, sir."

"What if I don't want to? What if, instead, I want to slide into your sweet pussy and fuck you until you beg me to stop?"

She panted heavily in response.

"What if I want to flip you over onto your hands and knees, take my belt to your ass, and make you come in my mouth before I come all over your back?"

A shudder wracked her body, and a little gasp exploded from her lips. That one. That was the one she wanted. It didn't really surprise me. Elle loved it when I did anything to her sweet, round behind.

Moving quickly, I undid the ties around her ankles and ordered, "Turn over. Hands and knees. Get that ass high up in the air for me, Elle."

She scrambled to obey, planting her face in the covers and curving her back so low it had to be painful. I ran a hand over her cheeks and spread them. Her pussy was so wet that her juices had dripped down her inner thighs. Unable to help myself, I licked the trail up her meaty thigh into her pussy and right up to her asshole.

She tasted like pure heaven.

As I retrieved my belt from the ground, I wondered if I was moving too fast. Her body was utterly pliant under my hands, my commands, but BDSM was about trust, and she was new to the game. It was easy to forget that, given how beautifully she submitted, but I didn't want to take her too far because she was ready. Her absolute trust in me was too precious to squander, her body too beautiful to brutalize, her mind too steeped in past sexual abuse to ever allow me to take her sexual sincerity lightly.

Sensing my hesitation, Giselle wriggled her ass in my face and said, "Sir? Please."

"Please, what?" I asked, running a hand over her buttocks again to comfort her, to comfort me.

"I, I want you to take your belt to my ass. I want you to, um, make me come on your mouth, and then I want you to come on me," she murmured.

*Fuck*, but she was perfect. Too good for me. But I was a selfish guy, and I was willing to take it despite my merit.

Without further qualm, I looped my leather belt in my hands and gave my siren what she and I both wanted.

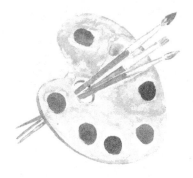

I sat in the dark hours later, the light of my laptop screen the only illumination in our suite. Giselle was asleep on the bed, exhausted from our hours of rigorous play. I hadn't been easy on her—her ass was red from my belt, stripped like a candy cane, and I had left no place untouched by my fingers, tongue, and cock. It was too much when she was already tired from our play on the plane, and I'd acted like a rookie Dominant playing with a shiny new toy. But the truth was, even though I had had her before, I'd never *owned* her. Not like this. My dick stirred in my pants even as I thought about it. The fact that I could mark her now, brand her with sex and pain, my name carved into her voice box with every grateful shout of her ecstasy, wasn't something I imagined I would ever get enough of.

My mind wandered to all the things I could introduce her to in the lifestyle. I didn't want to dominate her outside of the bedroom, not really, but I loved the idea of sending her to the gallery without panties on, of making her touch herself in the bathroom, and of ordering her to wait by the door for me when I came home, her forehead to the ground and her naked ass raised in offering the second I came through the door.

As if conjured by my runaway, deviant thoughts, my email pinged with a note from Elena. I stiffened, my cursor lingering over the notification. I deeply wanted to ignore her and isolate myself from the reality of New York so that I could fully enjoy my time in Paris with Giselle, but I also knew it was my responsibility to Elena to deal with the situation.

So I opened the email.

*To: Daniel Sinclair <danielsinclair@fairedevelopments.com>*
*From: Elena Lombardi <elenalombardi@fieldshardinggriffithllp.com>*

*Subject: Your Depravity.*

*Daniel,*

*I meant what I said yesterday. If you cannot respect my wishes regarding your immediate extradition from my family dynamics, I will be forced to divulge not only the nature of our separation (i.e. your infidelity) but also the truth about your sexual proclivities. You may think I know nothing about your disgusting 'scene,' but I'm a lawyer. I've researched and even represented victims of the "BDSM" lifestyle. Do you not remember my involvement in the Gian Gomeshi trial last year? You like to hit women, Daniel, you get off on causing them pain and forcing them to do things that they normally never would. I don't know how you live with yourself for that. It would be another thing if you tried to restrain yourself, but obviously, you've found some poor victim to take your deviancies out on, and that is why you are no longer attracted to me. I'm not sorry that I never let you beat me, but I am sorry that I thought for even a moment that you were capable of a normal, loving relationship. For her sake, I hope the whore you are supposedly 'in love' with has good health insurance. And I hope she knows whatever sick relationship you have isn't real love.*

*The bottom line is this; stay away from my family, or I'll let the world know your deplorable secrets. I can't imagine the conservative Mr. Paulson would be too happy to hear about those now, would he?*

*Cordially,*

*Elena Lombardi*

I sat back in my chair and closed my eyes as the truth of Elena's email poisoned me from the inside out.

Logically, I knew that properly practiced BDSM could not only be healthy, it could be healing. But I also believed what Elena said about my desires being disgusting. Would Giselle have ever found submission, the pleasure to be had from pain and complete acquiescence, if I hadn't forced them on her? Even now, was she only so interested in the power dynamic because it was the only way she thought she could have me?

I thought back on the four years of my vanilla relationship with Elena and winced. Our relationship had never been about sex, but I could see looking back that I had been deeply unfulfilled by it. Fortunately, it explained my single-minded focus and control as I built Faire Developments from the ground up. If I couldn't have power in the bedroom, I could exert it in all other areas of my life.

Only now, Giselle had alerted me to the possibility of a life as a total Dominant. I wasn't a switch, and I'd also been a powerful force in all aspects of my personality. I didn't want to give up control to anyone; I didn't want to kill the urge to push other people to do my bidding, to see how far I could push someone past their own limits to achieve a goal they had been previously too afraid to attain. Did that make me a sociopath?

The answer, at least at the moment, was a resounding *yes*.

Giselle was what I wanted beyond all things, not just a random submissive to act out my desires upon. I owed it to Giselle to show her that I could love her wholly, without the trappings of a lifestyle that I had missed and longed for. Elena had forced me to give up on the Dom within me, and it had been like living a half-life. Wouldn't that be the same thing for Elle if I forced her to be a sub when that wasn't really what she wanted?

I dragged a hand over my face as my mind surged with doubt and fear. I needed to wake up Giselle so she could have time to get ready for our dinner with my colleagues, but I didn't think I could face her in my current state.

Quietly, I walked over to take a seat on the edge of the bed so that I could look down at her. Her red hair spiraled around her head, bright and glossy like sienna oil paint even in the darkness. Even her thick eyelashes were red, dark against the pale gold of her soft cheeks. My heart ached as I looked down at her. I knew then that a vanilla future was the only way forward for us. It would take some adjusting on both our parts, but Elena was right. I owed it to Giselle to try.

# Chapter Four

*Giselle*

Nerves bounced on my diaphragm, trampolining and cartwheeling in my stomach like circus performers as we walked through the cold night to one of Sinclair's favorite casual restaurants in Paris.

He held my hand, and people gave us appraising looks as we passed them by. It was a heady feeling to realize that they were admiring us as a couple. I squeezed Sin's hand and beamed up at him when he glanced down at me. The soft light of the shops and old-fashioned lampposts spilling into the street turned his hair to pure copper and cast his features in shadow.

"I never thought we would be able to do this," I admitted, somewhat sheepishly.

His eyes were kind, though, his version of a tender smile. "Now you can know that there will never again be a time when you *will not* be able to do this."

He raised our joined hands to place a kiss on my knuckles.

I swooned a little, rocking on my heels, but Sin steadied me with a soft huff of laughter. "Have I worn you out, my siren?"

"The nap helped but yes, a little."

This time his laugh was big and loud enough to attract attention. I stared at his throat, mesmerized by the way it moved with his humor.

He stopped the moment he looked back over at me, his face frozen mid-expression.

"What?" I asked.

"You have this way of looking at me."

"A way?"

"Mmm, a way. A way that tells me that you think of me as the very best kind of man, a person in possession of a very good heart."

"You are that," I agreed easily even though I could tell that he was moved almost to discomfort by the idea.

"I don't want you to be disappointed in me." He said it so softly I had to lean in to be sure of his words. "I will try harder than I ever have before to be that kind of person, but you will have to forgive me my mistakes when I inevitably make them. I wasn't this kind of man before I met you."

His words made my soul ache. I couldn't believe that no one had ever told him how intensely beautiful he was. Though I had met his parents, understood them to be self-serving, I couldn't really fathom how Elena could have refrained from telling him every other moment how special he was. I honestly felt like it was my honor to get to love him, to know him, and take care of him.

I told him so.

He stopped walking and slowly turned to me, slipping one hand through the hair at the nape of my neck and the other around my hip. We stared at each other with wordless feelings in our eyes as he slowly walked me back against a wall and pressed himself close to my body. I relished the heat between us, tipping my head back to maintain eye contact.

"Thank you," he whispered, and I felt, more than heard, the words against my lips.

I pressed a soft kiss to his mouth in response.

When he broke away, he pulled back to smile a ridiculously adorable grin. "Are you ready for some *déjà vu*?"

I frowned but then realized we were in front of *Chez Dumonet*, where we would meet his friends and colleagues from Mexico. It was my turn to grin.

"Lead the way."

I had never been to this restaurant before but only because I had always been too poor for such extravagancies. I loved it on sight for its subtle opulence and quintessentially French features, but I also understood that I was biased by the sight of the Mexico crew sitting around the best table by the window.

"Giselle," Robert Corbett bellowed as everyone stood to greet us.

I couldn't help but laugh as he embraced me in a huge bear hug. Though he was sixty-five years old, he had the kind of virility you would have expected in a much younger man.

When I embraced Duncan Wright next, I couldn't help but note the difference between the two men. The CFO of Faire Developments comported himself with a humble, almost subservient calm and kindness that would have seemed much better suited to a man of Robert's age and slight stature.

Margot only deigned to smile slightly in my direction, but I found myself surprisingly happy to see her. After all, she had been the one to urge me to pony up and claim Sinclair as my own.

Richard hugged me next, but it was a short embrace because Candy was pushing him out of the way before he even had his arms around me.

"I'm the best friend," she explained haughtily as she delicately wrapped her arms around me and then snapped me close with a brutal force that shoved the air from my lungs.

I laughed even as I tried to catch my breath. "Hey, best friend."

"How are you feeling?"

My heart panged. "Like I sacrificed my entire world for the only thing that really matters."

"That was pretty poetic," she said as she pulled away from me and made a face. "But it makes sense. Even though you made the only choice you could, it doesn't make it any less difficult."

"You owe me two hundred big ones," Richard said to Duncan.

I turned to the meek young man and watched him blush furiously.

"I, um, I don't..."

Richard guffawed. "Don't be embarrassed, Wright, you lost fair and square."

"You placed wagers on my relationship with Elle?" Sinclair asked in that perfectly glacial tone that immediately froze everyone in place.

Duncan cleared his throat before stuttering, "Well, logically, you see, I mean, it was obvious to everyone who could see you two in Mexico..."

"Oh, get off your high horse, Sin. We made a bet on you two getting together. Big whoop. Turns out our instincts were correct, which is probably what makes us such invaluable employees too," Candy said.

"And the best of friends," he added, drolly.

Her eyes widened, and she placed a hand over her chest. "You think we're friends? I'm touched, truly."

I laughed at their antics as everyone took their seats. Even though I didn't know the group very well, I felt connected to them because they had been there at the very beginning of Sinclair and me. If anyone could understand the magnetic, inexorable pull between us, it was them.

And they proved their understanding by being nothing but polite and delightful through the entire evening. It was amazing to relax with friends and feel comfortable leaning into Sinclair when he fed me a morsel of beautiful beef bourguignon from his plate and kiss him when I returned from the restroom. Candy coyly commented on the silver and turquoise cuff Sinclair had given me, the very same one that I had admired with her in Mexico, and I was even thrilled when they began to question us about the future as if it were only natural to assume the two of us would be together for a very long time.

"Where will you live when you return Stateside?" Robert asked.

I looked at Sinclair with a deep frown because I hadn't thought of that. We couldn't very well shack up at Cosima's together for a variety of reasons.

My Frenchman didn't look at me, but he squeezed my knee beneath the table. "We'll figure that out when we come to it."

Richard narrowed his eyes at us. "You haven't told anyone yet, have you?"

"No," I admitted, suddenly fascinated with the delicate stem of my red wineglass. "It's a bit easier said than done."

Candy snorted indelicately. "That is officially the understatement of the century."

"Candace," Sinclair warned softly.

"As much as I love to disagree with Candy, she does have a point," Margot chimed in. "What do you do in this situation? Call up your sister and say, 'hello, Elena, you know that man you planned to marry and spend the rest of your life with? Well, I'm sleeping with him.'"

"Boy, I don't envy you that conversation," Robert said with a wince.

"It's not about the sex, though, or at least, it wouldn't be for me," Candy admitted with a guilty look in my direction. "It would be that Sinclair was choosing you to spend his life with and not me."

My heart rattled and rocked on the turbulence of their words. My previous levity drowned beneath the waves.

Sinclair's hand moved soothingly back and forth over my thigh, but it didn't bring me any great comfort.

"It would be the sex for me," Margot countered. "Knowing that my man thought my little sister was hotter? Horrible."

"Quiet," Sinclair ordered, his voice steely. "You are speaking about a situation that is impossible to understand from the outside looking in. More importantly, you are being insensitive to Giselle. She has done nothing wrong."

"Except for having knowingly slept with a taken man," Margot muttered.

Her words found their bull's-eye in the center of my chest.

"You know nothing." Sinclair's eyes blazed bright as a lightning strike as they landed on her. "I will explain something to you which is none of your business even though you seem to think it is. My past girlfriend thought my sexuality was *disgusting*, you understand? She found me repulsive and vile, and when we did have sex, it was never making love. I have great respect for Elena, but she never loved me, not my entire soul. To stay with her would have been a great wrong for both of us. Giselle is my partner now and forevermore. If any of you have a problem with it, I do not care to hear it."

Utter silence fell in the wake of his bitter speech. Even I was a bit afraid of the bristling fury he kept barely contained under that ice-cold façade. Gently, I tangled my fingers with his on my lap.

"I'm sorry," Margot said, more to my surprise. "I didn't mean to cast judgment. I can't say that I fully understand your connection, but I do respect you, Daniel, and if Elle is the woman for you, I won't stand in your way any longer."

"She is the *only* woman for me," he stated imperiously.

I dragged in a shaky deep breath of relief. God, I loved this man.

"Okay." She nodded at him before looking at me. "Okay."

He turned to stare at his other colleagues, daring them to speak out.

Surprisingly, it was Duncan who blinked twice and said softly, "Sinclair, man, we knew she was the one in Mexico almost from the very start. Why do you think we stayed quiet?"

"We want you to be happy. You're happy." Robert shrugged.

It was a lot more complicated than they made it seem, but I could see that their approval meant a great deal to him by the way Sinclair's frown turned to one of confusion and then melted away.

"Now, Elle, how would you feel about a personal tour of the

building site tomorrow?" Richard interjected smoothly. "I could always use an artist's eye."

My laughter eased the tension at the table. "I would love to."

"Speaking of an artist's eye," Candy said, "I've had another three offers for the *Dreams Under Water* painting, Sinclair."

"No."

"Sin... At least consider it. You don't even like it."

I looked back and forth between the two of them—at Candy's frustration and Sinclair's adamancy.

"What are you talking about?" I asked.

"Sinclair's biological mother's painting," Candy explained.

"Excuse me?"

Sinclair's mother had been an artist? How was it possible I didn't know that?

"Candace," Sinclair warned.

"Your mother?" I asked him.

Richard let out a low whistle. "Damn, man, you didn't tell her about your mother?"

"When did you expect me to tell her? I *just* made her mine, and you are jeopardizing that by making it seem like I am keeping secrets from her."

Candy bit her lip. "I'm really sticking my foot in it tonight, aren't I?"

"Yes," Sinclair agreed, but his voice wasn't cold because it was obvious Candy was upset.

I was too. "Tell me about your mother."

He closed his eyes briefly to hide the flare of pain that turned them deep and soft as wet velvet. "My mother was an artist. It was how she met my father, Alain Sinclair. She was selling her paintings at a fair in the countryside outside of Nice. She left her family, her caravan, for him without ever looking back. I think they had known each other for only a few days when she took off with him."

"Oh," I said because I didn't know what else to say.

It was a romantic story, a Frenchman falling in love with an exotic, artistic gypsy, but I knew it had a sad ending, one where

Sinclair was orphaned at the age of seven. His mother's abilities made it obvious where his love of art had come from, so I wondered why he seemed to be so sensitive about her paintings.

Reading my thoughts, as he so often did, Sinclair explained, "My mother, Apolline, produce a lot of work, mostly nature-inspired abstracts. When I had the means, I tracked down as many as I could. The one that hangs over the reception desk is the only one that I have real memories of. She painted it when she discovered she was pregnant. I remember her telling me that she had dreamed of permanency, of a home, a husband, and a baby since she herself was a child, but she always thought it was an impossible dream."

"Hence the name, *Dream Under Water*," I murmured, getting it.

He nodded.

I looked into his face, seeing the pain at the tight corners of his eyes and the strained press of his lips. Talking about this wasn't easy for him, especially in front of others, but he wanted me to know him, and he was trying to open up in a way I was sure he had never opened up before.

"Love you," I whispered.

The tension in his muscles eased as he leaned forward to press a kiss into my hair.

"*Toujours*," he whispered into my ear.

$\mathcal{T}$hat night, Sinclair declared we were too tired to play. I was definitely exhausted from all the emotional upheaval, our two previous, rigorous rounds of sex, and jet lag. I also knew that I would *never* be too tired to play with Sinclair. I told him so, but he only smiled slightly before ordering me to get ready for bed.

"Have you seen my pill pack?" I asked, rummaging through my suitcase.

Candy had done an excellent job packing, but of course, she hadn't included my backup pill packet, and the one that I always kept in my purse had temporarily gone missing.

I looked up at Sin anxiously as he popped his head out of the bathroom to stare at me for a long moment before shaking his head.

"*Putain,*" I muttered under my breath, but he heard me.

"Is everything okay?"

"Yes, but if I can't find it in the next day, I need to find a clinic to get a refill. It's dangerous to miss more than two days in a row." I bit my lip. "If we want to be one hundred percent careful, we should probably use condoms until I can get this figured out."

Sinclair frowned at me. "Do not be ridiculous, Giselle. You are mine now. What is the point if I can't take you bare?"

I laughed as he meant me to and decided to look again in the morning when I was less disorientated from a long flight and emotional exhaustion.

Happily brushing my teeth beside my Frenchman, washing my face and moisturizing while he took a quick shower and then slipping into bed together in our pajamas was its own kind of distracting bliss. He wore charcoal gray drawstring pants that rode low on his narrow hips. They exposed those ridges of muscle that arrowed straight into his groin. I decided they were the best pants in existence and thought about asking him to wear them every day, all day. But then I thought of him in his three-piece suits and kept my mouth shut because those were incredibly sexy as well.

Suddenly, I was overwhelmed by the fact that if I wanted to

dictate his dress, I could because it was something women did when they had a man. They played dress-up with him and for him. I was already planning my outfit for the next day when I would get a tour of the building site for the hotel they were constructing. I wanted to look good to the people we met with because I was a reflection on Sinclair and I wanted them to be proud of me.

On that thought, I tipped my head up on Sin's chest to look at him. "I don't really know much about you."

"You know enough to love me."

I shivered because I was in his arms, and those were good words.

"But I don't know the little things," I stressed.

"The little things are little for a reason. You know what's at the heart of me. Do you need to know what my favorite color is?"

"Yes," I said immediately. "What is it?"

"Giselle..." he said, partly exasperated, partly amused.

"Sinclair..." I mocked him.

There was laughter in his voice when he said, "I'm partial to Titian red."

I blushed as his fingers filtered through my hair. I'd known he loved my hair, and it didn't take a genius to see he was into redheads given he had also been with Elena.

Which led me to my next question. "How many lovers have you had?"

He burst out laughing.

Seriously.

One second we were lying with me tucked into his side, my arm around his belly and his hand around my waist, languid and cuddling. The next, he was frozen mid-crunch, his stomach rock hard beneath my hand and his entire body jerking so much with laughter that my body was thrown off his.

I was so surprised I just stared at him.

When he was finally finished except for the odd chuckle, there were tears at the corners of his eyes.

"Are you quite finished?" I asked, a little enthralled because I had never seen him laugh so hard but also annoyed because what I had asked wasn't funny.

"Oh, Elle." He chuckled before reaching over to tug me back into his side.

I resisted.

He sighed around his smile but gave in, crossing his arms behind his head. I tried not to notice how his biceps bulged, and his abs drew taut.

"Do not be angry with me, *mon amour*. I was only laughing because you bring me so much joy."

"Yeah, right," I muttered, swinging upright so I could cross my legs and fold my arms over my chest.

He bit back a laugh, a chuckle rumbling around stuck in his chest.

"You would really like to know how many lovers I've had?"

"Yes."

"Fourteen."

He searched my face for my reaction, but I was surprisingly relieved. Fourteen wasn't a massive number, and I realized that I wouldn't feel any jealousy about the number anyway as soon as he spoke the words. Sinclair and I were different. He loved me so much that he'd left his orderly life and perfect partner for me, an inexperienced artist.

"Okay," I said as I dropped down at his side again. "What's your favorite meal?"

His arm instantly slid around me again, securing me firmly to his side. His squeeze told me that he was happy with my reaction to his confession.

"Anything with duck."

"I love duck too!"

I couldn't see his face, but I knew he smiled.

"Who are your favorite musicians?"

"Elle, it's been a very long day, and as much as I would love to play twenty questions with you, I also have to be up in four hours to be on-site."

"Okay," I said, a little disappointed.

Sin's hand slid up from my waist into the hair at the back of my head, curling it into his fist so that he could tug my head back in order to look at me.

"We have time now, Elle. There is no need to rush."

Emotion surged up my throat, so just to be safe, I didn't open my mouth to speak. Instead, I nodded.

His other hand slid out from behind his head so that he could gently run his fingers down my jaw. "All the time in the world," he emphasized.

It might have been wishful thinking, but I believed him.

# Chapter Five

*Giselle*

When I woke up the next morning, Sinclair was gone. I vaguely remembered him pressing a kiss to my hair before getting out of bed, but the jet lag had lulled me into a deep, dreamless sleep, and I couldn't wake up enough to give him a proper goodbye.

There was soft music playing throughout the suite, a throaty French voice that I recognized as Jacques Brel. I stretched the lingering laziness out of my muscles before I rolled out of bed to investigate. A shiny silver iPod was plugged into a dock on the antique rolltop desk with a note tipped against it.

ANY SELF-RESPECTING FRENCHMAN LOVES JACQUES. ANY TEENAGE FRENCH
BOY LISTENS TO ENGLISH POP, SO I ALSO ADMIT TO LOVING THE BACKSTREET
BOYS AND CHRISTINA AGUILERA AT ONE POINT. NOW, I LISTEN MOSTLY TO
JAZZ, AS YOU KNOW; MILES DAVIS, FRANK SINATRA, NORA JONES, AND
DIANA KRALL. I COMPILED A PLAYLIST WHILE YOU SLEPT LAST NIGHT.

BISOUS,
SINCLAIR

I grinned down at the note. Even though I knew what he said last
night about knowing the important things about him was right, I still
longed to know the trivialities, the quirks, and fears, and desires that
made Sinclair the love of my life.

I listened to the eclectic playlist as I showered in the gorgeous
wood-paneled bathroom, shaking my booty to Britney Spear's "*Oops, I
Did It Again*" before crooning along to Edith Piaf's "*La Vie En Rose.*"

I had plans to meet Richard at eleven o'clock at the hotel in Saint-
Germain-des-Prés, my old stomping ground, and I wanted to make a
good impression on anyone I might meet who was close with my Frenchman. Candy had packed my bag, and she had done well. I chose a thick
cable knit oatmeal turtleneck sweater with exaggerated braiding and an
inky black pencil skirt that I paired with wicked high heeled black
leather boots Cosima had bought me as an early Christmas present.

As if sensing my thoughts, my phone rang just as I finished
brushing out my curls and stepping into the footwear. My sister's
name flashed across the screen.

"*Bambina!*" Cosima shouted when I answered. "Where are you?
There is a sale at Barney's, and when I was walking by the other day, I
saw this amazing eggplant dress that would be incredible on you. I
don't care what you are doing. Drop it and come shopping with me."

I smiled into the phone. "I would love that, but I'm actually out of
town at the moment."

There was a long silence that I felt physically like Cosima had run
into the wall of my words and was reeling.

"Out of town," she echoed softly.

"Yes."

I bit my lips as I grabbed my purse and heavy jacket before leaving the hotel room. As much as I wanted to focus entirely on my potentially devastating phone call with my sister, I didn't want to be late to meet Richard.

"Okay," Cosima said finally, still soft-spoken. "Do you want to tell me where you are or who you are with?"

"I can... but I'm not sure you want to know."

Another long pause. My heart was beating in my throat. I always suspected that Cosima knew about Sinclair and me, but this conversation was proving it. I just didn't know what she thought of it, and it wasn't exactly something that I wanted to get into over the phone when we were across the Atlantic from each other.

"Oh, Gigi." She sighed. "Please take care of yourself, okay?"

"I am, Cosi. For the first time maybe ever."

I waited for her censure or a reprimand at the very least.

Instead, I got another gusty sigh, and when she spoke again, her voice was tender as a caress. "You are a beautiful woman worthy of epic love. I've always wanted that for you. But love is hard, the epic kind the hardest."

"You sound like you're speaking from experience." Not for the first time, I wondered what horrors my sister's young life had held.

"I am. When you get back from 'out of town,' I will tell you a little bit about it, and you can tell me a little bit about your vacation," she said.

It was both a threat and a promise.

I had better be ready to divulge everything to her when I returned.

Strangely, the thought comforted me. If she wasn't screaming at me for my adulterous ways now, I had hope that she would be at least mildly supportive of Sin and me when I finally told her the whole truth.

She further confirmed this by saying, "I will tell the family that you took a brief vacation. Say hi to him for me and take care, *bambina*."

Before I could respond, she hung up.

I stared at the dark phone screen as I stood in the underground waiting for the metro to take me to the hotel. There were so many subtle layers to our short conversation that I was still processing them when I arrived at the site of what would be a Dogwood International Hotel.

It was set close to the narrow sidewalk that was characteristic of the neighborhood, but there were beautiful wrought-iron gates and green plants lining the walkway up to the white-stone façade. Sinclair had told me that they weren't building a new hotel so much as transforming two adjacent classic French homes into one building. The small space between the two edifices was breached by a new glass and wrought iron atrium that housed the lobby. I stepped through one of the double sets of tall black wooden doors into the marble foyer and gasped at the beauty I found there.

Drop cloths and building supplies still littered the white-veined marble floors and the huge multifaceted windows were grimy with drywall dust, but I could already tell that the space would be extraordinary and utterly Parisian.

"I was going to ask what you thought, but I can tell by the beautiful expression on your face that you like it," Richard boomed as he strode toward me from the left side of the building.

He was wearing a dusty denim button-up and blue jeans, decked out in a Canadian tuxedo that he somehow pulled off. I laughed as he embraced me in his strong arms, enjoying his scent of stone and fresh sweat.

"It really is gorgeous, Richard. You have fabulous taste."

He nodded as he pulled away, prompting me to laugh again. "Sinclair does as well. He is a very detailed man and, frankly, a pain in my ass most of the time. But the result is always worth his breathing down my neck, ordering me to redo the blueprints a thousand and one times."

My Frenchman enjoyed control in all things. "He's a man with a plan."

Richard gave me an appraising look. "He is, indeed. You should be prepared for that."

"Excuse me?"

He took my hand and tucked it into the crook of his arm. "I have a feeling he has a number of plans for you."

"He dated Elena for four years without much forward momentum. I think we are happy to take things slowly."

Besides, we hadn't even told Elena or the rest of my family about our relationship yet. If I was being honest, I was dreading more than anticipating that. Just because I had decided not to live without Sinclair didn't mean that I was eager to sacrifice my family, especially when we had just reunited.

"I think we both know that Elena wasn't right for him. Now that he has the right woman, I have no doubt that he will want to charge ahead. But don't let him sweep you into anything you aren't ready for. He has a habit of doing that to people."

We walked into the left side of the hotel, where the elevator bank to this portion of the hotel was. The one we took was beautifully appointed with a red velvet bench at the back and wood paneling that harkened back to historic French designs.

"I appreciate that you've known him longer than I have, but I really don't think you are right about this. It was hard on Sinclair to make the decision to choose *me*. I think we just need easy now, probably for a while. It's a massive adjustment for both of us but mostly for him."

I mean, as of under a week ago, Sinclair was living with another woman.

That woman being my sister.

Yes, we were definitely going to take it slow.

"How do you even know that I'm the right woman for him?" I asked softly because, despite his declarations, it was difficult not to compare myself to the elegant and successful Elena or find myself unequal to Sinclair's own brand of movie-star-quality good looks and too-good-to-be-true awesomeness. And I meant that in the traditional sense of the word; I was in awe of him.

"If the only thing I knew was that Sinclair, a man I know to be steadfast, whip smart, and intensely loyal, had left Elena and his beloved well-ordered life to be with another woman, I would know it was the right choice. As much as he has succeeded in his professional life, he lived like a robot for years, and I'm sorry to say, your sister has too. They enabled each other. Now, especially when I have had the pleasure of meeting you and more, knowing you, I can assure you that no woman is more perfect for Daniel. He needs light, love, and creativity. You seem to need the things that he has always been ashamed of; his intensity, his need for control, and his deeply hidden sensitivity."

"Oh," I responded because I was struggling under the beautiful weight of his words.

He grinned at me. "So, I wouldn't be so sure about his desire to move slowly. If I'm right, you let me know if he's speeding too fast for you, and I'll have a word with him, okay?" Richard led me off the elevator onto the tenth floor and into a corridor lined with crown molding and subtle floral-patterned silver wallpaper.

He looked down at me while giving my arm a squeeze. "I've worked with him since he was twenty-one years old and hired my firm to renovate his club. Even though he is technically my boss now, I like to think we are friends and maybe even that he thinks of me as a father figure." He hesitated. "I know I think of him as the son I never had."

It was my turn to squeeze his arm as his words flooded me with warmth. From what I had seen of Mortimer Percy, he seemed like a nice enough man, if not completely self-consumed. In direct contrast to him was Richard Denman, Sinclair's right-hand man and, apparently, a nearly lifelong friend. It thrilled me to know that even though Sin underutilized his loved ones, he had them in spades.

"I'll let you know," I promised.

He searched my face for sincerity, and finding it, he nodded curtly. "Okay, let me show you our latest baby then."

*A*fter a long morning of touring the hotel with Richard, I left to walk around the surrounding streets of my old neighborhood while Sinclair finished his meetings somewhere across the city. Habit kicked in, and somehow, my feet took me to *L'École des Beaux-Arts*. It was the safe place I had found, thanks to Cosima and Sebastian's generosity, after the hell I had fled from in Naples. It was the same place that had nourished the creative spirit of masters like Henri Matisse and Anne Rouchette. There was no other place in the world that felt more like home to me than the world-renowned university, and even though my years studying there had been the loneliest of my life, I wouldn't have changed the experience for anything.

I smiled as I slipped through one of the buildings on a whim to find Madame Claremont's studio. It was a large space lined with big square windows on three sides, and currently, a small class of artists-in-training was set up at easels painting a live nude model who reclined comfortably across a raised pedestal. I took a moment to appreciate how technically challenging it would be to reproduce the exaggerated curves and graceful rolls of the large woman on display before I swept the room looking for my mentor.

She stood in the corner farthest from me, but her eyes were

already trained my way, studying the changes in me with the highly trained eye of both an artist and a friend. I took a moment to do the same with her, noting with surprising gratitude that she was absolutely in no way changed. Odile Claremont was the daughter of a poor farmer from Alsace who looked more Germanic than French, with long blond hair she braided across the crown of her head and blue eyes so pale that they appeared colorless. She was in her sixties but looked forty, her pale skin unblemished because she never spent any time in the sun.

I finished my examination and nervously waited for her to do the same. She had more changes to the catalog, so it took her a good few minutes. I tried not to squirm and immediately come to the conclusion that she hated what she saw. The last time I had seen her, the day before I left Paris, she had expressed her joy at seeing my natural red hair for the first time, but since then, I had evolved in more than physical ways, and I knew she would see those.

"Continue. I will be outside in the hall if I am needed," she told the class in a French murmur that somehow carried across the room.

I loved the sound of her Alsatian accent, so despite my anxiety, I was smiling at her when she came my way. Without a word, she grabbed my hand and tugged me into the corridor, closing the door behind us.

"Giselle," she said into my hair as she enfolded me in her arms. "You look so well."

I dragged in a deep lungful of her turpentine and lily of the valley fragrance, feeling my worries evaporate.

"I missed you more than I realized," I said as we pulled away.

She kept my hands in hers as she smiled at me. "And I, you. You promised to write, yet you did not."

I blushed under her reprimand. "Things were... absorbing in Mexico and then New York. It would have been impossible to tell you in print how my life has changed."

"Yes," she said, casting another critical eye over me. "I can see it has changed fast and drastically. Tell me about the man."

"How do you know it's about a man?"

She made that French sound, a huff of breath exploding between her lips, a punctuation of sound. "No woman looks like this for any other reason."

"How do I look?"

"Terrified, happy, and *alive*."

I laughed. "Okay, yes, there is a man. You'll love him."

"He's here?" she asked, her pale eyebrows raised.

"He brought me here to get away. Our situation is a little... unorthodox," I admitted.

"*Chérie*, I am French. We are the kings and queens of unorthodox relationships."

I laughed again because that was true. The former president divorced his wife for his longtime lover, a model and singer, while he was in office. Such a thing would have been unheard of in the United States.

"I'll tell you all about it," I promised. "And I have a show coming up at *DS Galleries*. It's a bit different than anything I've ever done before, but I think you would be proud."

"Do you have pictures?" she asked, excitement making her bounce lightly on her toes.

"I do."

"*Parfait*, I will finish with this class in half an hour, and then you and I will go for wine, yes?"

I pursed my lips, desperately wanting to but worried that it would interfere with whatever Sinclair had planned for that afternoon.

Understanding inherently, Odile shook her head in mock exasperation. "Text your lover and tell him that I insist on stealing you away. I will return you drunk to your hotel, and he will thank me for it."

I laughed again, knowing she was right.

While I waited outside the building in the courtyard, I found out she was right. Sinclair texted back immediately to let me know he would reschedule our afternoon because it was important for me to spend time with my mentor. I loved that he supported me so wholly. Not many men in Sinclair's world, one of business and money, would understand the life and business of an artist, so I was grateful for his mother's profession and for his own investment in the arts.

Our affair in Mexico was also the kernel of inspiration that gave root to my collection. He was the man who had introduced me to the wild passions and delicious shadows of the erotic world, who made it safe for me to explore those depths after Christopher had tainted them.

It was impossible not to think of the Englishman who had ruined my childhood now that I was back in Paris. I had fled to the city because of him and eventually fled from it when he had found me again. I had no doubt that one day he would discover me once more; he was a tenacious but patient stalker. He would never suspect that I had joined my family, though, partially because he had worked so hard to tear us apart.

I mulled over the similarities and differences of the two love triangles I had shared with my polar opposite sister. Christopher had never presented as anything but a gentleman. Mama had loved him, Seamus had relied on him to take care of us when he himself was absent on a drinking and gambling bender, and he had spent considerable time teaching English to us kids. He was all but promised to Elena, a girl nearly eighteen years years younger than him, from the time she was sixteen. With her, he was kind, courteous, and wise, if a bit aloof. They spent hours talking about politics, history, and literature, their heads together over an open book at the kitchen table while Mama cooked, I sketched, and the twins ran around the house playing games.

With me, as soon as I turned thirteen and developed the kind of body that was hard for men to ignore, Christopher was impassioned. It began with innocuous touches, murmured endearments, and encouragements to touch him back and tell him that I loved him. It had taken me years to realize that even though he didn't beat me, he was still a monster, one who brandished love as a weapon of manipulation instead of his fists. He had groomed me to be his since I was a young girl.

The sexual acts didn't start until I was fifteen, and they never escalated to vaginal sex. That, he always said, he wanted to keep for our marriage night. Mama didn't suspect anything untoward when he took me 'out for gelato' or into Rome to see some art gallery or another. I often spent the night with him with my mother's blessing. He never hurt me, but I was always scared, nonetheless.

I didn't know something was really wrong with our relationship until I mentioned it to Sebastian and Elena one day when they were bickering about Sebastian's exploits with a local girl. I'd innocently divulged that kissing was nice, the only thing I liked about sex. Even though I was eighteen at the time, I didn't understand the consequences that my naïve comment would bring. Sebastian had immediately asked if Christopher and I had made love, and when I assured him that we hadn't, not fully understanding the question, he had relaxed slightly but told Mama that I wasn't allowed to be alone with Christopher anymore.

Two weeks later, Cosima had sent a letter telling me that she had the money to send me to *L'École des Beaux-Arts,* and I knew that the twins had orchestrated it to get me away from him.

Elena had reacted differently, obviously. We had never been close, but after that confession, she was cruel to me, calling me names and inviting Christopher over nearly every day but never letting him out of her sight, kissing him in front of me in a way she had never done before. She must have known how desperate he was to get me alone, how much yearning filled his eyes as he stared at me while his lips were locked with hers, but she wasn't angry with him for it. She was angry with me.

I was happy to leave them four months later to start school in Paris. By that time, Sebastian had left, and Cosima was long gone. I was alone in Naples, and I would be alone in Paris, but at least I would be without the two malevolent presences in my life.

Cosima told me years later that Christopher asked for my information all the time, that Mama began to notice his erratic behavior and that she still allowed Elena to move in with him. She also told me that for that half a year our eldest sister had lived with him, he had not been kind to her. I didn't know the details, and I'd never really delved into it before, but it wouldn't surprise me to know that he had sexually and emotionally abused her, taking out his heartbreak and desperation on her because he couldn't have me.

At least, that was the narrative I thought up in order to excuse Elena's blatant hatred of me over the years.

A year after I left, the twins found enough money to move Mama and Elena to New York City, and they left Christopher behind. I didn't know the story there—whether he was happy to see them go or if they fled him like I had. He wasn't something that I had ever talked about with anyone, even Cosima. That was, until the demons he had left me with cropped up in Cabo with Sinclair.

Of course, the situation with Sinclair was different but not totally so. If you wanted to strip it down to brass tacks, the way I knew Elena would when she eventually found out about Sinclair and me, it would be fair to draw the conclusion that in both triangles, the man had chosen me over her. It wasn't as simplistic as that. It wasn't fair to either circumstance or either man. It wasn't even fair to Elena or me. But it was what she would see, and it was one of the reasons, maybe even the core reason, she would never forgive me.

# Chapter Six

*Giselle*

"How was your evening with Madame Claremont?"

I was lying on top of a sweaty Sinclair, my entire body aligned with his, pressed front to front. My fingers were in his hair, threading through the damp strands. We were both exhausted from jet leg and a vanilla but vigorous bout of lovemaking that I'd instigated the second I was in the door from drinks with Odile. As promised, she had plied me with enough wine to make me just the right amount of intoxicated and definitively horny. Sin had taken immediate advantage, but it was the first time in a while that the Dom Sinclair hadn't taken me. It didn't bother me, but I definitely noticed the difference and drunkenly wondered about it before moving on.

"It was amazing. I forgot how libertine the French are. Infidelity and affairs are par for the course, so obviously, she wasn't judgmental about us."

In fact, Odile had been positively *thrilled* about my romance with Sinclair. She had waxed on about how I was finally living my life for me instead of hiding behind ugly clothes, ugly hair, and an ugly outlook on love. It had helped that I'd shown her photos of my paintings for the collection. If the path I'd taken toward sexual deviancy surprised her, she hadn't expressed concern or disgust. Instead, she had informed me that she wasn't one to judge as she was simultaneously dating three *much* younger men. At which point, I had begged her to paint all of them together for the show. She'd agreed, and we set a date for Thursday at her private studio in Montmartre.

I told Sinclair this, my words slightly slurred together from tiredness and a lingering intoxication that made me feel heavy and content.

"Interesting woman," he noted when I was done. "No wonder she helped inspire your talent so beautifully."

I tipped my head up so that he could see my smile, but I was too lazy to open my eyes to see how he received it. Happily, I could tell he was pleased because he slid a hand down the curve of my back to rest it on one of my ass cheeks.

"Are you enjoying Paris then, *mon amour*?"

"Yes. I honestly didn't think I would come back, but I am happy to be here, happier than I thought I would be. I love Paris," I said on a dreamy sigh.

"We could move here if you wanted. It would take me a while to organize the transition of Faire Developments' offices, but it could be arranged, especially as we are doing so much business over here now."

My body tightened with shock. "Are you kidding?"

I let out a squeak as he rolled us before I could protest. I stared up at him with wide eyes, drinking in his intense scowl with mute interest.

"Do I look like I am kidding? I meant what I said when I was wooing you, Elle. I want to be with you in every conceivable way. If it were socially acceptable, I would cuff us together and never let you out of my sight. Not because I don't trust you but because I love every minute with you, watching you react to the world, react to me as if I am some kind of world wonder. It makes a man feel fucking invincible. You give me that? The least I can do is concede to living anywhere in the world that you want to be most."

"When you say things like that, I can't believe you're real," I admitted, placing a shaking hand on his cheek.

He bit the edge of my thumb where it lay against the corner of his mouth. "You have time to get used to it. That is what I have been trying to tell you. Forever, Elle, I mean it."

I let out a shuddering sigh, trying to expel the acidity in my chest that was worry for the future and the pain of the past.

He sensed my struggle, and his hard face softened. "I don't want to go back to the city before you feel secure in this, in us. We will have to face a number of monumental challenges in order for me to give you a happy ending, and if you don't believe in my love for you, we won't be able to overcome them."

I agreed with him, but I didn't know how to respond because I *was* unsure. For weeks, he had seemed content to stay with my sister even though he claimed to love me. I knew he loved me, but I didn't think love was enough. He didn't know me enough, I figured, to see the deep fault lines that ran through my character. He could always change his mind about me, about how well I fit into his beautifully constructed life. The son of the governor of New York, the CEO of a successful real estate development company, and a man of his incredible character deserved the best. I wanted that for him. I wanted to *be that* for him. I just wasn't sure if I was up to muster.

"In a couple of superficial ways, I think Elena is better suited for you," I confessed.

It was hard to do, but I wanted to be honest now that I had the opportunity to be. Sinclair was finally in my arms, in my life in the way I wanted him to be, and voicing my insecurities was a risk to that but not talking them out, giving them license to fester and haunt, was a greater one.

"In no way is that true," he countered immediately. "I told you back in Mexico that I can't say anything bad about Elena. She doesn't like my kink, of course, but that isn't something to hold against her. She is a beautiful, talented, classy woman who I spent four years of my life with. I do not regret those years."

A shiver tore through me, and because I was in his arms, he felt it even though I didn't want him to.

"They led me to you, Elle. You were always my destination, *d'accord*? I feel this, and I know this in every way a man can know that he has found the right woman. I told you that I would fight for us, and I will, even if it means fighting you and your own insecurities."

I stiffened again, but he knew why and addressed it before I could even fully digest the reason myself.

"I am not saying that your fears are baseless. I gave you a reason to doubt me. I am just telling you that I am going to rectify the pain I caused by lavishing you with love and protecting you from anyone who may harm you. Until you feel utterly secure in that truth, I want to stay here in Paris. Are you okay with that?"

Stay in Paris, hidden away in my favorite city with my favorite man so that I didn't have to face the awful consequences of our completely not awful love?

"I can do that," I whispered.

"It may mean being here for Christmas," he warned.

I hadn't thought of that but when I did, I only felt relief. I couldn't imagine spending Christmas with my family when everything was still so unresolved. It would mean either pretending I wasn't with Sinclair or tearing apart my family just in time for the holidays.

"We will have to push back the date of your gallery showing too," he warned.

It was currently scheduled for January, so this was true. If we stayed any longer than a week or two, it would need to be pushed back, and I wasn't sure how I felt about that.

"We could reschedule it for Valentine's Day," Sinclair suggested. "Fitting, no?"

I grinned because it was.

"Let's stay here," I said, going into a crunch so that I could gently bite his chin and then place a kiss there, a physical representation of the apology I wanted to give him for still having so many doubts.

"We'll stay here. I'll contact my office and Rossi to let them know the change in our plans tomorrow," he said, holding me closer for a moment before readjusting us so that I was faced away from him and he was spooned up against me. "Now, get some rest because tomorrow we are going to spend most of the day exploring my girl's favorite place in the world."

"Okay," I said as exhaustion crashed down around me. "Love you more than anything in the world, Sinclair."

"My love for you is bigger than the world, my siren," he said into my ear just before I fell into a heavy sleep.

# Chapter Seven

*Giselle*

*I* made a stranger take a picture of us.

The primary reason for that was because I realized we had no photographs together. As an artist, I collected photos, pictures, magazine clippings, sketches, and swathes of material, *anything* really to document my life and inspire me. I only had the photos of Sin from Mexico when he was driving the boat to our little cove and then a few more that Elena had given me to start the painting she had wanted to commission.

The second reason was more base, selfish, and common in a way that I didn't care to shy away from. We cut a striking image that afternoon. Sinclair was in total black, from the tips of his Italian leather loafers to the button-up he wore beneath a thick black cashmere V-neck sweater and the long Burberry trench he wore over it. He wasn't wearing socks, which may have seemed like a strange thing to notice and like, as in *a lot*, but I did, and I did. The subtle slice of brown skin when the rest of him was covered was so unbelievably sexy that I had actually salivated a little when I met him at the café around the corner from our hotel that morning.

In direct color contrast to him, I wore a pale oatmeal cashmere sweater dress that fit my body like a glove and complimented the knee-high chocolate brown boots that I had splurged on at a small local boutique that morning. I'd also had my hair done at a small hair spa that I had walked past countless times as a student but had never had the money to afford. They hadn't done much but cut in a few layers and form the heavy mass into thick dips and curls across my shoulders and breasts. But I loved it, and Sinclair had responded favorably to the stylish cut if the movie-quality kiss he landed on me was anything to go off.

So, vanity was definitely involved.

But we also had an absolutely amazing day, the kind of daylong date that I never would have imagined happening. After waking up together, we had parted ways so that Sin could go to an early meeting in the 2nd arrondissement, and I could treat myself to the spa and some shopping. I still wasn't rolling in cash so I hadn't seriously thought about hitting any of the city's amazing shopping districts, but Sinclair had pressed his credit card into my hand on his way out the door and ordered me to use it before I met up with him. He didn't give me time to protest, and I was actually thrilled for the opportunity to buy a new outfit to show off for him, so I did as I was ordered.

Later, we met for brunch at an amazing Franco-Taiwanese restaurant, Le 37 m2, before we went Christmas shopping in the Marais. Afterward, Sinclair sent the bags back to the hotel while we walked along the Seine hand in hand, enjoying the surprisingly unpopulated promenade and the crisp bite of the winter air.

In a word, heaven.

Now, we were at the doors of my favorite place in the entire world.

*Le musée d'Orsay.*

Sinclair was an art lover, but I was fully aware that he watched me react to the multitude of paintings and amazing sculptures more than he viewed the pieces himself. He followed me as I bounced from my favorite work to my next favorite, skipping from exhibition to exhibition like an eager child. I was too happy to care that I wasn't being chic, and Sin didn't seem to mind either.

"This is one of the pieces that inspired my collection," I blathered on, as I had been since we entered the hallowed halls.

I had already shown him Edouard Monet's *Olympia* with the reclining naked woman with her velvet collar and the famous *Luncheon On The Grass* with the naked woman bracketed by two fully dressed men, but we were now stopped before *L'Origine du Monde*.

"When I was a student, I used to come here every week, nearly every day in the first year I was in Paris. I tried to focus on a different exhibit each time, but inexorably, I found myself in front of Gustave Courbet," I explained, standing to the right and in front of Sinclair so that I could have a minimal amount of privacy. It was difficult to explain my struggle with sexuality, but I wanted him to know.

"Sex had never been a good thing for me, so I had never really explored my own desires. Even when I got up the courage to date Mark in my second year here, we didn't do much more than kiss and fondle each other over our clothes. Pathetic for a twenty-one-year-old," I said, pulling a face.

"Elle," Sinclair protested, but gently so that I would continue.

"I was so drawn to the erotic images here, especially this one. I would just stand in front of it like the closet pervert I was, trying to make sense of the trauma Christopher had left me with and the latent sensuality I felt creep up my throat like bile each time I looked at this painting."

I paused, warring with the echo of that feeling in my gut. It was easy to look over my left shoulder and imagine my younger self—undernourished, swimming in colorless, oversized clothes, and drab under all that harsh black hair. I had been so unhappy and so confused yet utterly oblivious to it.

I turned to Sinclair, finding him braced like a sailor on a rocking deck, and I knew that my confession was hurting him because my pain was his own. He had put himself in charge of my protection, and this was one thing he would never be able to change.

I stepped forward to press my palm lightly to his chest over his heart.

"You took that tangle of angst and desperation, Sin, and you unfolded it for me. You barely knew me, yet you saw my struggle, collected all the broken pieces that I couldn't reconcile, and bound them together. That week in Mexico wasn't just magical because you made me fall in love with you. You made me fall in love with myself."

"Elle," he repeated, but this time the word was a benediction, a prayer of reverence.

He stepped close, bringing both hands up to cup my face lovingly. "We made each other whole, Elle. I was just as broken before you rearranged my life and brought it into focus."

I leaned my forehead against his, grasping his wrists in my hands to feel the strong pulse there.

"I want to inspire that confidence and security in others. That's why my collection is the way it is."

"I know," he murmured.

"I know you do," I admitted. "You know me better than I know myself." I pulled back slightly, but he kept his grip on my face. "That's probably why you make such a good Dominant."

The softness in his expression glazed over with ice, hardening into a mask that hid his true self from me. I frowned up at him because I couldn't understand what I had said to prompt the change.

"Sin?"

But he wouldn't answer me. I knew before I even opened my mouth to appeal to him. When Sinclair decided to close off, it took a sledgehammer to crack him open again, and unfortunately, the middle of a museum was not the place for that messy business.

We continued our tour of the cavernous, converted train station, but we didn't recover our levity. I bided my time, trying to figure out where I had gone wrong, but I kept coming up blank. A part of me wanted to blame myself anyway, but Sinclair had taught me to be strong, and I didn't want to jump to a conclusion where I was in the wrong.

We went for a quick but delicious dinner at *Chez Berber* after watching the sunset from the top of the extraordinarily ugly Montparnasse Tower. He teased me about how effusively I complimented my lamb *tagine* to the waiter and told me stories about his youth growing up with Cage in the orphanage, but it was as if his frequency had changed to another setting, one that threw just enough static into the mix of our interactions that I couldn't fully enjoy it.

It wasn't until we were back in the hotel getting ready for bed that I knew something was seriously wrong.

I had used the half an hour between getting my hair done that day and meeting Sinclair to use the other part of the spa to get a fresh Brazilian wax. So, I was fully expecting a deliciously volatile reaction when I emerged from the bathroom in nothing but a sheer black baby doll and a matching G-string.

Sinclair sat on the end of the bed in those amazing drawstring gray pants, his torso on prominent display as he leaned back on his hands. I wanted to play his abs like a xylophone with my tongue, so I was momentarily distracted from seeing the clench of his jaw and the flash in his eyes that spoke to anger.

When I did look up, I only caught the tail end of it. I was about to question him when he stood abruptly and moved past me, placing a chaste kiss on my forehead like I was a goddamn *child* before he went into the bathroom.

I stood in the middle of the bedroom, stunned and reeling. It was the first time I had really done anything like that, taking the initiative.

And he had totally brushed me off.

My stomach fell out of my body, along with my ability to breathe. I couldn't orientate myself, the room twirling around me, because the foundation I had been building with Sinclair had suddenly, crudely, been pulled out from under me.

"What the fuck just happened?" I whispered, just to hear my own voice.

Oddly enough, it helped.

I said it again louder so he could hear me in the bathroom. "What the *fuck* just happened?"

Sinclair appeared in the doorway and leaned against the frame, his pose deliberately casual as if everything was fine when it so clearly. Was. Not.

"Elle," he said as if beginning a sentence, but then he didn't continue.

"Yes? Are you going to explain why you just brushed me off like that?" I asked, hands on my hips in my own power pose.

"We've had a long day, and I'm jet-lagged."

"*Merde*, Sin, that is a lie and not even a good one. What is going on?"

He stared at me for a long moment.

It struck me how much he looked like one of those beautifully carved marble statues that I admired so much in the *musée d'Orsay*; gorgeously constructed but utterly cold because it was not alive.

"Don't go back to that cold man who treated me like shit in Mexico because he was scared," I breathed, the flaming anger gone and replaced with the glacial chill of fear.

"I know you aren't well-versed in relationships, but most couples don't have sex all the time," he explained calmly, condescendingly.

"I can't believe you would say that to me," I said, pressing my hands to my stomach where I felt the wound that his words had inflicted like a physical agony.

His eyes squeezed shut, woven tightly closed behind his thick russet lashes. I could see the tension in his body and realized how much he hated what he was doing to me. So why was he acting this way?

"Don't you want to touch me?" I breathed, not in despair this time but with feminine authority.

I walked forward with slow purpose as his eyes snapped open at my tone and found me. Those blazing blues carefully cut across my skin like knives, erotic but dangerous. I could sense the tenuous hold on his restraint.

"I'll make love to you," he conceded, but it wasn't enough, and we both knew it.

"I want you to take me," I said, stepping close and up on my toes so that I could drag the edge of my teeth across the sharp angle of his jaw.

His sharp breath gave me confidence.

"Please, sir, I need you to help me."

I ran a finger between my breasts, watching his eyes follow its path as I dipped into my panty-covered mound and emerged with a wet, slicked finger. I tried to bring it to his lips, but his eyes cut to mine with a warning that hit me like a thunder strike.

Instead, I brought it to my mouth, flicking my tongue out to taste myself. My moan was overtaken by the rumbling growl that emerged from his chest.

"I need you to tell me what to do," I begged softly. "I need you to teach me how to make myself come."

A vicious shudder ripped through his body, but he held still. The predator in him, the part of himself that he called savage, called out to me from the cage he had locked inside him. I could practically hear the rattle of the bars, the baying howl at the moon. Each muscle and tendon was starkly delineated under his dusky skin as he strained against his primal urge to take and dominate.

Why was he resisting me?

"Sin," I begged, an edge of desperation to my voice.

He didn't move, but his eyes burned, burned, burned hot but suppressed like the destructive force trapped under the cap of a volcano.

Locking his eyes to mine, I back away slowly to sit in the old-fashioned armchair in the corner by the scroll desk and shed my underwear. I sat down and hooked my legs over each arm to completely expose my pussy to him.

The muscle in his jaw ticked like the secondhand of a clock.

I swallowed the minimal discomfort that my prudish former self might have felt and slid two fingers down to my core, opening myself blatantly under his scrutiny. His regard was so intense that his gaze was a physical caress against my slick folds.

"Should I touch myself here, sir?" I asked, dipping one, then two fingers just inside.

His head tipped further so that he could really watch, but still, he didn't move, didn't speak. I think we both knew that if he did, he would be done. Mine.

"Or here?" I asked on a gasp as I twirled my index finger over my throbbing clit.

I set up a steady thrum across the sensitive bundle of nerves, licking my lips deliberately as I latched eyes on the erection almost comically straining the front of his pajama pants.

"Would it hurt if I pinched it, do you think?"

Sinclair flinched as I did so, and my back arched steeply at the sharp swell of pleasure that arrowed up my spine.

"Do you want to see my fingers inside me?" I asked, trying to channel what Sinclair might order me to do.

It wasn't the same as his commanding presence, but I enjoyed the thrill of playing with a predator, the danger I was knowingly putting myself in. Prey could only dance so long before a true animal before they gave into their nature and *took*.

At least, that was what I was banking on.

My lids shifted to half-mast, matching Sinclair's hooded gaze as I stared intently at the fingers playing over my wet core.

"I need you," I panted.

He jerked slightly, and I knew I had him, just one more little push...

The mechanical vibration of a cell phone cut through the room, bringing us both to a complete halt. We both stopped breathing and looked over at the phone buzzing away on the nightstand.

Sinclair was the first to move, swiftly walking to the phone and answering in a clipped voice. He didn't look at me as he dived into a rapid-fire French exchange and moved out of the bedroom into the suite's living area.

I sat in the chair for a long moment while I listened absently to the exchange. My mind refused to acknowledge that Sinclair didn't want me. He did. I had never doubted that, not through any of the turmoil we had been through. Yet now he denied what we needed?

Robotically, I got ready for bed, letting muscle memory and habit guide me through brushing my teeth and moisturizing before I slipped beneath the covers and turned off the lamp beside my bed. I stared into the darkness for a long time, well after Sinclair finished his phone call and hung up.

Eventually, he came back, stared at my back for a few minutes, and then got into bed. He rolled into me immediately, tucking me tightly into his body so that we were pressed inch for inch, front to back.

"My love for you is bigger than the world," he murmured into my ear after he pushed my hair away from my neck. "I love you more than my need to dominate."

He thought I was asleep, obviously, so I tried to keep my body from going hard with shock and then soft with relief. It wasn't me he was disgusted by but himself. I should have known that, and it irritated me that I was so slow on the uptake when he had been struggling with his sexual deviancy for years before he met me. Now that I knew what the problem was, there was no way in hell I would let it defeat us, not when I finally had the love of my Frenchman after months of longing.

# Chapter Eight

*Giselle*

The next morning, I was up before Sinclair, and I took immediate advantage of the fact. Normally, I wouldn't breach his privacy so flagrantly, and I had a momentary pang of guilt as I checked his phone for any evidence of contact with my sister and his ex-girlfriend. Elena was the only person I knew who had the power to turn Sinclair against himself like he had last night, so I followed my gut and was rewarded when I found an email from her in his inbox.

Rage ignited like a bonfire in my belly, rushing through my blood until it had burned everything clean and clear.

She was officially a bitch.

I didn't care how badly she might have belittled me, but subjecting her lover, former or current, to her unfair biases was absolutely *not* okay.

I worried that the crushing force of my fury would wake up Sinclair, so I carefully closed down his phone and lay in bed beside him as I struggled to digest the news. In a way, it made me feel better to know that at least I hadn't done something to turn Sinclair away, but at the same time, I was disappointed he hadn't shared the email with me so we could talk it through. If our situation had been reversed, he would have expected, no *demanded*, that from me.

Slipping out of bed, I tiptoed over to his computer and fired up the search engine. Before our one night together at Cosima's apartment, I had done a bunch of research on BDSM, but I wanted to know more. I wanted to know everything. The small taste that I'd had of the power dynamic was addictive. It was more than just my attraction to Sinclair that had wooed me. It was the idea of being under his control. The messy mass of desires, shame, fear, and power that made up my complicated sexuality was tamed by the skilled touch of Dom Sinclair. My traumatic history with Christopher also ceased to exist when I was under Sin's spell. I refused to give these things up, especially when Elena's influence was the driving force behind his sudden need to live vanilla and not his desire.

I looked over at him as he laid peacefully asleep, the crest of his thick lashes casting long shadows across his cut glass cheekbones, the fall of his rich mahogany hair across his forehead. He was so achingly beautiful, so deeply perfect for me in every way. I just needed to remind him of that.

Moving into the other room, I made the call I needed to make in order to set my rash plan into action. Thirty minutes later, Sinclair was still in bed with a note I had left explaining that I'd gone into Odile's studio to paint for the day. I met Cage at *Quotidian* to have a tartine and enlist his help.

"Absolutely not."

"But Cage—"

"*Jamais. Pense-tu que je sois con?*" he asked me incredulously.

"No, I don't think you're stupid." I looked up at him from under my lashes, my eyes wide with sincerity. "I thought you were a friend, that you would *want* to help me with this."

He scoffed, unmoved by my act. "You know better than to ask me this, I think, *chérie*. Sinclair would kill me without a second thought if I took you to such a place without him."

"I love Sinclair, but we need this," I leaned in to whisper. "He won't dominate me since Elena sent him that awful email. Last night, he wouldn't even touch me!"

"Even without the kink, he is still more passionate with you than he has ever been with another woman. Maybe he doesn't need it like you think he does."

I gave him a look.

He opened his large palms wide and sighed. "I will not deny that he needs *some* level of control in the bedroom, *d'accord*? But he has lived the past four years of his life thinking it was inhumane to dominate his partner. Do you really think that is something you can bounce back from overnight?"

I hadn't thought of it that way. Elena had been condemning him for years about his sexual preferences. That sort of thing left a mark on someone.

I tilted my chin in the air. It was something Elena did when she wanted to get her way, and even though appropriating her behavior was the least of my transgressions against her, it still felt wrong.

"I'll go without you," I threatened.

Cage glared at me, but humor sparkled in his thickly lashed eyes. "Ah, well that changes things, doesn't it?"

"I think it does."

He chuckled darkly and leaned back in his chair, the big, strong leather-clad rocker in a tiny chair in a feminine French restaurant. A thick fingertip traced his ridiculously full bottom lip as he contemplated me.

"*Je suis d'accord, chérie.* I will let you play, but I will not take you to some club, *oui*? My friend, *Madame* Claire, holds a monthly soiree for like-minded people. I will take you to this, but I have to warn you again, even this is not for the faint of heart."

"I'm not some shrinking violet," I retorted.

He gave me a long, languorous perusal. "*Non*, not anymore, but this change is recent. You may change your mind, and then where will Sin be, ugh?"

"I would never leave him," I said, and I had never meant anything more.

Cage waved a dismissive hand through the air as he knew that already. "He will kill me, you know this? If he finds out I took you out as my submissive."

I frowned. "Your submissive?"

Cage nodded. "I will not take you to something like this unclaimed. As it is, you will garner too much attention as a newcomer and looking like you do. You'll have to be mine for the night. Don't worry, *chérie*, I will try not to enjoy it too much." He winked.

I laughed nervously. "When is it?"

"So eager. We will go this Thursday. Can you get away from Sinclair?"

I bit my lip but nodded. Sinclair was supposed to be going to a business dinner with Paulson and a few other investors in the Dogwood project, so it should be easy enough to slip away.

"Do you have anything to wear?"

"Excuse me?"

Cage sighed dramatically. "I cannot take you to something like this without the appropriate attire. We'll have to go shopping."

He stood and placed a few euro notes on the table before pulling on his beautiful black leather coat.

"Come," he encouraged when I just sat there.

"Oh, right now?"

He grinned, extending his huge hand to help me up. "Yes, right now."

*H*e took me to Agent Provocateur and laughed at my expression of intimidated awe as we swept through elegant displays of delicately webbed lace and gorgeously constructed corsets. Cage stopped briefly at various racks, picking out things that caught his eye and transferring them into the hands of an eager and beautiful saleswoman who followed us around the store. He didn't ask for my size, but I knew enough about Cage Tracey to know that he would make an accurate guess.

It occurred to me that Sinclair would be furious at the idea of someone else dressing me in racy lingerie, of another man taking me to a public playroom. I didn't want him enraged with me or anyone else, but I truly felt that the only way to convince him of my investment in the scene was to pursue it independently of him. If he could only see what submitting did to me, he would have to understand.

And maybe if I were a better sub, he wouldn't be able to keep himself from me like he had been.

"You'll invite him then?" I asked Cage as I followed him into a spacious change room.

I was only mildly surprised when the saleswoman left us alone inside. This was Paris after all, the city of romance and not America, which Sebastian often claimed was run by prudes.

I began to strip, unashamed in front of Cage. He was a rock star, for God's sake. He'd seen way more appealing naked bodies than mine.

For his part, he averted his eyes as he took a seat on a velvet bench.

"I will. We will get you settled first, and then I will let him know you followed me to the event. Give it fifteen minutes, and he'll show up in a rage." His obsidian eyes flickered my way and widened. "Especially if you are wearing that."

I blushed as I pulled up the last stocking and attached it to the garter belt strap. I struck a silly pose for him. "Do you like?"

His eyes smoldered, but his posture was casual as he leaned his back against the wall. "If you do not take your own sexuality seriously, Elle, how can you expect anyone else to? Look in the mirror and tell me what you see."

I swallowed hard past the knot of insecurity growing in my throat but did as he said. Even though I knew Cage wasn't as into the scene as Sinclair was, he still had a very effective Dom voice.

The woman staring back at me wore a tight black corset with stiff lace embroidery and sheer panels that nipped in her waist to extreme proportions and highlighted the creamy swell of her full breasts above the rise of the sweetheart neckline. Inky black thigh-highs encased her curvy legs, exposing a panel of white skin that was somehow extraordinarily sexy against the starkness of the black lingerie. Her red hair spilled like wine across her shoulders and down her back, and her lips grew wet with moisture as she chewed on one.

"Look at yourself and tell me the truth, that you have never seen a sexier woman before in all your life." Cage's voice reached me through the haze of my own self-infatuation.

"I wouldn't go that far," I protested on a breath.

"Then you are wrong," he retorted. "Maybe this will be easier for you. How would Sinclair react if he saw you like this?"

I could picture the exact shade of blue his eyes would darken to, the color of the sky just before it tips into nightscape when it is still just barely electrified with light. His jaw would clench and tick with restraint, and his voice would wind itself around me, seductive and heady as drug smoke.

My entire body shivered and flushed.

"Exactly," Cage agreed, satisfied with my response. "This is the one you will get. And this, you will wear as well."

He got up swiftly and gently tied a length of black velvet ribbon around my neck, like a makeshift collar. It reminded me of the painting from the museum, *Olympia*, with the woman collared in much the same way. My fingers fluttered against the ribbon as my pulse hammered.

"Hopefully, by the end of the evening at Madame Claire's, Sinclair will give you a collar of your own, but for now, this will do."

I swallowed heavily and straightened my shoulders. "I'm going to get him back, Cage."

He nodded soberly. "I've no doubt of it."

Despite both our confidences, my knees shook as I took off the expensive garment and gave it to Cage to pay for as my Christmas present.

If things didn't go the way I needed them to, Thursday could very well be the last night of my new relationship with Sin.

*M*adame Claire lived, unsurprisingly, in *Montmartre*, the trendy, artist neighborhood built on steeply curving streets surrounding the *Sacré Coeur*. Her apartment was two floors but oddly constructed because the top level had at one time been the servant's quarters. Now, it was a spacious, open-concept space where nearly everything was visible as soon as you opened the door.

Which was why I froze in the doorframe while Cage moved further into the foray.

My eyes danced over the scantily clad people present, some talking innocuously over glasses of champagne while others took up more daring poses. A man in leather chaps kneeled on the floor on all fours with a tray of drinks balanced on his back. Another man, this one dressed in an impeccable suit, pet him on the head as he spoke with a friend. A woman wearing nothing but scarlet red nipple tassels and a matching leather collar was strapped onto some kind of enormous cross. The man before her was carefully but brutally laying into her with a red leather cane, leaving vivid red stripes along her skin.

My own flesh tingled at the thought.

I jumped when Cage reached out and tugged me farther into the room.

"It's a St. Andrew's Cross," he whispered in my ear.

A quick flash of Sinclair strapping me into such a thing made goose bumps break out over my skin.

Cage chuckled. "A bit advanced for you, Elle."

"Isn't that the point?" I countered.

Sinclair and I had made love once in the four days since Elena had sent him that email. He had done a relatively good job of avoiding me, throwing himself into work and encouraging me to visit with Odile and spend time with Candy and Cage. I knew it was because he couldn't control himself around me, which gave me some level of comfort, but not much.

I missed him acutely.

I had tried to talk to him about the problem, mentioning Elena's cruelty at Thanksgiving, how wrong she was to condemn him for his interest in BDSM. He had shut me down with a flick of the wrist before he removed himself from the room to take a call. I was trying to be patient with him even though he was hurting both of us with his obstinate behavior but having a plan made it easier.

Four days was long enough.

It was time to bring my Dom back.

A slight smile pulled at Cage's full lips, but he ignored my comment in favor of leading me toward an older woman reclining in an antique chair while she used a naked man as a footstool at the back of the room.

As we drew closer, I could see she wasn't very attractive—her features were too broad and plain for that—but the elegance of her bearing and the cutting wit in her dark eyes was enough to arrest me.

"Madame Claire," Cage purred as he inclined his head toward the woman. "May I introduce the lovely Elle?"

"You may," she replied, but her sharp eyes reprimanded me as they trailed over my body. "Is this how you wish to present yourself?"

Without thought, I folded to my knees and tilted my head toward the ground, my hands clasped behind my back. Immediately, my mind cleared of anxieties and I let out a deep exhale of relief when I felt Cage's approving hand on top of my head.

"Better," Madame Claire praised. "It is unlike you to have a pet, though, Cage."

"Yes, she isn't mine. In fact, she belongs to Sinclair."

I didn't have to look at her face to feel the surprise this elicited.

"I have not heard that name in a very long time. As I understood it, he had settled with some *vanilla* American," she said with disdain.

"He has rectified his error," Cage said with faux sobriety. "Elle is both his woman and his sub now."

"Then why is he absent, *mm?*"

"May I speak, Madame?" I ventured.

A pause.

"You may."

"The vanilla American accused his kink of being sexually

abusive." Even repeating the words made me irate, but I gritted my teeth and sank further into my pose to find calm.

Madame Claire sniffed loudly, in that quintessentially French show of derision that I had always loved.

"Monsieur Sinclair has suffered from this fear for too long. Look at me, sub," she ordered softly, waiting until I looked up at her before she continued. "We will do what needs to be done to get your Dom back, *oui*?"

My smile was almost painful as it blasted across my face. "*Je suis d'accord.*"

Sinclair was having a late dinner meeting until nine o'clock, so Cage insisted on taking me on an introductory tour around the room to acclimatize myself to the situation. I protested at first, but it was a good idea because the nervous, bouncing tics of my diaphragm like a precursor to hiccups, disappeared after making a few rounds of the room.

We paused before a scene where a Domme had bound her bulky male submissive at his wrists, elbows, and ankles so that he was prone on his knees, ass in the air on the floor. She played idly with his erection, with the beautiful muscular swell of his ass while she spoke to him at length about everything she was preparing to do to him. From his throaty groans, I knew he was ready for whatever she deemed worthy of him.

I was most excited to talk to the woman in red who was now cradled in her Dom's lap after their session. Her eyes were half-closed as if even that effort cost her energy that she no longer had to expend.

"Laurent, Miss Pascale," Cage greeted warmly, clearly familiar with the couple.

"It has been too long," the handsome Laurent noted with a wide, affectionate grin.

I knew better than to judge a book by its cover, especially after witnessing the dynamic between the Paulsons, but I was still surprised that the Dom who had handled Pascale with such deliberate cruelty could have such a boyish, open face. His curls of sandy hair fell into his wide gray eyes, and his smile revealed twin dimples. Of the two, Pascale, with her striking dark features and sharp pixie cut, seemed better suited, physically, for the role of Dominant.

"This is Sinclair's woman, Elle," Cage introduced.

"Sinclair?" Pascale asked, roused from her post-orgasm daze by the sound of my man's name.

Jealousy flared through me.

She noticed, addressing me with a soft smile. "He was a good friend to my Master once, Elle, that is all. I have never had the pleasure of playing with him."

"Good," I said with a smile to dilute the edge of my possessiveness.

She laughed musically and wriggled closer to Laurent. "Sharing is a special thing. Not everyone is into it."

"I am not," Laurent admitted with twinkling eyes. "Pascale is for my hands, cock, and mouth only. But she gets off on sharing me, which is why we come to these soirees."

My eyes widened, comically apparently because Cage and the couple laughed.

"If you are interested, I would love to watch him play with you?" Pascale suggested seductively, biting the tip of her pink tongue.

I stepped closer to Cage, who wrapped a protective arm around me, but it wasn't because the idea held no appeal to me. If Sinclair had been there and deemed fit to share me, I would have been thrilled.

"You like that idea," Cage ducked down to whisper in my ear.

I shivered as his breath wafted over my neck.

"Tell me, *chérie*, what would you do if Sinclair shared you with me?"

Honestly, the thought had never occurred to me. Cage was sinfully beautiful, the kind of handsome that was intrinsically linked to thoughts of sex. I remembered thinking that if I hadn't met Sinclair first, I would have found Cage the most beautiful man who I had ever laid eyes on. We were good friends, so I never would have entered into a sexual relationship with him. There wasn't that inherent chemistry between us, but would I have objected if Sinclair brought him into our bedroom?

I looked up into his glittering black eyes. "If Sinclair wanted it, it would be my pleasure."

I watched with a feminine thrill as desire blasted across his features, stark and harshly highlighted before he could get it under control.

A thought occurred to me, though, an uncomfortable one.

"You like Elena," I said softly because I wasn't sure, but I suspected.

His lips twisted in a cruel mockery of a smile. "Maybe I just have a thing for sassy redheads?"

I laughed lightly because it was clear he wanted me to and that he wouldn't talk about his unrequited crush with me, at least not then.

"Are you ready?" he asked me after another few minutes of conversation with Laurent and Pascale. "Sinclair will be here soon, and we want to be prepared."

I nodded, and before I could fully process what had happened, we had confirmed my goals, limits, and safe word, and I was strapped into the device Cage had called a St. Andrew's Cross. My cheek was pressed to the cool, smooth wood while my back and bottom were exposed to the crowded room. No one was paying me much attention yet, probably because they were used to the sight and also because a powerful tool of domination was denial—of touch, sight, and acknowledgment. I was living evidence of its success; my flesh was raised with goose bumps, my inner thighs slick with my arousal even though no one had touched me.

Cage's dark voice wafted across the back of my neck like smoke. "He's on his way. Just a few more minutes, *chérie*."

"She's gorgeous," another masculine voice said from over my shoulder. "Are you in the mood to share, Cage?"

"She isn't mine to share."

"If she's without a Dom, I'll ask her directly." There was a shuf-fling sound behind me. I didn't need to see to know what was going on. Cage had stepped in front of the curious man, his chest puffed and legs spread.

"You will do no such thing," Cage growled.

But he didn't have to because I could feel the change in the air, the static current that suddenly zinged through the room like an electrical storm.

Sinclair had arrived.

The room quieted so much that I could hear each sharp clack of his expensive leather loafers cross the hardwood floor. I shuddered violently when they came to a stop just behind me, the space between us thick with crashing neutrons.

"No one will be touching her. We're leaving."

I gasped as the sound of his voice vibrated against my skin. It took me a moment to recognize his words from within my fog of desire.

"No," Cage said, and for a second, my confused brain thought I had said it. "She needs this. *You* need this."

"I do not." Sinclair's voice was glacial.

"Fine, you think you don't need this. You want to be miserable, that's your decision. But Giselle has a choice, and she's made hers."

"I want this," I said, my voice strong and clear despite the awkwardness of my positioning.

"Giselle—" he began, but I cut him off.

"No. If you don't want to be a part of this lifestyle, then Cage is right, it's your decision to make, and that's fine. I need this, though. I need the submission, to be in the hands of a man who will take me through my darkest desires with dominance and calm. If you can't be there for me, then I need to find someone else to take care of those desires."

His body was suddenly pressed to mine, the coolness of his suit against my skin only serving to further fuel my flushed body.

"It doesn't mean I don't love you," I whispered as I strained to move closer to him.

It was also an empty threat. I would never let another man handle me the way Sinclair did. At least, not without him there.

He was quiet for a long minute.

I focused on breathing in tandem with him, craving even that small harmony.

"Do not make me do this," he began, and the pit of my stomach fell out like a false bottom, "unless you truly desire it."

My relief was so acute that I slumped against the hard wooden cross.

"Please," I begged.

Immediately, a new tension overtook him. I shivered at the feel of his entire body hardening with resolve and desire against my pliant flesh. He tilted his head down so that he could speak against my ear.

"You want to be punished before these people, don't you, my siren? You want them to witness my claiming of this gorgeous body." His hand swept down the curve of my hip and roughly squeezed my bottom.

"Yes, please, sir."

"Good girl," he practically purred before he stepped away from me, leaving my skin cold but my insides burning with anticipation.

"You remember your safe word?" he asked.

"Yes, sir."

"Tell me."

"Heartbeat."

My senses were heightened by my lack of vision, pressed up against the wall as I was, and coupled with my knowledge of the dozen other inhabitants of the room, I was already trembling with need. It also comforted, the idea of being claimed before strangers, and a small part of me knew it was because he hadn't yet claimed me in New York.

I wanted everyone to know that this magnificent man owned me.

His breath whispered against my ear. "Are you ready, siren?"

"Yes, sir."

His response was to drag the tip of the bright red cane I had seen earlier down the curve of my cheek, under my neck, and down my spine until it tickled the crevice between my ass cheeks. He paused there, sliding the end back and forth, deeper and deeper until it dragged achingly slow through my wet folds.

"So wet for me already," he noted, loud enough for the entire room to hear. "You always did like the thought of having an audience, didn't you? The room service waiter in Mexico, the door open to your hall so that anyone could see you kneeling before me in Cosima's apartment. So beautiful, so eager for my cock. You want everyone to see what a good girl you are for me, don't you?"

"Yes, sir," I breathed, barely audible because I was so focused on the throbbing under the tip of that leather strap.

"Louder, let everyone hear you," he ordered.

"Yes, sir, I want everyone to see what a good girl I am for you," I said, my words ending on a ragged moan as Sinclair brought the cane up and back down hard across the swell of my right ass cheek.

I squeezed my eyes shut and gritted my teeth as the sting deepened and rushed like a river through a broken dam down to my sex.

He didn't stop.

The cane striped my ass, upper thighs, and the outside of my sex in a continuous rhythm that made me rock and sound like an instrument under his beating hand. The pain was bright at first and then sank to my very bones where it pulsed hotly, building and building to a crescendo that I knew would break me into pieces. There were no thoughts in my head, no words. Instead, the hypnotic crack of the whip, the bass-like moans from deep in my belly, and the harsh sound of Sinclair's excited breathing played behind my closed lids like a symphony of colors, red, black, and gray strobe lights that lulled me into subspace.

My legs were pulled so far apart that my sex was wide open for the bite of the cane. His cadence changed. It grew faster, sharper still, with an emphasis on the wet slick of my inner thighs. The edge of the hard leather caught the lips of my sex and made me jerk hard against the cross.

"Sir," I cried out as my legs trembled in their straps.

I needed something more, something to shatter me so that he could reform me, reclaim and forgive me for pushing him over the edge.

"Yes, my siren?" he asked in that cool, immaculate voice that made the brutal sensuality of his beating even sexier by contrast.

"Please, I need to hear you, need to see you. If it pleases you," I added hastily, panting so much that the words barely came.

Sinclair landed two more hard swats to my burning ass before he stepped away, cool air stirring over my hot, sensitized skin. I moaned, both from the loss of him and the new sensation of air. It astonished me somewhere deep in the lost recesses of my rational brain that I was at the point where a light breeze could tip me over the edge.

"Cage, Laurent, I need your assistance," Sinclair spoke to his friend and the Dom I had met earlier as he stepped close again to undo me from the thick cuffs binding me to the cross.

I slumped forward as I was freed, but Sin caught me on his shoulder and gently turned me around so my back was to the cross and my front was to the audience.

I watched through blurry eyes as Cage and Laurent stepped forward by some unspoken command to take either arm and pull it around their respective waists. Sinclair bent forward to fasten my legs against the cross again, but this time, the men held my arms bound behind them in a tight grip, their sides pressed up close to mine like parenthesis.

I shivered at the contact, and the desire that had begun to ebb away as they readjusted me flooded back in.

Sinclair was suddenly in my face; his wide, lightning-blue eyes the only thing I could see. "Cage and Laurent are going to hold you down and play with your beautiful nipples while I make you come with my fingers."

I trembled violently at his words.

He smiled wickedly. "You are not allowed to orgasm until you receive permission from all three of us. Do not disappoint me, my siren."

"I won't, sir," I promised.

At that moment, I would have laid prostrate on an altar, bared for an entire congregation to gawk at if it meant Sinclair would touch me. I loved knowing that an entire room watched our exchange, how completely I gave myself over to him. I wanted them to watch how explosively he could make me come.

"You look so beautiful like this, *chérie*," Cage murmured huskily in my ear.

I shivered again as two of his blunt, rough-tipped fingers plucked at my left nipple.

"Watch us play with you," Cage ordered as Laurent also reached up to twist and pull at my other nipple.

I looked down to watch their dark fingers brutally manipulate my flesh and shuddered at the corresponding pull deep in my pussy.

"Isn't she magnificent?" Sinclair asked, drawing my attention back to him.

It was impossible to be unaware of him even when I focused on the other men, though, because I knew they were touching me at his behest. That he was in charge of the pleasure I was feeling, even if it was different hands on my skin.

I sank further into the shadowy depths of submission.

I arched my back, pushing myself further into those unfamiliar hands with a guttural noise I normally would have been ashamed of.

Instead, all I felt was overwhelming need.

"So greedy, my woman," Sinclair noted casually.

"*Oui*," Madame Claire agreed, standing just behind and to the right of our scene, her arms crossed like his, as if both of them were viewing a painting at the *Louvre*. "So beautiful in her greed. Will you give her what she wants?"

Sinclair cocked his head, his face impassive. "Eventually."

"Please, sir," I begged, rolling my head on my neck, restless with desire.

"Sin," Cage asked, an edge of pleading in his voice. "May I take her in my mouth?"

Sinclair's eyes flashed, not with anger but with the joy of possession. He liked the effect I had on Cage, the power being his because he wholly owned me.

He inclined his head magnanimously. "You may."

I gasped as Cage and Laurent dipped in unison to take my

straining peaks into their hot mouths. They held me tight to their sides so that I couldn't thrash despite my best efforts, and the feeling of being restrained ratcheted my arousal into previously unknown dimensions.

"Are you worthy of an orgasm, Elle?" Sinclair asked conversationally as he stepped before me again. "You deceived me, tried to top me from the bottom by forcing me into this scene. Now, tell me, who has the power?"

"You, sir," I practically shouted as his fingers ghosted between my thighs.

I humped at the air, desperate to bring them back to me when he pulled away.

"Yes," he hissed. "Me. I can do whatever I want to you, even order these men to take you in their mouths. I know you like their tongues on your sweet nipples, but you know that they are really my mouth, my tongue on your flesh, don't you?"

I groaned in agreement because his fingers were back in the dripping pool of desire between my legs. I was so wet that I could feel the trickles of desire slide down the backs of my thighs. The squelching noise Sin's fingers made as he thrust two, then three fingers brutally deep into my clutching sex was one of the sexiest noises that I'd ever heard.

"Very good, Elle, so wet for me."

God, how could I be anything but? I was dialed to ten and still cresting. The orgasm that loomed large and dark in the distance was terrifying. I knew it would obliterate me, crash through me, and eviscerate everything but the bliss he gave me.

The hard smack of his palm hitting against my sloppy, wet pussy brought me back to him.

"Pay attention. I'm going to make you come now," Sinclair ordered.

He dropped to his knees but even in the lowest position of our quartet, he still emanated power. His face pressed into my left thigh so that he could watch up close the way his fingers began to churn through me, driving me higher and higher.

"Beg us for permission to come," Sinclair reminded.

"Please, please, please..." I began to recite, rising from a whisper to a near shriek as I was seized with excruciating tension, suspended in the moment when a glass hits the floor but before it cracks.

"Show us how prettily you can come," Cage spoke with his teeth against my nipple.

"Come for your Dom," Laurent demanded.

Simultaneously, the two men bit viciously into my nipples and chewed.

"Come now." Sinclair's voice lashed out like the cane against my pussy as he added his thumb, slick with my damp, into my ass.

I rocketed into space. My body lashed hard against my restraints as my mind broke open. I tumbled headfirst, screaming wildly into the darkness, distantly aware that Sinclair would catch me when I fell.

# Chapter Nine

*Giselle*

"Thank you," Sinclair said into the early dawn.

We were back in our bed at the hotel the morning after Madame Claire's, folded together with precision and closeness like a carefully wrapped present. My face was pressed so close to his that I had to go slightly cross-eyed to look into his serious gaze, but it was worth it to see the apology there, the need and gratefulness.

After my orgasm, I had passed out briefly, and when I came to, I found myself in Sinclair's arms as he sat on a velvet loveseat talking to Madame Claire and her sub Dominic about the recent French presidential election. He had clutched me tighter in recognition of my wakefulness and gently drawn me into the conversation, trying to normalize things after the intense scene. It worked. I'd happily talked about the National Front and the protectionist leanings of Marine le Pen and the relief we all felt that she had not won. Cage had joined us at one point, winking at me roguishly as he sat down across from us. I'd blushed but felt no real awkwardness about the intimacy we had shared. Sinclair touched me continuously, petting my hair, stroking the slope of my cheek and the swell of my lips. Reconfirming our connection, I knew, and it made me warm with success.

I had brought him back to me.

"You don't ever have to thank me for reminding you that you are safe with me," I said now, after the first good sleep I had had in four nights. "If anything, I should apologize to you. I thought that I had made it clear that I loved you *and* the sexual freedom that being a submissive gave me. Clearly, I didn't do a good enough job of making you feel accepted."

His arms pressed me closer still. "No, it was through no fault of your own. I let Elena's spitefulness get to me. The truth is, Willa came across me fucking one of my girlfriend's bound to my bed when I was in the twelfth grade and laid into me using the same language Elena always had. It was hard for me to believe that a woman I cared about could accept that part of me when the other two could not."

I made a soft whimper of empathy.

He continued, "I caused you pain. That is unacceptable, especially when I promised you that I would protect you from judgment. I turned right around and judged us myself." He made a noise of disgust and buried his nose in my hair. "*Désolé, ma sirène.*"

"You are forgiven," I said because I knew he needed to hear it even though I didn't actually feel the need to do it. "Let's move on from it, okay? From this day forward, we talk about things that concern us instead of closing each other out."

He smiled against my cheek. "Look at you, Elle. When you first came to me in Mexico, you were this unsure, timid thing with a deep well of gumption and fierce feminine power that you had no idea how to tap into. Now, you are a siren come into her own."

"You had everything to do with that," I said because it was true.

"You would have found it eventually."

I disagreed, but I decided to leave it at that because we were having a moment. I knew there would be more trials in the future, so I thought it was important to luxuriate in the peacefulness, the absolute rightness, of our togetherness while I could.

Our phones buzzed simultaneously on the table beside Sin, and he reached for them.

"The day has officially begun," he murmured dryly as we both checked our notifications.

"You were the one who wanted me to have a phone," I pointed out. "I was happy without one for twenty-four years."

"You needed one. How else can I send you orders to ready yourself for me before I get home at the end of the day? You also need a camera phone to send me pictures of all this gorgeousness while I am away on business trips. A phone was a necessity."

I laughed, the sound trailing off as I read the email from Stefan.

"Sin, Stefan is in town," I crowed, delighted for the opportunity to see the Greek shipping magnate again.

"Joy."

"Sin..." I giggled. "He is a very nice man. And, as I told you, he was the one who encouraged me to go after you that night when you had blatantly tossed me aside."

His lips flattened at the memory. "I am so fucking lucky you have the patience of a saint."

I laughed and snuggled closer. "You make it all worth it."

"You read the email, and I'll be right back. I have a meeting in an hour, but I want to have a bath with you before we leave for the day. You must be sore from last night."

He pressed a sweet kiss to my forehead. I watched him get out of bed, his naked body gilded with weak winter sunlight as he walked into the bathroom. My throat was tight with emotions, but I swallowed them back and turned my attention to my phone.

"He wants to meet for lunch," I called so Sin could hear me as I read the note. "He has a proposition for me."

My words were met with a heavy silence, and I bit my lips against my stupidity.

"I think it was something to do with my art," I amended.

No response.

"I still haven't found my pills, so I'm going to head to the clinic I used to go to in order to get a new prescription," I said again, hoping to distract him.

He didn't say anything, so I took the time to quickly send off a response to Stefan agreeing to meet him at noon at *Le Cinq* in the George V Hotel off the *Champs-Elysées*.

When I entered the bathroom, I took a moment to love the rich wood paneling and the emerald-green tiles that encased the deep bathtub that Sinclair was filling with steaming water and a plethora of lavender-scented bubbles.

"Get in," he ordered, moving away to press play on the music system.

The smooth jazzy refrain of Melody Gardot's music flooded into the room.

I was naked already, so I just swept my hair up into a messy bun and stepped into the nearly painful heat of the soapy water. I sank down, hissing from the sting, and closed my eyes to absorb the heat.

When I opened them, Sinclair was sitting on the side of the tub with a soft white washcloth that he dunked into the water. We locked eyes as he leaned forward to softly run the fabric from my neck down over my shoulders and arms, firmly around each finger, releasing tensions that I hadn't even known I harbored.

"That feels so good," I murmured.

"It feels good to care for you," he responded sweetly.

I opened one eye to make sure he was real before closing them again so I could better feel the friction of the cloth against my heat-sensitized flesh.

"I don't want you to wear panties to your meeting with Stephan today."

My eyes flew open. "Excuse me?"

"You heard me. I want you to go without panties."

"Ugh, I would have thought you would want me as clothed as possible."

A smile tugged at the edge of his mouth. "You would have thought wrong. I want you to go feeling the breeze tease your bare cunt under your skirt, knowing that the moment you get back, I will have my mouth on you and that you will already be wet, knowing that is what I have in store for you."

"Oh," I said because that seemed really nice even though it was a little possessive.

Maybe because it was a little possessive.

He grinned fully at me. "Now, lean back and close your eyes again. Let me take care of you."

There was something about the George V Four Seasons that was both horribly and magnificently cliché. It was a beautiful, quintessentially French decorated building and the temporary home of many rich and famous visitors who came exactly for the cliché Parisian experience. Despite the triteness of that, the hotel was still a joy to strangers and locals alike. It was an institution in Paris that might have been hated once but was now embraced, much like the Eiffel Tower.

I loved that Stefan had chosen to stay there because it spoke to what I already knew about his character. He further delighted me by waiting for me in the lobby in a perfectly tailored, formfitting burnt orange suit that somehow looked utterly fantastic on him.

I threw myself into his arms because he opened them for me.

"Giselle," he said into my hair.

He smelled amazing, some kind of strong, manly cologne designed to cut women off at the knees.

"Stefan," I beamed at him as I stepped away, clutching our hands and swinging them between us. "You look fantastic."

"As do you." He cast a critical eye over my form, encased in black trousers, a Gucci belt that Cosima had given me, and an amazing pearl-buttoned white blouse. I wasn't wearing panties, and the seam of the denim kept rubbing against my clit. I was mildly concerned about the effects of pussy lubrication on jeans. "Happiness looks good on you. Let me guess, the Frenchman won you over?"

I laughed at him as I took his arm, and he led us into *Le Cinq,* but I didn't answer until we had been seated at a table by the window.

"He did," I confirmed. "The painting you sold him helped that. Thank you, Stefan."

He made a face. "I was loathe to part with it, but he told me about your upcoming collection, and I knew I could replace it with something new and inspired by you."

I blushed. "It's different than my normal work."

"I'm counting on it," he said with a wink. "You are a different woman since Mexico, no?"

"I am. Sinclair makes me feel strong and sure of myself."

"You have many reasons to feel that way outside of your relationship with that man. Your art alone is reason for a considerable about of arrogance," he offered as the server came to fill our water glasses and take our drink orders.

Stefan ordered us a bottle of Domaine Romanée Conti.

I didn't object.

"You flatter me," I said when the server swept away.

"I do not. Your art is actually the main reason I wanted to meet with you." He eyed me for a long moment before coming to a decision. "First, you fill me in on your life, then I tell you about what I had in mind."

I was curious, but I hadn't spoken to him since the first and only email I sent to him on my return to Mexico, letting him know that Sinclair was, in fact, dating my sister. So, I settled in to tell him the entire sordid story and was rewarded by his occasional bark of laughter and lascivious comments.

"So, you ran away again?" Stefan concluded, taking a sip from his glass of extraordinary burgundy wine.

I frowned, hesitating to bring a morsel of codfish, spinach, and raisins to my mouth. "We didn't exactly run away."

"Giselle, darling, do not fool yourself. You ran away from Naples, you ran away from Paris, and now you have run away from New York. You are a runaway girl."

Carefully, I placed my fork back down and propped my chin in my hand to think about Stefan's accusation.

He was right.

I was a runner. I had just never realized it.

Was I that cowardly that I couldn't face the consequences of my actions?

I felt, momentarily, ill.

"We're going back," I said.

"I am not criticizing you, Elle. You left behind a steaming pile of *merde* each time you ran away, so the desire to do so was not unwarranted. In fact, I'm looking to enable you." He dabbed his lips daintily with his napkin before replacing it in his lap and leaning back in his chair to commit himself to staring at me.

"Yes?" I prompted after several moments of his unnerving contemplation.

"A friend of mine is one of the senior editors at French *Vogue*. They need a new art editor, and I thought..." He trailed off with a wave of his hand at me. "You would be perfect. Of course, it means that you would have to relocate to Paris, but given the circumstances especially, I do not think that would be so hard."

I blinked at him in total shock. Editor at French *Vogue*? How was this even a remote possibility? I was just a relatively unknown artist from backwater Naples.

"I don't deserve an opportunity like that," I expressed.

Stefan glared at me. "Bullshit. As we spoke about in Mexico, you have begun, and I dare say have now finished, the transformation from an 'ugly' duckling to a swan. You are a competent, intelligent, and talented artist with a degree from one of the most prestigious art schools in the world. You have four successful shows under your belt and another one upcoming in New York that has already generated much talk, even in Paris. You deserve this opportunity and any others that I or anyone else can throw in your path."

"Wow, that was very impassioned," I said stupidly because I couldn't believe he was being so kind.

"I am not saying it to be kind or because I am your friend," he said, reaching across the table to take hold of my hand. "Though, I am that, your very dear friend, I hope. I am saying this because you deserve the opportunity, and I would be doing my other friend a favor by setting up an interview with a promising employee."

It was hard to speak through my suddenly parched mouth, so I took a long sip of water before saying, "Can I think about it? It just... It seems too good to be true."

"Of course, you can. Talk it over with your lover and let me know. Interviews begin the first week of January, so you have time."

I nodded, looking out at the rain-slicked streets of Paris, feeling the love I had for the city and the awe I had at being presented with such an amazing chance. It would mean giving up the purity of being a full-time artist, but it would also give me the ultimate *in* into the art world of Europe.

"Thank you, Stefan," I said, pouring as much gratitude and love into those words as I could.

Somehow, I had landed more than just the love of a good Frenchman on my trip to Cabo. I had also secured the kind of friendships I had never really had before, with people who would always strive to take care of me. It was *awe*some to realize that.

Stefan smiled lovingly at me. "Anything, anytime, Giselle."

"I hope you know you can ask the same of me," I returned.

His smile turned into a grin. "Excellent, then I call first dibs on that new collection of yours. Send me pictures of the completed paintings and expect me to choose at least three of them for my own collection."

I laughed at him. "Deal."

# Chapter Ten

*Giselle*

It was easy to forget everything but my love of Sinclair and the City of Lights. We established a schedule of sorts, where Sinclair would wake up early and work until two in the afternoon before meeting me at the tiny café around the corner from the hotel. From there, we would head out on a different adventure, reacquainting ourselves with the city we both loved but had been forced to leave. We ambled through the steep and crooked streets of Montmartre, bought charcuterie and cheese from *Marché Place Monge* before heading to *Jardins des Arenes* for a picnic among beautiful Roman ruins, and watched films at the *Parc de la Villette* open-air theater, tucked up in blankets with steaming cups of hot chocolate to keep us warm.

While I waited for Sinclair every morning, I practiced the French art of being a *flaneur*, a person who walks through the streets with no goal in mind but observation and meditation. Sometimes, I made friends with people as I ducked into patisseries, sharing my beloved Maison Kayser chocolate chunk cookies with a family of German tourists or dancing with a young Australian couple to the music of the violinist who was a permanent fixture in front of the *Sacré Coeur*.

Most of the time, though, I walked and sketched to my heart's content. Odile let me use her private studio whenever I wanted so I had made progress on my collection even without my usual supplies.

This included three pieces I was doing on Odile and her three delicious younger men. I was calling the trilogy *The Power of Three*. Each canvas depicted a different facet of the relationship, from a tangle of bodies that were barely discernible as female or male to three sets of thick male hands on a dainty female form, and finally a subtle depiction of them out on a date, the view of the men's hands fiddling with her under the table. At the same time, they dined and chatted casually above.

Even Madame Claire agreed to pose for me, using the same man who had been her footstool that night at her party to serve as a prop for my pictures. I loved the audacity of French sexuality and found myself discussing it openly in a way I never would have before Sinclair, before we had come to Paris to explore together.

Before I knew it, we had been there for two and a half weeks, and it was Christmas.

Paris at Christmas was a revelation. The dark latticework of naked trees lining the narrow streets and broad promenades were ribboned with tiny lights, lampposts boasted large red bows and every storefront was tastefully rearranged according to a different holiday theme. Elegantly dressed Parisians walked leisurely through the city, stopping into lesser-known chocolate shops to seek out *chocolat chaud* and Christmas confections between last-minute gift shopping.

The lavishly decorated Christmas tree that dominated Notre

Dame Cathedral's main plaza drew tourists and locals alike, especially as they had canceled the installation last Christmas due to the
November terrorist attacks. People had placed flowers beneath the
tree like presents to those who had passed away, but the atmosphere
was jovial nonetheless, the air filled with laughter and ample cries of
*Joyeux Noël.*

It was a gorgeous place to spend Christmas Eve, but I couldn't
shake the melancholy that had stalked me the past few days. It made
me feel ungrateful to feel this way, especially when the love of my life
was beside me, currently holding my gloved hand. He had sensed my
mood, of course, and taken the past few days off work in order to
throw himself into entertaining me. We ice skated at the Trocodero,
ate at all my favorite haunts, even the cheap café under Place de
Madeleine, and now we were simply walking the crowded streets on
our way from meeting Candy and Cage for drinks.

"You are unhappy," Sinclair noted.

I bit my lip, unwilling to spoil our beautiful day with my stupid,
self-indulgent thoughts. "Just thoughtful."

His eyes narrowed. "You know how much your thoughts are
worth to me. Please, tell me."

"As happy as I am here with you, I still feel restless. Unresolved."

He nodded. "That's understandable. Even though we are finally
together, this is a dream world, one where we don't have to reap the
consequences of our actions."

I bit my lip. "Well, I am feeling one of them. I miss my family, and
the worst part is that I know this feeling won't go away anytime soon
because when I see them again, I'll have to tell them about us, and
then they will deliberately go away."

Sinclair pressed my hand between his. The gesture reminded me
of the way one preserved a flower between the pages of a book, and I
knew it meant that he wanted desperately to conserve my relationship with my family, at least with Mama and the twins.

"You don't know how they will react. They might be supportive."

"Honestly, I think the twins know already. At least, Cosima."

"Oh?" Sinclair asked though there was sharpness in his eyes that said he wasn't that surprised. "She does know both of us well enough to sense something amiss."

"Well, I've definitely been distracted, but I can't see you giving yourself away. Obviously, I didn't know you before, but you seemed to act the same."

"I was happy, Elle, incandescently so. That was a change that everyone noticed."

I sucked in a deep breath between my teeth, surprised by his words but more surprised by the impact they had on me. When would I get used to the fact that Sinclair had always wanted me? That maybe he always would?

"Do you miss her?" I asked. "I'm not trying to trap you. I'm honestly just wondering. It's only natural after spending so much time with a person that you would miss them."

Even though I said the words, and a large part of me meant them, there was still an echo in my chest that urged me to compare myself to Elena. I resisted, drawing on the strength of Sin's hand in mind in order to do it.

"I do and I do not," he admitted. "I miss talking to her because she was smart and curious about the world, a great conversationalist. I think our favorite times together were spent reading the Sunday *New York Times* and hashing out the events of the week and doing the crossword puzzle."

I felt a pang but not a large one. Sinclair and I didn't read the paper together like that, but we would establish our own routines, and we had countless topics to talk about it.

"I do not miss how savage she made me feel for wanting to tug her hair or talk dirty to her. She made me ashamed of an essential part of myself. More than that, I don't miss the life we lived together, stuck in these strict routines and bound by everyone else's rules, including my parents. That's not what any relationship should be about. So, mostly, no, I do not miss her."

He slid a thumb down the line of my jaw and pinched my chin to tilt it up, so I was looking him in the eye. "Do you?"

I shook my head before I could even process his question logically. "No, I never had much of her to miss."

His lips flattened. "The way she treats you... I knew she was never your biggest advocate, but for a sister to treat another sister that way, I think it's disgusting."

"You're just protective. I'm sure plenty of sisters have issues with each other."

Sin shot me an eloquent look.

"Okay, maybe not issues as deep-seated and malicious as ours."

"It's good to acknowledge that. And thank you for bringing her up, for sharing with me. I told you that nothing can harm what you and I have as long as we are open with each other. Do you believe me now?"

He was asking if I believed enough in our love to brave the obstacles in our way together. It was a question that he had proven he had the answer to in innumerable ways, from the moment he declared his love for me after Thanksgiving dinner, through his week of wooing me, and the entire time we had been in Paris together. He had stumbled a little after Elena's email, but that was so understandable that it still broke my heart to think of the self-disgust she had instilled in him after all these years.

Nothing was disgusting about my Frenchman.

With that in mind, I answered his question in a way I knew he would understand. "I know we talked about your willingness to move here for me, especially after the job opportunity at *Vogue* came up. I hope you know that I love you for supporting me, but I think it's time we went home. I'm ready to face the music, and our lives are in New York."

"Are you sure?" he asked, and I knew my potential confirmation meant a lot to him.

France had been both of our homes for a long time, but it was in our past. Our future was in the States.

"Absolutely," I said.

He groaned, a sound that seemed to be wrenched from the very soul of him, as he drew me tight against his body and buried his face in my hair.

"Mine," he claimed on a ragged whisper.

"Yours," I agreed.

We stood in the middle of the Notre Dame plaza for a long time, holding each other, and it felt like its own Christmas miracle to have my arms around a man so perfect for me I could not have even dreamed of him before meeting him. Yet there I stood with a man so perfect for me and so perfectly *mine* as much as I was his.

I stood on my tiptoes to murmur, "I have an early present for you. Let's go back to the Wilde room."

"Only if you promise to get wild with me." He chuckled and then groaned. "That was terrible, and I apologize profusely."

I beamed up at him, arms wrapped around his waist. "No apology necessary. As long as you're smiling, I can put up with your shitty puns."

His laughter rang out over the holiday music and made me grin all the way back to our room.

*I* was folded on my knees beside the bed, a strip of red satin over my eyes with another one binding my hands together in a bow behind my back. I had pre-tied the bow and practiced tightening it around my wrists while they were awkwardly pressed behind me so that I could present myself to Sin as his Christmas present exactly like this.

Of course, I had also gotten him a real gift, a painting that Odile had done of me before I had left for New York. I had posed in a nude workshop for one of her advanced classes, and the painting depicted me from behind, my head tilted so that my riotous curls flooded like a lava spill down one side of my back, and a sliver of my profile was revealed to show me biting my lip. My ass was round and pert with shadows and highlights, and something about the deep line demarcating either side of my back where my spine rested was unspeakably erotic. I knew he would love it even more than I did.

But for now, I was giving him this, me.

I could feel the still air shift, molecules activating with the power he brought to the room as soon as he entered.

"Look at you all wrapped up prettily for me," he murmured as he came to a standstill in front of me. "It turns you on to present yourself like this for me. I can see how wet your sweet pussy is between those thighs, how your rosy nipples strain, begging for me to twist them, bite them, mark them with my tongue."

I began to pant.

"You look pretty as a picture, Elle. I couldn't have drawn you better myself, but I still want to add my mark. You would look magnificent with my come on those flushed cheeks."

"Yes," I gasped because I wanted it.

"I have something else in mind, though, to make this even more beautiful. Would you like it?"

"Yes please, sir."

"So polite," he crooned as I heard him snap something open.

Then he was wrapping something cool and textured around my throat.

My heart leaped into my mouth and stayed there while he clasped the necklace behind my nape.

"Collared," he whispered into the profound silence. "Mine."

I shivered under the power of his ownership. It felt so final to have his brand around my skin. I hoped it was something I could wear every day so that even if strangers didn't know its significance, I would.

"It's a pearl choker, Elle. You never have to take it off if you don't want," he said, reading my thoughts again in that way of his that thrilled and terrified me.

"I don't want," I murmured.

"Good girl."

He pressed his foot between my spread knees, pushing his calf bone hard against my clit. I groaned at the friction of his crisp hair against my flesh. My hips bucked before I could still them.

"Now, you have a choice here, Elle. It is Christmas and I just collared you, so I am feeling generous. I will let you get off on my leg before I do what I want with you or you can wait and see if those plans involve you orgasming."

I shuddered. I didn't really think he would leave me hanging. Sinclair wasn't that kind of man or that kind of Dom, but the thought of getting off on his leg was so dirty, so delicious that I started gyrating back and forth before I had even made a conscious choice.

"That's right, use my leg to get yourself off," Sin murmured.

I pressed my face into his upper thigh, discovering that he wasn't naked and his erection was trapped within the confines of his boxer briefs but angled right at my panting mouth. I moved faster, shamelessly as I tongued his cock through the fabric.

"You want me in your mouth, Elle?"

"Yes, please, sir." My mouth was already dripping with saliva as I imagined the taste of him exploding across my tongue.

"No, I want you to get off on my leg first."

I increased the tempo, humping his leg hard, grinding my clit into his shin.

"You're dripping all over my foot," Sinclair noted, and for some reason, his calm observation drew the coil tighter in my belly.

I loved the debasement of being on my knees in front of him, bound and finding pleasure in the simple act of humping his leg like a dog. I was too deep in subspace to find the degradation anything but electrifying.

I started whimpering, little sounds of pleasure exploding from my mouth as the climax crawled up my back and took hold of my spine before I could even notice its descent.

"Ahhh," I moaned as I thrashed against his leg, almost losing my balance with my hands clasped behind my back.

My sex was still spasming as he abruptly lifted me to my feet and pushed me over the side of my bed. I shouted hoarsely into the sheets as his fingers drove into my clenching pussy, curling and driving deep to draw the orgasm on and on and on. My legs shuddered, unable to hold me up as his mouth sought my clit and clamped on.

"No," I screamed as a terrifying orgasm dropped on top of the first one before it had even finished.

I lost control of my body, my muscles snapping like elastic bands as I collapsed on the bed, only my hips still moving, thrusting back against his fingers and tongue. Sinclair growled into my cunt and ate like a mad man, lapping up the juices that flooded from me.

He adjusted me again just as I was regaining any degree of consciousness, pushing my legs up on the bed and under me so that I was in his favorite position, my hands bound behind my back and my ass presented to him high in the air over my steeply curved spine.

Instead of taking his fingers from me, he added a thumb to the tight pucker of my ass. When I lurched forward, he tugged me back with an arm banded under my belly.

"Does my siren like to be filled?" he asked coldly before biting into the back of my shoulder.

I shuddered against him. "Y-Yes, sir."

"You tied yourself up so nicely for me. Does that mean I can take whatever I want?"

"You can always take whatever you want, sir."

"And why is that?"

"Because you own me," I breathed, a shiver clutching as me as I spoke my absolute truth.

This man totally and completely owned me but only like this, when I was literally twisting myself into a pretzel to please him, did I really feel alive with his possession.

"Yes, I own this pussy," he said, sliding a third finger inside and twisting it savagely so that I moaned and hissed at the pleasure-pain combination. "I own this pretty pink asshole, and I am going to take it as my Christmas present."

I opened my mouth to say something, but only a ragged groan emerged when he landed a hard smack on my ass. He unwrapped his arm from around me and used it to add two fingers to my clutching bottom, twisting and turning them inside me in a sinuous rhythm that had my entire body clenching, quickening again.

"I, oh God," I blathered incoherently as he worked both my holes.

"Hush," he murmured, and I could feel him staring at our connection, watching how I opened and closed around him. "So pretty."

"Please, oh, please," I begged, for what I didn't really know.

"What do you need, *ma jolie fille*?" he husked.

"I need to come again," I panted. "I want to come on you."

"On me where?" he urged me to say. "You know I like your voice."

"Please, sir, take my ass and let me come again."

Before I even had the words out, his fingers were gone and he was surging, sure and steady into my ass. I screamed into the duvet, sweating and moaning and aching as he spread me open over his huge girth.

"Oh God, oh God," I murmured into the blanket at he seated himself fully inside me and then slowly pulled out.

He continued to fuck me tortuously, so slowly that I could feel every ridge and vein in his cock as it entered me.

"Please," I begged.

He pulled out, ignoring my murmured protests and ran his finger around my gaping opening. It was such a possessive, intimate touch that I nearly lost it as he ran his thumb around and around my closing muscle, dipping the tip of his digit into me from time to time.

I could feel the puddle of my arousal at the base of my knees, soaking the bed.

"So fucking pretty," he groaned. "This ass, this pussy, this woman."

"Yours, all of it," I gritted out through my teeth.

"Mine," he agreed, heaving into me again.

This time he set a brutal pace, each time pressing his entire length into me before taking almost the entire thing out again. He pushed and pulled me off his dick, slamming me back and forth against his hips so that I was rocking like an agitated pendulum.

"Work yourself against my cock," he ordered and I threw myself back against him with an athleticism that I hadn't known I possessed.

"Are you going to come with me in your ass, Elle?" he asked me, his cool voice cracking like breaks in the ice at the end of his question.

It spurned me on. "Yes, sir, if you will allow it."

He fucked me harder, slapping my ass with each cruel thrust. The pain gathered at the base of my spine and spooled into golden pleasure.

"I'll allow it. Come then."

A hoarse shout ripped from my lungs as I went completely rigid, the orgasm tearing through me, paralyzing me from the inside out for one shocking moment before it electrified me, shaking and rolling every single molecule in my body together until I was only a churning mass of matter, not even human any more.

Vaguely, I heard his gruff shout of triumph before he released warm and deep inside me.

After a few moments, he gently left me and smoothed me out on the bed so that I was laying straight and tied on the mattress. He unbound my hands and pressed a kiss to each wrist before he undid my blindfold. His hands ran down my back, rubbing and soothing my back, bum and thighs for a few moments before I was a complete puddle of melted woman against the bed. Only then did he go to the bathroom to clean up.

When he returned, he pushed a button for the AC and I sighed softly as it stirred beautifully over my sweat soaked skin.

"Thank you," I murmured as he got into bed beside me.

"No, Elle, thank you for trusting me with yourself. Best Christmas present ever."

I grinned at him even as I fell into a deep sleep.

# Chapter Eleven

*Giselle*

It was on New Year's Eve when I got the call.

We were at Cage's massive apartment where he was throwing a 1920s themed party. It had been an amazing night even though my stomach was a little off so I wasn't drinking. Sinclair looked absolutely dashing in a traditional black tuxedo, and his eyes flashed every time he took in the four rows of perfect blush pearls that lined my throat. I had only been collared for six days, and it was still thrilling to both of us.

We were also just straight-up happy. We had found harmony together, living side by side, that I never could have guessed would be so easy or so blissful. I knew we would go back to New York soon. We had talked about going at the end of January, but for now, we were finding our way in our new relationship without the strain of outside judgment.

So happy.

Then I got the call.

"What?" I yelled into the phone, pressing a hand to my other ear to block out the sounds of revelry.

It was long after the countdown, and the party, unsurprisingly as it was populated with musicians and BDSM worshippers, had slipped into loud, jovial debauchery.

"Cosima," Mama cried, "She's in the hospital. They have her in surgery right now, but *bambina*, it does not look good."

My phone clattered to the ground as I stared off into the party-goers thrashing on the dance floor.

Cosima was in the hospital.

It was not looking good.

God, what could have happened?

Sinclair swooped down to pick up my phone, appearing beside me even though I had left him in the kitchen to take the call. He watched me as he spoke into the phone, but I didn't look at him. I was paralyzed with fear and pretty certain I was going to throw up.

"Sebastian?" Sinclair was saying. "Yes, expect us soon. We'll catch the next flight out."

I didn't remember much of what happened after that except for a vague recollection of returning to the hotel to change and pack our bags before catching a taxi to the airport at some time just before dawn. I didn't even remember enough to say a proper goodbye to Paris. When I woodenly mentioned this to Sinclair, he had kissed my hair and promised that we would go back.

Now, I was so afraid that I was physically sick with it. Sinclair had held my hair as I repeatedly vomited on the plane back to New York. I would have been embarrassed, but he sweetly reminded me of how he had fallen under my spell when I was sick on the plane to Mexico and that this was nostalgic somehow instead of gross. It was pure lies, but I appreciated his efforts too much to say anything. Besides, I was too busy making use of the toilet to talk back anyway.

By the time we landed and dragged ourselves into the waiting Town Car, my body felt weak and saturated with grime like a wrung-out dish towel. Sinclair held me tightly against his side as he responded feverishly to emails on his phone. We had to leave in such a rush that he had left a mess of things back in Paris. A part of me was grateful for his distraction, both because it took his mind off Cosima's dire situation but also because it gave me room to think things through unobserved. If he hadn't been preoccupied, he would have easily picked up on the rod of discomfort in my spine that kept me from sinking into his warmth.

My anxiety only increased as we entered the city and headed straight to the trauma ward at St Vincent's Hospital. I hated that my overwhelming fear for my sister was undermined by the drama that had become the cornerstone of my life. Elena didn't know about Sin and me, which meant that as soon as we entered those sliding glass doors, we would effectively cease to exist as a unit at exactly the moment we needed each other the most. I tried to give myself a stern talking-to like a tough coach before a big game, but no matter how much I berated myself for being selfish, reminded myself that this was the least I deserved, told myself that I was a strong, independent woman capable of handling emotional distress without someone else's help, I kept coming back to the desire to whimper like a freaking baby.

Sin pressed his lips to my hair and breathed deeply. "Visiting hours are almost over, but the family will still be there with her. As soon as we are finished here, I booked rooms at the St. Regis."

Of course, because we hadn't talked about what our living situation was going to look like now that we were together. Sinclair was without a home, and I couldn't very well live with Cosima. It would be incredibly unfair to make her choose sides, especially when she couldn't actually speak for herself at the moment.

It took me a moment to understand what he said, but I blamed it on the lingering nausea.

"Rooms?"

Sin picked up his phone and nonchalantly scrolled through his inbox again. "Mmm."

"Why the plural?"

"I need to give Richard a call before we get to the hospital if you don't mind."

"I do mind. Why did you book multiple rooms, Sin?"

He sighed, tugging on a lock of his overlong hair. "I wasn't sure if you would want to stay with me, given the current situation."

Maybe if he had voiced it differently, emphasized his own discomfort with the living situation, with the fact that there would never be a good time to come out to our family but that it most definitely was *not* now, I would have felt insecure about the comment. Instead, my heart melted a little inside my chest because I knew that it was Sinclair, my enigmatic, in-control Frenchman, who was experiencing a moment of doubt.

I got to my knees on the seat in order to take his face in my hands. His eyes were squinted defensively, but their color was pure and velvety with sadness.

"If it wasn't completely callous of us, I would demand to move in with you this very second and take out an ad on page six of the *Times* so that everyone in the entire city would know it," I said.

Sinclair's corresponding grin was so large that I could have counted every single one of his pearly white teeth. "I love you."

"I love you. And I'm going to miss you the second we get inside that god-forsaken hospital," I admitted.

Sin ran his knuckles down my cheek and lifted the hair from my neck to swing it behind my shoulder. I tilted my head to give him access to my throat. The pads of his fingers pressed gently against my fluttering pulse while his other hand slid up my bare thigh, under my skirt, right to the edge of my panties. We both felt the increase in my heart rate.

"Your body and soul, your very heartbeat are mine, Giselle. Remember that even when I'm across the room from you, pretending otherwise. I will still feel every hop and skip of this pulse, feel every emotion that plucks at this chest, and I will remember every single one so that I can console you properly later." He laughed at the flush of arousal that I could feel blooming under my skin. "Such a dirty girl, you know what I meant."

"I do," I said before leaning over to nip his strong chin between my teeth. "I was just hoping you would also console me physically."

His chuckle was deep and smoky as he gripped my chin and brought his lips against mine. "That goes without saying."

The driver pulling in front of the hospital and knocking lightly at the partition interrupted our searing kiss. I clutched to Sinclair, my nails digging into the quilted muscles of his back, my lips sucking hard at his, for one desperate moment before I pulled away.

"Let's go see Cosima," he said, reminding me gently why we were here in the first place.

I was up and out of the car in less than a heartbeat.

It was my first time in a hospital. When I was growing up, the hospital was almost as bad as the police station. No one went because it meant having to disclose why you were injured, and in Napoli, home of the Camorra, death that stemmed from tattling was worse than any other fate.

The whir of equipment and the faint shush of Crocs shuffling across the laminate floor immediately disturbed me. I didn't like the pressurized silence, the forced smiles the nurses gave me as I passed through the lobby, up the elevator, and into the trauma ward. Everything was white or beige, sterile and chemically scented. The antithesis of Cosima.

Sinclair wasn't with me, opting to wait downstairs for a few minutes so that it wouldn't seem suspicious that we had arrived together. I understood the need for duplicity, but I wished fervently that he were beside me, his cool control like a balm to my flustered spirit.

I rounded the corner of the nurses' station, about to ask which room Cosima occupied when I caught sight of a tall, dark, and handsome man emerging from behind a drab curtain.

"Sebastian!" I called out, too loudly, too desperate for the muted ambiance of the hospital ward.

By the time he turned around, I was already barreling into his arms. He caught me in a death grip, squeezing so hard it was hard to breathe. I relished the sensation.

"*Bambina, bambina,*" he murmured over and over into my hair.

It took me a moment to realize that he was trembling beneath my embrace, that under his spicy cologne, he smelled like stale sweat and cigarettes. Things were bad whenever Seb picked up his smoking habit.

"Let me look at you," I said, gently extracting myself from his arms.

He kept hold of my hands but allowed enough distance for me to observe his appearance. My heart tightened painfully as I noted his grimy, tousled hair and the deep purplish trenches beneath his glassy eyes. He looked incredibly ill as if Death himself stalked his every move. He might as well have, I figured, because if Cosima didn't pull through, I really couldn't see Sebastian surviving without her.

"You look like shit."

A glimmer of amusement flared in his gold eyes. "You look more beautiful than I have ever seen you."

*I'm happy*, I wanted to say but didn't. Instead, I shrugged and tugged him by the hand closer to the room he had just left.

"Tell me what happened. Mama only had time to tell me that Cosima was in some sort of accident and that she was in the ICU."

Seb scrubbed both hands over his face, absentmindedly taking mine along for the ride as we were still clasping palms. He didn't notice, and I didn't say anything.

"She was having dinner in the Bronx at this tiny Italian deli she likes even though the prosciutto tastes like shoe leather. According to witnesses, she was eating alone, but she seemed to be waiting for someone. She even bought an extra sandwich and a bottle of Chinotto Neri—"

"She hates soda," I interjected automatically.

"I know, and I can't think of a single damn person in her life who would drink that stuff."

"Only an Italian," I said, because it was our version of Coca-Cola but bitter, the Neri brand quintessentially Italian too.

"Obviously," Seb agreed, his jaw taut with agitation. "I was fucking useless when the police questioned me. She is my twin sister and best friend in the world." His voice cracked, and he cleared his throat. "How can I have been oblivious to this?"

I thought about the secrets our sister kept hidden close to her skin, closer even than her twin brother and best friend in the world could be.

"Continue," I urged because I didn't have anything comforting to say.

"She had been waiting for about fifteen minutes when a black SUV pulled up in front of the shop and opened fire."

I gasped, the scene playing out in my mind like a film reel. My beautiful sister sits at a table near the window and waits patiently for some unknown man like a heroine in a tragic romance novel when the gunfire starts.

I felt sure it was a man she was waiting for, not least of all, because Cosima didn't particularly like women, and they didn't particularly like her. It was clear to me too, that this wasn't a random attack. Who would target a nearly empty Italian deli in the Bronx just for kicks?

If I rephrased the question—who would target a nearly empty Italian deli just to take someone out?—I knew the answer. *The Mafia.*

I swallowed hard and snuck a glance up at Sebastian who was absorbed in his own painful reverie. The face of Dante, the black-eyed mafia man who had appeared one day in Cosima's apartment a few weeks ago, flared to life in my memory. He had something to do with this. I knew it as surely as I knew that it had been wishful thinking by our family to think that Cosima had fled the confines of Naples unshackled. After she had left, and Seamus, our family had been left remarkably untroubled by the local made men. Mama had put it down to God and her devout prayer, Sebastian to the departure of our gambling, addict father, but I had always wondered, and I knew Elena did too, if Cosima hadn't signed away her soul for our freedom.

As we were standing in a hospital with her lying ten feet away, struggling for her life, I was desperately afraid I already knew the answer to that question as well.

"She was just sitting there," Seb said quietly, almost to himself.

"Giselle?" Mama's voice drifted out into the hall, and my heart tripped over the familiar, tender notes.

I spilled through the doorway and tumbled straight into the arms of my mother. She pressed me against her breast, hushing my suddenly laborious breaths and random whimpers of pain. Now that I was there, in the awful hospital that was such a contrast to my vibrant sister, the reality of her situation came crashing down around me. Before I could lose it completely, I pulled away from the faint citrus and semolina scent of my Mama and turned toward the hospital bed.

Cosima under a thin white sheet, thin and pale as a cadaver used in medical school experiments. There were deeply purple bruises under her eyes and a brackish, yellow-brown discoloration over the left side of her face. She had always been svelte, but in the harsh light, she seemed skeletal, impossibly dead.

I gasped and then choked on a bulbous sob.

Mama stroked my hair as I turned and threw up in a bin that Sebastian thrust under my chin.

"*Bambina, bambina*," she crooned.

"What happened?" I whispered through the bile rising at the back of my throat.

"She was shot three times in the torso."

I tilted my head to stare at Elena. She sat in an absurdly orange plastic chair beside the bed wearing a beautiful turtleneck dress. Her hair was still shiny and supple, curled around her beautiful face perfectly. Hatred rose with the bile to pool at the back of my tongue. How dare she look so composed when Cosima was practically dead beside her?

Elena continued, even though my glare should have eviscerated her. "She hit her head on the way down, and they have her in a medically induced coma until the swelling goes down."

I wrenched my gaze away from Elena and my unfair rage against her to look at Cosima again. Her skin was papery under my fingers when I reached over to brush my fingers against her cheek, and her normally lustrous hair was brittle. Another sob rose in my throat, but I swallowed it painfully. Crying would only prompt my family to do the same.

"*Cane*, let me through!" A roughened voice demanded from down the hallway.

"Get your act together," another voice bit out, "or I won't let you see her."

A moment later, Sinclair led a disgruntled Dante into the room. I gasped at the sight of the Italian man, his inky hair completely disheveled and his black eyes wild with grief. He immediately tumbled into the room and sat on Cosima's bed, his hands shaking as they gently skimmed over her face.

"*Mia bella ragazza*," he murmured over and over again as he stared at her.

I was deeply surprised and even strangely moved when tears began to roll down his cheeks.

"Who the fuck are you?" Sebastian demanded after the moment of shock passed.

Dante ignored him. Instead, he pressed his forehead against Cosima's and continued to mutter in Italian under his breath.

Sebastian took a menacing step forward but stopped with Dante let out a choked sob. His hand shook as he stroked it down Cosima's brittle mane of hair.

"What happened to you?" he whispered in anguish.

Sebastian vibrated beside me, but I knew he wouldn't rip the mafia man away without asking questions first.

I opened my mouth to do just that, but Elena interrupted me.

"What are you doing here, Daniel?"

It took me a moment to process what she was doing. When I whirled to face her and saw the sincerity in her expression, I was furious for a different reason.

"Elena," I snapped before I could temper my response.

Sinclair held up a hand and stepped forward. "Elena, this isn't the time."

Mama looked between the three of us with sharp eyes that saw too much. "What is going on, *ragazzi*?"

"Daniel and I are," Elena paused delicately, "going through a trial separation."

Sinclair frowned but didn't correct her. I wanted him to so badly that my muscles twitched, but I tried to understand why he remained silent.

Mama barely batted an eyelash. "I agree. This is not the time, Elena."

"No, it is the time for this *cafone* to tell us what he got Cosi into," Sebastian growled as he moved forward to plant a heavy hand on Dante's shoulder.

The made man stilled, his lack of movement filled with threat.

"I didn't get her into anything," he said quietly.

"*Stronzo*, do not lie to me about my sister."

"I would never do anything to harm her," Dante whispered again.

Was it absurd that I believed him? He was looking at Cosima with a tenderness that echoed in my chest.

"Tell me the truth," Sebastian roared, yanking him back by the shoulder.

Dante was on his feet in a flash, his forearm across Seb's throat as he held him against the wall. My brother was tall, over six feet, but Dante was practically a giant, closer to seven feet than six, with muscles defined and bulging like coils of rope beneath his skin.

Dante leaned close to Sebastian's face and calmly repeated, "I didn't get her *into* anything. I *saved* her, *patatino*."

He knew his family nickname.

Who was this guy?

Dante stepped back with a snort of disgust and turned to face Cosima again, his face soft with anguish again. He took her hand but spoke to Sebastian, "I understand your anger but know that I have lived with it for much longer than you, this rage against the people who dare to touch this woman." His fingers tenderly brushed her hair away from her face. "She kept you in the dark because you weren't strong enough to deal with her demons."

Sebastian growled, but I stepped forward to press a hand to his arm.

"She never gave us the chance," I said softly. "Maybe you can?"

Dante looked over at me, his eyes large and wet with tears. For a moment, I could sense his desire to connect with us. There was no doubt in my mind that he loved Cosima and the outsider in him longed to be accepted by her and by association, her family.

But the expression flicked and died a quick death when Elena snorted at my comment and Sebastian bared his teeth.

The family that couldn't even accept their own would never accept him, and by the look in his eye, he knew it.

"It is not my story to tell, not really," he finally said.

"Cut the bullshit," Sebastian said. "I want to know what happened to my sister."

Dante shrugged as if he didn't care, but his eyes were tight. "I can't know for sure. She knows more than one dangerous person, myself included, who could have swept her up into the middle of a feud. She always was too curious for her own good. Too defiant."

"So, you had nothing to do with this?" I clarified because I was pretty sure Sebastian needed to be reminded.

He had the wet black look of murder in his suddenly dark eyes.

"No, but I will find out what happened to her," he vowed, more to Cosima than to anyone else. He leaned closer to her until their noses were almost touching. "And I promise to rip them apart with my teeth, *tesoro*."

# Chapter Twelve

*Giselle*

There was no way to prepare for something like this. Of course, there wasn't a handbook that offered advice to adulterers on how to calmly confront the wronged party about their infidelity. How did a person condense their sinful actions, endless excuses, and genuine apologies into one carefully constructed monologue? Even if you accomplished such a thing, there was no way in hell the person was just going to sit there and listen to you.

"This is impossible," I murmured, my hands clutched around my cold cup of coffee.

Sinclair was cleaning up in the kitchenette after our quick breakfast of croissants, baguette, and fresh plum jam. Or at least, Sinclair's quick breakfast. As soon as I had touched a piece of toast to my mouth, I had run to the washroom to throw up. I was still feeling physically ill from the trauma of Cosima's accident and now, from the stress of confronting Elena, it was impossible to keep anything down.

There was a smudge of purple jelly left on the right side of Sin's mouth that I fixated on as he competently moved around our suite at the St. Regis. I loved to watch the economy of his actions, the contained grace with which he carried his lean build. It didn't disturb me anymore to know that I could spend hours watching him.

Who needed Netflix when you had a hot Frenchman to stare at?

Normally, he was enough to distract me, but I was going to coffee with Elena this morning. To call it a coffee date was misleading and wrong, but I didn't know how else to phrase it except to say that it was a date made to ruin her life, and it didn't have the same ring to it.

We had only been Stateside for three days, all of which were filled with extended hospital visits to a still-comatose Cosima. It felt wrong to tell the family about our relationship during a time like this, but it felt like more of a betrayal to hide it from them during a time like this, so I was meeting with her this morning.

"Elle, we have spoken about this. If you don't want to be the one to tell her, I am more than prepared to do it myself."

I blinked up at him where he leaned over the other side of the island, his gaze direct and strong. I had no doubt he was prepared to do the hard part for me. In fact, I was sure he would have preferred it.

I shook my head. "No. I'm her sister. We may not get along very well, but I owe it to our family bond to tell her about us to her face. I just don't know how to go about it gently, you know?"

"I do know. I know that something like this, it cannot be done gently."

I sighed into my nearly empty mug. It felt doubly wrong to break the news to her, given what was going on with Cosima, but it was for exactly that reason that I knew I had to do it sooner rather than later. If God forbid something worse happened to Cosima, Sinclair and I would need each other. Besides, we were ready to move forward together, and keeping that a secret in the face of everything seemed reprehensible.

"Giselle," Sin said softly, rounding the marble counter so that he could take my cheek in his cool palm. "There is no candy coating this. You are in love with your sister's ex-boyfriend. I do not think words exist in any language that will make that more palatable to Elena."

God, I hated how true that was.

"We made the right decision, the *only* decision, but it doesn't make it seem any less selfish," I admitted.

His thumb brushed tenderly over my bottom lip before he dipped down to press a kiss there. When he tried to pull away, I abandoned my coffee cup to link my hands behind his neck and clasp him closer to me. He smiled against my mouth before kissing me more deeply, his tongue warm velvet against mine.

"The only thing worse than being so selfish, I've found, is not owning it," he said after a minute, pressing his forehead to mine. "We may have acted immorally, but we did it for a purpose. We did it for love, and there is no shame to be felt in that."

"No," I agreed because I couldn't imagine being ashamed of the man I held in my arms.

"Do not show her regret. She is a shark, your sister, and she will sense blood in the water. She will make you pay for that shame."

I sighed loudly against his face and pressed another kiss to his lips. "You're right, of course."

"Of course," he agreed with a smile as I pulled away to scoot off my stool. He gave my bum a playful slap as I moved past him to get ready. "Go get 'em, tiger."

*I* was happy that Elena had chosen our location for coffee because I fully planned never to set foot in the place again. Like a nuclear blast site, it would remain toxic for the next forty years. As it was, the place suited my sister entirely, posh and trendy without being hip, with black and white photos on the wall and tons of smartly clad businesspeople milling about even on a Saturday morning. We both sat at a small bistro table in one of the large bay windows, holding our cups of coffee tightly as if to make up for the intimacy lacking between us. We had been sitting there for five awkward minutes in silence while I worked up the courage to begin.

"How have you been?" I finally asked lamely.

"Well, thank you. I've told you before that I'm on the partner track?"

*Only a thousand times.*

"You may have mentioned it once or twice. That's very impressive."

Elena nodded graciously.

Awkward silence reigned for an excruciating minute.

"Mama told me that you just got back from France. You went to visit friends?" Elena asked.

Her words hit my hollow heart with a dull thud. She was actually trying.

"I did. It was good to go back. It will always be home for me in a way that Naples never was."

She nodded, her eyes glazed over as she looked out the window at the softly falling snow. "I know what you mean. I have absolutely no desire to ever return there, even to Italy. Do you know, I tell people that I am American?"

I wasn't surprised, but she did shock me by elaborating.

"It took me over a year of constant study and practice to rid myself of that common accent. It was the r's that frustrated me. The flat English sound took me forever to master."

"Why is it so important to you?"

She was startled by the question as if I should know the answer. "Italy stands for everything that I abhor. It is gritty, dirty, violent, and fundamentally debased."

"Have you ever thought that you might be substituting the half for the whole? Yes, our childhood could be defined by those things, but does that reflect on our country or only on our circumstances?"

Elena blinked at me. "Does it matter? The half contaminates the whole. The poison spreads."

I swallowed thickly. "You're saying that you cannot forgive Italy for the desperation of your childhood?"

"I see no reason I should."

"Yet you forgive Mama for raising you like that?"

Finally, Elena looked uncomfortable. "She didn't have the power to control it."

I arched an eyebrow at her.

She pursed her lips. "I understand the point you are trying to make, but it isn't valid. Mama tried her best to raise us right. There was nothing more she could have done, and she has more than made up for her mistakes every day since we got out of that hellish place."

I sucked a deep breath into my lungs like a drowning man who knows that will be his last breath.

The stage was set, however poorly, and I couldn't put it off any longer.

"Elena, I actually asked you to meet me here today to talk about something kind of difficult."

She stilled so completely that it brought into stark relief the motion of the coffee shop flowing around us. It was a popular spot at a busy time, and I had to swallow the impulsive panic that everyone was suddenly listening to us.

"I know that you and I have always had a... hard relationship, and I wish so much that it was different." I looked into her eyes and flinched at the lack of compassion there. She shared no such desire. "Our family has been through so much, and it has been our strength and loyalty as a unit that has gotten us through. I admire and respect you so much—"

"Cut the crap, Giselle. What is it that you want to say to me?"

My throat was so dry that it hurt to breathe. Pain shot up my arms directly into my off-beating heart. I wondered if I was having a heart attack.

I gasped for one more lungful of air before willingly falling on my sword.

"I am in love with Sinclair."

Silence.

Total and complete silence.

A non-reaction.

For a moment, I wondered if I had even spoken.

Then she blinked in that slow way of hers that hypnotized you, and when her eyes opened again, they were narrowed with laser-like intensity.

"When?"

The word flung me like a dart through a butterfly's wing, pinning me to the wall, helpless against her scrutiny.

"We met in Mexico. I had no idea he was your boyfriend, and he had no idea I was your sister. We knew each other only as Sinclair and Elle. We, well, we spent a lot of time together that trip, and I fell in love with him. I fell in love with the person he made me believe that I could be."

"An adulterer?" she asked mildly.

I had never been as afraid of anyone, not even Christopher, as I was of my sister at that moment.

"I left him thinking that I would never see him again, but then there he was in Mama's kitchen. There he was as your boyfriend."

"He was more than a mere boyfriend," she hissed.

I nodded. "I know. I knew that he was yours; that this was the man you had been with for the past four years. I knew that you two seemed perfect together."

"We were. We are."

I choked on her words and coughed. "We both refused to acknowledge what had happened. We wanted it to be in the past where it belonged, but..." I chewed on my lip, focusing on the pain there instead of how hurtful it was to look at my sister, to prostrate myself, my heart, before her even though I knew how it would end.

Bloody, with her hand on the knife stuck deep in my chest.

I tried to remind myself that I deserved it, but it didn't ease the pain.

"We became friends again, just friends," I whispered, more to myself than her.

Elena just sat there, cloaked in righteousness and arctic cold disdain.

"But I loved him so much even in those moments. I loved him so much, Elena, that it became bigger than anything else. Bigger than morality and sin, bigger than our circumstances, bigger even than our love for you."

She was staring at me so hard. I could feel the weight of it like punishing gravity, crushing everything inside my body, folding me up into a crumpled little unrecognizable ball of waste. The beautifully pleated lines and contours of the origami figure I had constructed over the past few months with Sinclair, all those beautiful qualities I had grown to know that I had possessed, were destroyed with one slow blink.

I began to cry, which disgusted me because she was the victim, but I couldn't stop.

"I fought it so hard, Elena. We both did. If you believe nothing else, please believe that we didn't want to do this to you. But this wasn't about a choice. If I denied myself my love of Sinclair..." An ugly sob burst through my lips and slapped wetly against the table. "I would have destroyed both him and myself."

"So, instead, you chose to destroy me," she said quietly.

I cried harder, burying my shameful face in my hands. Snot-laced tears ran through my fingers and dripped to the table.

Elena watched me cry.

"You let him defile you, don't you?"

I recoiled at her sharp question, my head flying up so that I could look at her.

She was sneering at me, her red lips twisted like a bloody smear.

"You let him beat you, don't you? You like it when he hits you, when he ruts into you like a wild beast and marks your body as his own." She laughed at my gasp, the sound sharp and high pitched like an auditory weapon. "You stupid slut. Daniel doesn't love you. He is just using you."

A whimper lodged in my throat. I wanted to beg her to shut up, but I deserved her hatred, so I kept quiet.

She leaned forward, her gorgeous face more animated than I had ever seen it, warped harshly with revulsion. "You think he loves you? What is there about you to love? You are just the same meek, stupid, self-centered little girl who always gets what she wants and is shielded like a baby from every bad thing life throws at her. Do you know why Mama and the twins do that? Hmm? Because they know you are weak. They don't love you so much as pity you. If your family can't even respect you, how do you think a man like Daniel Sinclair could ever *love* you?"

She lifted her chin and looked down on me like the queen of hearts condemning one of her subjects to the guillotine. "Daniel is the best person I have ever known. He is an intelligent, successful businessman and the son of the New York State governor. And you think he loves you?"

Her laughter sliced me into ribbons. All I felt was pain, and still, I sat there and absorbed it, ever the masochist.

She sat back in her chair with a comfortable confidence that was somehow cruel. There was a small smile on her lips when she said, "Did you know, when I first found out he was having an affair, I was concerned? Thank you for alleviating my fears. Daniel doesn't love you, Giselle. When he inevitably grows tired of you, no matter how much you let him slap you around in bed, he will beg for a real woman, a woman of power and substance, to take him back. And that destruction you were so afraid of? It will eviscerate you. You will not have your family or Daniel at your side. I haven't wanted you to be a part of this family for a long time, and I always knew Daniel needed to get his perversions out of his system." She laughed lightly and took a sip of her coffee. "Two birds, one stone."

I sat, my mouth gaping wide open like an angry wound. There were no thoughts in my head or emotions in my chest. I was nothing, just as she and I had always secretly suspected.

Elena searched my face for a long minute, her gaze scalping me, before she nodded, assured of my overwhelming pain. She stood swiftly and tugged on her coat.

"Tell Daniel to call me when he's through with you. Oh, and Giselle, stay the fuck away from my family and me. If you don't, every person in New York City will know what a gold-digging whore you are."

# Chapter Thirteen

*Giselle*

I couldn't go back to the St. Regis after that. Instead, after Elena left and I threw up for twenty minutes in the café restroom, I wandered around Manhattan like some kind of urban zombie, both hollowed out inside and rotten to the core. I was empty of thoughts. In a weird way, it reminded me of what it was like to be in subspace, incapable of coherency but eloquent with emotions. They crashed over me in tidal waves, drowning me in dark pools of pain and guilt.

I knew that if I went to Sinclair, he would make it all go away. He would murmur sweet condolences in my ear, stroke my cheekbone in that way of his that made me feel priceless as a statue, more beautiful than anything rendered by Auguste Rodin or Botticelli. He would, as only he was capable of doing, as he always did, soothe my ugly, crumpled edges and fold me back into an origami swan.

I didn't deserve that peace. A small, protected piece of my mind argued that I did deserve it, that I was worthy of Sinclair's love and that maybe all was fair in love and war. But I also knew that if I went back to him before I had somehow disassembled and portioned out the immeasurable mass of self-hatred and grief churning through my system, I would leave him.

Margot had been right when she said Sinclair deserved more than a coward. It was difficult before when no one knew about the affair. We had been disciples of immoral subterfuge and intense yearning, torn between our past and our dreams for the future. We had barely been able to see each other through the mess of obstacles between us.

Now, I had him. The thought sent a zing of happiness down my spine even in the thralls of my guilt. Daniel Sinclair, the beautiful, misunderstood Frenchman with the seemingly perfect life, had risked his reputation, his family, and his career on *me*.

Elena's vindictive words echoed through my head. He was too good for me, on that we wholeheartedly agreed. I doubted that there would ever be a time when I believed myself worthy of his love. So few people ever found their soul mates, let alone had reason to believe in the concept, and there I was, finally, with mine. Whether or not I deserved such luck, I was not going to take it, *him*, for granted.

I had made my decision, and now I had to live with it.

I wasn't surprised when Mama's restaurant loomed before me, the gold lettering of *Osteria Lombardi* glittering in the lower-level window of the brick brownstone. I floated down the few steps to the entrance and entered before I could run away in fear.

One of the servers directed me to the kitchen where Mama was preparing for dinner service. It was that awkward time of day in the restaurant industry when it is too late for lunch and early for dinner, when most of the day's prep had been done by the day crew before the night lineup came in, so Mama was alone at a long stainless-steel countertop hand-rolling *orecchiette* pasta when I pushed through the swinging doors.

She was so absorbed that she didn't notice me, so I took a minute to watch her work. Her long silver threaded black hair was woven into her habitual braid, and her soft features were arranged into an expression that was the foundation of a smile before it springs. Her nimble fingers gently folded the dough into tiny ear-like shapes before setting them aside to dry, and she hummed as she worked. It was a different setting, but the sight of her like that took me back to the hot, dry afternoons in the Naples of my childhood.

For one insane moment, I wished I was back there.

"Giselle, my French baby, what do you do here?" Mama asked, startling me out of my past.

I smiled softly at her, filled with tenderness. I indulged myself by hustling toward her for a hug. Immediately, she opened her flour-coated arms and pulled me close.

This time, when I cried, the tears were silent.

Mama soothed me like a child with indecipherable cooing noises.

"I love you so much, Mama," I breathed.

"*Sempre*," Mama murmured as she brushed my damp hair away from my face. She searched my eyes for a long time before wrapping me up even more tightly. "What has happened?"

Somehow, it was harder to tell Mama, a woman who had raised me to be better than deceit and infidelity. My betrayal meant the end of a relationship with Elena, but did it have to mean the dissolution of the bonds that tied the rest of my family together?

Fuck, I hoped not.

"I have something that I need to tell you," I whispered.

She sighed softly before steering me toward the other side of the counter where she pulled up a steel stool for me to sit on. Once I was settled, she nodded and returned to her pasta making. Love seared my insides as I realized what she was doing, giving me space to confess.

I stared at the way her hands carefully formed the dough,

mesmerized by the repetition. It helped me gather the edges of my shredded thoughts.

"Mama," I choked on a sob and cleared my throat. "Mama, I want you to know how much I love you, how much I respect the struggle you've been through in order to keep our family whole and successful. You've been a wonderful inspiration for me, the epitome of grace and goodness. Please, don't let what I'm about to tell you be a reflection on your parenting or how I feel about you."

She nodded but didn't look at me, her eyes fixed on her work even though I knew she would do it blindfolded. Her lack of attention gave me the comfort of a confessional. I knew she was on the other side of the pretend indifference, listening and trying not to judge. It gave me hope.

"I had an affair, Mama, with a wonderful man who I met when Brenna sent me to Mexico. I didn't mean for it to happen, I knew he was in a meaningful relationship, but there was this pull between us that I couldn't ignore. He was the most beautiful man I had ever seen, and he made me feel worthy, good, and free of my insecurities." I sucked in a shaky deep breath. "I fell in love with him even though I never planned to see him again. Only, I did. I saw him that very same day, later that night, in your kitchen at my surprise party."

Mama stilled, just for a beat, in her movements, but it was enough for me to realize that she knew where I was going with my story.

I rushed on.

"I was so ashamed, we both were, when we realized the truth. We avoided each other for weeks, but there was still the agonizing magnetism between us. I really thought we could be friends..."

"Never," she said, so softly that at first, I wasn't sure she had spoken at all.

"I loved him too much for that, and apparently, he felt the same way."

"You began an affair again," she stated.

"We began an affair again," I agreed on a whisper. "We were only physically intimate once or twice before he left her, but either way, it was an emotional affair. I don't know. Maybe that's worse."

"*Si*, it is."

I bit my lip so that it wouldn't tremble, and for the first time in years, I spoke to my mother in our native tongue. "*On posso vivere senza di lui.*"

*I cannot live without him.*

"And he feels this way?" Mama asked.

The memory of Sinclair declaring his love for me in his office after the horrible Thanksgiving dinner, how impassioned and primal he was in staking his claim on my heart. I knew without having a mirror that the thought of him lit me up like a traffic light.

"He does."

Mama hummed, the way both she and Elena did when they were processing things.

"I love him more than I have ever loved anyone, and"—I swallowed—"he made me love myself too."

A long silence followed my words. I could have said more, I could have definitely clarified who I spoke of and what our future plans entailed, but instead, I chewed on my lip. Meanwhile, mama finished shaping the last of the semolina dough and braced her hands on the table. I waited with my heart in my throat for her to look up at me, yet I was jolted out of my skin when her rich brown eyes found mine.

They were eyes I had stared into for the majority of my life, and her gaze was the one I had grown up looking to for guidance, support, and redemption. So, I think a large part of me was expecting to see the acceptance that I had always found there even though I knew what I had done was at least mildly despicable.

Only, there was no acceptance there.

No, Mama's eyes were filled to the brim with disappointment and condemnation.

"Have you told your sister?"

The urge to weep clutched me by the throat and held me captive for a minute before I was able to nod.

"I should go to her," she said.

A noise of complete distress, something like a dog's yelp, leaped from my lips before I could slap a hand over my mouth. I knew she was right. Elena deserved Mama's time and attention right then more than me. Yet Mama's pure dismissal of my admission and obvious guilt hit me like a freight train on repeat. I struggled not to hyperventilate; I didn't want Mama to take pity on me for medical reasons when she was clearly as disgusted with me as I was by myself.

"I understand," I said.

Mama's eyes narrowed. I sat still, my posture straight and strong despite my innards caving in on themselves. I remembered Sinclair's advice about holding strong, remembering that I had made a *choice*, a premeditated decision to serve the greater happiness of two people, not just myself. It was horrifyingly easy to picture Sinclair five years from then with Elena, his soul subdued, and his work his true mistress.

He belonged with me.

I tilted my chin higher and said, "I'm willing to accept your judgment, Mama. I'm even willing to accept that for, at least a little while, you might not want to see me." I couldn't help the tears that began to race scalding hot down my cheeks, but I didn't let my voice wobble. "I can almost bear the thought of not seeing you and the twins at Christmas and birthdays and for our weekly lunches even though I'll be miserable without you. But what I could not ever bear, what I will never again even entertain, is the thought of being without Daniel Sinclair. He's it for me, and if he is the only family I have now, I can deal with it if I have to."

She stared at me, still for an eternity. At one point, I began to tremble because my body was physically incapable of maintaining its structure under the crushing weight of her scrutiny.

"I am glad for that, *bambina*," she said softly, "because as you say, for a little bit at least, I will not see you."

My lips rolled under my teeth to lock in my scream.

"I do not mean to punish you for finding love. Love..." She sighed heavily. "I know what a person will do for it, and I will never say the consequences are not worth the love. But, Giselle, there will be consequences, and losing me like this temporarily is one of them. I cannot speak for the twins..." Her face crumpled as she thought about

Cosima, slowly recovering in the hospital. "But I have a feeling they will feel the same."

I nodded as I slipped off the chair, glad that I hadn't taken off my coat. She was reacting properly. She was right, and I was wrong. I let those words repeat in my mind, finding the words and assembling them so that I grew numb to them.

"Thank you for listening to me," I murmured, ducking my head as I turned to leave.

I had to get out of there before I imploded.

"*Stammi bene, bambina,*" she said as I pushed through the swinging door.

Happily, they swung shut before I started sobbing.

I felt mildly better when I was out in the street, absorbed by the myriad of New Yorkers with better things to do than observe my pity party. Even though I had never in my life felt so utterly devastated, so unbearably *raw*, I also felt a profound sense of relief. I was glad that I had put myself through the ordeal of Elena and Mama in one day. I couldn't imagine how long it would take for me to digest this grief, but at least the accusations closest to my heart had been dealt with. Now, I only had to worry about the judgment of my siblings, who I truly believed might be vaguely supportive, and New York as a whole. Daniel Sinclair was a vital part of its high society, and I fully expected them to lend their voice to the criticism laid at our doorstep. The thought of more was frankly harrowing, and for a while there, as I wandered aimlessly around the city, I seriously wondered if I would have a nervous breakdown.

My phone rang in my pocket. I pressed ignore, but not before I saw the lineup of notifications across the screen. Sinclair had called me six times and sent two texts.

*Frenchman:* No matter what happens. No matter how awful she makes you feel about yourself. Remember the woman I fell in love with. The brave woman with flaming hair and bold eyes who capti-vated me from the start. It wasn't your beauty that drew me in, my love. It was your capacity to *feel*, to filter every emotion and experience through your body so that you can better understand life. You are so utterly alive that you even succeeded in bringing me to life. Feel for Elena, feel grief for what you have to give up for me (I am more sorry for that than I can say) but then release the grief. If you can forgive me, you can forgive yourself.

**Frenchman:** *Et aussi, je t'aime.* Come home to me when you are ready. I have a surprise that I would like to share with you.

My heart ached and throbbed like a mortal wound as I read and reread his words standing in the middle of 7th Avenue as people jostled and rushed past me. The loneliness that had crippled me like a physical condition my entire life seized me in its iron fist. Memories assaulted me: Cosima leaving followed by Seamus and then Sebastian, arriving alone in Paris to make a new life, fleeing it to get away from the threat of Christopher, the distance that remained between my siblings and me. The agony of solitude whipped around me, swirled me into a vortex of pain and then left abruptly.

I placed my hands on my knees and panted lightly from the intensity of my revelation.

I wasn't alone any longer, and if I had the strength to accept the repercussions of my relationship with Sinclair, I never had to be again.

# Chapter Fourteen

*Giselle*

Sinclair was practically vibrating with excitement. His knee bounced up and down under our clasped palms as we sat in the back of the cab that was transporting us to a surprise location. He had seemed incredibly relieved and then uncharacteristically giddy when I'd arrived at the suite, dropped my things, and dived into his arms. He'd held me in silence until I collected myself, and then he had asked me to go with him somewhere. I didn't tell him about the ordeal with my sister and my mother. I wasn't ready to unleash my grief onto him, but I'd sealed the promise that I'd made myself—to devote myself to our future—with a long kiss.

"We're going to Brooklyn?" I asked now, surprised.

His boyish enthusiasm was immediately snuffed out by the incredulity of my tone, and his mask slipped back in place. He raised a cool brow and said, "You dislike Brooklyn?"

"Not at all." I smiled. "In fact, I kind of love it. It's a hipster haven after all."

"You are not a hipster," he said, appalled by the thought.

I laughed. "No, but I am an artist. I like the grittiness that still lingers here, the cool little shops and the community feel. Besides, this is where we spent our first 'date' after we found each other again."

His grin was back.

I shook my head at him as our cab pulled up to a building near the water overlooking the Manhattan skyline. He was out of the car and opening my door before I could pry my eyes away from the gorgeous nightscape.

"I've never seen you like this."

He tugged me out of the car and into his arms, one hand firm on my chin so that I was looking up into his eyes. "I've never been like this."

The air was cold and bitingly fresh in my lungs as he led me to the gorgeous building right beside the Manhattan Bridge overpass.

"Mr. Sinclair," a professionally dressed older woman greeted from beside the entrance. "It's lovely to see you again."

"Meagan," he said, shaking hands with the statuesque blonde. "How are you this evening? I appreciate you meeting us here at such a late hour."

She blushed. "Don't be silly, I'm happy to accommodate you. After all, how much business have you sent our way in the past eight years?"

He inclined his head to acknowledge her words and tugged me forward by our joined hands. "Meagan, this is the woman I was telling you about, Giselle Moore."

To my surprise, she beamed at me and took my hand warmly in both of hers. "It's a pleasure to meet you, Giselle."

"Oh?" I asked, sliding a glance up at Sin.

"Of course. It's not often Sinclair can't shut up about something other than work," she joked.

My eyebrows were somewhere startlingly close to my hairline as I stared up at my Frenchman. He raised one of his reddish brows at me haughtily, as if such behavior was to be expected.

"Who are you, and what have you done to my enigmatic, aloof Sinclair?" I asked.

He chuckled darkly and leaned close to my ear to whisper, "Trust me, your Sinclair is still in here, waiting to have his wicked way with you."

I gulped as his words ignited that ever-ready powder keg of desire in the base of my belly.

"Shall we go in, then?" Meagan was saying as she buzzed through the glass doors and into the lobby.

I followed mutely after her, listening vaguely as she explained the building's amenities and the appeal of living in Brooklyn's trendy DUMBO neighborhood. Sinclair's thumb swooped rhythmically over mine as he conversed with her in the gorgeous glass elevator that took us impossibly high in the converted boxing warehouse. A sense of impending wonder and anxiety churned in my gut as the doors slid soundlessly open to reveal a massive open concept kitchen and living area.

My mouth hung open like a flytrap as I stepped into the space, pulled instinctively toward the massive glass-faced clock at the center of the far wall. Through the wrought-iron face, I could see the entire western layout of Brooklyn. I swiveled around to gape at Sinclair who stood with his hands deep in his pockets, watching me with his usual neutral expression. I caught sight of another identical clock face in the wall perpendicular to me and rushed toward it. This one offered an unparalleled view of the Manhattan Bridge and the sparkling lights of the big city.

I turned again to Sinclair, unable to speak.

He stepped into the recessed living room but kept a wide swathe of space between us. Meagan, the good real estate agent that she was, made herself scarce.

"Sinclair, what are we doing here?"

He pulled a hand through his hair, cleared his throat and shrugged one shoulder. "It is obvious, no?"

"No," I said. "Not so much."

"If you don't like it, we can find something in Manhattan. I would offer to leave the city entirely, but my business is based here, and it would take some time to move the base of operations. I thought Brooklyn was a good compromise, a place close to our family and our old lives but a new neighborhood, one we could explore and learn to love together. We wouldn't run the risk of constantly running into people we knew."

He stepped forward slowly as if he was approaching a cornered animal. When I bristled at his touch, I realized I was giving him reason to act like that. Struggling to relax, I gave him my hand so he could lead me toward the staircase.

"It's rather large; three floors and three bedrooms," he explained as we ascended the stairs to the second level. "I know it might be hard to imagine our lives here, so I took the liberty of labeling a few things."

I moved forward silently to read the large label on the master bedroom door, *Our Room*. Swallowing a sob, I explored further, finding each closet labeled *his* and *hers*, a drawer marked *Giselle's sexy underwear* and another *fishing attire* in Sinclair's neat, sloping script. A sticky note on the main wall was a placeholder for a yet-untitled work of art by Giselle Moore. *I want to sleep beneath your art*—read the caption.

Crying now, I left the bedroom to explore the rest of the floor. The guest bedroom was equipped with a list of approved guests—Cage, Seb, Cosima, Brenna, Santiago, and Katarina but under *no* circumstances Stefan Kilos. There were random red sticky notes on floor-length glass windows, in closets, on the glass elevator doors, and the banister that merely promised *sex here*. I laughed wetly through my tears, aware that Sinclair was following me at a respectful distance. He would be nervous, but of course, he put my feelings first.

God, I loved him.

And that was before I stepped in front of the other bedroom's closed door and frowned at the lack of a label.

"I wanted to explain this one before we went inside," Sin said from behind me, close enough to touch but deliberately avoiding it.

"I want you to understand that this isn't me trying to rush you into anything. Honest to fucking God, I didn't even know if we would survive the night. This is me showing you what I've had a hard time telling you, what I've never had to tell anyone before. I love you, Elle. I love you like there is a second heart inside my chest that beats just for you."

One of his cool hands found my hip while the other pushed open the door before us. I held my breath as we took three steps in tandem into the room.

A purple sticky note on the wall opposite us read—*baby's room?*

I felt my body light up like a flare, leaving only my heart bloody and beating loudly on a pile of ash on the floor. All thought, all reservations, fell away as if they had never subsisted, and all I felt was shock and awe.

"We are going to be faced with a lot of acrimony for making the decision to be together, but I know we can get through it. And on the other side of all those obstacles is a future where we belong to each other, and we can have whatever life we want together. *Mon amour pour toi est plus grand que le monde.*"

My love for you is bigger than the world.

It was. Our love was something colossal, so heavy and uncompromising that it ground to dust everything that stood before it. It had its own gravitational force, wrote its own law of physics and code of morality. It was separate from anything that had ever existed before us and would ever exist after.

How could I ever have thought it possible to walk away from him?

I walked over to the wall and gently unpeeled the sticky note, folding it before putting it in my pocket. Sinclair watched me, his anxiety like static in the air. My Frenchman wasn't used to giving up power, and I loved that he was doing it for me.

My feet carried me back to him as if on a cloud. I placed my hand firmly over his heart, felt the quick patter of his pulse, and smiled up at him.

"Too much?" he asked with a wry twist of his lips.

I canted my hips against him, moved his arms around my waist so that he was holding me. "Never."

"I want to move in immediately," he warned, but his hands clamped over my hips and pressed me closer against him.

"Yes," I agreed, licking at the pulse that was beginning to throb in his neck.

He groaned. "Should we christen our new bedroom, my siren?"

"Isn't Meagan downstairs?"

He leaned back to look at me with cold, demanding eyes. "Does that matter?"

I shivered in anticipation. "No, sir."

"Good girl."

I wanted to spend the night in our new apartment, but we didn't even have a bed yet. Sinclair convinced me to go back to the St. Regis, but he promised me we could move in the very next week as long as I was okay with his interior designer decorating the place for us to expedite things. I'd never had my own home before, so I was eager to leave my stamp on things, but I understood Sin's desire to rush. Having a permanent place of our own lent our precariously placed relationship a stability that we both desperately wanted. So, Sin sent me Emma Meyers' email, and we were already communicating about color schemes and designs. I took a liking to her immediately, especially as she was originally from London and understood my desire for a European-style home.

I looked up from the screen of my phone, drawn by the feeling of Sin's eyes on me. He stared at me from over the thin sheets of *The New York Times*, his eyes aglow with love and the morning light filtering in through the windows. Even though we were in the States again, we still tried to have a coffee together every morning before heading our separate ways.

"What are you staring at?" I asked, playfully annoyed.

"The love of my life."

Heat suffused my cheeks. "Has anyone ever told you that you're almost unbearably romantic?"

He reached across the little table and brought my hand to his lips. I gasped when he bit one of my knuckles and then gently laved it. "I am unbearably greedy. I have finally captured my siren, and I have no desire to let her go."

I laughed, my heavy heart lightening under the bright light of his attention. "Careful, or you will spoil me."

"Count on it," he said with a wink as I got up to rummage through my tote bag for my birth control.

He watched me intently as I popped one in my mouth and swallowed it. I narrowed my eyes at him in question, but he only shrugged one shoulder before returning to the paper.

It wasn't until I sat down again and plopped my feet in his lap that he asked, "You really like the apartment?"

"I love it. In fact, I'm going to spend the morning at the gallery and then head over to meet Emma this afternoon. Are you sure you want me to go full steam ahead on the decorating?"

"Absolutely. Carte blanche as well."

"Sin..."

"I won't argue about this. It will be the home of our future children one day, yes? So, it must be perfect. I'll leave my card on the counter, and I insist you use it for everything. Later today, I'll arrange it so you can have a card in your name on the account."

Something fluttered in my belly, but I bit my lip to quell the questions that bubbled up inside me. I had been so certain Sin didn't want kids. Wasn't it one of the reasons he and Elena were so ill-suited?

The buzz of Sinclair's phone disturbed me from my thoughts, and I watched distractedly as he answered. My Frenchman never really stopped working. It wasn't unusual for him to take calls at all times of the day and spend extra hours on the site of his new project. It was no wonder that he and Elena had made such a good pairing when she spent eighty-plus hours at the law firm each week. Sinclair was sensitive to my mood, and I could sense his apprehension whenever he took a call or came home too late for dinner, but there was no reason for it. I enjoyed his work ethic and single-minded intensity; they were two of the qualities that he had applied so ceaselessly to his relationship with me. My showing was in less than a week, and though I was close to completion, I still had two pieces to tweak before I felt secure in the collection, so I was busy as well, especially with the time we had taken off in Paris.

I *was* lonely, but it had nothing to with the amount of time I spent with Sinclair. I missed my family with an acuteness that echoed like church bells from my heart throughout my body at every hour of the day. It seemed as though I had been chasing after the dream of a complete and perfect family since I was a child, poor and lonely in a dirty house abandoned by my father, sister, and brother, left only with a broken mother and a hostile Elena. But even then, there had always been hope, the belief that sometime in the future we would be reunited and peaceful again.

I'd eradicated that future like a bug beneath my heel.

"Stop with the baseless accusations, Paulson," Sinclair bit out, standing up abruptly and slamming his hand down on the table.

My head snapped toward him as he began to pace through the small living area of the suite.

"I did no such fucking thing, and you know it. We have been business associates for years. I have known about your proclivities, and you mine for *years*. I would have nothing to gain and everything to lose from telling the press—"

He cursed under his breath in French and tugged a hand through his overlong hair. I bit my lip as I watched him, apprehension crawling over my skin like a dozen spiders. Suddenly, he stormed back toward the table and slapped open the paper he had been reading to the society section. I caught a glimpse of the name Paulson, and a portrait of both husband and wife before Sinclair's hand crumpled it up under his fist.

"Believe me, Paulson. I will get to the bottom of this. Give me forty-eight hours." He gritted his teeth and hissed an exhale through his clenched teeth. "Fine. Thirty-six hours then."

He shut off the phone, threw it to the table, and watched as it skittered across the glossed surface before falling to the floor.

"Fuck," he roared, roughly pulling both hands through his hair.

I remained quiet while he reined in his anger. I'd never seen him so frustrated, and I wasn't sure how to handle it. The relief I felt when he finally turned to me with anguish, and not anger, in his eyes, surprised me.

"Someone leaked the Paulson's BDSM lifestyle to the press."

My mouth fell open in a horrified O.

He nodded and dropped down into his chair with a loud sigh. "He's blaming my camp and threatening to pull out of the Dogwood Hotels deal. It's a multimillion-dollar contract that I've spent two years securing. It means constructing hotels in four countries, including a casino in Vegas, over the next five years." He closed his eyes. "It would have secured Faire Developments as one of the leading development firms in North America."

My heart stuttered. "Who do you think could have done something like that?"

"Honestly? Not many people. I want to be furious with Paulson for accusing me of doing something so unscrupulous, especially when it's crippling to me as well, but I'm one of only a handful of people who know about what goes on behind closed doors in that house, so I can't blame him for not thinking clearly at a time like this. The man's entire reputation is built on frankly puritan values. This is devastating for him."

"And for you," I reiterated, reaching forward to grab his clenched hands. "What are we going to do?"

A slight smile pulled his lips to the left. "*We* aren't going to do anything, my siren. You are going to continue your day, spend the morning at our home, work on your art, and visit your sister, and I promise to be in a better mood when I next see you."

I pursed my lips, but I understood. "Probably not tonight."

"No, probably not. I can't rest until I figure this out." His eyes pleaded with me to understand, and I could see by the grinding of his teeth that he was anxious to be off on the hunt.

I cupped his tense cheek, leaning forward to kiss the muscle jumping in his jaw. "*Bonne chance, mon chasseur.*"

He smiled tightly but pressed a firm kiss to my lips before he took off, his phone already to his ear as he barked orders to Margot.

I tried not to despair of our run of bad luck as I downed the rest of my now cold coffee and pushed away from the table to get ready for the day.

*J* decided to stop at Cosima's apartment first. Hades was still there after all, and the poor cat needed some food and affection. I felt the echo of my sister's vibrant spirit the moment I opened the door. The lingering scent of her, rich honey and warm spices, made my eyes tear but in a good way. I knew she would recover from this, not only because I needed her to and she had never before let me down, but also because she was the best and strongest person I knew. She could pull through anything, even a coma.

Hades squawked at me, tripping me up as I retrieved his food from the cupboard and set some down for him in a clean bowl. While he ate, I sorted through the mail piled up on the kitchen counter, dividing them into urgent and non-pressing piles for both Cosima and myself.

I frowned when I came across an envelope with my name written in vaguely familiar script across the front with no return address, no postage stamp. With a sense of increasing premonition, I extracted the letter folded inside. Most of the page was blank but for a few words written in red pen.

*I've found you again, mia cara.*

Something gentle pressed against my shoulder and I screamed, the paper falling from my hand as I spun to face the intruder. It took my panicked brain a moment to realize that the person I thought would be standing there, the same person I was almost sure had written the letter, was actually Dante.

It took me a second more to absorb the fact that he was standing in my sister's kitchen wearing nothing but an indecently tight pair of white boxer briefs that fought valiantly to contain a morning erection.

I looked up at him with wide eyes and stuttered, "What, what are you doing here?"

He frowned at me. The left side of his thick head of dark hair was sticking up from sleeping on it funny, disturbing the overall effect of his intimidating stature. I focused on that instead of his absurdly defined body. Lord, the man must have worked out religiously.

"Hades."

"Excuse me?" I blinked.

He gestured at the still feasting cat. "Cosima would have wanted someone to care for Hades. I figured that I would stay here until she was well."

"Huh, you just figured that? And how did you get up here exactly?" There was a doorman, a key fob for the elevator, and another key needed to enter the apartment.

He grinned rakishly. "I have my ways."

I narrowed my eyes at him, absently noting that my primary fear had dissipated. Dante was a big, scary man, there was no hiding that, but after seeing his love for Cosima, it was impossible to think he would truly bring me harm.

He chuckled, rubbing at his bare stomach. I tried again not to notice that he had something like a twelve-pack going on down there. "She gave me a key when she bought the place."

"She trusts you."

I'd had every reason to believe that before this revelation, but Cosima believed her home was sanctuary, and she would never allow anyone less than family to harbor a key. My eyes skirted the long, cut man in front of me with a new appreciation. What had this scary man done to make my sister love him?

"*Si.*"

I shook my head. "I want to apologize for my family yesterday and for my reaction just now. Cosima is just usually so open with us about everything. It's difficult to imagine that she would have kept something, *someone*, like you hidden."

Dante stared at me intently, his eyes huge and entirely black. I wanted to shiver, to tear my gaze from his and flee the apartment, but I stayed still, letting him take his measure. Before everything with Sinclair, I may have cowered, but he had made me stronger and now I relished Dante's scrutiny, even if he did see the immoral stain of my affair on my skin.

"Your sister has kept dark secrets from you all your life," he finally said, his voice a beautiful mixture of British and Italian.

He sighed, gesturing for me to take a stool at the counter as if this was his home and not mine. Despite his arrogance, I did take a seat because I could tell he was about to open up to me.

He walked over to the wall where two of my paintings were propped. I watched as he ran a finger down the edge of one canvas, the one of the dark-haired woman bound in a shibari-style by ropes of her own hair.

"Cosima would do anything for you. She has done *many* things for you in the past, things that she would castrate me for telling you, so I will not. But you must know that she has continually sacrificed her happiness for your own, for your family. She always had a special place in her heart for you, though, her *bambina*."

I smiled at her endearment for me even though the fact that he knew it made me shiver. How could he know so much about her, about our family, yet we had never even known he existed?

"Are you her lover?" I asked before I could censure myself.

I blushed when his eyes slid to mine with heated amusement.

"No, I have never been with her romantically." He laughed at my shock, leaning back against the opposite counter as if we were having a normal conversation. "I love her, but because she is *mia sorella di scelta*."

*My chosen sister.*

"We met when she lived in England. It is a long story, one that I have said before is not mine to tell. The only thing you must know is that she is under my protection." His expression was fierce as a warrior before battle, his posture that of a soldier. I had no doubt he could protect Cosima. The man was basically a heathen.

"Why should you need to protect her?"

He crossed his arms across his expansive chest but didn't answer.

I gritted my teeth in frustration. "Fine. Who are you to offer protection?"

His full lips twitched. "Now, you are asking the right questions. I told you before, you will hear about me. I am Don Salvatore."

Even though I had forsaken my country of birth years ago, there was something in my Italian blood that reacted instinctively to the presence of a made man.

I gasped, scooting back on the stool until I nearly fell over. "You are in the mafia."

He shrugged one massive shoulder. "I am in the business of money and power."

"Do you know anything about Cosima's attack?" I demanded.

His lips thinned. "There is no reason to share details with you. I am working on it."

I shivered at the raw threat in his words. Whoever had hurt my sister would pay brutally for doing so.

"My family won't warm to you, not when you remain so enigmatic," I explained. Not to mention, we all abhorred the Mafia, the men who had so ceaselessly stalked us in Italy. My fear was warranted, and I was grateful for it. A naïve person might have seen the threat of violence, the money, and the power as glamorous, but I knew it only meant death.

I shuddered.

"Your safety comes before everything else. Cosima would want that," he countered.

He was right, so I didn't argue with him. Instead, I decided to trust in his ability to get to the bottom of Cosima's accident. No matter his motivation, it was obvious that he loved Cosima and that he was ruthless, a mafia man with the same soulless eyes I had seen so many times around the house in Naples.

Which reminded me of the letter I had let slip from my fingers. I searched the ground for it, spotting it just beside Dante's feet. My gaze drew his to it, and before I could move, the paper was between his fingers. He glowered at it.

"Who wrote this to you?"

I bit my lip, unwilling to tell him. Even though I had my deep suspicions, I didn't want them to be true. I'd left Paris to escape, and I deeply wanted to refuse the idea that he could have found me so quickly again. I closed my eyes, though, because I had been incredibly incautious about the publicity for my upcoming show. Though I had changed my name to Giselle Moore in hopes of creating a new identity, my cover had been blown when he found me in Paris.

"Giselle," Dante called me back to reality. "Who wrote this?"

"A man," I said, unhelpfully.

*A man who has been stalking me for the last four years.*

"Christopher?"

My eyes snapped to his. "How do you know about him?"

"Your sister. She told me a little about him. This is the man who abused you, *si*?" His eyes sparked with anger and the hand that held the letter shook with tension.

"I don't like to talk about it."

"Well, you bloody hell should talk about it to someone," he bit out, his British accent more pronounced. "Does your man know that this sociopath is back in your life?"

"It may not be him," I countered, but there was a sinking feeling in my gut as I remembered the odd candid photo of myself that had been sent to me, the feeling that I'd been having of being followed.

When Christopher had found me in Paris, he had confronted me right away. It seemed that now we were playing an extended game of cat and mouse.

I watched Hades pounce on an imaginary foe on the carpet in the kitchen and swallowed thickly. It was only a matter of time before

Christopher confronted me again. I couldn't imagine what he was waiting for, but whatever it was couldn't have been good.

Dante watched me while I digested this before finally shaking his head. "You need to tell your man about this, immediately. Call him while I change. Were you planning on going to the hospital today?" I nodded. "Good, I will escort you."

He stalked off into Cosima's bedroom.

I desperately didn't want to call Sinclair. He was dealing with so much already with the Paulson scandal, and I was pretty sure I could handle things on my own. Christopher was a sick, twisted man, but he wasn't a murderer. He wouldn't rape and pillage me. Besides, now that I knew he was back, I would take extra precautions to stay in a group or on busy streets. He wouldn't approach me unless I was alone. There was no reason to make Sinclair crazy with worry over it.

Happy with my decision, I slipped off my stool and had my coat on by the time Dante came out dressed to leave.

"You informed him?" he asked me with dark, narrowed eyes.

The expression was meant to be intimidating, but I'd had practice with mafia men far more scary than him, so I was able to smile casually and nod.

"Good. Let me know whenever you want to go to the hospital, and I will escort you, okay? No need to take unnecessary risks. One Lombardi in the hospital is enough."

I nodded mutely but couldn't help but frown at the contradictory man who opened the door to lead me out of the apartment. Dante was clearly a devoted and passionate man to those he loved, yet he was a self-proclaimed made man, which made him any combination of murderer, thief, and liar. What role could he possibly have played in my sister's life?

# Chapter Fifteen

*Giselle*

I didn't see Sinclair for the next three days.

He had warned me that he was a workaholic, that he often spent weekends and evenings sequestered in his office high above the city. I tried not to remember the part where he told me it would be different once we were together. It wasn't fair of me to be angry with him, not when he was working on saving a deal that he had lusted after for years, not when our relationship was the reason for its currently precarious position.

But I missed him. It was lonely living in a hotel room in a city that had become my home, without my family to comfort me. I had made my decision to put Sinclair first. I didn't regret it, but my isolation highlighted my change in circumstances like a neon pen. Though he texted, I found myself worrying about our longevity, if we could withstand everything coming at us in droves, and about his stance on BDSM, if he would waver without frequent scenes and fall into shame again.

To make matters worse, my pill pack had disappeared again even though I ransacked the suite looking for it. I made an appointment with the doctor to get another one, but I considered switching to an IUD or a contraception shot given my recent bouts of forgetfulness. I didn't worry Sinclair about it because I didn't think it was cause for worry. I had missed one or two pills in Paris without consequences. Sinclair didn't really want kids or marriage or the white picket fence, and I was okay with that. I'd never had the same longing that my sisters did for children of my own, but I was fully prepared to rock the cool aunt role.

I threw myself into furnishing our new apartment to take my mind off everything. Armed with Sinclair's black AMEX, Emma Meyer's professional opinion, and way too much angsty energy, I hit the best of New York's stores. Though we had already purchased a variety of things online or through Emma's connections with auction houses, warehouses, and antique stores, it was fun and somehow mandatory to touch most of what would be in my home before I bought it. We were searching for a French provincial style sofa to match the coffee table we had found at Jung Lee's when my phone rang.

"Giselle," Sinclair said in greeting.

The one word was laden with meaning; his longing and the relief he felt at being able to talk to me, his continued frustration at the collapsing Paulson deal, and his resulting bone-deep exhaustion.

My heart ached for him.

"Sin," I said, infusing the one syllable with the very same love and yearning I'd sensed in his voice.

He sighed gustily. "There, that is better already. Tell me what you are doing so that I can pretend I am with you, where I am supposed to be, instead of here in the office."

"Emma and I are still shopping. I thought it would be overwhelming to furnish an entire, *massive* house, but Emma has this system where she catalogs everything we've bought into folders on her iPad so that we can always refer back to them and make sure everything is copasetic."

"Excellent," he said. "We wouldn't want to live in a mismatched house. I cannot think of a worse fate."

"You're teasing me."

"I am."

"You miss me."

"If you only knew how much, you would be here as quick as a cab could carry you."

I bit my lip. "I've been desperate to do just that, but I worried that I would be distracting you."

Another sigh, this one short and punctuated with irritation. "You would. Especially as it has been three interminable days since I had you. No, the next time I lock eyes on you, Elle, it will be in a private place where I can take you properly."

A little shiver shot down my spine as I sighed in longing.

"That little gasp you make when I've been teasing you, and I finally dip between those sweet thighs," Sinclair continued in a voice that pebbled my skin and drew my nipples tight like a sluice of cool water. "I crave those little sighs and moans you make when you try to keep yourself still under my fingers. Such a good girl."

"Sin," I breathed, my thighs pressed together as I stood, helplessly turned on, in the middle of a furniture warehouse.

"Are you wearing a skirt today?"

I looked down at the dark gray of the raw silk dress I was wearing. It was a cold but snowless winter day in New York, so I paired it with thick black hold-ups and knee-high black leather boots.

"Yes."

"Good, when you get off the phone, I want you to go into the restroom, take off your panties, and put them in your purse. Then you are going to touch yourself until you make those little noises I like so much, but because I am not there to hear them, you will not come. Do you understand me?"

"Yes, sir," I whispered.

"I have to go, but I promise I'll be back tonight. Wait for me naked on your knees by the door at seven o'clock, *d'accord*?"

Emma chose that moment to return. "Giselle, I need you to look at this gorgeous loveseat they have. Neoclassical French. You'll die. And I know you wanted to wait to pick out the bed with Sinclair, but there is this huge black wrought-iron affair that I know you would both love."

"Ugh, Sin, I have to go," I said into the phone.

"Get the bed."

"Excuse me?"

There was a smile in his voice when he said, "Get the bed, Elle. I love the sound of wrought iron. It will be easy to tie you to the head-board that way."

I swallowed thickly as his disconnection cut off his smoky chuckle.

"I have to use the restroom, but when I come back, take me to the bed," I told Emma. "And is there any way we could put a rush on delivery?"

*I*t was early evening before I got the chance to visit Cosima in the hospital, later than I usually went, so I wasn't surprised that someone else was there to visit her. I was surprised, unpleasantly so, by whom it was, though.

Elena sat in a chair pulled up beside the bed with Beau, her best and only friend. I hadn't seen him since my welcome back party in the fall, but previously, we had always enjoyed an amicable friend-ship. He was very beautiful, proudly gay, and had an insane sense of fashion. I didn't know what he made as a lawyer's assistant, but it was enough to keep him in Boss, Prada, and, on the rare occasion that he dressed 'down,' Lactose.

My lips were smiling before my brain could register that he was glowering at me. Actually, glowering was probably not a strong enough word to describe the absolute hatred that he emitted. It thrummed and throbbed through the room, making me somehow motion sick.

"What are you doing here?" he snarled even though Beau was a smart man, and it was obvious I was there to visit my potentially dying sister.

"Cosima," I murmured.

"Get out." That was Elena, her eyes still focused on our sister in the hospital bed. "You aren't welcome here."

I wanted to get out. I wanted to run out of the room, out of the hospital, out of the state, and across the Atlantic back to France because if I let myself be propelled by the sheer force of her hatred, that is where I would have ended up. Far away from her.

Her eyes cut my way blazing with inner fury, and I readjusted; not just far away from her. Elena wished I was dead.

She affirmed my belief by saying, "It should be your lying, cheat-ing, fat ass in this bed and not Cosima's."

I reeled, my stomach tossed backward, my heart hitting hard against the back of my rib cage. My foot caught me before I fell on my ass, but only just.

The Mean Girls snickered.

I opened my mouth to say something without any idea of *what* exactly to say when a large presence at my back made me stiffen.

"Excuse me," an incredibly posh British accent ordered.

I whirled around to face the man, and my mouth fell further open. The man in front of me was even taller than Dante, some impossible height that was made even more astonishing by the fact that he was perfectly proportioned, not as deeply muscled as the Mafia man but close. That was where the similarities ended, though, because this man was not rugged. His dark blond hair was pushed back from his regal forehead like a golden crown, highlighting the aristocratic features that I honestly didn't think I could have re-created with paint or brush. He was so exactly symmetrical, so beautifully colored in tones of all gold but for the bright glint of steely silver at his eyes. They weren't black, those eyes, but I recognized in them, as they bore down on me, the same ruthless, violent capabilities that lived in the eyes of the made men I'd known in my youth.

This stranger was not a good man.

Elena seemed to have surmised the same thing. She stood swiftly, moving to the front of Cosima's bed to block our vulnerable sister from the newcomer. It was a beautiful gesture that made me feel better about her as a person and worse about her as my sister.

"You have the wrong room."

The blond prince—seriously, he could have been King Arthur reincarnate—looked down his nose at us. "I do not."

"This is Cosima Lombardi's room," I offered.

Elena dug her sharp elbow into my soft side.

"Perhaps *you* are in the wrong room. This is Cosima Davenport's room."

"What?" I breathed.

"Excuse me?" Elena asked harshly.

The blond stranger was completely unfazed by our horrified expressions. In fact, he idly adjusted the gold cuff link at his wrist and said, "The woman you are trying to hide from me is my wife."

Oh my God.

Oh my *God.*

*Putain.*

Who was this guy?

"Who are you?" I asked, my voice still breathy with incredulity.

"Her husband," he said, standing straighter, proud and so tall even Elena, who was tall for a woman at five foot eleven, had to tip her head back to maintain eye contact with him. "You may call me Alexander, seeing as we are family."

Still reeling, Elena, Beau, and I stood mutely as he walked briskly around us and took the unoccupied chair up against Cosima's bedside. He sat down on the very edge, looking stupidly big for the tiny orange chair, and immediately took her hand.

"My beauty," he murmured, his hard mask collapsing as he took in her lank hair, the deep bruises that were turning yellow over the left side of her face.

"Cosima isn't married," Elena said, the first to recover.

"She is. I was at the ceremony."

"She would never get married without telling us," Elena snapped, moving forward to point a finger in his face. "You are some *freak* stalker who has seen her in magazines and fixated on her. *Get out!*"

Alexander stared at her without expression. Even though I was used to Sinclair's immaculate mask, something was terrifying about this British man's blank face. Sinclair hid behind his propriety, his beautifully honed manners and perfectly enunciated speech both because he been trained to do so by his adopted parents and then because it gave him a degree of necessary separation from others.

Alexander was not wearing a mask. He truly seemed devoid of feeling. So, the way he stared at Cosima with devoted yearning sent shivers of revulsion down my spine. I wouldn't have been surprised if this man was a psychopath. Was this the man who had put those deep bruises around my sister's wrists when she had visited England before Thanksgiving?

His unfeeling gaze cut to mine, and I had my answer.

"I would say your goodbyes," he said quietly. "Visiting hours are over, and I am the only one who has been granted the choice of staying the night with her."

"Like hell you are," Elena snapped. "How do I know that you are who you say you are?"

"He is her husband," Dante said from the doorframe, his voice uncharacteristically low and subdued.

We both swung his way.

"They were married years ago in England. If you press him, I am sure he will show you the marriage certificate," Dante continued.

"What the hell is happening?" Elena demanded. "First you and now, this maniac who claims to be her husband?"

"Stop."

Everyone froze for one eternal second before leaping into action, converging on the hospital bed like a carrion around a scrap of meat.

"Cosima," I breathed out on a sob, reaching out to grasp her calf because Elena and Alexander both had hold of her hands already.

"Bambina," she croaked, her eyes barely slatted open. "Water."

Alexander was already tipping a small plastic cup to her lips so that she could sip. "Just a little bit, my beauty. You do not want to make yourself sick."

"I'll go get the doctor," Beau said before dashing out the door.

"You scared me," Elena breathed in a voice I hadn't heard from her since she was a little girl. "You terrified me, Cosima. What would we do without you?"

"You would survive," Cosima whispered hoarsely.

Elena's hand spasmed against hers. "No, I wouldn't. So much has happened..."

Cosima's eyes darted to me, and I knew she understood just exactly what had happened during her absence.

"You will survive," she repeated, giving both of us a slight smile.

"Everyone needs to leave," Alexander demanded with the kind of authority I had only ever felt before from Sinclair.

"We don't need to do shit," Elena cursed, clearly beyond her breaking point.

"Xan," Cosima scolded softly, tilting her head on the pillow so she could address her apparent husband. "You came."

His face softened, growing so handsome that both Elena and I gasped softly. He leaned forward to smooth her hair out of her face.

"I am the only one who hurts you, remember?"

I shared a look with my sister, completely disconcerted by the entire situation, but mostly by the increasingly-more-likely-a-psycho-than-not Alexander Davenport.

Cosima had no such reservations. She leaned into him and dragged a deep breath in like it was the first and only breath she had ever taken.

"I know," she agreed.

We watched them share an intimate moment before Elena cleared her throat. "Cosima, I know you just woke up, but what the actual *fuck*? You are married?"

"Yes," she whispered, closing her eyes and resting back against the pillow. "I know you are worried, but Alexander cares for me. He is here to take care of me, and so is Dante."

The doctor hustled into the room at that moment, bracketed by a small contingent of nurses who somehow bustled us out of the way as they went about checking out Cosima.

"You need to leave," the doctor, a stern man by the name of—no joke—Kyle Steele, demanded.

"I am her husband," Alexander said, throwing back his shoulders so that he seemed to take up the entire right side of the room.

Dr. Steele stared at him for a moment. "Fine, but stay in the corner. The rest of you, out."

"It's okay," Cosima assured as we stared helplessly at her. "I am awake now. I'll see you again soon, *si*?"

We both nodded woodenly, and though we didn't speak on our way to the elevator and rode down together, I knew we were both more worried about our sister than she had been even when she was in a coma.

*S*inclair stood in the doorway, one long line of gorgeous French man, and even though I wondered absently why he didn't come closer, I was happy for the opportunity to soak him in after days apart.

All that thick mahogany hair was pushed back from his forehead but curled slightly around his ears, overlong once more and striking against his dusky skin, his incandescent irises. His suit was one I hadn't seen before, a light, luminescent gray that hugged his tall, lean form like quicksilver. I took a moment to note his expression, its blankness, and then to hunt for his little tells. His eyes were dark under heavy brows, his mouth firm, unyielding, and his stance strong.

A little shudder zipped my spine closed vertebrae by vertebrae until I stood ramrod straight. Because my Dom stood in front of me.

I had called him immediately after leaving the hospital to tell him about Cosima waking up with the strange addition of an honest-to-God husband at her side, and I had assumed that we would table the play for the night and talk about what was happening with her.

Apparently, Sinclair had other plans, and as I had grown wet the moment I set eyes on him after a long three days apart, I was rearing to go.

"When you finish undressing, go into the main room and sit in the chair positioned for you, close your eyes, and do not move until I tell you to do so."

My mouth was dry around the words, all the moisture in my body rushing to between my legs. "Yes, sir."

I shed my clothes on the move, so eager to have his hands on me, his voice in my ear commanding me to please him that my fingers were shaking.

The chair was in the middle of the small living room, and the other furniture had been pushed to the side, isolating the chair, isolating *me*, in the empty center. I took my seat with my pulse already pounding between my legs.

It felt like a long time later, but it was probably only ten minutes when I felt Sinclair's presence behind me. He loomed over the back of the chair, and I could tell his body was curled over mine, not protective and not threatening, just close enough to bear down on me with nothing but his presence.

"I bought you a gift, my siren. Would you like to open it?"

I was surprised, too aroused to immediately respond to the non sequitur. He chuckled as his hand appeared from around my back to offer me a large, flat, black velvet box. My fingers continued to shake as I took it from him and flipped open the lid.

My breath caught as I took in the large, blush pink pearls coiled within the satin. They gleamed dully in the low light shed from a lone lamp in the corner of the room, but I knew they were expensive, utterly beautiful. They perfectly matched the pearl collar I wore at my throat.

"Sinclair," I said, his name full of thanks.

He stayed behind me but leaned forward to pluck the strands from the case, lifting one long necklace and then another and finally, two more. They reminded me of the 1920s girls that dripped with pearls in Paris's hottest jazz clubs.

"I love them."

"Good," he murmured, finally coming out from behind my chair.

He was still wearing his suit pants, but they were unfastened, revealing the tantalizing trail of dark hair that led down from his naval. I watched raptly as he crouched before me, his lean muscles undulating. Gently, he took my left hand and wove one strand of pearls around my wrist while he began to explain to me.

"Really, these are a gift for both of us. You are such a lady, Elle, when we are in public, in your feminine dresses and classy accessories. It's fucking delicious," he leaned forward to breathe against my lips as he wrapped the pearls and, therefore, my left wrist to the arm of the chair. "Do you know how hard it makes me to see you like that knowing that you're mine? All that innocence and purity, mine to corrupt."

I shivered as he bound the other wrist to the wooden arm. There was no room for me to move, but the restraints, being delicate pearl necklaces, would be easily broken if I thrashed or pulled too hard.

Sinclair read my mind. "You'll have to stay very still for me. Can you do that?"

I swallowed hard. "What are you going to do to me?"

His eyes grew cold a second before his palm smacked loudly, though not painfully, against my inner thigh as he spread them in order to bind my ankles to each chair leg. "Is that how you address me?"

"Sir." I panted when he pressed his nose to the curls above my clit as his nimble fingers finished fastening me. "Sir, what are you going to do to me?"

"If you keep very still, I'm going to fuck this sweet pussy with my tongue until you come all over my face. And then, after I do it again, I'm going to make you lick yourself off my lips before I fuck your beautiful face."

A soft sigh escaped me.

"Would you like that, Elle? Would you like to give me your sweet cum?"

"Yes, please."

I was devastated when he stepped away from me, straightening so that he could take me in, bound with pearls to the chair.

"*Putain*," he swore harshly, his hand going to the hard ridge straining his pants.

My mouth dried up as I watched him stroke himself through his pants.

"Let me do that, please," I offered, begging already, and he hadn't even really touched me.

"No."

"*Please*," I tried again after I saw his hips buck into his touch.

God, I wanted him in my hands, in my mouth, even just against my skin.

His face hardened. "I just told you what I had planned, Elle. This is the second time you have asked me to derail my plans. Would you rather have my cock than come on my tongue?"

"Yes," I gasped immediately. "Please."

He stared at me for a long minute, and I was giddy at the thought of him giving in to my desires. I could already taste him on my tongue. His scent dazed me as he leaned over me, hands over my bound wrists so he could lean into me.

"Well, I do not want to give you my cock, and it's my choice, isn't it? What happens to this body? I control that."

A shudder violently seized my spine, but I stared at him through it. "Yes, sir. Sorry."

"You'll be forgiven if you give me that orgasm," he said matter-of-factly. "You have two minutes to give me what I want, Elle, or I'll untie you, leave you wanting, and I will jerk off in the shower alone."

I whimpered as he dropped to his knees and ran the flat of his tongue up the seam of my sex, parting my wet folds. He stroked either side of my slick flesh with his thumbs, his eyes on mine.

"Two minutes," he warned again.

Then his head descended, and his mouth was on me. There was nothing gentle or slow about the way he attacked my pussy. No, he fed from me, sucking up all my juices and driving his tongue deep inside me to scoop up more. When he touched my clit, he didn't play with it. He sucked it deeply into his mouth and even gently grazed the hood above it with his teeth so that I jerked against the pearls.

The only sounds in the suite were my heavy panting and frequent gasps and murmurs, and the incredibly erotic slurp of Sinclair as he fed from me. His dark head between my paler thighs was so sexy. I could have come from the sight alone.

"Sin," I groaned out, long and low.

"Such a sweet cunt," he whispered, his lips moving against me as he spoke.

He pushed his hands under my legs, curling them over my hips so that they pressed into the tops of my thighs, pulling me tighter against his hot mouth.

I gasped and my legs shook when he pressed his nose hard into my clit and fucked me with his tongue. Thirty seconds later, my body was drawn so tight, straining against the pearls so hard that I was certain they were going to break. That anxiety coursed through my pleasure-soaked system like lighter fluid, so when Sinclair reached a hand up to put hard pressure against my womb, and the other descended between my legs to drive two fingers into my drenched hole, I went up in flames, the stress of keeping still ratcheting up my orgasm until nothing else was in my head but velvet black bliss.

"Good girl," Sinclair said as I came down, his fingers sliding languidly in and out of my clenching sex. "Under two minutes."

His praise washed over me, giving me goose bumps.

He reared up from his knees to brush his wet lips against mine.

"Taste how fucking sweet you are," he ordered before his hand came up to firmly pinch my chin, and his mouth slanted over me.

I moaned against the silky, delicious invasion of his tongue.

He was right.

I tasted good.

So good that my pussy quivered with the aftershocks at the dirtiness of having the taste of my orgasm in my mouth.

"What do you think?" Sin asked me as he took himself away from me. "What is sweeter... your cum or mine?"

My eyes practically rolled into the back of my head.

Sinclair grinned wickedly at me, his eyes dark, dark, dark.

He stood and pulled his gorgeous cock out of his pants. There was already a bead of arousal on his crown, making my mouth water.

He stepped closer, and I realized that the chair was low enough to take him in my mouth without him having to bend his knees. My mouth dropped open automatically to catch him as he moved his wet cock like a paintbrush against my lips. I moaned as his hot flesh pressed against my cheek. He held himself there as he stroked a hand down my hair. He smelled so good, musky and male, edible.

"Does my siren want my cock in her mouth? You like the taste of cum, don't you? Yours and mine. Well, you'll have to work for mine. I'm not going to come in under two minutes."

I could tell he was smiling, high on the power he held over me, but I was too far gone to care. We hadn't had this in three days, and the submissive in me had been beyond nurtured since we got together. She had been spoiled. And she wanted his cum in her mouth more than her next breath.

I pushed all that desire into my eyes, into the single lush word from my lips. "*Please.*"

His hand ran softly over my crown and then fisted hard in the hair at the nape of my neck. "Open wide."

I did.

He slid in smoothly, right to the back of my throat and down. I gagged slightly around his girth before I remembered to breathe through my nose.

"Now, stay still while I fuck you," he ordered as he began to thrust in a steady but controlled rhythm, using my mouth, using me to get himself off.

My clit throbbed powerfully, and my arousal slid down my thighs and pooled under me on the wooden seat. He fucked my mouth for so long that my jaw began to ache, and my eyes teared up, but I loved it. I loved how the drool spilled down my chin and how I had to fight to accept each thrust down my throat. The effort turned me on because I was doing it to please him, and there was nothing sexier, nothing more rewarding than finally, so many minutes later, taking the prize of his hot release on my tongue.

He kept himself in my mouth as he started to soften, and he looked down at me as he tenderly stroked my hair back from my face.

*"T'es tellement belle," he whispered.*

You are so beautiful.

I smiled when he slipped from between my lips and closed my eyes to better absorb his compliment. They were still closed when he moved away and came back with a glass of cool water, which he brought to my lips so I could drink.

"Uncomfortable?" he asked after a few minutes of petting my head and feeding me water.

I shook my head because even though the pearls were tight against my skin, I liked the way they felt.

"Good," he leaned down again to look me in the eyes, and I found his were still delightfully dark. "Because in about three minutes, I'm going to make you come on my fingers and then again on my cock."

I smiled, so happy I felt high. "Thank you."

His lips didn't even twitch, but his eyes sparkled. "You're welcome."

We shared the moment before he right himself and his Dom mask was back on.

"Now, let's test how strong those pearls are, hmm?"

# Chapter Sixteen

*Giselle*

I woke up the next morning with vomit in my mouth.

I scrambled out of bed, kicking Sinclair in the shin as I did so that I could make it to the toilet in time. I emptied my stomach, but my stomach still roiled and churned like the sea during a monsoon. I doubled over the toilet, desperate to vomit and so nauseous it brought tears to my eyes. I groaned, long and low like a bleating cow.

"Giselle?"

I *really* didn't want Sin to see me like that.

"Leave me alone," I called, my voice breaking on the last syllable as bile flooded my mouth, and I finally began to throw up again.

I didn't hear him come into the bathroom, but I wasn't surprised when cool fingers collected my sweaty locks and held them away from my face, and his minty breath wafted across my neck.

"You should know by now that I will never leave you alone, especially when you need me."

I could only groan in reply, wracked by dry heaves. One of his hands rubbed soothing circles on my back. I rested my forehead over my hands on the porcelain rim of the toilet and sighed, exhausted.

"I don't know what's wrong with me," I said shakily. "I've been feeling so out of sorts the last couple of weeks. I think it might be the stress."

Sin was conspicuously silent for a few minutes, running his long fingers through my hair before tying it back in a ponytail. He prepared my toothbrush for me and watched while I erased the gunk from my mouth.

When I was done, I sighed again when he sat down against the wall and pulled me into his lap. His smoky scent surrounded me, as warm and tangible as his arms pressed against my skin. I gripped a handful of his shirt, tipping my nose up into the hollow of his throat to take a large handful of that fragrance into my lungs.

"Thank you," I breathed.

His arms constricted slightly around me. "Don't thank me for something I'm happy to do. It's my privilege to take care of you." He sighed. "I haven't been doing a great job of it lately, or ever actually."

"Hush," I said, mocking his habitual use of the word. "I'm the happiest when I am with you. This life... this life is only good with you in it."

Sin pressed his lips to my forehead and squeezed me tighter.

I laughed at his somber aura. "What is the matter with you, Mr. Serious?"

"A lot is going on in our lives right now."

"*Mais oui, comme toujours*," I agreed because our lives were always dramatic.

"Elena still hasn't forgiven us and likely never will. Cosima is..." He sighed so heavily that I felt the weight of his breath fall on my face like a stone. "Cosima just woke up from a fucking coma, and now her never-before-seen husband has shown up. Your show is in two weeks and I don't know what the fuck is going on within my own company. It's a lot."

"Yes," I said again. "I'm well aware, Sinclair. What's your point?"

He maneuvered me quickly so that I was straddling him. I locked my ankles around his waist and sunk my fingers into the back of his overlong hair. He needed another haircut, but I wasn't going to tell him that because I liked his roguish locks. I smiled as the silky strands passed through my fingers, but the expression fell off my face when I looked down into his serious electric-blue eyes.

"Sin?" I breathed, nerves fluttering in my vacant tummy.

His beautiful face was perfectly impassive, but those too blue eyes flared with suppressed anxiety. He took a moment to gather himself before saying, "I think we might have another thing to add to the list. I only hope you think it's a blessing and not another tribulation."

"You're scaring me."

He nodded. "*Je suis désolé, ma sirène.* I'm nervous."

"No," I said with faux dramatic shock, "not the ever-unflappable Daniel Sinclair!"

A reluctant smile tipped his lips as he shook his head at me. "You are aware that I'm crazy about you, correct?"

"Correct. Now tell me what has you acting so strangely."

He tipped his forehead down to press it against mine. I swallowed the irrational fear that was building in my chest because I knew that whatever faced us next was no match for the two of us together.

"I think you're pregnant."

The bottom dropped out of my hollow stomach.

Sin leaned back to take my cheeks between his large palms so that he could properly scrutinize my face. My brain had blown a fuse, so I didn't know what he could have been reading in my expression.

"Elle?"

"Mm-hmm?"

The corner of his lips twitched. "How are we feeling here, siren?"

I blew a gust of air into his face. "I'm not pregnant, so I feel fine."

One red brow rose.

"I'm on birth control!"

"Because no one has ever become pregnant while using contraception."

Guilt seeped into my mind as I searched my memories, recalling how many times I had been forced to double up on the pill in the last few months. I wanted to blame the total upheaval of my life or even Sinclair, for being so distractingly sexy...

I choked on my exhalation and looked up at him with wide eyes. "You wanted this."

His eyes were clear and bright, unrepentant. "I hoped."

"Sin!" I shoved him in the chest and scrambled to get out of his grasp, but he only held me tighter to his chest. "You can't just *do* something like that. Did you throw out my birth control in Paris? What kind of person would manipulate their partner into getting pregnant?"

"The same kind of person who fell in love with their girlfriend's sister," he said with exceptional calm. "Before you get angry, let me ask you this; is the idea of having a baby with your hair and my eyes so horrific to you?"

Before I could help it, the image of a toddler with a shock of red curls and cerulean blue eyes appeared behind the screen of my closed lids.

"We would have good-looking babies," I whispered, mostly to myself.

"We *will*," he corrected me, running his knuckles down my cheek so tenderly it made my heart ache. "I want a little girl just like her mother."

I groaned. "So did I, but eventually, not now, not when Elena hates us so viciously, and our family is completely at odds. Not to mention that you and I have only been together for a few months!"

"Hush," he said.

I opened my mouth to protest, but his lips caught my breath, gently crushed against my own in a searing kiss that I felt all the way to my toes. I sighed into his mouth, surrendering to the craziness of our love, the inexorable pull between us. My hands locked in his hair and pulled him even closer.

He smiled against my lips. "Please, tell me you are happy."

I pressed one hand to his cheek, ran my thumb against the prominent ridge of his cheekbone. It still bewildered me every day that somehow this ridiculously perfect man was *mine*.

"You own the lease on my happiness," I murmured, reminding him of the night we had finally succumbed to our attraction and slept together again despite all the things working against us.

Our life wasn't easy, but that didn't mean our love had to be difficult too. As long as we focused on each other, I knew that I would live happily ever after no matter what happened.

"My love for you is greater than the world," Sinclair said, pressing his forehead against my own. "And I will feel the very same about our daughter."

"Son," I said automatically, my hand flying to my stomach. "I think we are going to have a son."

"Want to bet?" Sin asked with a raised eyebrow.

"Are you really going to bet against a mother's intuition?"

He groaned softly. "Is it strange that I am incredibly attracted to you, right now?"

I tipped my head back to giggle. "If I had known the image of me barefoot and pregnant was all it would take to pin you down, maybe I would have tricked *you*."

He scowled at me playfully, so I laughed again.

"I guess I need to make a doctor's appointment," I mused.

His silence was conspicuous enough for me to notice.

"Sin..."

"Mmm?"

"Did you already make me a doctor's appointment?"

He shrugged. "You haven't been feeling yourself for a while. It was just a precaution." When I slanted him a look, his lips twitched. "We have an appointment on Wednesday with the preeminent Ob/GYN in the city."

"Of course we do. Nothing but the best for me, right?"

"Exactly," he agreed solemnly, despite my sarcasm.

"You are crazy. Have I ever told you that?"

"Only a few dozen times in the past four months."

We grinned at each other, our smiles so broad that they folded the skin of our cheeks into hospital bed corners. Then we were laughing, laughing so hard that tears leaked from our eyes and ran down our cheeks. It was the first time I had cried happy tears in much too long, and I clutched Sin tightly, almost painfully, even amidst our mirth because the only thing that terrified me in this life was the idea of losing that, losing him.

It was the weekend, and Sinclair and I were in our new furnished apartment. Emma had worked absolute wonders, and I couldn't believe how beautifully everything had come together. Even Sin had looked pleasantly shocked when she had shown us around the apartment that morning. Everything was absolutely perfect, but Sinclair confirmed it by kissing my breath away as soon as Emma left us alone.

"This is absolutely perfect," he had said after breaking away from me. "The only thing we need to do is furnish the baby's room."

So, Sinclair had called Rossi and Eddie to pick up painting supplies while we laid out spare sheets in the future baby's room. Sinclair wanted to paint a mural together for him or her.

He'd caught me when I had literally swooned at the idea.

"What do you want to paint?" I asked as I came back into the room after changing into an old, paint-splattered pair of overalls and a pink crop top.

Sin stared at me for a second with heat in his eyes. "What?"

I grinned. "What do you want to paint for the baby?"

"I thought we would do a beach scene, like Cabo," he explained unnecessarily as he came over to me and placed a firm hand on my abdomen. "Where it all started."

"You are so poetic," I said with an eye roll to mask the fact that I wanted to cry.

He smiled softly at me before placing a kiss on the tip of my nose. "Should we call over more friends to help us? We could turn it into an impromptu housewarming party."

"That sounds awesome," I said, but he caught the glimmer of despair in my eyes.

Neither Elena nor Mama would come.

We wouldn't even bother to invite them.

I had tried to reach out to Mama a number of times since our conversation, but she remained radio silent, and I wasn't surprised by it. Of course, my understanding didn't soften the blow of hurt I felt each time her phone went to voicemail, each time something new and exciting happened in my life that I wasn't able to share with her.

It was hell, but not having my mother and one of my sisters wasn't the worst fate I could have been dealt with as far as consequences went.

Sinclair and the beauty he infused in my life every single day were a testament to that.

By the time the sun was setting on our Saturday, I had been further proven right.

Cosima had arrived on the arm of her husband, Alexander, both of whom had mostly kept to themselves because my sister was still recovering, and Alexander wasn't exactly a comfortable man to be around. She hadn't divulged much about her relationship with him, only that she cared for him and that she would give us the full story when she was feeling stronger. Still, it felt marvelous to have her alive and well on my new couch in my new apartment while the rest of us, Rossi, Eddie, Candy, Richard, Emma, Duncan, and Sebastian, all painted the nursery.

Sebastian had pulled me aside as soon as he'd arrived because we hadn't had time to speak alone since Cosima's accident.

"I suspected," he began, straight to the point. "It was obvious that there was some serious chemistry between you the moment I saw the both of you in Mama's kitchen the night you finally came home to us. From then on, it just became increasingly more difficult to ignore."

He sighed, his gaze cutting over my shoulder to where I knew Sinclair was arguing with Rossi over the type of music that should be played for a baby in the womb. They had been bickering about it for the last half hour, Rossi for classical, Sinclair for jazz, but they didn't seem to be running out of steam.

"He loves you," he said with another dramatic sigh. "It's always been so fucking obvious that I'm surprised either of you took so long to act on it. We both know that Elena and I aren't particularly close and that you, *bambina*, have always been my girl, but I just have to say, what is happening here, as beautiful as it is for you two and as happy as I am about it, it's a nightmare for Elena. I haven't seen her much, but I know she's hurting. Unfortunately, you did that to her. I hope that you can understand when you see her in the future. She never had any reason to be mean to you before, but now, well, I think you know she has a reason."

"I can understand," I said after swallowing back the acidic taste of guilt in my mouth. "I'm not mad at Mama for taking her side, and I'm not mad at you for saying what you need to say to me. I did a bad thing, and I regret so much that it hurt her but..." I bit my lip, and my hand found my tummy.

I had only known that I was pregnant for a few days, the pregnancy tests that Sinclair had gone out to get for me that morning confirming it, yet I was already so *aware*. My breasts were sore, swollen slightly already, and there was a tight sensation in my womb as it swelled with our baby. Sin and I had both already geeked out and bought nearly every book known to man who was written about pregnancy.

I had never imagined a man like Sinclair loving me, and I had certainly never imagined having a child with that man, but now that it was happening, I was loving every single minute of it.

In fact, part of me was sincerely convinced that I was the luckiest person in the world.

"But I have never been happier," I finished, looking up into Sebastian's burning gold eyes. "And I'm determined to enjoy it."

My brother stared at me, a war raging in his eyes. He had spent his entire life providing for me, protecting me from the real-life monsters that haunted our reality. Sinclair had now, effectively, usurped his role, and he had done it in a way that my brother had a hard time with. He was the man of our family and more a father to me, even though he was nearly two years younger than me, than our own father had ever been. Now, the man I wanted to spend the rest of my life with was also the man who had broken the heart of another one of his charges.

I went on my tiptoes and pressed my hand to his cheek. "I'm sorry to put you in this position."

He closed his eyes, leaning into my palm. "As long as you can tell me, every day, and Gigi, I am going to be calling you every day for a while now, that you are happy, then I will be happy for you."

"Thank you," I said earnestly.

He nodded curtly and cleared his throat. "Now, I'm going to go say the same thing to your future baby daddy." He looked down at my stomach and shook his head. "He sure doesn't waste time when he really wants something, does he?"

I giggled, "No, he does not."

Now, all of us were settled in the sunken living room, having ingested far too much Di Fara's pizza. Brooklyn was a gorgeous miasma of lights and inky blackness outside the massive windows in the clock face that sat in the center wall of the living room. The men were drinking beer, Cosima and I were sticking to tea, and the atmosphere had relaxed a little since Sebastian had his requisite talk with Sinclair, and Alexander Davenport had bent enough to join the conversation.

After hours of fun and work, the mural was shaping up to be extraordinary even though we had non-artistic people helping. At one point, Emma, Eddie, and Cosima had sat beside each other and started a Pinterest board for the nursery that they were determined to turn into a reality.

"I can't believe my *bambina* is pregnant," Cosima said now, her head on my lap so that I could stroke her hair.

She was still pale, and there was a long line of stitches on the left side of her hairline that was still an ugly red.

"I can't believe you are married," I half teased, half scolded her.

She closed her eyes. "Don't bug me about it. Gigi, I told you that I would tell you everything soon. I just want to wait until things are less volatile."

"What do you mean?" I asked with my hand paused mid-stroke.

"Can't we just focus on how beautiful this afternoon has been? Look at all the people who love you," she said, gesturing to the assorted member of my gang.

Warmth seeped into my heart at the sight of Sebastian with his tongue between his teeth as he read one of my baby books. Sinclair, Richard, and Candy were talking about an upcoming event for Romani International, Eddie and Rossi were bent together over the Pinterest board they had created on my iPad, and Emma was actually flirting with the nerdy but adorable Duncan Wright.

It was a good scene, and it hit me hard that Sinclair and I had created this family for ourselves, this network of good people who only wished good things for us. I wished that Stefan and Odile could have been there, Brenna too, but it was enough to know that they would be there if they could. Cage was out of town for an interview on Ellen de Generes in LA, but I couldn't wait to show him our place and tell him about the baby when he got back.

I closed my eyes to absorb the beauty of having a home, a man, and a family for the first time in my life before I looked down at Cosima. She was staring up at me with pride and satisfaction.

"You just successfully distracted me," I admitted.

She smiled. "Good. You deserve this, Elle. Mama will come around, especially when she hears that you are pregnant. Her first grandbaby? She will be at the door in a second."

"I would rather you didn't tell her," I said.

Sinclair and I had talked about it, and I didn't want the world to know yet. We weren't that far along, and more, I didn't want to take Mama away from Elena. She needed someone in her corner that was assuredly not in mine, and I wasn't ready to take that away from her yet.

"You are too good to her," Cosima said, understanding.

I flinched. "I don't know how you can say that, knowing that I cheated with Sinclair."

Her eyes glazed over with painful memories as she tipped her head up slightly to look at Alexander, who sat with her feet in his lap at the end of the couch. He had picked up one of the baby books that littered our new glass coffee table, and he seemed completely absorbed in it.

"I encouraged you to go for it when you asked for my advice back in Cabo, and even knowing that it was my other sister you were hurting, I wouldn't have advised you any other way. I've known Sinclair longer than both of you, and I have never seen him like *that*," she said, pointing over at my Frenchman as he laughed loudly with Richard and Candy.

He caught my eye and winked.

I beamed back at him.

"See?" she said softly. "That is exactly why I do not begrudge you the affair or the secrets you kept from us for so long. Not only because you have that unspeakably epic kind of love with Sin, but also because, as you now know, I've kept my own secrets too."

She sighed deeply and bit her lip before continuing, "I have to go away from a while now, *bambina*, and I cannot say where I am going or for how long. I need you to be okay with that."

"I'm not," I said immediately.

"Well, then, I'll just disappear."

"That's what you are saying that you are going to do anyway," I pointed out.

She stared at me with those beautifully intense golden eyes until I was lulled by them. "You need to trust that I'm doing what I need to do to be happy, to be better."

I slid a glance over at Alexander. "Does it have anything to do with him?"

"Yes. I know you don't understand, but Xan is a huge part of my life. I would do anything for him just as you would do anything for Sin."

I closed my eyes, overcome with worry. "What do you want me to say to that Cosi? That I am okay with you disappearing with a man who I don't know anything about except maybe for the fact that he likes to seriously cause you pain?"

"I know that you and Sin don't exactly have a normal relationship," she pointed out with flashing eyes.

"He would never leave deep purple welts on my wrists," I countered.

Cosima lay stiff as a board in my lap, but her voice was soft, pleading as she said, "You won't see me again after tonight for a while. I'm not even telling Sebastian."

"He wouldn't let you go," I interjected.

"No, he wouldn't because he can't understand. I thought, hoped, you would at least try to," she said.

I sighed heavily because there was nothing else I could do. Cosima was her own woman, and she would do what she wanted.

"Okay," I said. "As long as you can promise me that you'll be happy wherever you go and that *eventually,* at least, you'll come back to us."

"I promise," she said solemnly, turning her cheek so that she could kiss that hand that I rested at her hairline. "Thank you, Gigi."

I leaned down to press a kiss to her forehead as there was a knock on the door. Sinclair and I locked eyes before he got up to answer it, but we both had a bad feeling about who may be on the other side.

We were right.

"You *fucking* adulterer," Elena screamed as soon as the door was open.

I closed my eyes for a brief second to gather my wits before I gently pushed Cosima's head off my lap and scurried to the door to be by Sinclair's side.

Elena's red face turned to me, and she shrieked so fiercely that spittle flew across my face. "You are the biggest bitch I have ever met! I cannot believe you are my sister, you spiteful, hateful shrew. You think that you can just take whatever you want, don't you? First, you take all of Mama and the twin's affection because you are so fucking fragile and pathetic that they need to waste all their time taking care of you."

She had stepped through the door and was stalking me, forcing me to move backward until I hit the glass wall of the elevator in the middle of the room. Sinclair was beside me, keeping a wary eye on Elena, but he let her get it out, and I thought that was good of him.

"Then you took Christopher and turned him into a fucking psychopath. He was good to me before you corrupted him. He took me to museums and festivals, he read to me, and so patiently taught me English even though I sucked at it. Then you grow those goddamn tits, and suddenly, he only has eyes for you," she sneered at me. "You practically begged for his attention, yet you go crying to the twins as if he raped you. Do you know what that made him do? Do you know what a man goes through when he is accused of rape? It turns him into that fucking animal."

"Elena," I breathed because she was confirming my worst imaginings.

"Yes, Giselle. Christopher couldn't have you, but he could have me, even when he didn't want me, and he *raped me for six goddamn months*."

My heart was beating in my throat, and my sensitive stomach was thrashing against my other organs violently. I needed to throw up so badly that my entire body shook.

"Elena," Sinclair said quietly, authority still clear but calm in his voice. "Please, take a deep breath, and let's talk about this privately."

I had forgotten that we had an audience.

Apparently, Elena didn't care.

"Finally, years later, I find a man who I care about, that cares about me. I get out from under the weight of Christopher, of that stinking fucking Naples and all that poverty, and actually make a life for myself. And what do you do? You show up and fucking. Ruin. Everything. *Again!*"

Elena moved forward so quickly that Sinclair couldn't stop her. She grasped my shoulders and brought my head back sharply against the glass wall as she shook me.

"He leaves you for me, and now Margot tells me that you are GODDAMN PREGNANT?"

"Elena, please," I said, trying to ignore the ache echoing out from the base of my skull. "I am so, so sorry."

"Elena," Sinclair said, his voice cutting into her so hard that she flinched a full foot away from me, releasing her grip before she could even consciously be aware of it. "You will not touch Giselle like that. I understand that you are angry, and rightfully so, but you do not touch a woman, your sister, or a pregnant woman like that, for *any* reason."

"Fuck you, Daniel. You are just as bad as that slut, and everyone is going to know it."

Sinclair vibrated with fury, and it was Elena's turn to retreat as he moved closer. She might have played at being a predator, but Sinclair was the ultimate alpha wolf, and her manhandling of me had caused him to shed his thin veneer of civility.

"If you think that you can come into my house and hurt my woman, physically, mentally, or emotionally, then you are just fucking stupid. We hurt you. Fuck, if we don't feel that regret every day. There is nothing to do for it but apologize but empathize. We have kept as far away from you as we can and allowed you to treat us, particularly Elle, with absolute cruelty. That is done now. I hurt you, Elena. It was me who did this and me you should be angry with just as it is Christopher that you should be angry with and not your little sister. Have you ever thought that treating her like shit for her entire life may have led her to this? Maybe she would have tried harder to resist if you'd given her any kind of love or warmth over the years.

"As it is, I'm fucking glad she didn't because she is *mine* now, and no one messes with her, not even you, not even if you think you deserve to. So, get out of our fucking house and stay away unless you can pretend to be fucking civilized."

His voice was not loud like Elena's had been or coarse with an excess of emotion. Instead, it was stripped of anything but cold, cold malice, and I watched as every word hit Elena like a physical blow. In the end, she stood shaking in the doorway, her eyes skirting over the entire space, over our collection of friends, including Cosima and Sebastian in the living room, before they landed on me again over Sinclair's shoulder.

"You took everything from me," she breathed, so broken that it was painful to look at her. "And somehow, I'm the bad guy."

I wanted to say something, but the bile in my stomach had finally flooded over, and when I went to open my mouth, I threw up all over the floor.

"Dammit," I heard Candy curse as she dashed over to me, holding my hair back as it came flooding out of me.

Sinclair appeared a moment later with a small copper trashcan for me to heave into.

"I think it's time everyone went home," Eddie said softly over the loud sounds of my sickness.

By the time I finished dry heaving minutes later, everyone but Cosima, Candy, and Alexander were gone. Sinclair scooped me up, vomit-stained clothes and all, and strode with me up the glass staircase two steps at a time until we reached the master bathroom. Candy had followed us up and immediately turned the bath on while, surprisingly, Alexander, turned the shower on.

Sinclair was busy undressing me, his jaw ticking like a countdown to another explosion.

"Sin," I croaked through my sore and dry throat. "It's okay. She needed to do that."

He paused after stripping me naked to look me in the eyes, his utterly haunted. "I am so sorry."

"*Mon amour*," I breathed, placing my hand over the thudding heart in his chest. "Please, don't be."

"Get in the shower, honey, then the bath will be ready once you've rinsed off," Alexander said softly.

He looked me in the eyes, not once at my bare flesh. I was too hollow to thank him for that, but I noticed it all the same. I nodded and stepped through the open door to the walk-through shower. Surprisingly, Sin came with me, clothes and all. I hiccoughed as he tugged me into his arms and pressed my cheek to his chest. I burst into tears when he stepped us both under the hot spray.

"Let it out, my siren," he cooed over and over again as he gently gathered my vomit splattered hair and lathered it with my honey-scented shampoo.

He moved me like a precious doll as he tended to me, washing and conditioning me before picking me up in his arms to transfer us both into the waiting bubble bath. He arranged himself behind me in the huge white tub and tucked both his arms and legs around me.

"I've got you," he whispered into my hair once we were settled.

"We hurt her so badly," I breathed, completely wrecked by my puking and the crying jag.

"We did," he acknowledged. "It was awful, but it is over now. You let her have her freak out, and she doesn't get any more. This life we've fought for does not include her bullying or her bitterness."

"Sin," I protested, but he stopped me with a finger to my lips.

"No, Elle. We didn't fight for this relationship only to have it poisoned by her every single day. We did a bad thing, a really fucking horrible thing to someone we both cared for, but *it is done*. We cannot keep retreading that path, or we will never be happy."

God, he was so right. I knew it, but it didn't seem right to be so incandescently happy when she was so miserable.

"We aren't good people," I said because I needed to acknowledge it.

"We did a bad thing," he repeated. "So, maybe we aren't the best people, but I do not really fucking care. I would rather be a villain with you than a good person with anyone else."

We sat in silence for a long time after that. Distantly, I could hear Alexander, Candy, and Cosima cleaning up in the kitchen.

"Where did Seb go?" I finally asked.

"After Elena," he explained.

"Good."

"We're going to be fine, my siren. Even if it was just you, me, and this baby, I would make sure that we were the happiest family in the world. But we are not alone. We just had a whole group of people happy to congratulate us on our new house, on our baby, and our new life together. We're going to make it through this, and I am going to give you a happily ever after. *D'accord?*"

"*Je te crois,*" I murmured back because I believed him, even if it was hard to imagine it at the moment.

# Chapter Seventeen

*Giselle*

*I* was beginning to wish that Sinclair wouldn't read *The New York Times* anymore.

"Fuck," Sinclair cursed as he slammed the paper down and reached for his phone. "Fuck!"

"Sin?" I asked, uncurling from the deep chaise lounge we had on our upper level deep.

We were drinking our morning tea—Sinclair had decided to forgo coffee as well in a show of moral support—and enjoying the beautiful late winter morning sunrise over Brooklyn. We both loved the dual view of the Brooklyn and Manhattan bridges, and it was the perfect way to begin every morning. Sinclair had made the pot of herbal tea, wrapped me in a blanket, and brought me up the stairs to present me with the only breakfast I could stomach, a thin slice of extremely toasted bread.

I had just finished, and we were idly discussing the party he was planning in celebration of my gallery showing in two weeks when something in the paper turned him instantly on to beast mode.

"What the fuck?" Sinclair bit out into the phone. "How the hell did this happen, Margot?"

I listened to the one-sided conversation with my lip between my teeth.

"And I'm supposed to believe you? Was it you who tipped them off about the Paulsons too? Bullshit, M, Elena showed up here last night fucking livid, putting her hands on Elle, who is fucking pregnant, as you well know, saying that you told her about the baby. So forgive me if I don't believe you when you say that you had nothing to do with the Paulsons or this new article."

I zoned out after that in favor of leaning forward to snag the offending paper of the little table it lay crumpled on.

*Faire Developments CEO and son of Mortimer Percy, New York State's governor, has a torrid affair with longtime girlfriend's sister.*

Okay, yeah, I could understand why Sinclair was furious.

The article went on to state some of the intimate details of our affair; how we met in Mexico, the subsequent reveal that Elena and I were sisters, our continued affair, and finally, how we were now living in sin in Brooklyn. It also mentioned that I was an upcoming artist with a gallery showing in two weeks.

"Fuck," I echoed.

"I'll deal with this," Sinclair said, suddenly crouching in front of my chair. His face was harsh with contained fury, but it was his eyes that slayed me, filled with panic. "Fuck, this is too much for you to deal with right now."

I reached out to take his head in my hands. "Sin, please, I am okay right now. It sucks that someone felt the need to out us to the press as if we are some reality program, but at least everyone knows now, right?"

Sinclair did not laugh at my lame joke.

"Honey, seriously, I am okay. It might mean that some people might not come to my showing, but I can live with that. I'm worried about what it means for you."

And I was, the Dogwood deal was hanging by a thread, and Sin still hadn't found the person who had released the information about Mr. Paulson to the press.

He sighed. "I think this will be the end of that."

"No," I said immediately. "You can't be serious? Paulson would really pull out of the contract because of *gossip*? Can he even do that?"

"It isn't only Paulson, but the investors he brings to the table, and they all follow him because they share the same sensibilities," he explained.

"I'm sorry," I said.

He leaned forward to press a hard kiss to my lips. "Enough of that. We aren't doing this to each other. I do have to go, though. I know it's a Sunday, but I need to manage this."

"I understand."

He nodded again and gave me another kiss, this one with tongue so that I was panting slightly when he moved away.

"Later," he promised.

I nodded and watched him walk away. I stayed in the chaise until I was sure I had given him enough time to get ready and leave before I got up to do the same myself.

*I*t was hard to forget how opulent the Paulson's apartment was, but the massive chandelier in the foyer seemed even bigger than the one in my memories. I waited there while Gus, the butler, went in search of his mistress.

I was nervous. It could turn out to be a massive mistake to show up unannounced and somehow beg for them to continue to honor Paulson's deal with Sinclair, but at this point, when Sinclair was so uncharacteristically resigned, I knew I had to risk it.

"Giselle, what a surprise," Terry said as she swooped into the room.

I couldn't help but smile at the sight of her. She wore her signature hoop earrings, and her huge hair was out to *there* in teased curls. It was still midmorning, but she was already decked out for the day in a leopard print blouse and black cigarette pants. She looked like one of the Pink Ladies from *Grease,* and I loved it.

"Terry," I greeted, still smiling. "I hope I'm not intruding, but I brought you and Paulson a gift."

Her eyes widened with joy before she could subdue herself. I watched her bite her red-painted lip and struggle with what to say.

"Oh fudge, I can't be mad at you. It's not like you're involved in this whole sordid mess anyhow, right? I mean, I told Pauly right from the get-go that Daniel Sinclair was not the type of man to play in gossip, but you know men. They get so *angry* and so *stubborn* that it's hard to convince them of anything."

"Trust me, I know."

She laughed her awesome hyena laugh at my dry tone and came forward to wrap me in her heavily perfumed arms. "I missed you, girl."

"Same here, Terry," I murmured into her cloud of hair.

"Okay, okay, before I get mushy and ruin my makeup, let us go get Pauly. He is just about to go into the office, so you have good timing," she said as she linked our arms and led us down the vaguely familiar hall to her husband's office.

"I read about the whole affair thing in the paper this morning. Horrible stuff having your personal life displayed like that." She wrinkled her nose at me. "Anyone who sees you two together, though, will know that it was no tawdry thing. Don't you worry, hon."

"Thanks," I muttered as we pulled up to the door, and Terry knocked perfunctorily before leading us inside.

When we entered, Paulson was sitting behind his palatial desk talking on his Bluetooth, and I had a *déjà vu* moment. He immediately hung up and glared at his wife.

"What is she doing here, Teresa?"

"Don't Teresa me, Pauly. Giselle is our good friend," she warned.

"A good friend who is dating a man who I am not certain I should trust at the moment."

"Excuse me, Paulson, but Daniel Sinclair is not the kind of man to play games, especially when they would hinder more than help him. He is intelligent and fair. You know him well enough to know that as fact," I said, my voice strong despite his glower.

When he didn't respond, I squeezed Terry's hand and let go in order to take the awkwardly large brown wrapped canvas out from under my other arm.

"I came here to remind you of his goodness but also to remind you that we are just as vulnerable to gossip as you, as evidenced by the article in the paper today about us. Sinclair and I live a BDSM lifestyle too. We understand and accept the sanctity of that kind of relationship, especially how easy it is to misconstrue. I'm sorry that happened to you, Paulson, but if I may, I have some advice. People know your secret now. The only thing you can do is hold your head high and *own it*. Otherwise, people will always judge you and do it easily because you let them shame you."

I waited a beat for my words to sink in before I placed the canvas before me and ripped off the front of the paper. "This is my gift to you, regardless of how you choose to proceed with Sinclair."

They both stared at the large-scale painting I had revealed to them. There were no faces, only the broad chest of a man sitting behind his kingly desk, his legs spread beneath it to accommodate the woman on her knees under the desk, her pert ass balanced on the knife-like edge of her high heels.

It was a subtle rendering of a bold power exchange. There was dominance and affection in the hand that lay on the women's shining dark curls and power in her submission as she serviced him, knowing she was giving him pleasure.

I loved it. It was one of my favorite paintings in my collection, but I wanted them to have it.

Finally, Terry cleared her throat and looked up at me with shining eyes. "I always admired your work, knew you were freaking talented, lady, but this is beyond perfection. I couldn't love or appreciate it more."

I smiled slightly, but my eyes moved to Paulson when he cleared his throat.

"You understand that there is grace in such a thing," he said gruffly. "Beauty in it, even though I'm not a man who gets beauty much, 'less it's Teresa. This is a gift of beauty, and I will honor it, Giselle, just as I will honor my deal with your man."

Relief passed through me, making me shudder from the surreal thrill of it.

"Thank you," I breathed out.

"*Thank you*," Paulson boomed in his usual radio announcer voice.

"Now, should we call that man and get him over here to share a celebratory drink?"

"We should," I said as Terry jumped up and down, clapping.

When Sinclair arrived, I was sitting on a gold brocade couch with Terry drinking sparkling apple juice while she had champagne. Paulson sat straight but oddly comfortable in an antique wooden chair that looked like something from a torture chamber.

Sin came immediately to me, lifted me into the air and planted a deep, long, wet kiss on my lips. By the time he pulled away, my legs were wrapped around his waist, and both of my hands were twisted in his hair.

"Hi," I breathed against his mouth.

His hands flexed on my bottom. "I love you so much. You have evolved into such a beautiful, fierce woman, Elle. Exactly like a swan."

I blushed like crazy under the praise and butted my forehead lightly against his. "I can be fierce for you."

"Evidently." He chuckled.

"Care for a drink, Sinclair?" Paulson asked, his voice tinged with humor.

Sinclair pressed one more kiss to my lips before he swung around to sit on the couch beside Terry with me in his lap. "That sounds about right, Paulson. I'll have what you're having. We seem to have similar tastes."

They shared a moment of meaningful eye contacted before they both laughed, Sinclair more subdued than the other man's bellowing chortle.

"So," Terry said when they had recovered, and Sinclair was nursing scotch on the rocks. "Who do you think leaked your story?"

"Unfortunately, it's not much of a mystery," Sinclair said with a wince. "Elena showed up at our new place last night because a colleague of mine discovered that Giselle is pregnant."

Both of the Paulsons gasped and then expressed their heartfelt congratulations, which we both accepted with a smile.

"She was less than impressed, and it wasn't the first time she threatened to tell the media about us, but I think it was the final straw," Sin continued to explain.

"Well, damn. I know it must be hard on her, but love is love, things happen, and family is the end all be all right?" Terry said, her nose scrunched again in disapproval.

"It could be argued that if family is the end all be all, then I wouldn't have done what I did," I pointed out softly.

I was willing to move past our indiscretions and wrongdoings, but I didn't want to forget them or underplay them.

Sinclair placed a kiss on my hair.

It was Paulson, though, who offered the best advice I had heard so far. "She comes around, or she doesn't. She's hurt, but if she had handled things differently, you all could have healed together, found a way through that didn't ruin your family. She chose differently, and that's on her."

His words settled the last pieces of sharp-edged grief digging into my happy heart, and I closed my eyes as they shift and smoothed out.

"Happy," Sinclair both asked and reminded.

"Happy," I agreed, nestled on his lap with people we admired, his business deal saved, and a baby on the way.

Yeah, I was definitely one of the luckiest people in the world.

# Chapter Eighteen

*Giselle*

After weeks of no communication, the esteemed governor of New York and his wife invited Sinclair and me for a formal dinner at their estate upstate.

To say that I was nervous would have been a gross understatement. My stomach rolled and bucked like a rabid stallion as we made our way through the beautiful country roads of Suffolk county. There wasn't anything left in my belly but a few saltine crackers Sinclair had forced down my throat that morning, but it was just enough to make me gag a few times behind my hand, hoping he wouldn't notice.

He did.

"We can still cancel," he offered for the twelfth time that day.

"No, we can't."

I didn't want the Percys to have any more reason to hate me. Yes, I had stolen their son from a perfectly adequate mate while I myself was just a bohemian artist with loose morals whose greatest asset was her breasts, but no one would ever love their son more than I would, and I was determined to make them see that.

"So stubborn, my siren," Sin scolded, but his hand squeezed my thigh tenderly. "I just don't want you to set unrealistic expectations. My father is a kind man, but he doesn't take an interest in anything outside of politics, so he will probably leave you be. You know my mother. She will be looking for any reason to speak down to you, to belittle our relationship."

My heart clenched. I knew he was right, but our love was still so new, so unbelievably unbelievable that I didn't have the emotional fortitude to weather much more censure. It was impossible for me to reconcile the moral *wrongness* of our relationship with the absolute *rightness* of our connection.

Everyone wanted to condemn us, and as a person who had spent her life trying to avoid conflict, to stay firmly out of any kind of spotlight, it was wearing thin on my soul.

I linked my fingers through Sinclair's and immediately felt soothed.

"We can do this," I said.

He ran a thumb over the back of my hand. "We can do anything."

"You are so cheesy," I teased, even though his words warmed me.

"Only with you." He shot me a small smile before looking back out the window. "I want to tell them that you are having my baby."

My tumultuous stomach heaved painfully. "What?"

"I don't want to hide," he said, mulishly. "We've done that. I want the world to know I own you, my siren. I've told you this before."

"Sin, I really don't feel comfortable telling your parents." I felt more than uncomfortable. I was terrified by the thought of it.

"When do you plan to tell them? When our child is two, twelve or thirty-six?"

"Don't be deliberately cruel."

"*Et toi?* I am not the one who refuses to acknowledge our unborn child."

Guilt and anger coursed through my veins like hot lead. I opened my mouth to say something but the sight of an enormous brick mansion secured behind beautifully constructed wrought iron gates distracted me.

It was exactly the kind of place I expected the Governor of New York and his socialite wife to live in, from the gabled windows to the perfectly symmetrical hedges lining the drive. As if I wasn't nervous enough already, my heart leaped into a sprint.

"*Putain,*" I cursed under my breath.

Sinclair chuckled softly before parking in the cobbled driveway that looped around a central water feature. I waited, mostly because I was frozen with anxiety, for him to open the door for me.

"Giselle," he said, after gently helping me out of the car and pushing me back against the closed door.

His voice came to me like I was underwater.

"Giselle."

It was the warm stroke of his thumb across my cheekbone that stirred me. I blinked up at him owlishly.

He smiled tenderly. "You look beautiful, and I am very much in love with you. Have I told you that today?"

"No," I couldn't help but pout, drawn in by his unusual playfulness. "Not for at least twenty-six hours."

"Well, that won't do at all."

He pressed his body flush against mine. Even with the layers of silk and cotton between us, I could feel his heat.

"What I wouldn't give to take you back home and leave this godforsaken place. I would tie you spread eagle to our bed and worship you for hours."

"Why don't you?" I breathed, completely forgetting where we were and why.

A smile ghosted along his firm lips. "I cannot run away and hide between your thighs every time I am afraid of losing you."

"It's impossible."

"I know, I own and operate my own company. As enjoyable as it would be, I can't afford to go bankrupt," he teased.

"No," I insisted, hauling him even closer by the lapels of his ludicrously expensive suit. *"C'est impossible que tu passes ne serait-ce qu'un jour sans moi à tes côtés."*

It is impossible that you will ever be without me.

That was my truth. As long as Sinclair wanted me, I was his.

He softened, wrapping me up in my arms so that my cheek was pressed to his chest and his nose was in my hair. I smiled while he drank in a deep lungful of my scent.

"Okay, my siren, are you ready for the den of dragons?" he asked.

I threaded my fingers through his and looked down my nose at him. "I was born ready."

*I* wasn't ready.

The Percy mansion was the American equivalent to a French chateau or an Italian villa but without any of the serenity or warmth. It was like a mausoleum.

A real-life butler with a large mustache answered the massive oak front door. He immediately gave us a cordial greeting and seemed delighted to shake hands with Sin, but I was too intimidated to smile at him.

Sinclair smoothed his thumb over the back of our joined hands as we entered the main hall. Dark wood glistened beautifully from every corner, swooping down in a double curved staircase that framed the entryway. My heels wobbled on the plush Persian carpet we stood on as I took everything in.

I caught my reflection in a large gilt mirror to the left after I wood-enly handed my coat to the butler. My cheeks were pale under wide anxious eyes, and my curls spilled like dark blood over my shoulders in the dim light. I was wearing a demure dress, thinking that the black satin and the high-necked halter would read as sophisticated. Instead, it flowed down my curves like an oil slick, highlighting the nipples that had hardened immediately from the cool air outside and the arrogant curve of my ass. The black made me look like a slut, not a lady, and even the pearls at my ears and the elegant pearl collar at my throat could do nothing to elevate my class.

Sinclair's hand found the skin of my bare back, his fingers toying with the long silky ribbon holding my dress together at my neck. "The only thing that will get me through this is the thought of unrav-eling you like a present at the end of the night."

I shivered and blushed fiercely while the butler pretended not to notice. It took me another moment to notice the faint murmur of voices floating from a room further down the left hallway.

My gaze flew to Sinclair.

It sounded like more than just his parents were there for dinner.

"Hainesport?" Sinclair asked in his dangerously mild tone. "I was under the impression it was just my parents, my girlfriend, and me for dinner tonight?"

The mustached Hainesport cleared his throat awkwardly. "You are mistaken, Mr. Sinclair. Your parents are having a small gathering to celebrate your father's announcement."

Sin stiffened. "Announcement?"

"Yes, sir."

"*Putain*," Sin swore under his breath.

He looked down at me, a muscle ticking in his jaw. I reached up to press the spot with my fingers, offering support even though I had an awful feeling that this night was already taking a turn for the worse.

"They are waiting for you in the dining room," Hainesport said, already making his way toward the party.

I looked up at Sinclair without masking the panic in my eyes. His own flashed with protectiveness, but he only reached down to press a hard kiss to my lips.

"Bigger than the world, my siren."

For the first time since he had uttered that phrase, I didn't take comfort from the words.

I followed after him with my heart in my throat, beating so strongly it threatened to choke me. The sense of doom I felt stalking after us made me want to pick up my skirts and run away, but I reminded myself that this was important. If I wanted to be with Sinclair, I had to accept this part of his life, the elevated, refined society he had been transplanted into upon his adoption. I wished fruitlessly that Cage could be there, but I knew he neglected his foster parents as much as they did him.

When we rounded the corner, we were greeted with the sight of over two dozen elegantly dressed guests. Sinclair cursed softly again.

As if drawn by the sound, conversations fell quiet, and eyes swiveled loudly to look at us. I watched with grim fascination as they cataloged my wanna-be-classy-but-still-slutty dress, the harlot red of my hair, and the hand clasped within my own.

For one half of half a second, they seemed perplexed. They were trying to reconcile past meetings with Elena and what they remembered her as with the woman before them now. They wrinkled their collective noses.

Had Elena always been so... garish?

Another second and they had their answer. I saw it in the tightening of their eyes, how the women searched subtly for their men and how they, in turn, searched my body subtly for further evidence of my curves.

This wasn't the up-and-coming New York City lawyer they had

met and admired. This was someone else, and she was considerably *less*.

I tried to tell my insecurities to give it a rest, but their combined gaze was the definition of judgment.

"Daniel," Willa separated herself from the crowd, gliding forward in an exquisite icy blue dress that Elena might have worn. "We worried you wouldn't make it."

Sin's lips tightened at the passive-aggressive comment. "It's nice to see you too, Mom."

He kept my hand in his as they exchanged cheek kisses.

She frowned up at him. "You need a haircut."

I saw the smile try to claim his mouth and took pleasure in knowing it was because of me.

"I like it this way."

"It looks unkempt."

"I prefer to think it looks piratical," he retorted before turning slightly to wink at me.

I giggled softly.

Willa finally deigned to look over at me, her eyebrows prematurely raised in condescension.

"Giselle Moore, I wish we were meeting again under different circumstances."

"Oh? Are we commiserating or celebrating tonight?" I asked, deliberately obtuse.

Her eyes narrowed, trying to discern if I was being smart or not.

"I'm speaking, of course, about the fact that you are here as my son's date and not, as you are meant to be, as his future sister-in-law."

Wow.

I blinked, stunned that she had the audacity to just come right out and lay battle lines. My anger warred with exhaustion; I was so tired of fighting.

Sinclair, apparently, was not.

He stepped forward with his hand wrapped securely around my waist, and though he spoke quietly, his words were forceful. "This is the woman I love, Mom. If you love me or respect me in any way, you will treat her with the kindness she deserves."

Willa stiffened, a muscle ticking in her strong jaw. Sin might not have been her biological son, but I could see where he had inherited his arctic freeze temper.

"I mean it," Sinclair warned.

"Oh, I know," she said softly. "Hence my shock."

She studied me out of the corner of her eye, cataloging everything about me with the precision of a 3D scanner. I stood straight and tall before the scrutiny, secured in my confidence by the feel of Sin's hand on my hip.

"And my begrudging approval," she added.

My head snapped around to look at Sin's reaction, but he seemed just as mystified as I was.

Willa laughed. "I may not be the most maternal woman in the world, and I certainly cannot approve of the inception of your relationship, but if you rebelled against every single thing I taught you about morality and success in order to be with this woman..." Her nose scrunched delicately. "In order to be with you, Giselle, then I won't waste my time and alienate my only son."

The words 'Cage is your son too' pooled on my tongue like excessive saliva, but I refrained from saying anything.

"Welcome to the family, dear." She smiled again, but it was wooden as she leaned in to whisper conspiratorially, "Next time, we'll go shopping together before an event."

*Bitch.*

I smiled demurely, ignoring the huff of amused breath from Sinclair next to me.

"Thank you, Willa."

She inclined her head regally. I could see clearly how she would have liked Elena. They both wore their artifice and insincerity like a string of highly polished pearls.

Without another word, she turned and made her way over to a small group that I recognized as a congresswoman, a prolific political advisor, and a journalist from the *NY Times*.

"*Merde.*"

"Careful, most of the people here speak French," Sinclair reminded me.

"As if I wasn't intimidated enough already," I muttered under my breath.

Sin smiled at me, but before he could say anything, a short man in a suit with his sparse hair carefully arranged around his bald crown approached us.

"Daniel Sinclair, it has been a very long time," he said while stabbing his hand toward us.

"It has. How are you, Mr. Carroll?"

My eyes widened before I could curb my reaction. Mr. Carroll was one of the most famous defense attorneys in the country. I knew this, of course, because Elena had been obsessed with the little man/big lawyer for years. It was her dream to battle against him in court one day and beat him. She had mentioned once that whenever she went into court, she pretended Mr. Carroll was her opposing council.

I imagined the shrill sound of my self-esteem rushing from the puncture hole in my confidence. How in the world was a poor artist from Naples supposed to converse with such a man?

Happily, Mr. Carroll took care of the job for me. He turned my way with a small but genuine grin that made him fair more comely.

"Miss Moore, it is my absolute pleasure to meet you. My wife and I have been deep admirers of your work since your second exhibition in Paris. I believe it was in 2013?

"Oh yes," I said, miraculously harnessing my shock. "It was my first nude collection." And this esteemed man had bought some of that work.

I tried not to freak out, settling on what I hoped was a demure smile instead.

Sinclair squeezed my hand in support.

Mr. Carroll chuckled. "Yes, I remember well. My wife is a good friend of Terry Paulson. It was she who turned her on to your art. I must admit, we bought one of your pieces at your last showing, and my wife was incredibly disappointed she didn't get to meet you. She will be furious that she missed dinner tonight."

I laughed, charmed by this innocuous-looking yet charming man. "You must give her my card and tell her to call. I left a few pieces out of the collection if she would be interested in a private viewing?"

His eyes widened comically. "I would have brownie points for *years* if I could secure that. We were looking at the preview catalog for your next collection just the other night and already put a hold on one of the pieces."

This time, we all laughed.

"Well, I'm happy to do it. May I ask which piece you bought?"

To my delight, he blushed faintly. "*Candy.*"

He'd bought the painting of Candy Kay sucking salaciously on an oversized red lollipop. I was proud of both Sinclair and myself for remaining sober.

"One of my favorites too," Sinclair said with a wink.

God, I loved that man.

Mr. Carroll grinned. "Of course, you must be incredibly proud of her, Sinclair. A man has to wonder what a gorgeous artist is doing with a workaholic, fuddy-duddy like you, eh?"

I snorted before I could help it.

Sinclair looked bemused by the comment but shrugged good-naturedly. "You can understand when I say she brought color to my life, Isaac."

He nodded. "I can, I can. Now, if I may insist, I would love your card, dear girl."

I opened my mouth to explain that I had left my cards in my coat, but Sinclair beat me to the punch, pulling out his slim leather wallet to retrieve one of my cards. He chatted briefly with the man before he handed it over, but I was oblivious to the conversation. I was focused on the man who kept my business cards in his wallet and happily shared his love for me with almost strangers.

Everything awful in life was worth having this man by my side.

When Mr. Carroll had excused himself, Sin looked down at me

with a broad grin. The expression slipped slightly, replaced by passion-narrowed eyes and tensed lips. His hand tightened in mine.

"Do not look at me like that in public, siren, or you may not like what I will do to you in front of these many eyes."

I swallowed thickly, tilting my head back to expose my throat, like a beta wolf before her Alpha. "I think I would like it."

Sinclair smiled down at me wickedly and whispered, "If you are a good girl, my siren, I promise to reward you for the tedium of this party."

A shiver coursed down my spine. I couldn't understand how deeply attracted I was to this man. Though, of course, he was absurdly handsome, and his tightly leashed control only served to emphasize the depth of his hidden passions. At first, I thought maybe the taboo nature of having an affair added an extra explosive element to our chemistry, but my theory was contradicted every time he touched me. We had been living together, however unconventionally, for three months, and the kindling that he had ignited within me in Los Cabos was only growing, now a raging inferno that threatened to devour all other rational thought.

Sin turned slightly in front of me, shielding me from the majority of the curious onlookers so that he could gently pinch one of my tightly furled nipples between two knuckles. "Would you like that?"

"Yes, sir. I promise to be a good girl," I breathed.

He smiled sharply and abruptly twisted my captured nipple so that sweet pain radiated through my chest.

"I know you are self-conscious with these people, but you are the color amid all this black and white bullshit. Do not let them take that away from you."

I bit my lip. As punishment, he pulled hard on my nipple, making me gasp.

"I am so out of my league here," I murmured.

Sinclair's soft chuckle stirred my hair as he pulled me against his chest. He gently kneaded my hips with his fingertips, every press of his fingers against the silky material of my dress made my breath catch. Even though I knew we were in the corner of the room and that most people could say we were inappropriately close to each other, my slight worry over what the guests would think only heightened my arousal.

"Do you remember that second night in Mexico?" He breathed against my ear.

"Mmm."

"I was hard the entire night thinking of all the things I wanted to do to you after Iago's party."

I panted slightly as his grip suddenly tightened, pressing me tightly to the arousal tenting the front of his trousers. I pressed a hand to his chest and felt the heavy thrum of his pulse. It was intoxicating to know that his heart beat for me.

He dipped his head low to lick a path around my left ear before blowing on it. "I want you to focus on all the wicked ways I will pleasure your body later tonight. How I am going to bind you to our bed and spend hours between your sweet thighs while these pert nipples strain beneath those painful metal clamps."

Fuck, I was panting now.

"I want you to focus on how you will beg me to let you come on my face, how wet your sweet little pussy will be when I finally slide into you from behind, your ass red from my hand."

"Sinclair," I moaned.

I swear I could have orgasmed just from listening to him speak to me in that voice like smoke and leather.

He chuckled darkly and pressed a sweet kiss to my nose. "Focus on that, my love. Now, are you ready? I believe dinner is being served."

A ragged groan tore from my throat, aroused and enraged by his flippancy. He only chuckled again and tucked my arm firmly in his to escort me to the dining room.

The room was absolutely gorgeous with vaulted ceilings that sparkled gold in the light from three delicate chandeliers.

"Wow," I breathed as images of *Beauty & The Beast* flooded my head. "I can't believe you grew up here."

"I didn't really. Boarding school, remember? In the summers, we usually went traveling. I still have a designated bedroom here, but I can count the number of times that I've actually used it."

"Still..." I drifted off, overwhelmed by the splendor.

Sin chuckled under his breath while he settled me into my seat before taking the one beside me.

"Daniel, darling, your place card is up here next to your father," Willa called lightly from the head of the endlessly long table.

Sin stiffened midway through sitting down. I watched him with curiosity as he moved away from me toward his mother. He stopped beside the empty chair at her left, dipped down to place a chaste kiss on her cheek, and plucked the place card from the table. Willa watched with vague surprise and amusement as he reclaimed his place beside me and switched out the name cards.

There was a rush of whispers across the table, but Sinclair ignored them. Without looking at me, his gaze sweeping across the startled guests, he lifted our clasped hands to place a lingering kiss on my knuckles. I blushed, but thankfully, everyone became distracted by the beautifully presented first course that arrived before us.

Sinclair was quiet as we ate despite the numerous attempts by other guests to chat with him, but I was happy to engage with the middle-aged matron beside me, a Mrs. Hastings, who regaled me with tales of her youthful glory days. I was laughing at one such story when I noticed Sinclair had stiffened beside me.

"It was the idea of children, wasn't it?"

I turned to face the young man questioning Sin. He was around the same age as my partner but boyish looking with his floppy curls and dimpled smile. I remembered his face from the news and magazines. He was the son of the New York senator and one of Sinclair's friends from boarding school.

"It's nothing to be ashamed of Sinclair. God knows, I don't see the appeal in spawning little brats," Liam Reed continued to say. "Deal breaker for Elena, though, huh?"

"Don't be stupid, Liam," a beautiful blonde said from the other side of him. "Everyone knows he left Elena for the sister." She inclined her head toward me with pursed lips. "Didn't you read about it in *The Times*?"

Liam looked vaguely surprised before he threw his head back with laughter. "You dog. I never would have guessed you for a cheat."

Sinclair was still and cold as an ice sculpture, his jaw so tight that I wondered if his teeth would crack under the pressure.

"Don't get me wrong..." Liam leaned forward to wink at me. "This one is a lovely little thing. But you can't tell me kids didn't play a role in it?"

I clenched and unclenched my sweaty hands in my lap, worried that Sin would say something and worried that he wouldn't.

I was right to worry.

Sinclair leveled his freezing glare on both Liam and the blonde, staring them down until they looked away nervously. "Marriage and family were never the problem, at least not with the right woman. Giselle, *the lovely little thing*, who has done me the greatest honor by consenting to be with me despite the havoc I have wrought on her life, is that woman for me. In fact," he paused dramatically, and I realized that the entire table had quieted to listen to his little speech, "we're expecting, and I could not be happier about it."

The silence that blanketed the room was so heavy that it crushed the air from my lungs. Sinclair reached for my hand under the table and took it in his, rubbing his thumb comfortingly back and forth. I tried to take reassurance from it, but the anger and shame that warred inside me beat it back.

"Sinclair?" Willa asked, her voice uncharacteristically soft. "Is this true?"

"It is," he confirmed.

I watched his face transform with a glorious smile, his cobalt blue eyes alight with pride and joy.

Damn, it was going to be hard to stay angry with him.

Willa struggled for a moment with the news. She stared down at her plate, blinking rapidly, before she looked over at her husband at the head of the table. He inclined his head at her, his smile gentle.

"Well," she finally said, "I cannot believe it. I'm finally going to be a grandmother!"

It was my turn to blink rapidly as tears rushed forth and spilled over my cheeks before I could help it. Sinclair tugged my chair closer and put his arm around my shoulders as he began to accept everyone's congratulations.

I decided to rest my head against his strong shoulder, smiling weakly at everyone as they beamed at us. Apparently, procreating trumped the shame of adultery, at least in the high circles the Percy family ran in. I was both relieved and repulsed by their congratulations, but after months of antagonism, I was willing to take whatever niceties I could get.

"*T'es fâchée?*" Sinclair murmured into my hair when we had a moment to ourselves.

"I'm not angry even though that would be justified." I scowled up at him. "How can I be angry when you are so excited for this baby?"

His fingers skimmed over my satin-clad belly and rested there, but it was his eyes, brighter than I had ever seen them—so blue that they were almost neon—that captured my total attention.

"I have never been happier."

I swallowed the sob that rose in my throat. "Me too."

"Sinclair, I would like to speak with you," Mortimer Percy said, suddenly appearing over our shoulder.

He frowned at his father and then me before nodding. "Okay, but Giselle is coming with me."

Mortimer stared at me for a moment before inclining his head in consent.

I puzzled over him as I followed them both from the room. He was a mystery to me in a way that Willa was not. I understand that the woman lived for her role as a matron of New York society, that she loved the power bestowed upon her as a governor's wife, and that, in her own way, she loved the son she had found and molded in France.

But Mortimer was a different entity, one that Sinclair didn't talk much about. I knew that he wanted Sin to follow in his political footsteps, and that he was charismatic and generous. But whatever his qualities, I knew that he too had used his adopted son for his own gains, and I would never forget my Frenchman's sadness as he related that to me in that little cove in Mexico.

So, I was wary as we all settled in Mortimer's office, a place of cedar, leather-bound books, and manly red walls. Sinclair had me sit in a chair in front of the desk beside Willa, who had followed us in, but he remained standing even when his father took his place behind the desk.

"It was you," Sinclair started.

I couldn't see his face, but I knew from the tone of voice that he had discovered something horrifying.

It took me about two seconds to clue in, so I was gasping when Mortimer nodded. "Yes. I was the one who told the press about Paulson's unique... tastes."

"How did you know?"

"You forget that I am the one who introduced you," Mortimer said simply.

"Daniel," Willa interjected when the two men just continued to stare at each other. "We didn't mean to cause you real problems. We just wanted to... give you a push in the right direction."

"Meaning?" he growled.

"Meaning, we wanted you to take your rightful place in politics," Mortimer explained calmly.

"You are kidding me, no?" Sinclair asked in his glacial way.

Willa froze over accordingly, her eyes wide with fear. I wondered if she was worried about what other people would think if they found out or if she truly regretted crossing the line and the risk doing so now posed to her relationship with her son.

"Unfortunately, no," Mortimer said before heaving a huge sigh and focusing on a point over Sinclair's shoulder. "I know we didn't go about it the right way, trying to manipulate you into following my path. It was wrong of us. I can see that now. But you have to understand; every single Percy since we settled in this country from England has been in government. You are my son. I don't care if we don't share the same blood. I wanted that legacy for you."

"That's so fucked up," Sin breathed out.

It totally was.

To his credit, though I didn't really give him any, his father nodded sadly. "Agreed. I know we haven't been the best parents—"

I snorted, unable to keep quiet anymore. "You have been *abysmal* parents as far as I can tell. And before you say that I have no business in this conversation, you are wrong. If it involves Sinclair, it involves me. You two made the deliberate choice to be his parents, and you have never done right by him."

"We gave him the best education money could buy, the tools to succeed in this life," Willa snapped, aghast at my audacity.

"I have no doubt that Sinclair would be successful even if he had remained an orphan on the Côte d'Azur. What he needed, what you promised to give him by adopting him, was love."

"We love him," Willa mouthed, her voice lost to the grief those words stirred in her. She turned to Sin with both her lips, and her eyes opened wide, punctured with remorse. "We love you. You know that, Daniel."

He cocked his head to the side as he studied her. "I do. But Giselle was the one who taught me how to love properly with my whole heart. You don't use your loved ones to better yourself in society."

"That is not what we did," Willa objected sharply.

"It wasn't what we meant to do," Mortimer amended quietly.

The two of them shared a long look before Willa turned to Sinclair with wet in her eyes. "Sinclair, my darling boy, I've always loved you. Since the minute I saw you on the streets in Nice, I loved you."

I watched Sinclair swallow hard. "Honestly, I don't really care anymore. I'm done with family drama. I have Elle now, and we are going to have our own family. If you want to be a part of it, you will do what you can to rectify the mistake you made in contacting the press about the Paulsons, and you will start treating both of us like family."

He looked down at me, and despite his little speech, I could tell he was rattled—both by the betrayal he felt and by their sincere remorse for it.

I took his offered hand and followed him to the door, but we paused when Willa called out to us.

"I just want you both to know that we are going to do better." She shot her husband a look and gathered her composure so that when she looked back at us, she was once again the immaculate society lady. "I want to be in my grandchild's life."

"Do better, and you will be," I said.

Sinclair squeezed my hand, and together, we left.

# Chapter Nineteen

*Sinclair*

I wanted to marry her. The thought consumed me to the point that it was affecting my work. Margot had caught me browsing Tiffany's website for engagement rings when I should have been in the Town Car on my way to the construction site on the Hudson River. She'd paused dramatically before suggesting that Giselle might prefer something more unique, an antique or something custom made. She was right, and the fact she had warmed up toward my relationship with Elle was enough to make me cast her a massive grin. Her shocked but happy reaction made me realize that Giselle was right. I didn't smile enough.

I knew I had to wait, though. Giselle wouldn't appreciate me asking when we were already going through so much, moving at a pace that would have scared the fuck out of me even six months ago. I took immense comfort from the fact that she was pregnant, though. The savage in me rejoiced in knowing that a part of me grew inside her. I'd worried she would be mad about the pregnancy, but the look of confusion giving way to the pure joy that eclipsed her face when I'd convinced her of it would remain with me forever. She had never been so beautiful.

I hated that she wouldn't let me tell anyone, though. It was fucking ridiculous to keep it a secret, especially given that she was probably three months along. I hoped that after our appointment with Dr. Adams that day, she would change her mind.

When I arrived at the office, Giselle was already there, curled up in a small chair with her travel sketchbook in her lap. I took a moment to watch her gently bite the end of her pencil as she stared into the distance at a place only her vivid imagination could construct. Her fiery hair curled over the cleavage exposed by the long wool dress she wore. My dick twitched in my pants even as my heart warmed at the sight of her.

She was so fucking pretty and so fucking mine.

As if she could sense my predatory thoughts, her eyes snapped to mine, clicking in place like magnets. A slow smile claimed her features, and I couldn't help but beam back at her. There were other people in the waiting room, but I paid them no mind as I strode over to my siren and fell to my knees before her, first planting a gentle kiss on her tummy before claiming her lips in a possessive kiss. My hand found her throat, my thumb at her pulse, and I squeezed gently just to feel her heartbeat throttle before I moved away to take the seat beside her.

She blinked dazedly at me before breathily saying, "Hi."

I grinned in pure masculine satisfaction. "Hi."

"I know I just saw you this morning, but I've missed you," she admitted with a faint blush.

Her words liquefied me. I reached out to gently cup that pink-stained cheek. "I missed you too. How are you feeling today?"

"The nausea is pretty bad. I thought I had a handle on it this morning, but I ended up puking in the Paulson's gold plated toilet." She made a face that had me laughing. It was one of my favorite things that she didn't take herself too seriously.

"It's normal," I assured her because I might have gone a little crazy with worry when she wouldn't stop throwing up one morning last week.

"I know, I know. I guess..." She looked off into the distance so that I couldn't see her expressive eyes.

I tapped her chin lightly with my knuckles. "What is it, love?"

"I guess I wish that I could talk to Mama about this. She's done it three times, so I'm sure she knows what to expect."

Fuck, she had the power to absolutely gut me. It was like my heart lived in her small hand, and her moods dictated its every beat.

I simultaneously wanted to kill Caprice for turning her back on her daughter and sell her my soul in order to bring her back to Giselle.

This love thing was so illogical.

"I'm sorry," I said because, at that moment, I really was.

"For what?"

"For being such a selfish bastard. I did this to you." I pressed my hand to her slightly swollen stomach.

"It takes two to make a baby, Mr. Sinclair," she sassed me.

She was so sexy when she sassed me.

"And thank God for that. What I meant specifically was that I deliberately hid the pills from you, tried to make you forget to take them... I really wanted this despite the timing and what it might mean for you."

I wasn't feeling guilty for getting her pregnant—no part of me could feel anything other than pure jubilancy at the thought of our child—but I hated how much pain my love brought her and how she had to choose me over everyone else she loved.

"Hey, hey now," she said, taking my chin in her hand this time. Her eyes were huge, a crystalline gray brighter than pure silver. "I won't argue with you about some of that. You should have just talked to me about having a baby; I had no idea that was even something you wanted in the future, let alone right away. And it is pretty bad timing. We just moved in together, and we are still so new..." She trailed off at the look on my face, and I quickly tried to resurrect my cool façade so she would continue her honestly, but it was too late. "It feels like you and I have been together for years, like we were always meant to be together. As crazy as it sounds, I think you and I are ready to be parents. We will make a perfect nuclear little family. It's the extended family that I'm worried about. I don't think Elena will ever forgive me for also getting pregnant with you, especially so soon after you ended things with her."

"Elle." I pressed her palm to my face with my hand. "I hate to break your heart, but Elena was never going to forgive you, regardless of this."

Tears welled in those beautiful eyes, but she bit her bottom lip against shedding them and nodded a few times to shore up her strength. I kissed the inside of the wrist holding my hand, then dropped our linked hands to my lap so that I could lean forward and kiss her sad-softened mouth.

She sighed gustily when I retreated. "I'll have to tell Mama and the twins at some point."

"You will, but you can decide when that is. We can keep it quiet as long as you'd like." God, but it hurt me to say that.

She side-eyed me before smiling. "How much did it cost you to say that?"

"Just don't make me say it again." My dry comment was rewarded with her laughter. I soaked it up like sunshine.

"Miss Moore?" We turned to a nurse in pink scrubs that stood with a clipboard before us. "If you could come with me, the doctor is ready to see you now. Mr. Sinclair, I'll come out to get you if you want to be part of the ultrasound."

"Of course," I bristled, annoyed she would even ask, that she would even consider barring me from the process.

Giselle placed a calming hand on my arm before getting to her feet to follow the nurse. "Be calm. I'll see you in a few minutes."

I watched her disappear through the door before I opened my phone.

"*Mon frère, ça va?*"

"What's with all the noise?" I asked Cage, wincing at the cacophony of sound in the background.

He laughed. "Give me a second." I waited while he moved somewhere quieter. "There, that's better. How is my favorite redhead?"

"We're at the doctor's office."

There was a long pause while he digested that.

"Okay, I am going to guess that she isn't sick. Otherwise, you'd be going berserker on me. So..." He burst into ruckus laughter. "You old fucking dog, you knocked her up."

I couldn't help my grin. "*Mais oui.*"

"Just when I think you've completely turned your back on the French, you do something so quintessentially francophone like knock up your mistress."

"She is not my mistress."

"Whoa, ease up. I was just teasing. If you tried to make Giselle your mistress, I would happily cut off your balls."

"You're a good friend, Cage," I said dryly, which only elicited another chuckle from him.

"How is she dealing with it?"

"It was a surprise, but she seems happy."

"*Bon.* I am very happy for you, Sin. You've got yourself quite the woman."

Pride sluiced through me; Giselle was the ultimate woman.

"Listen, I need your advice." I waited for him to stop laughing before continuing. "I agree, you're an idiot, but I need someone to talk to, and apart from Elle, you're family."

Cage cleared his throat roughly. "Any time, *mon frère.*"

"I want to marry her."

There was a loud whoosh as Cage exhaled in shock.

"This is a joke?" When I didn't respond, he blew a raspberry into the phone. "Wow, I am shocked. Daniel Sinclair wants to get married."

"He does. Tomorrow wouldn't be early enough."

He chuckled. "Okay, then I don't really understand why you need advice. Marry the woman."

"Her mother has basically disowned her, one of her sisters hates her, and the other just came out of a fucking coma, her brother is on location somewhere in the California desert, we have only been dating for a few months, and we just discovered that she's pregnant."

There was a long pause.

"Seems like a bunch of excuses to me. You want to marry her, then do it. When a man finds a woman like that, he does everything he can to tie himself to her."

*Fuck yes.* I knew if anyone could understand my primitive need to claim Giselle, it would be my best friend and brother of choice, Cage. Unlike me, he had never tried to civilize himself. He was happy with being a blunt, gluttonous badass even when people turned their noses up at him. Even when our parents did.

The guy had balls of steel, and finally, I felt like he wasn't the only one who did.

"I'll need you to help me pick out a ring," I said. "And I have an idea. It's crazy impulsive, but I don't think I wait to make her mine, legally. I'll need you to help me organize it."

"Done. I'm busy with the new album, but any time, man, I'm there."

I tipped my head back against the wall and let out a massive breath that I wasn't aware I'd been holding in. "*Merci, mon frère.*"

"She brought you back to you, Sin. There isn't a hell of a lot I wouldn't do for her, and you know there is nothing I wouldn't do for you."

I swallowed the stone lodged in my throat just as the nurse appeared in the waiting room again to beckon me forward.

"I'm about to see my baby for the first time."

"Damn," Cage said. "You're a lucky man."

I got up and followed the woman into the hallway. "Trust me, I know."

When I entered the small room, Giselle was reclined with her legs propped up and open over stirrups and covered modestly in a blue blanket. Her eyes were wide with nerves and excitement as they caught on mine. Wordlessly and instantaneously, she reached out her hand to me.

I tried once again to force that stone out of my throat and made my way to her side, linking our fingers.

"Mr. Sinclair, I'm Dr. Madison Adams," the older woman situated between Elle's legs smiled kindly at me after I sat down. "The physical examination showed that Giselle is approximately nine weeks along, but we will be better able to determine the exact date of conception with the ultrasound."

"Excellent," I said, giving Elle's hand a squeeze.

She was fidgeting in her seat, uncomfortable with her exposed position and very nervous. It was her nerves that concerned me. I'd been fairly certain that she was happy about the pregnancy, despite the shock of it, but seeing her now seemed to contradict that.

Before I could ask her, the doctor was gently telling us about how she was going to proceed. She lubricated the end of a vaginal ultrasound wand and disappeared under the blanket. Giselle squirmed against the intrusion, her fingers cold between my own.

I leaned forward to press a kiss against her hair, and she immediately turned her face into it, searching for more comfort.

Two seconds later, there a percussion noise filtered throughout the room. I watched Giselle look at the monitor beside the doctor, wanting to see her reaction before I looked myself. I was thrilled that I did. Softness descended over her features, smoothing the frown from her brow and setting her lips into a trembling smile.

"Sin," she breathed. "Look at our baby."

My heart was beating so hard that I thought I might die, but I did what she asked and looked at our baby.

It was just a little thing, etched like a pencil drawing in black and white. I had been expecting it to look like a little peanut, not really human, but there was a little head, tiny fisted hands, and two little feet curled up underneath it.

"It looks just like you," Giselle decided firmly.

I blinked then threw my head back to laugh.

When I settled down a bit, my siren was smiling softly at me, awe in her eyes and love tucked into every curve of her beautiful face.

"I'm serious," she said.

"Okay," I agreed, because she was being ridiculous, but I was ridiculously happy, so it seemed fitting.

"It looks like you are eight weeks and four days, which puts the date of conception at November 26th." She smiled kindly at us. "Any special significance for you?"

"Yes," I said.

The good doctor frowned at me, and I realized I might have snapped at her. Giselle gave me a squeeze because she understood my gruffness was a product of emotion, *fucking great* emotion, and not anger.

"It was the first night we officially got together," she explained softly.

Dr. Adams beamed at us.

She was a nice enough woman and the best damn woman's doctor in the city, but I was done sharing the moment with her.

"Is it possible to have a moment alone?" I asked, even though it was stated more as a demand.

I'd found people reacted positively to thinly veiled orders. The trick was to underlay the suggestion with casual authority so they responded automatically before ego kicked in and they remembered to argue with you.

It worked beautifully on Dr. Adams, who smiled again at Giselle before moving swiftly out the door with a murmur that she would be back in a moment.

As soon as the door was closed, I moved into Elle. I pressed my forehead to hers, sinking one hand in all that red hair at the back of her neck so that I was cupping her to me. The other hand, I pressed gently but firmly on the minuscule swell of her abdomen.

"I never wanted my own family," I began, working the words through my irritatingly tight throat. "After my parents died and I went to the orphanage, I met Cage, we become brothers, but I knew in my heart that I would never have a real family again. Not even for an instant when Willa and Mortimer adopted me did I think we were a family. They were good to me, they liked my looks, my intelligence, but they eschewed Cage, fostering him for years with their house-keeper in Paris instead of keeping him with us."

They had been lonely years, that handful of years I had spent studying hard at Trinity's to make up for my deplorable lack of early education, trying so hard to impress my new guardians. I'd always been a fairly serious child, but Cage had brought levity to my world, reminded me to relax and smile. With him gone, I realized now, I'd begun the slow but sure process of becoming the man Elena had met and loved, an automaton replica of the man I wanted to be.

"When Cosima came into my life, she settled herself in it, dragged the rest of your family into my life in a way that was intimate and permanent. I met Elena, but by that time, the idea of family had disappeared and in its place was obligation. We were suited; we shared the same interests, enjoyed each other's conversation, and I found her attractive. But my heart wasn't truly in it because I had stopped using that muscle when my parents died. Honestly, I was happy never to use it again."

I watched Giselle's lips tighten. It could have been discomfort at the thought of my feelings for Elena, or more likely, it could have been because those very feelings made her soft heart sad, that I had thought love was made like that and that Elena had too.

"So, still, no family."

Elle's silver eyes were wet with tears.

"Then you." I paused because how could I properly explain how profound her entry into my life had been? This was why people recited poetry. It was easier to steal words than come up with my own. "I fought it. We both know, I fought it. But I knew from the moment I said goodbye to you on the plane that even if I never saw you again, my life was no longer enough. I needed a family. I needed love and a woman who was wholly mine. Now, in the span of five months, against so pretty impossible odds, I have one. You gave that to me, Elle, and I cannot express how fucking grateful I am of that."

I smoothed a thumb over the tears that slid down her cheeks and into her hair, watching as her lips trembled and her eyes shone. She was so pretty I felt it in my chest.

"I don't know what to say to that," she admitted. "It was so beautiful. Anything I say will just sound stupid."

I grinned at her. "Don't say anything. I just wanted you to know. This baby you're giving me means the world to me."

"Me too. And obviously, I will love him or her no matter what, but I really hope we have a Sinclair lookalike on our hands."

Then I kissed her because there was no other thing I could do.

# Chapter Twenty

*Sinclair*

Things were moving quickly.

Thank God.

I was tired of the subterfuge, of the games and the back and forth over something I knew in my fucking bones was eternal. Everything was falling into place; Giselle was pregnant, and her showing at my own art gallery was just around the corner. The nonsense over the Paulsons sexual proclivities and my affair with Giselle had ceased to matter to the crème de le crème of New York City society (not that I cared when it had). There were only three things that needed to get in line in order for me to deliver Giselle her happily ever after.

One of them, the question of our legal union, I was already orchestrating with the help of Cage and Candy. I wanted to include Cosima, but as she had promised Elle at our pseudo housewarming party, both she and Alexander Davenport had disappeared without any way to contact them. It was hard not to feel anger that she would put the family through that after everything they had been through with her accident, but the crushing worry we all felt, myself included, dominated the irritation. I hoped desperately that she was safe and was using any means necessary to secure the information, both for my own peace of mind and Giselle's.

I hoped I wasn't overstepping by essentially planning everything about our wedding. Most girls dreamed their entire lives of their wedding day and all of its details, but I figured my woman wasn't one of those girls. She was too busy surviving to think about her future, too busy dreaming of the fantastical to focus on her own desires.

So, I was a man planning his own elopement. As unconventional as it was, it was also surprisingly fun. Especially picking out her wedding dress, a creamy collection of lace and weave that would look astounding on her generous curves against all that flaming hair.

I had called Sebastian, who was on location somewhere in the California desert to film a movie about outlaws, to ask his permission. It was an outdated practice and one that I personally found fairly misogynistic, but I knew the Lombardi clan was close-knit and old-school enough to find my gesture both charming and necessary.

Our conversation went something like this.

"Hello?"

"Sebastian, I hope you are well. I'm calling to ask you a rather serious question, if you have a moment."

Pause.

"I have a moment."

"Good. I would like to ask for your blessing to marry Giselle."

Another pause.

This one longer.

Then quietly, he asked, "Are you sure you have the right sister now?"

It could have been a passive-aggressive statement, but the way he spoke softly, carefully, let me know he was just acknowledging the differences here; between Elena and Giselle, and between me with each of them. I didn't blame him. Elena's Daniel had delayed marrying her for four years, and now there I was, asking to marry her sister after only six months of knowing her.

"I have the right woman now."

"She would be happy to live with you in sin forever. She doesn't need marriage," he said because I'm sure he felt that he had to.

"I wouldn't be."

Another dramatic pause. I was used to them. Sebastian was an actor both on and off the screen.

"I'll walk her down the aisle."

She would love that, so I said, "Thank you."

It was a much easier conversation than I had planned for, but I had always liked the only male Lombardi, and I found that he was often surprising.

So, one thing down and two more to go before I could rest easy in my new life.

Those two things were Caprice and Elena Lombardi.

I started with the easier of the two.

Osteria Lombardi was only two blocks away from my office, so I stopped by after work to duck into the kitchen. They were used to me there, the staff knew that I was dating one of the Lombardi women, probably the wrong one, but they let me back without protest, so I didn't care to check.

Caprice was arguing with her head chef over something on the menu, but it wasn't yet busy with the dinner rush. She caught my eye immediately and continued to look at me as she finished her conversation. Without a word, she flicked her finger at me to follow her out the swinging doors and into her cramped office.

She sat down and gestured for me to do the same. Her face was set in a fierce scowl that rivaled Cosima's, and that girl could level a grown man twice her size with one of her looks. I reminded myself that Gisele had gone to bat for me twice now, with Paulson and my parents, and it was my turn to do the same.

"I'm marrying her, Caprice," I started because I wasn't one to beat around the bush and because I knew she would flinch the way she did. I was angry with her for causing Giselle pain, so I enjoyed it.

"You refuse to marry my Elena for years, and now you want a union with my *bambina*?" She snorted. "I do not think she will have you."

"You are wrong. Giselle loves me more than anything," I said, never confident of anything more in my life. "I know this because I feel the same, if not more, toward her. She is it for me, Caprice. I am sorry that Elena was only a step, a necessary one, along the way. I am sorry she was hurt because I found my soul mate through her, but a man doesn't throw away a gift like that just because it causes someone else, of frankly even himself, pain."

She blinked slowly at me. "So, you don't throw her away. You marry her before she can realize what a *stronzo* you are?"

I smiled slightly, but it was sharp, mean. "I am certain that Elle already knows how stupid I can be. She has stood by me through some of my worst decisions yet, and I know she would stand by me still. I am going to marry her, Caprice, and treat her like the queen of my fucking heart for the rest of our lives because that is what she is to me. I am not here to ask your permission. I am not even here to ask your forgiveness. I am here to tell you that I unequivocally love your daughter, Giselle, and I am going to make her my wife."

I wanted to tell her about the baby so badly that the words burned in my voice box, made it hard to swallow and breathe without uttering the news. I resisted. That moment was for my siren to share with her mother if she chose, and I knew that for now, she was sacrificing that comfort in order to give it to Elena.

God, my girl was selfless. It was both beautiful and hard for me to bear.

Caprice's lips were thin with strain as she stared at me. "I have known you a long time now, Daniel Sinclair. I was happy to meet you and give you one of my daughters. You chose wrong, it seems. I know that happens because once upon a long time ago, I chose wrong too, and I hurt my children in doing that. I do not like to see them hurt more."

"I understand that," I said slowly. "But you are hurting Giselle by blindly siding with Elena on this. I get that Elena needs you, and I still care for her, still want her family for her. But Giselle loves her mama, and you've taken that from her. I just wanted to let you know that we are creating our own family. If you stay away too long, you might find that she doesn't need you when you deem her worthy again."

I stood and buttoned up my blazer again as I tilted my head to her. "Despite your bad choice, you made beautiful babies, Caprice. Thank you for that."

Then I left, leaving the matriarch of the Lombardi clan feeling as if she had lost her daughter, and I was glad for it because if she continued to hurt Giselle, I wasn't going to let her have her back.

*I*t was strange to walk up to the apartment I had shared with a woman for years and have it not be my own, have no desire for it to ever be again. Giselle thought that I was unnecessarily cruel to Elena when we had interacted since the breakup, but I didn't have it in me to fabricate kindness when she treated the woman I loved like dirt and me not much better. It killed me to draw the parallels between Willa and Elena, but as soon as I did, it was impossible to stop. They both loved me, but the way one loved their show pony or Best in Show breed. They loved me for what I could give them.

The world would have to forgive me if I was tired of that shit.

Still, when I knocked on the door, I did it without anger. I wasn't sure exactly what I wanted out of the exchange, but I hoped it would bring Elena some closure.

She answered the door in her lounge clothes, a long cashmere cardigan over a matching silk short and camisole set. Her hair was pushed back from her face with a velvet headband, and she had her black-framed reading glasses on her nose. She looked absolutely beautiful, yet not a part of me wanted her.

Good to confirm.

"Elena," I greeted, holding up a bag of Sushi Yasaka take-out and a bottle of her favorite sake. "May I come in?"

She hesitated sweetly for a moment before opening the door further. I swept in, went to the kitchen to gather plates, chopsticks, and napkins and met her at the coffee table where she had her papers laid out.

"Put those away, and let's eat," I ordered as I pulled out her favorite rolls and set them in front of her before pouring out the sake into the little ceramic glasses we had bought together a few years ago.

"Why are you here, Daniel?" she asked in an aberrantly soft voice. "To yell at me again?"

"No, darling," I said, softening toward her when she curled up into a ball on her side of the couch with her tray of sushi propped up on her knees. "I'm here because we haven't really talked since the breakup, and I wanted to give that to you."

Her lips twisted. "I can't decide if that's really nice of you or kind of douchey."

"Probably both," I said before popping a spicy tuna roll into my mouth.

We ate in silence for a while because I didn't really have anything to say. I just wanted to be there for her one last time in case she had something she wanted to say.

Finally, she spoke, "You really love her, I guess."

"I do," I said, firmly even though I felt a brief flare of guilt.

I loved Elle so much more than I had ever loved anything.

As if I had said those words out loud, Elena flinched then sighed. "Yes, I guess I could tell that."

"Yeah?"

She nodded. "You were so weird when you got back from Mexico. Moody. Happy one day and so sad the next. It was so out of character that I should have known it was someone else making you feel that way. You were never moody with me."

"It's called emotional, Elena. You should try it sometime," I said, joking but completely serious too. "Maybe not as explosively as you did at my house the other day, and maybe not so much it makes you vindictive enough to go to the press..."

She blushed furiously. "That was terrible. I still can't believe I did that."

"You were angry."

"I was. And," she hesitated, "I've hated her for so long. You know a little bit about that. I never really said anything kind about her to you. Christopher, he, well, he pitted us against each other from a young age, and I was never strong enough to get over it."

"Maybe it isn't too late," I suggested even though I knew it was.

"It is," she confirmed softly. "She has everything I ever wanted."

"I truly believe that you will find something that you want more," I said, facing her fully so that she was forced to witness my intensity. "We were not right for each other, and that's okay. Not just for me because I have Giselle now, but for you, because now you can find someone who will truly make you happy. I never did that for you."

She didn't protest, but I knew she wanted to.

We finished our meal in more silence.

"I have these for you," I said after I had cleaned up. I handed her the documents that I had my lawyer draw up. "This legally gives you the apartment."

She stared at the stack of papers in my hand before taking them with a hard nod. "Thank you, I love this place."

I never really had because I hadn't spent much time in it. I already loved my house in the clock tower so much more; the mural on the wall of the nursery, the studio I'd had installed on the top floor in a room full of windows, the bed I shared with Giselle.

I wanted to get back there.

"I'm leaving," I said, crouching in front of her. "I won't be back again, but if you ever need me, you can call me, yes?"

I meant it. Elena was the kind of woman who was really a queen. She deserved knights and footmen and kings bowing at her feet, taking care of her every need. I thought that was one of the reasons I was drawn to her in the first place.

I didn't want to leave her alone.

"Promise me," I said, looking into those big gray eyes, so much darker than Elle's but still so familiar to me. "I know it seems like a poor consolation, but I will always be here for you."

She swallowed hard twice before she nodded. "You can leave now."

"Okay," I said, staring at her for a second more before I did just that. "I don't blame you for the anger, for the scene at the house or the article in the newspaper. I have to live with what I did to you, and it won't ever get easier."

"Good," she said without fire.

"Good," I echoed before casting one more look at the place I had called home for almost half a decade and the woman I had thought was mine.

*Good*, I thought as I closed the door behind me and set out with a clear mind to get home to Brooklyn as quickly as my Porsche would carry me and the traffic would allow.

When I told Giselle that night, holding her in my arms after taking her hard in our bed, about my visit to Elena, how it had felt like closure, she too had murmured *good,* and I knew she felt clear of it as well.

# Chapter Twenty-one

*Giselle*

It was finally time.

My life had taken on the quality of an Italian soap opera since meeting Sinclair, with so many incredible highs and lows that it felt we would never settle in to our life together. I hoped that the excitement of the gallery opening would mark the end of the many consequences we reaped from being together and herald a new, calmer beginning for us.

But calm, I was not.

"Are you serious?" I asked, my voice shrill as a teakettle whistle.

Rossi laughed kindly. "I am. *The New York Times*, Robin

Cembalast from *ARTNews*, and Jerry Saltz from *New York Mag* have all confirmed their attendance tonight."

"I can't breathe," I said with the last of the air left in my lungs.

"Yes, you can," Eddie said, rubbing soothing circles on my back. "You have to breathe so that you can answer all the lovely people who are coming to see *your* exhibit tonight."

I shook my head manically, my hand over my tripping heart. Stars and black spots flashed before my eyes.

"Giselle, darling, people are going to begin arriving in half an hour. You need to calm down," Rossi scolded.

"Can't," I squeaked.

Everyone was going to hate my work. It was the edgiest I had ever been. The most subdued of all the paintings was the one of Mama with a deep swatch of sweaty exposed bosom in front of a stove. I was already mildly notorious for my affair with Sinclair. What was my flagrantly sexual display going to do to his reputation? I tried to inhale and choked. How had I been so selfish?

I looked around frantically, trying to find an escape from everything, when I felt two cool hands descend on my shoulders, stilling me immediately.

"Ladies," Sinclair's cultured, slightly accented voice crooned over my shoulder. "What seems to be the problem here?"

Both Eddie and Rossi slumped in relief at the sight of him.

"She's having a mental breakdown," Eddie said candidly.

"Eddie," Rossi rebuked, but it was okay. It was the truth.

"I think I'm dying," I told him, leaning back into his strength so that I didn't collapse.

"Well, we can't have that, can we?" There was amusement in his voice, but the arms that wrapped around my waist and the hand that subtly covered my slightly swollen abdomen were kind and supportive. "If you'll excuse us for a while, I think I'll take Giselle into the back to calm down."

Rossi looked at him critically. "Fine, but don't mess her up too much, and she needs to be out on the floor by the time the doors open at seven."

"Of course," he said somberly, but I could sense his amusement as he gently led me into the small kitchenette off the gallery rooms.

He placed me in a chair and set about making me a cup of tea. I didn't particularly like tea, but ever since we'd found out about the pregnancy, Sinclair was a stickler for sticking to health guidelines, which, unfortunately, included banning me from coffee.

Only when the kettle was set on the stove to boil did he come and kneel between my legs, both his strong hands braced on my thighs so that his face hovered just in front of my own. I stared into his cobalt blue eyes, searching for a safe place to anchor myself amid the turmoil in my own mind. He let me stare at him for a long, silent minute while his thumbs rubbed gently across my thighs.

"You are scared," he began, his voice as cool and refreshing as spring water. "I understand that this is a nerve-wracking endeavor, your first show in New York City. As a patron of the arts in this ruthless city for years, I do not take that lightly. But you must also understand that as a man who is your partner, who has grown as you've grown and witnessed you blossom with confidence, that I am nothing but excited for you tonight. This evening the world will be introduced to my siren, a woman of skill, sensuality, and a keen observation of the dark side of the human psyche. They will find your artwork stirring and visually appealing, as those are facts, my love, and not a matter of opinion. So, whatever nerves you are feeling, feel them, but know that when this is all over, and you are lying in our bed tonight, you will do so with pride and satisfaction at a job well done, *d'accord*?"

His powerful words lingered in the air, and I greedily sucked them in through my mouth to better absorb their potency. The trust and respect of a man as powerful as Sinclair was not something that could ever be taken for granted. If he believed in me, it was impossible not to believe in myself.

"I love you so much," I breathed, weak with relief.

He smiled as I pressed my forehead to his shoulder. "And I you, *toujours*."

"Do you think she'll come tonight?" I asked after a moment.

He didn't ask who I spoke of. "I can't say. She was always prideful, and given that she is in the collection, I'd imagine she would at least come to see that you didn't do her a disservice."

"Do you think I did?" Worry had been eating away at the lining of my stomach since I had completed the last piece of the collection, the one of my sister wrapped in melting ice sculptures.

"Enough worry," he said, shifting away from me to look into my face. His eyes were cold and shuttered, and I knew even before he spoke that his next words would be an order. "Get over my knee."

Instantly my core clenched. I hesitated briefly before settling over his lap, not because I didn't want the spanking but because I had been secretly craving such a release all day. Nothing could eradicate my demons like the glowing space I occupied when I submitted to my Frenchman.

"I can feel your eagerness," Sinclair murmured darkly as he caressed my bottom through the silky material of my skirt. "This is not a punishment, siren, so I do want you to enjoy it. This is about release."

I let out a shaky sigh when he pulled up my dress and hoisted the edges of my half-bottom panties so that they slid deeply between the crease of my ass. I squirmed against the pressure it put on my already sensitive clit, but he stilled me with a firm hand to my lower back.

"Still, I expect you to thank me for each one," he said, in that unflappable voice.

I shivered in anticipation, moaning when his hand smacked against my skin.

"Thank you, sir."

He rubbed the sting hard with his fingers. "Mmm, you are welcome, siren."

The next hits came one after the other, alternating between one cheek and the other. Each stinging pain lulled me further into subspace. I could hear my breath panting loudly in the space, punctuated only by the harsh slap of his palm against my flesh.

Somehow, I remembered to thank him each time.

Eventually, his hand moved from my lower back to the sopping wet place between my legs. His fingers slid through my folds, barely dipping inside me. I wriggled and moaned, wordlessly begging him to finish me off.

"Use your words," he reminded sharply.

"Please, sir, may I come?"

"I don't think so," he said, boredom dripping from his words like my arousal was from his fingertips.

"Puh-please," I begged as he swiftly pressed two fingers inside me and curled them toward my front wall, pressing against the small patch of tissues that always made me detonate.

"Tell me what you are thinking about," he demanded.

Thoughts swirled around my head before disappearing too quickly to verbalize.

I groaned.

The next spank was especially brutal. I hissed through my teeth and teetered closer to orgasm.

"Not good enough. Tell me; are you worried about the show, about what anyone may think of your art, of yourself? Or are you thinking about me, about my fingers inside your sweet, wet pussy, and my hand branding your ass a nice, scarlet red?"

"Your hands, your fingers," I panted, pressing harder into the erection I could feel poking my stomach. "Want your cock."

He chuckled wickedly. "Good girl. I should be the only thing on your mind. I am the master of this body, the owner of your thoughts. When I touch you like this"—he plunged another finger inside me while circling my asshole with his arousal-dampened thumb—"you know who you belong to."

"You, sir," I cried out, so close to climaxing that my vision was growing dark at the corners.

"Yes, *me*. Come for me now," he ordered.

A second later, I was lost. Blackness surged toward me, hot and cold, a swirl of sensation that pummeled my body and made my skin sing from the inside out with sensitivity. Every negative sensation that had weighed down my body was obliterated by the welcome darkness, and I think, for a least a moment, I blacked out.

When I came to again, Sinclair was cradling me to his chest, and my clothes were righted. He smiled against my hair as he stroked it, satisfaction oozing from him even though he hadn't been the one to orgasm. I loved that as a Dominant, he got off on orchestrating my pleasure as much as I did from experiencing it.

"I'm going to keep your underwear in my pocket, and you are going to walk around this gallery tonight knowing that I own you, feeling that and only that between your thighs." He paused to let the words sink in. "Are you ready now, Elle?"

I tipped my head back and beamed up at him. "Let's do it."

There were dozens of people. Every time I was introduced to someone new, another person over my shoulder was waiting for an introduction. Some of them I knew immediately, like the art critics Jerry Saltz and Holland Cotter, Jace Galantine, the famous movie star that Sebastian kept a wide berth from, and Louis Vuitton Foundation's CEO Bernard Arnault who had first championed my work in Paris. They *all* had something nice to say about my paintings. I tried and probably failed to be cool about it.

Of my family, only Sebastian was there, having flown in from filming his new movie in Los Angeles just to be a part of opening night. He apologized on behalf of Mama, who was at the restaurant managing a private party, but I knew that she wouldn't have missed it for the world if she had wanted to be here. It made me sad for a moment, Mama's continued distance and Cosima's inexplicable absence, but I had reason to be happy still. All the friends I had in the world were there to support me, including Stefan, Santiago, Kat, Richard, Duncan, Robert, and even Odile, who Sinclair had flown over as a surprise for me.

The Paulsons were there too, their first public outing since the scandal. Mr. Paulson looked mildly uncomfortable, but after their experience being ground through the rumor mill, he seemed lighter somehow and was less careful about his gestures of affection and dominance over Terry.

Even Brenna showed up.

"C'est une blague," I exclaimed in French when I found her lingering by a portrait of Sinclair.

She laughed, but her expressive face didn't light up the way it usually did. "Not a joke."

I leaped at her, completely oblivious to the persona I had tried to cultivate throughout the night. She caught me, staggering backward under my weight as I squeezed her roughly.

"Je te déteste," I told her over and over again, as I rained kisses down on the top of her golden head.

Her shocked laughter quickly dissolved into silent tears as she brought me closer still.

"I missed you too," Brenna whispered.

"I was always right here," I reminded her gently.

She nodded and squeezed me once more before taking a step back. I watched her wipe the tears from under her eyes and noted that she was healthier looking than the last time I had seen her, depressed on the arm of her famous husband.

"What has happened to you?"

Her smile was shaky but bright. "Almost as much as has happened to you, it looks like. I'm sorry I didn't respond to your emails and calls, but I had to go off the grid for a while. When I logged back into reality last week, I devoured all of your notes, but I still feel like I've missed so much."

I followed her excited gaze over my shoulder and saw Sinclair standing across the room speaking with Cage. As soon as he felt my eyes on him, he turned unerringly in our direction. My breath hitched at the quiet possession in his eyes as they dragged over me, checking in on my state of mind and my companion. Finally, his lips twitched into a slight smile and he dipped his head to acknowledge Brenna's presence.

I bit back a smile.

"Let's start with *him*." Brenna laughed, linking my arm through hers. "And then move on to what possessed you to create this amazingly provocative art. The Giselle I knew didn't know anything beyond the practical value of rope, chains, or handcuffs, and now I find you exploring BDSM?"

It was my turn to giggle as we paused in front of the portrait of Madame Claire using Dominic as a footstool, her face hazy behind a cloud of looping cigarette smoke. The oil painting was done in somber hues but for the brilliant red soles of her stiletto heels crossed over the corded muscles of his back.

Brenna licked her lips as she stared at it. "This is deeply titillating stuff, Elle."

I grinned. "I have you to thank for all of it. If you hadn't sent me to Mexico in your place, this would never have happened."

I frowned, though, because I had never really thought it through. If Sinclair and I had met as future in-laws, would the sexual chemistry between us have remained dormant?

Awareness pulled my spine straight like a zipper, locking my posture in vertebrae by vertebrae. I shivered as Sinclair took the final step forward to stand beside me and discovered that I had the answer to my question; no matter the meet-cute, Sin and I would have eventually ended up together.

"Brenna Buchannan, I'm a fan of your work, both as an actress and Giselle's best friend," Sinclair was saying when I clued back in to reality.

My best friend grinned and giggled like a little girl. "It's always nice to meet a fan. I'm sorry it has taken us so long to be introduced."

"She was worried," he admitted with a scolding frown as he tucked me into his side.

Brenna blushed, but I stepped in to save her from Sinclair's scrutiny. "She wouldn't have disappeared without reason. I understand." I tilted my head up to stare at my handsome boyfriend. "Sometimes, we all need to disappear."

His eyes sparkled at the reminder of our trip to Paris. I swallowed audibly when one of his large hands wrapped around the back of my neck, his fingers running lightly over the pearl choker. It was a subtle cue to remind me that I belonged with him.

"I'm hosting a little after-party to celebrate Giselle's success after the gallery closes. I hope you are free to join?" Sin asked.

Brenna beamed at him, but I was distracted by the rest of their conversation by the sight of my sister standing frozen in the entryway.

Elena was dressed impeccably, as always, the cashmere backless black dress contrasted beautifully with her clear skin and dark red hair. A number of people had stopped staring at the art in order to evaluate her.

I swallowed thickly before excusing myself from the conversation with Brenna and Sinclair. He had no doubt noticed her too, but after a quick caress, he let me move forward to handle it myself.

"I didn't think you would come," I said as I approached her.

She didn't look at me, caught up in the massive canvas of Sinclair that dominated the small front wall that immediately faced the entryway.

"I didn't think I would either."

I nodded even though I was aware that she wasn't paying me any attention. So, I stood there beside her, staring at the portrait of a lover we had both shared at some point. The three of us hadn't shared the same space since the day Sinclair and I had returned from Paris to see Cosima in the hospital, but it was somehow more intimate to be staring at my image of him with Elena by my side. She was staring at the heart of the man I loved and, therefore, at the very heart of me. If she said something cruel now, as would have been her right, I knew it would eviscerate me.

"It looks just like him," she finally said, her voice softened by the Neapolitan accent she usually tried so hard to hide. "Yet, I've never seen him like this. Does that make any sense to you?"

I was careful to shrug casually even though it did make sense.

"It would have been hard not to notice how much you love him if this was the portrait you were planning on painting for me."

I cocked my head as I stared at the beloved lines of his form spread over nearly three meters of canvas. There was nothing overtly sexual about the image, it was just a very beautiful man in a very commanding position, but if you looked closely, there was no doubt about the sexual power that emanated from him; the way his fingers curled around the edges of the broad throne, how the veins in his corded forearms bulged and in the slight but provocative tilt of his full, firm lips. There was a glittering menace, a calculated coldness in his eyes that spoke to sexual deviancy instead of violence, at ruthless pleasures to be had if only you had the courage to let him exploit them.

I knew this was the man who I loved, the man who I knew him to be, but I had been worried about the subtlety of the image in the critic's eyes. Would they see him in all his constrained glory?

"It makes me realize how much I made him keep from me," Elena said quietly.

I shivered at the depth of remorse in her tone.

"I saw this in him at first, all the sex wrapped up in this controlled, intellectual gentleman. I think maybe a part of me was even intrigued by it, the fucked-up part of me that never got over Christopher's abuse." She sighed, crossing her arms tightly under her breasts as if she could physically restrain her emotions. "I can confess that I didn't love him the way I should have. We could have been right together if either of us had been willing to be brave, to stand up to the other and actually talk about all the things that made us broken." She shrugged. "I can admit that I could have loved him better, but I will never forgive you from exploiting that flaw, for taking him from me so goddamn ruthlessly."

I sucked in a deep breath, wanting to say something but having nothing to say.

Finally, she turned to face me. Her eyes raced over every inch of my being, setting me on fire with her condemnation.

"I always knew you had it in you. Mama, Seb, and Cosima saw this fragile little girl with her head in the clouds and thought you harmless. Only I knew how dangerous a girl made of fantasies could be." She laughed darkly. "Apparently, even knowing that wasn't enough, even avoiding you for years, you made your way back into my life and made it a fucking nightmare just so you could have your bloody happily ever after."

"Elena," I began, but she shook her head.

"No, don't. I came to say this stuff to you so that our family doesn't suffer. I don't love you, Giselle, and I think we both know that I haven't in a very long time. I don't forgive you either. You knowingly ripped my life apart. Our family will forgive you, society will forgive you, and I think you've already forgiven yourself, but my hatred is one consequence you will have to live with forever."

I nodded, too busy swallowing back the urge to cry to respond to her.

She nodded curtly and turned on her heel to walk away to another painting across the gallery.

I saw someone approach me out of my periphery, but I knew if anyone talked to me before I got a handle on the emotions wreaking havoc with my system, I would dissolve into tears, and the critics would have more drama to speak about than the scandalous nature of my art. With my head down, I sped toward the small back room, only stopping when I had slammed the door shut behind me. I cupped my hands to my mouth, trying to stuff the sobs back inside fruitlessly. Giving in to the misery, I curled forward into the only uncluttered corner of the room and squeezed my eyes shut.

# Chapter Twenty-two

*Giselle*

"I've missed watching you."

I froze mid-sob, my chest expanded in a shuddering breath even as my heart constricted inside me. There was no other voice that could make me feel so afraid, so instantaneously. It was a voice that had haunted my youth and eventually, chased me out of Paris.

Slowly, drenched in paralyzing panic, I straightened.

Christopher stood across the tiny, darkened room. He wasn't a large man, average height and build with an open, engaging face that was somehow quintessentially British. He had large, round eyes that were the soft blue of faded denim and that lulled you into trusting before he had even opened his mouth to speak. There was absolutely nothing threatening about Christopher's appearance, which made him all the more frightening.

"You are so beautiful with tears across your face, Giselle," he murmured, cocking his head slightly to the side in a predatory way that made me take a step back even though I was already pressed against the wall.

"You found me."

He nodded. "As I always do. I would urge you to stop running, as it inevitably leads to this moment, but I have to admit..." His grin was sharp. "I've grown to love the chase."

I was silent as I waited for my limbs to thaw free of the shock. There was a tingling in my toes that I took as a good sign.

"I think you like it too, sweet girl. You know that we are meant to be together, but you run for both of our pleasure. Well, I forgive you for making it more interesting, but now is the time to come together. I've searched for you long enough." He laughed. "It took me too long to realize that you had reunited with your family. I never thought you would do such a thing."

I bit my lip, trying to calculate if anyone would hear my screams. Running for the door wasn't an option when his position put him closer to it. The sultry music playing throughout the gallery had a deep bass, so the chances of being heard were slim unless someone was right beside the door.

Christopher's face darkened as he stepped toward me, stalking so slowly that it would have been comedic in any other situation.

"I've seen you with that man. It seems your taste for your sister's men hasn't waned, but we both know that Daniel Sinclair isn't right for you." He stopped right before me, looking at me for a long moment before his hand snapped forward and tugged brutally at my hair. "He may give you the pain you like, but he isn't me."

"No," I finally hissed. "Sinclair is *nothing* like you."

"What is the difference between us? He hurts you too." Christopher pulled tighter on my hair until my neck was bent back at an excruciating angle. When he was satisfied with my position, he thrust his body against mine brutally. "You love to be painted just like your canvases, all this lovely white skin colored with mauve and yellow and black."

To illustrate his point, his hand curled over my wrist and pressed. I bit back my whimper of pain because I knew he would enjoy it.

"You love the pain. You get off on it just like me."

His words stirred the rage sitting at the bottom of my gut labeled with his name. I had hated him for so long, but I had feared him for even longer, and the depth of my childhood trauma had overtaken the wrath but only for so long. Heat traveled through my previously frozen limbs until I vibrated.

"I get off on the control. And you have absolutely no control over me, not anymore," I practically spat at him.

His smile was disturbingly soft as he leaned back slightly to look over my face. "So beautiful. It's good that we are together again."

"Fuck you!" I yelled, spittle flying in his face.

He licked it from his lips, leaning closer to whisper, "Oh, I intend to."

Before I could move, he stood on my feet, anchoring me to the floor while one arm latched over my arms, constricting them against my torso. With his free hand, he quickly undid his belt and tucked the hem of my skirt into the collar of my dress, exposing my bare sex to him. I sobbed when his fingers brutally pinch my clit.

"I never had your cunt. I wanted to save it for a special occasion, for when you were truly mine, and now some other man has been inside you first." He bit my ear so hard that I could feel his teeth break the skin. "I will have to punish you for that."

I squirmed violently against his hold and opened my mouth to scream. He didn't try to stop me, even when I drew breath again and again to shriek for help. Instead, he laughed cruelly and pierced his fingers inside me in time with my screams. I was still wet from my previous interlude with Sinclair, but I quickly dried up, and his fingers chafed brutally against my delicate flesh.

"Don't fight this. We are meant to be together. I have always known that. Your mother wanted me to marry your sister, but we both know she would never do. Even that gorgeous slut Cosima wasn't good enough for me. I needed your purity. I needed to watch your corruption."

My throat was in agony as I continued to scream, the sound even lesser than it had been a minute ago. I was losing steam quickly. Christopher's erection bounced wetly against my hip. He was small, turgid, and an angry red that disgusted me, but it also gave me an idea. I wasn't strong enough to fight him, but I was strong enough to seduce him.

I reduced my screaming to yelling, interspersed with a reluctant and totally fake moan and groan. Christopher watched me in rapture as I pretended to give in to his touch.

"Yes," I breathed, sagging in his arms. "Oh, I forgot how good this was."

Nausea rolled through me, but I needed to be smarter if I wanted to get the baby and myself out of there.

"You love it," he groaned into my ear. "Tell me you want me."

"I want you."

"Say my name."

"I want you, Christopher," I said. "But I want you properly. I want you to take me for the first time in a bed, not in the back of the supply closet."

He pulled away slightly to look at me suspiciously. I tried to widen my eyes in earnest and ground down on his fingers.

"As much as I want you, I want our first time to be right. Please. There is no rush. You found me, so we have forever now."

I prayed to God that I had been gone long enough for Sinclair to start looking for me.

"You should never have run from me," Christopher said, his face softening as he brought me into a hug. "I would have taken care of you properly. I would have sent you to whatever art school you wanted to go to. You know I love you."

I shivered but clung to him tightly to mask my revulsion. That was the thing about Christopher. He really did believe he loved me, and he had never been physically violent toward me. The bruises and bite marks he had left me with were more a result of his desire to devour me whole, mark me as his, than from brute physical abuse. It was his sweet persuasiveness, and sometimes, when I was being particularly obstinate, his absolute authoritarianism that had made me succumb to his sexual advances. I was fifteen, the first time he had told me to get on my knees and show him how much I loved him with my mouth. It wasn't something a fifteen-year-old girl, sheltered as I was, knew how to refuse.

As if prompted by my thoughts, Christopher smoothed a hand down my hair before gently pressing on my shoulders.

"Be a sweet girl and get on your knees."

My stomach roiled. It was extra sensitive because of my morning sickness, and the thought of giving him head amplified it threefold.

"We should go before someone sees us," I urged.

He smiled softly, petting my cheek. "Don't worry, sweetheart. I have protection."

"What?"

I watched him reach behind his back and pull a small handgun from his waistband. I didn't know what type of gun it was, but it struck me that Cosima would know. She had been the one so well-versed in the Mafia men who came to visit our house in search of Seamus.

"Why would you bring a gun?" I asked, anything to keep him talking but also because he had never been a gun carrier before.

"Nothing will get in the way of me having you again, Giselle."

There was a calmness in his eyes, a surety that spoke of absolute conviction and total insanity.

"Get on your knees," he repeated, pushing harder at my shoulders this time.

I swallowed painfully and did as he asked, hoping even as I undid the zip on his pants tooth by tooth that Sinclair would find me.

His pants dropped to the floor, and his hand was wrapping one of mine around his shaft but still no Sinclair.

Minutes later, when more things, not the worst that could be happening, but *bad*, were happening, still no Sinclair.

Christopher's gun was the hand that held my head to him.

I counted to sixty.

Still no Sinclair.

Christopher was moaning when finally, I heard the door open.

I was pressed to the wall with him in front of me, but I could see sudden movement as the newcomer moved swiftly toward us. I braced myself against the wall when a scream tore through the air. Christopher stumbled, falling against me so I was brutally smashed against the wall. But I didn't care because someone was attacking him.

I rolled to the side when there was enough space and whirled to face the commotion.

Still, there was no Sinclair.

Instead, the body that clung to Christopher's and pummeled him with furious fists was my sister's.

Elena continued to yell, a warrior's cry that pierced the air better than any of my previous screams. She was wrapped around his upper back, landing punches to his neck as he tried to pull her off. She leaned forward and bit savagely into his earlobe, ripping away with her teeth still clenched. Christopher shrieked in pain as she pulled a large chunk of flesh from him and spat it over her shoulder. He tried to dislodge her by slamming her back against the wall, but she used the moment to push off and heave her weight the other way, which disrupted Christopher's balance. He almost recovered, but I scrambled to my hands and knees and threw myself in the way of the foot that sought to secure his equilibrium. I watched as they fell hard to the floor, terrified that she had taken the brunt of the impact before she scrambled over him, straddled his chest with her knee pressed into his neck.

Then she beat him.

And I mean, she brutally laid into his face with her fists, rearing back with her whole body to put ultimate force behind each exact blow. I watched her, hypnotized, as she turned his face into a bloody, pulpy mess.

I was vaguely aware of chaos at the door to the room, of yelling and people rushing forward to pull Elena, screaming and thrashing, off the comatose Christopher. People came to crowd me, but no one touched me. They were talking to me, but I couldn't focus. I couldn't take my eyes off my sister.

Elena finally settled in the corner, panting in Cage's restraining embrace. Her eyes were, surprisingly, on me.

Something passed between us, through that momentary connection forged over threats and violence. The man bleeding on the floor between us had groomed us both. It had never brought us together, mostly because the similarities his influence had formed in us were too damaged for us to connect over. Besides, from the very beginning, he had pitted us against each other, and even when he had gone, we had continued to live out the competition he had constructed for us. He had fucked us both, mentally and physically and in every fucked-up way a person could fuck up two people. It was Christopher, not Sinclair, who had torn us apart. I'd always known that, but it became clear, at that moment, to both of us, I thought, that since the moment Christopher had entered our lives, we were doomed. Our sisterhood was dead.

But at that moment, when her eyes, so similar but darker than mine, bore into me, they were filled with a protective fury for me as well as her own righteous wrath.

*No one fucks with you, but me. Her eyes seemed to say.*

*I tilted my chin to her. I'll take whatever you have to give me.*

I meant it to. She was allowed to hate me. It made sense, and I was happy to give her a villain. We would never be friends. We would never be anything but sisters by blood, not by choice. I knew it, and I accepted it. But she had attacked Christopher, and it had at least a little something to do with me.

So, no matter what I'd done, no matter how she might act, I knew that Elena loved me. Not a whole lot, not in a way that she had chosen. But she loved me.

I'd never known before this moment that she did.

"Giselle." A familiar voice pulled me away from our moment of clarity, but I let it because I could hear the panic there.

"Giselle," Sinclair said again.

He was crouched in front of me, between me and the prone body of Christopher. He had one hand on the man's throat, checking his pulse maybe, and the other was busy righting my clothes. He was on lockdown, his eyes cold and hard like marble, inhuman. His hands were perfunctory against my skin as they checked to make sure I was unharmed, but there was a haste to his movements that belied how fucking terrified he was.

"Sin," I murmured.

He ignored me.

"Sinclair," I repeated.

He paused, his eyes doing an intense sweep of my face but skirting past my gaze. I grabbed his hand and put it to my cheek.

"I'm okay," I whispered because there were tons of people in the room now, and this was a private moment, an important one.

I watched his Adam's apple bob once, twice. He struggled, and I watched the fury, the pain, and terror roll through him. I drew strength from it, from his obvious love.

"Nothing happened, not really. I'm okay," I repeated, meaning it.

Christopher had violated me again, but for the last time, I was sure of it. I had evidence of his stalker tendencies and witnesses to collaborate his sexual abuse. The law would deal with him, and if they didn't, I knew Sinclair would find a way to.

"Sinclair," I said again, "I'm still yours."

A vicious shudder wracked his frame before he allowed himself to sag forward, resting his forehead against mine.

"Thought he took you," he whispered brokenly.

My heart stuttered. "Oh Sin, he didn't. I'm okay."

"The baby?"

I had no pain in my womb, and he hadn't hurt me. "Just as fine as his or her mama."

"He is your nightmare," he said, his eyes closed. "Worse than that fucker in Mexico. He is your nightmare."

"Elena and I beat him."

His eyes flashed open, blazing so blue, and he pressed a soft kiss to my lips. "I'm taking you away from here."

"Okay," I whispered because I wanted to leave and because he needed us to.

"Now."

"Yes, okay."

"Brenna?" he said, and my friend appeared over his shoulder. "Take care of her for a second."

My grip on his hand tightened in panic. "Please don't leave me."

His face gentled, and I knew he was remembering how he had left me to Candy so he could beat the man who had assaulted me in Cabo.

"You aren't allowed out in society without me, siren, *d'accord*? Or I'll need to hire a full-time bodyguard."

My lips twitched because even though it was funny, he was being very serious. "Okay."

"I'm not leaving you. I just need to talk to the police when they arrive and check on Elena. I want Brenna to sit with you, but I'll be right over there." He pointed to just outside the supply room doors where Sebastian was keeping most of the guests away.

I nodded. "Can you bring Elena over here to sit with me while we wait?"

He stared hard at me for a moment, his thumb running back and forth over my cheek. "I owe her a debt I will never be able to pay for saving you from him."

My throat closed up.

"So, yes, of course, but only after I thank her myself."

He pressed a kiss to my forehead before straightening and walking off into the crowd. I leaned into Brenna, who wrapped an arm around my upper chest in silent support.

Together, we watched Sinclair crouch in front of Elena. I could tell from his profile that those glacial features were thawed with gratitude as he thanked her. She flinched against Cage's hold but didn't take her eyes off him. Pain and lingering anger contorted her features, but when Sin reached out to tuck her hair behind her ear, leaning close to press his forehead to hers and cup the back of her head to him, she closed her eyes and sagged into him.

I felt no jealousy witnessing the intimate moment because I knew Sinclair was mine as much as my name was my name and my hair was red. After all this time and all these trials, his love for me was just that irrefutable. So, I felt only warmth watching Sinclair reach out to my wronged sister, only happy that he offered her thanks *and* comfort because she deserved it.

"And I thought my family was complicated," Brenna murmured into my hair.

I laughed softly and leaned back into her. "The Lombardi clan has cornered the market on complicated, I think."

"You're pregnant?"

I froze against her as panic seized me. People knew, our Mexico crew, the Paulsons and the Percys, but not Mama and not the general populous. There was no way I was going to throw that grenade into the already volatile situation.

"I won't tell anyone, Elle. You're my person, my best friend. Besides, I'm well-versed in secret-keeping," she finished in a soft, sad voice.

"I'm pregnant," I confirmed.

Her arm gave me a hard squeeze. "Good, I've always wanted to be an Auntie."

Tears tickled the backs of my eyes. I let out a deep breath to curb the impulse to cry and watched Sinclair kiss Elena's cheek before he moved to the newly arrived police officers crowding the doorframe.

"Are you okay?" Brenna asked.

I was.

In fact, in a bizarre way, I felt better than I ever had. The threat of Christopher, his stalking presence throughout the entirety of my life, had been brought to an end. I felt good that I had figured out a way to avoid his rape. Yes, I'd still been sexually assaulted, but as long as I could wash my hands with industrial-strength soap for the next hour and a half, I knew that I could recover from it because I had recovered from worse. Sinclair had taught me to move past the memories. He had moved me through each sexual act that had been taken from me by Christopher and reclaimed it as our own. I knew he would do the same thing now. And even though I had him to help with this, I also knew that he had given me the tools to do it on my own, and that was somehow even more precious.

"Honestly, I am," I said and meant it.

# Chapter Twenty-three

*Giselle*

"I'm fine," I reassured Sinclair for the thirtieth time.

"I still think we should have gone to the hospital," he repeated for the thirty-first time.

"The paramedics on-site said that I would be fine, the baby is fine, and there is no lasting damage. I told you, Christopher didn't beat me."

We were in the back of Sinclair's Town Car. I was wrapped in a blanket Eddie had unearthed from somewhere in the gallery and cuddled up against Sinclair's side. My adrenaline had burned off, so I was finding it hard to keep my eyes open, but I didn't want to fall asleep with my Frenchman still so riled beside me.

"I wish it had been me to beat the bastard," Sinclair muttered.

I curled closer to him. "Elena needed that more than you did. I think it was closure for her."

We had sat beside each other while the police took our statements, close but not touching. At one point, she leaned close enough to press her shoulder to me as we watched Christopher taken away on a stretcher in handcuffs, but she didn't say a word to me until after the police had left and the guests had been ordered to leave for the night.

"Sorry about your show," she had said, surprisingly.

I shrugged. "Things happen."

"Don't we know it," she muttered.

I snorted, startled, before sliding her a sidelong glance. Her face was soft, softer than I had seen it in years. Our friends and family kept looking at us, waiting for a breakdown, but I knew that she and I felt the same. It hadn't been traumatic as much as it was cathartic to hurt and overcome our very own boogeyman.

"Thank you."

She tipped her head back against the wall and brought her knees to her chest. "No one deserves to be raped."

*Not even you.*

I nodded.

She sighed into the quiet after a few minutes. "It felt good."

"Yeah."

"Glad you're okay," she whispered, so quietly that I thought I imagined it.

Before I could question it, she had sprung to her feet and stalked off, tagging Sebastian to take her home as she went. My brother shot me a concerned look over her shoulder, but I nodded at him. She needed him more than I did.

As if to prove my point, Sinclair had returned to me and swung me up into his arms.

Now, we were in the car on our way home, and Sinclair was vibrating with fury.

"I'm happy, Sin. It's over. He ruined my childhood, forced me to leave Paris, and took a bunch of things from me that I never offered. It sucks." He growled at my understatement, so I amended, "Okay, it's horrible. But it is *over*. Now, I can forget the fear and the past and focus entirely on the love of my life."

He looked down at me so I could watch the ice in his eyes thaw and turn into liquid love. "He ruined a night that you've been working toward for months."

"True, but he isn't going to ruin anything else ever again, so I'll accept that."

The police had assured us that he would be deported, and Elena was filing a restraining order for me in the morning.

"I didn't protect you from him," Sin muttered, staring into my face as if he might never see it again.

I pressed my hand to his cheek. "You did. You gave me the tools to face him unafraid. You taught me how to love myself, how to be strong and survive. He wanted to abduct me, he had a gun, and still, we beat him. When I was a teenager, he wouldn't have needed the gun. I would have been on my knees because he loved me and perverted me, and I would have thought obeying him was right. Instead, I outsmarted him, and I *won*."

His eyes flashed.

"I need you to let this go and focus on everything good in our lives. I need you to do this because I'm living my dream, and I don't want to live it alone, or it's no dream at all."

"Elle," he breathed on a heavy exhale. "You are so exquisite. I don't deserve you."

"I don't deserve you, which is good because I'll never take you for granted."

"I'm falling in love with you," he said strangely.

I moved back a little to search his face, but he was very serious. "Um, I was kind of under the impression that you loved me already."

I watched laughter eat away at the anger in his eyes. "It's still happening. I fall further and further into you every day."

Okay, wow.

"You are so romantic."

His lips twitched. "I'm just being nice."

I laughed. "You don't have time to be nice, remember?"

He smiled gently and cupped my cheek. "For you, I can find the time."

Swoon.

I snuggled deeper into him.

"I know you have just been through an ordeal, but I had this planned before everything went to hell. If you want to just go home and rest, I completely understand."

"What are you talking about?"

His eyes danced. "How would you feel about a little celebratory vacation?"

"Sin! Are you going to make it a habit to whisk me away on a moment's notice?" I teased, but I definitely wasn't complaining.

"Yes, absolutely."

I laughed again. "Where are we going this time?"

"Cabo."

He watched me clap my hands and jump up and down in my seat, filled with childish delight and unashamed to show it. I smacked a loud kiss on his cheek.

"You spoil me."

"It's much more selfish than that. I like nothing more than to see you happy."

"Sin," I said, overwhelmed by him, by my life and my luck.

"You're up for it? Because we're on the way to the airport right now, and Candy packed a suitcase for you. It's in the trunk."

"Where it all began," I murmured, pressing my mouth close to his. "Of course, I want to go."

"Good, because no wasn't really an option."

I rolled my eyes.

# Chapter Twenty-four

*Giselle*

The soft, fragrant breeze wove through the open French doors to the balcony and wafted across the sweat cooling on my skin. Sinclair and I had finally ended up in the bedroom, the blankets pooled on the floor, and the sheet twisted around my torso, his legs, like some kind of toga. The air smelled of sex and lavender and that indefinable tropical scent combined with ocean brine, hibiscus, and almost metallic heat. My head rested on the mattress facing Sinclair so that my hair pooled in bloody tendrils over the white sheets where he could draw his finger lazily through the curls, and I could watch the way the pulse jumped in his brown throat.

I could have stayed exactly like that for eternity.

We had arrived at the Westin just after noon the day before and immediately proceeded to the very same suite Sinclair had stayed in all those months ago. There was champagne chilling on the bar, rose petals laid out over the huge canopied bed, and acoustic Spanish music filtered through the room from hidden speakers. I only had a moment to take it all in before Sinclair had me pushed up against the wall, his hands all over every inch of my body. There was passion in his haste but also a need for reassurance. Christopher had tried to claim and my Sin seeking to eradicate even the notion of such a thing.

He didn't have to work very hard to do it, but I appreciated the effort to brand himself on me against the door, then again that evening on the couch and after a delicious room service meal of *aguachile* and chicken *mole*, on the padded lounge chairs on the balcony.

Now, the morning after, my mind was so saturated with pleasure, with such a deep-seated contentment that I found the demons Christopher had plagued me with my entire life were laid eternally to rest.

"I have never been so happy," I told Sin because it was true and because it was all because of him.

Sin didn't open his eyes, but he hummed his approval and said, "Mission accomplished."

I laughed. "You are awfully smug."

He shrugged one shoulder in that French way of his, and even though he was lying down, his big body spread inelegantly across the breadth of the bed, the movement was somehow graceful. "I am a successful businessman with a gorgeous woman who is carrying my baby lying beside me after a pretty fucking amazing bout of sex. I think my smugness is justifiable."

I smiled so wide that it cut into my cheeks. He opened his eyes as if he could sense my expression, and they warmed until they were as blue and bright as the Pacific Ocean outside our window.

"You have that glow of a pregnant woman," he said, traveling his fingers through my hair until they brushed against my cheek. "Every time I look at you, I cannot believe you are mine."

"If you weren't so dignified, I think you would have your name tattooed on my lower back so everyone would know it," I joked.

His eyes darkened, his tone grew serious. "I do not have to do that for everyone to know that you belong to me. It is written in this tilt of your beautiful mouth," his thumb pressed to the smiling corner of my mouth, "in the way your eyes turn to liquid silver when I'm near. It's in how you turn yourself into my body whether you are standing beside me or across the room, like your body is a compass and I am your true north. And as you grow bigger," his calloused fingers swept down my side until they came to rest over my slightly swollen abdomen, "they will see what belonging to me has done to you."

Tears pricked at the backs of my eyes. I didn't think I would ever get used to the poeticism that lived inside my normally stoic and reticent Frenchman. Crying was a hazard of pregnancy, I knew, but I didn't want to ruin the moment with tears, so instead, I said, "What? That it makes me fat?"

His lips thinned in mock severity before he shifted, quick as a flash, to move fully on top of me, pressing my body, still pliant from his earlier caresses, into the bed. One hand plunged into the hair at the nape of my neck, holding me fast as he dipped down to speak against my lips.

"That it makes you wanton, incapable of keeping your legs closed against my virile charms."

I laughed into his face, but his lips closed over my smiling mouth, eating away the humor until I was writhing beneath him. I moaned in protest when he pulled away.

"I take my virility very seriously, Elle. It's nothing to joke about."

"No, of course not." I nodded, my eyes wide with faux sincerity, and my lips compressed against the monumental urge to laugh at him again.

His eyes narrowed further as he tried to read my solemnity, but there was my favorite kind of smile in his eyes as he nodded and pressed a kiss to the tip of my nose.

"I'm glad we've got that sorted. Now, get up and get moving," he said as he rolled off me and walked into the bathroom.

I spoke loudly over the rush of the shower as he turned it on. "Can't we just spend the rest of the day in bed?"

His head ducked back out of the bathroom; his face creased with boyish excitement. "I have a surprise for you. Now, be a good girl and get your gorgeous self in the shower before I lose control and take you again."

I stretched languorously across the bed, rolling my spine up so that my breasts rounded and presented themselves to him. His face tightened with desire as I got up and slowly sauntered over to him, my hips swaying like a pendulum, hypnotizing him. When I finally reached him, his eyes were dark as midnight and still trained down my body, taking in the heavy slopes of my breast, swollen even more with the pregnancy, and the faint tilt of my belly as it arrowed into my bare sex. I was sure that it was the swell of my belly that turned him on the most. The caveman.

I reached out to wrap my fingers around the base of his once more hard cock and gave it a firm tug. He shuddered and ground his back teeth together. With my other hand, I cupped the underside of my breast, weighing it in my palm before flicking my hard nipple with my thumb.

"Fuck, look at you," he groaned. "You are trying to make me lose my mind."

I grinned slyly. "Is it working?"

"*Desolé*, did you say something?"

My laugh was breathy. "Come shower with me."

"We really do have somewhere to be." He caught my wrist as I moved it over his dick. "It's important, Elle."

I paused because there was an urgency in his voice, and he wouldn't turn down sex for just anything.

"Okay... We'll make it quick." I launched myself at him, forcing him to catch me as he stumbled back into the bathroom.

"Elle..."

"Quit stalling. We have places to be, Frenchman. *On y va!*"

He laughed as he placed us both under the hot stream of water, and he was still laughing against my lips when I took him inside me again.

*L*ater, after we finally emerged from the shower skin wrinkled and satiated, I followed Sinclair into the back of a Town Car with no idea of our destination. I watched him as we drove, how his jaw clenched and unclenched rhythmically, and his eyes tracked the blurred landscape flowing out the car window. He held my hand stiffly, but whenever he noticed he was doing so, he made a conscious effort to relax his fingers and throw me a small, inauthentic smile.

For whatever reason, my Frenchman was nervous.

I bit my lip, wanting badly to pester him about it but also deeply intrigued by his uncharacteristic bought of anxiety. This was the man who handled multi-national land deals, who had faced the scrutiny of New York City society without a tremor and survived a childhood in a poor French orphanage.

Sinclair nervous?

I was both giddy and terrified of what that could mean.

When Puerto Los Cabos appeared through the windows, and we came to a stop at the familiar marina, I was even more shocked.

"Sinclair?" I asked as we exited the car, somewhat nervous myself.

He took my hand and smiled down at me, a real smile this time, but the nerves remained in his eyes. "My siren."

"We're going fishing?"

"Not this time."

I cocked my head in question, but he only responded by smiling tightly before he led us forward down the dock. Instead of going to the left, where all the fishing boats bumped quietly against the wooden partitions, we went right. Huge yachts and sailboats gleamed on either side of us as we walked down the planks. I readjusted my grip on my beach bag and wondered why Sin had asked me to bring a nice change of clothes and my makeup.

"Sin?"

*"Oui, mon amour?"*

"Why are you being weird? You are making me nervous."

He stopped, turning to me with his thick brows raised in surprise. I almost laughed because the expression was so foreign on his face.

"I am acting weird?" he echoed, staring over my shoulder for a moment as if looking through memories of the last half an hour to test the validity of my statement. Finally, he looked back at me, threw his head back, and laughed loudly. "I am. My apologies, my mind was in a different place."

I stared at him suspiciously, but he seemed genuine enough, so my mouth dropped into a pout. "I'm not enough to hold your attention?"

His eyes sparkled so brightly that I blinked against the shine. He took me into his arms in a bear hug and lifted me into the air, laughing. "You are always and, sometimes inconveniently, on my mind."

I grinned down into his face, placing my palm on the creases his smile made in his cheek. My love for him spilled out of my overfull heart and into my chest, pressing against my lungs almost painfully. I couldn't breathe, but I didn't really care.

"My love for you is greater than the world," I told him in English this time.

"*Toujours*," he said.

*Always.*

I smiled, at ease again, as I slipped to the ground and took his hand again, moving forward. He stilled me, and when I turned around with a frown, he gestured to a gorgeous yacht just over his shoulder.

"This is our ride."

My mouth dropped open.

"*Ahola, buenos dias, Signor Sinclair*," an older Mexican man appeared from around the side of the vessel. He was dressed in a sharp white uniform and captain's hat. "Welcome to *Cuatro Vientos*, I am your captain, Oscar."

I looked over at Sinclair in mute excitement as Oscar led us onto the deck. He grinned at me as we toured the massive ship, taking in the open concept gallery complete with a small grand piano and a gorgeous lacquered mahogany bar the same rich color as Sinclair's hair. There was a master bathroom with an en suite that housed a deep Jacuzzi as well as four other rooms for sleeping and three bathrooms. The kitchen was small but beautifully appointed and currently stocked to the brim with fresh produce and copious amounts of alcohol. There were two men already steering the boat out of the harbor from deep leather chairs, and they took a moment to explain some of the finer equipment to Sinclair when he leaned forward like an eager boy to examine the many panels of tech.

"This is amazing," I breathed as we finally emerged into the open air of the top deck.

The ocean spread out before us, an azure blue unblemished by a single white cap. The sun spilled fistfuls of glitter across the glossy surface like a trail for us to follow into the sunset. My heart seized at the sight, at the thought, because it invariably led me to think about my own happily ever after with Sinclair. Was this it?

I turned back to face him with my heart in my eyes, disorientated when I found him on the ground before me.

"Are you okay?" I asked, deeply puzzled.

His smile was dazzling, fully realized across his hard features. It was so beautiful, from the square edges of his white teeth to the pink stretch of his full lips and the manly crease that cut into his cheeks, that I lost my breath.

"I have never been so happy," he said, echoing my words from earlier that morning. I was distracted by the way the breeze ruffled his overlong hair, how it painted the dark brown with glittering copper and brilliant reds. That was my excuse for not noticing the way his hands cupped a velvet box the way a man might have cradled a baby, with reverence, joy, and a considerable amount of worry.

"Giselle, my siren," he said, drawing my attention back to his face. "Come here to me."

I breached the few feet between us and stared down into his face, cupping it with one hand because I still wasn't used to touching him, to the fact that I was not only allowed but encouraged to.

"Elle," Sinclair's voice was amused as he once again drew my attention back to what he was saying.

"Mmm? I'm sorry, I'm overwhelmed by how beautiful you look." I blushed and rushed on to explain, "I don't think I'll ever get used to being with you. It's impossible not to touch you, not to love you like this."

He made a noise in the back of his throat that was practically a purr. "If you were paying attention to me, you would understand that I'm asking you to spend the rest of your life loving me like this."

My eyes were drawn down to his hands as they presented me with a deep blue velvet box. I was gasping before it was even flipped open to reveal the most gorgeous ring I had ever seen. The large oval sapphire glowed like a midnight sky filled with lightning, glowing from the facets and the exact color of Sinclair's beloved gaze. A thin halo of diamonds surrounded the gem and encased the slim platinum band. My fingers shook as I reached forward to touch the ring, to test its reality.

"What's happening?" I breathed, too shocked to be embarrassed.

"I am asking you to be my wife. I am trying to claim you in every conceivable way so that there will never be any doubt in your mind, in mine or anyone else's, that Daniel Sinclair and Giselle Moore were made to be together and that they will remain together for the rest of their lives." He watched the tears begin to spill down my face, and his eyes warmed, his features softened with a vulnerability that only his love for me could produce. "I told you at our first meeting that I was afraid you would change my life, and you have. Elle, you have taken everything I ever knew and threw it into brilliant perspective with your generous soul and beauty. I have never felt more like a man, more complete and successful, full of fucking life, as I have with you."

"But..." A huge rush of air flew past my lips as I struggled to make sense of this. "You don't believe in marriage."

His eyes sparkled brighter than the sapphire diamond ring. "I believe in nothing as much as I do our love. I want to be able to call you my wife. I can think of nothing better than being your husband, except perhaps being the father to your children."

"Oh God," I sobbed, so inelegant with emotion, so saturated with love and hope and all those emotions that steal your breath away and set your mind to spinning faster than a top. "I love you so much. Of course, I will be your wife. I'll be anything you want me to be."

"*Vraiment? Tu seras ma femme?*"

"Yes," I cried, sliding my hand into his hair and the other over his dear, dear face. "Of course, I will be your wife."

I had never seen anything as wonderful as his face broken open with joy, his eyes so bright and his smile so wide. It almost hurt to know that I was capable of bringing such a man to his knees with elation.

He wrapped his arms around my waist and tugged me even closer so that he could place his cheek against my stomach. "I love you."

"I love you too."

He looked up at me with a slight smile. "Do not take offense, but this time I was talking to our baby."

I laughed, smoothed a hand through his wind-tossed hair. "I will never take offense to that."

He tugged me down to the deck, dragging me into his lap so that I was sitting there, my legs wrapped around his back, my face tucked into his neck and his arms wrapped securely around me. We stayed like that for a long minute, trying to absorb the monumental amount of joy saturating the moment.

"Marry me right now," he said, finally.

"Sin," I giggled, pressed a kiss to the pulse in his throat.

His arms tightened. "Marry me right now."

"Don't kid."

"I don't have time for jokes."

"I thought it was that you didn't have time to be nice?" I teased, leaning back so that I could look into his face.

It was a very serious face at the moment. "I don't have time for a lot of things. This is why I want to marry you right now."

I pursed my lips as I took in his utter sincerity. "Are you asking me to elope?"

The idea wasn't totally absurd. As it was, most of my family would have a hard time justifying attending our wedding, given that Sinclair had been with Elena as little as six months ago. I didn't even know if I was prepared for the society wedding that Willa Percy would want to throw us, and I certainly wasn't prepared for Mama's exclusion in the preparations. My heart panged. No, if I were going to marry Sinclair, as I was suddenly so desperate to do even though the thought hadn't ever really occurred to me, we would have to elope.

"No," Sin was saying, carefully looking into my eyes. "I'm saying that is why I brought you here."

"To Mexico?" I asked, surprised yet again.

He shook his head slowly. "No, here to the place where I knew for sure that I had fallen in love with you."

I frowned as he stood, offered me his hand so that I could get up as well. He led me to the side of the deck, gesturing dramatically to the scene in front of us.

It was the same beach we had spent the afternoon snorkeling at during our weeklong affair. I immediately recognized the huge outcroppings of red rock that acted like parenthesis for the long curve of sterling white sand and the gracefully arching palm trees and colorful fauna beyond that. But I registered all of that with the periphery of my mind because the sight of the people waiting on the shore, mingling amid white chairs before an arbor wrapped in bright hibiscus flowers, consumed me. I spotted Santiago and Kat Herrera, Cage and Candy, and the rest of the original Mexico crew, even Margot and Antonio, the Percys were talking to Eddie and Rossi, who had their arms around each other.

"Sin, what have you done?" I breathed.

His chuckle stirred the hair by my ear as he wrapped his arms around me as if he knew my knees were about to give out and I needed the extra support.

"I've tried to make us both happy by giving you a wedding filled with all the people you love, in a place where we fell in love."

"And how does this make you happy?"

"*Mon amour*, I would marry you in front of dumpster with sewer rats as witnesses if it meant I could marry you immediately. This seemed like a better option."

I laughed, turning in his arms so I could link my arms around his neck and press myself flush against him.

"I promise, I'm going to make you so happy," I murmured reverently.

His hand cupped the back of my head, and his sigh was full of contentment when he said, "Nothing else can but you."

We embraced for a long moment before someone on shore shouted our name, pulling us apart.

"Save that for the honeymoon!" Cage hollered from the beach. "Sinclair, get off that monstrosity so your future bride can get ready."

"Fuck off, Cage," Sinclair yelled back, carefree and full of good humor. To me, he said, "There is a surprise waiting for you in the bedroom downstairs. Why don't you go ready yourself to be my bride, and I'll meet you out on the beach whenever you are prepared?"

I nodded but felt a tearing sensation at my heart as he moved away from me and began to step down to the lower level. Sensing my yearning or maybe succumbing to his own, he paused and turned back to smile at me.

"Don't take too long, my siren. Thirty minutes tops, *d'accord*?"

I tipped my chin into the air with faux airs. "You cannot rush a woman on her wedding day, Mr. Sinclair."

"Thirty minutes, Mrs. Sinclair, or I'll carry you to the altar over my shoulder."

The witty reply I had prepared withered on my tongue as I gasped at the shock of hearing myself called Mrs. Sinclair. I drifted downstairs in a fog of fantasy and joy, pinching myself a few times to ensure that I wasn't dreaming.

Was it possible for the villain in a story to have a happy ending? Maybe authors just ended the book before they had to explore the potential for the antagonist's growth into someone *worthy* of such a thing.

"I can't believe this is happening," I said out loud as I moved into the master suite, hoping that saying it out loud would make everything more real.

"Well, you better believe it, *bambina*."

I spun around, unable to believe that Cosima could be standing there.

But she was.

My sister looked absolutely stunning, her skin a deep olive-brown and aglow with health, her curves fully recovered from the emaciated shape she had been in over a month ago when I have last seen her. Her long black hair rippled over her shoulders all the way to her waist, and her smile was easy, absolutely gorgeous.

"Cosima," I said because if she was a mirage induced by my happy delirium, then I needed to know.

"Giselle," she said, planting her hands on her slight hips and narrowing her eyes at me. "I hope you didn't think that you could get married without me."

"How?"

Her smile was gentle with compassion as she moved forward to plant a fragrant kiss against my cheek. She still smelled spicy and sweet like only she could.

"Sinclair reached out to Dante, who knew how to get in touch with me."

"Why did you leave?" I had to know. How could she have disappeared after such a terrible accident and left us all to wonder?

Her lips twisted. "I'm so sorry, *bambina*. I wanted to explain things to you, but they are so complicated, and now, well, it is not the time to share my long-winded, frankly horrifying story with you. Now is the time to ready my beloved sister for her wedding day."

I bit my lip as I digested her words. I wanted to press until she broke open under the pressure, spilling all those terrible secrets that had haunted her since she was too young to harbor them, but I also knew that she would never taint my day with her horrors, and it would be wrong of me to ruin the surprise of her presence with grim realities.

"Okay," I said, smiling.

"That was a lot easier than I thought it would be," Candy commented from her spot lounging on the bed. "If I ever disappear, I hope you're harder on me, girl."

I laughed as I launched myself at the bed, smothering Candy in kisses. She grunted under the assault even as her hands pulled me closer.

"Darlin', there will be plenty of time to be kissing later, and the person you'll be kissing is a damn sight easier on the eyes than Candy Kay," Brenna drawled as she emerged from the bathroom. "No offense, Candy."

"None taken. Sinclair is a serious hottie."

"Oh my God, I cannot believe this is happening," I said, my hands pressed to my flaming cheeks. "This is a dream."

"No, *bambina*, this is real, and I hope you are sure about it."

I froze, afraid to look over at the bathroom and acknowledge the woman who stepped out from behind Brenna. I hadn't spoken to her in weeks. The possibility of bursting into tears was pretty high if I turned to face her without steeling myself. So, I took a deep breath, reminded myself that I had survived motherless for four years in Paris and the only family I needed was Sinclair.

It was mostly bullshit, but it made me feel better, nonetheless.

Caprice Lombardi was a beautiful woman who looked nothing like me and everything like the twins, the long black waves and deeply olive skin, even the expression of intensity that seemed to arrest their features at all times. We shared the same curves, though, the figure-eight shape that I'd once been so self-conscious of and a similar smile, the way our cheeks dimpled slightly, and our lips stretched.

She was smiling at me now, and those soft arms were outstretched. "Come and give your mama a hug."

A sob rose in my throat. I didn't care that I was already crying by the time I folded myself in her semolina and lemon-scented embrace. Apparently, it was a day for tears.

She hushed me as one hand stroked down my hair, soothing me the way she had when I was a baby, pressing my head to her bosom so that I could take comfort from her heartbeat.

"Mama," I murmured, over and over in a small broken voice.

"*Si, mia bambina, tua madra.*"

"I'm so happy that you're here. I didn't think... I mean, I never hoped you would be at my wedding."

It was Mama's turn to cry. "Oh no, no, I could never miss this. You are my child. You are my *life*."

I sniffed. "You were so disappointed in me." When her face crumpled, I hastened to say, "No, Mama, I understood why you were. It was fair. It just hurt." I didn't explain how her apathy had crippled me; how my heart had skipped random beats, shuddering and clenching in my chest whenever I thought about her, which was often.

There was nothing like a mother's censure to paralyze the spirit.

"I did not like the way you came together, yes? The hurt you brought Elena, it was terrible and great. She deserved someone's loyalty, and I knew this, that she would not get that from the twins. They understand too much about the messiness of love, and they have always loved you almost like a parent loves their child. They would give you and forgive you anything. Elena needed someone, *capisci*?"

It made sense, of course. Elena was so alone, and even though she had played a large part in her isolation, it was my fault that it had become so starkly defined. I'd taken the love of her partner and the support of our family and any friends she had made through Sinclair. It disturbed me in a third-person kind of way that the greatest consequences felt by my affair had landed on my own sister.

"Okay, we are all happy and together, hurrah hurray! Now, let's get down to the business of making this girl into a bride, hmm?" Candy said, flouncing off the bed to drag me into the bathroom. "Wait until you see the dress your man picked out for you."

"It's a bit indecent for a traditional wedding, but I guess this is a beach ceremony," Brenna allowed, her Southern-born conservatism showing through.

Cosima snorted. "You will look like a vision. Sin won't know what hit him."

I smiled at the thought, but I still hadn't absorbed the blow that the presence of the best women in my life had dealt me. How long had Sinclair planned this for? How could he have known that this was exactly what I needed our wedding to be, in Cabo to bring everything full circle, with all our loved ones and no one else to judge what we had? If I hadn't known Sinclair loved me, there was no way to doubt it now. He was the man who turned all my dreams into realities, spun all my fears into golden desires.

He was the man I had always been destined to marry.

# Chapter Twenty-Five

*Giselle*

I knew immediately why Sinclair had chosen the dress for me. It was a delicately constructed mermaid-style dress with an open back, a v in the front that exposed a deep swathe of cleavage, and slight capped sleeves that frothed over my shoulders. The open weave, off-white crochet and lace patterned exposed flashes of skin without being indecent and pooled behind me in a slight train. It was bohemian, utterly unique, and gorgeous, but most of all, with my hair tousled in waves over my shoulder, I looked like a siren emerged from the depths of the Pacific dressed in sea foam come to find her sailor.

My bridesmaids and Mama went to shore first in a small motorboat after long minutes of reassurances, tears and embraces. I waited, fidgeting in the other boat that would take me to the beach, nervous as I'd ever been even though it was ridiculous to feel anything but excitement.

When I arrived on the sand, there was an aisle bracketed by small shells and coral leading up to the wedding arch, and Sebastian waited for me in the shallows to help me out of the boat. The cool ocean water kissed the bottom of my dress even though I held it up, but it felt appropriate to meet Sinclair with golden slippers of sand on my feet and salt spray on my skin.

"You look like a dream," Sebastian whispered as he took my arm, gently tucking it into his.

"Seb, you're crying," I noticed, shocked.

We hadn't had an easy childhood, one filled with violence or at least, the threat of it, poverty and fear. Through none of it had my brother—the man of our house since the tender age of seventeen but really, the true patriarch long before our father disappeared—cried.

His smile reminded me that he was a movie star before his words even registered. "I'm an actor, Giselle. I'm man enough to cry, and I'm damn pretty when I do it."

I laughed, the tension that I hadn't been aware of drained from my shoulders.

"I love you," I reaffirmed.

"*Sempre*," he confirmed. *Forever.* "Now, are you ready to become a Sinclair?"

I squeezed his arm and dragged him forward in answer, startling a laugh from him. Sinclair's eyes were on me, had been tracking every one of my movements since I appeared on the horizon, but I took a moment to check out the guests lining the aisle because I knew once I locked eyes with my Frenchman, he would be all I saw.

Cage grinned hugely at me, his arms crossed over his huge chest in a smug way that told me he thought he had played a vital role in bringing Sin and I together. I tipped my head to him, acknowledging the truth of it.

Dante was there too, bigger even than Cage but not as imposing as the man who stood beside him. I recognized Alexander Davenport and as I watched him watching Cosima instead of me, his eyes trained on her with a degree of possession and dark desire that was uncivilized, I knew that he was the reason for her disappearance, that she wouldn't have been allowed here without his permission and, apparently, his presence.

The Percys both smiled at me, Mortimer's was wide and uncensored with pleasure, and Willa's was appropriately bashful. She had tried to derail our union at every turn but now that it was happening, now that I was carrying her grandchild, she had wholeheartedly embraced me.

My Mexico crew, including, even, Margot and Antonio, all clapped as I passed, making me blush even as their approval filled me with joy.

I was ready to look at Sinclair, but his cool French-tinted tones beat me to it.

"Look at your future husband, *ma sirène*."

His words hooked my gaze and drew it directly to his. The blue of his eyes consumed me for a long moment. I would never find the right words to describe the vividness of the color, the shape of his lids, or the beauty of his russet lashes, let alone the ones needed to explain the look in his eyes at the moment. *Worshipful* was the word that came closest to the swirl of love, possession, awe, and gratefulness that seized him. I recognized it only because I could feel the very same thing sluice through my veins.

Inappropriately, I wanted to get on my knees before him and show him how much he was revered with my lips, teeth, and tongue, with long strokes of my fingers and sharp exclamations from my nails.

Sin's eyes flashed as they recognized the dirty path to my thoughts.

*Later*, he mouthed through the wicked smile pulling his lips wide.

My brother pressed a kiss to my cheek and carefully, appreciating the symbolism of it, placed my hand in Sinclair's.

"I've cared for her my entire life," Seb said, half benediction, half warning.

Sinclair surprised me by stepping closer, clapping a manly hand over Seb's shoulder. "You've done so well, *mio fratello*. Rest easy now. I have her."

Seb closed his eyes, swallowed thickly, and nodded. "*Si, tu sei la sua.*"

Thank God for waterproof makeup because I was crying.

Sinclair smiled brilliantly as my brother stepped away, and he turned to me fully. I laughed when he tugged me indecently close, our hips flush, one of his large hands at my hips and the other on my cheek, fingertips in the hair over my ear. His eyes bored into mine even when he said to the officiate, "You may begin."

I cried throughout the vows, but happily, they were silent tears, and when Sin dipped his finger in one that streaked across my face, bringing it to his mouth where he licked it away with sparkling eyes, I knew that he didn't mind. His voice was hoarse when he declared 'I do' and when the officiator began to say that Sin could kiss his bride, his hands clenched and unclenched on my skin in restless anticipation.

Finally, he hauled me tight against his body, his arm an iron band across my back and the other tightly woven in my hair so that he could angle my head to seal his mouth completely over mine. I moaned into the kiss, sucking at his velvety tongue as it dipped between my lips. Desire rocketed through me, heady like a drug rush and just as inappropriate to be experiencing at a wedding.

"I cannot wait to fuck my wife tonight," Sin said as he took my ear between his teeth and tugged.

I hissed, my knees weakening so that his arms were the only things holding me up. He took my mouth again in a passionate kiss. Vaguely, I was aware of clapping and catcalling from our assembled guests, but embarrassment was drowned out by pure lust.

Just when I thought I was going to have to climb him, rip off his clothes and ride him like an animal in heat, he pulled away to place his forehead against mine. His uneven breath wafted across my lips, heady and smoky as his fragrance.

Our friends and family were waiting to congratulate us, to party in celebration on the absurdly extravagant yacht that Santiago had lent us for the occasion but for now, it was just us, Sinclair and me.

"You look better than any fantasy I could have had."

I blushed.

"And this blush..." His thumb trailed over my pink cheekbone. "My wife has the prettiest blush."

"Your wife," I echoed, momentarily stunned. "We're married."

"Yes, that is typically the result of a wedding," Sin teased, his rare boyish grin appearing.

"Do you think we deserve this, to be this happy?" I wondered out loud for one tremulous moment.

His forehead pressed hard into mine, his fingers squeezed firmly where they clutched me. I knew if he had his way, we would be stitched together cheek to cheek, thigh to thigh, knitted forever as one person. That was how much he loved me, and more, how much he yearned to possess every inch of me. My mind spun with giddiness, pure euphoria.

"There is no way in my mind or in the minds of anyone here today that we were meant to be anything but together. Fuck the consequences, fuck the right or wrong of it."

Whatever the inception of our relationship, we had evolved and grown into something bigger than morality. We had cheated and lied and caused inexorable heartbreak in each other and those closest to us. We were sinners, undoubtedly, of the highest order. There was no way to deny or forget those truths. They just didn't matter anymore. Maybe it was about damn time the villain had a happily ever after.

I pressed my lips to Sinclair's, showing him how much I agreed with him, how much I only really cared about him, about us. How selfish my love was and how okay I was with it.

When he pulled away again, his eyes blazed with glory, an athlete who had trained and trained and imagined the win and who now, finally, held his prize in his hands.

"You are mine," he said in fierce triumph.

"*Toujours.*" I agreed.

*Epilogue*

*Giselle*

$\mathcal{I}$ was nervous.

There wasn't really any reason to be. Either way, I knew Sinclair would be thrilled. After all, this was our baby, his family, and nothing meant more than his new family.

Still, I was nervous because even though we'd spoken teasingly about it, I wanted to give Sinclair the baby he wanted. Obviously, it was out of my hands and in nature's, but that didn't stop me from worrying.

So I was fidgeting when I arrived at Osteria Lombardi and handed Clarabelle my coat to take before I weaved my way through the busy restaurant to the back corner where my Frenchman awaited me at the table Mama always reserved for family.

I knew he had sensed me the moment I'd entered because his head was up, eyes sparkling like faceted sapphires with anticipation as I rounded the corner and appeared before him.

He leaned back against the leather booth and shook his head, his lips slightly tilted as he took me in. I was wearing a sheer black dress and no underwear. Only strategically placed swathes of lace and jet beading kept the outfit from being entirely indecent.

"*Tu es manifique*," he said, recovering enough to stand to greet me. "Come give your husband a kiss, wife."

It had only been a month, and the newness of being Daniel Sinclair's wife had yet to wear off. I doubted it ever would.

I hop-skipped the final step to him even though I was in impractically tall heels, but his smoky chuckle as he caught me in his arms was worth the risk of falling.

"Hi," I breathed, looking into the face that had irrevocably changed my life.

"Hi," he whispered back, his eyes so bright with love they left sun spots in my vision.

"Elle?" he asked after a long moment of staring. "Are you going to kiss your husband, or is he going to have to take one from his wife?"

Immediately, I pressed my smiling lips to his. Sinclair made quick work of opening my mouth under his, slanting my head to the side with a firm hand in the hair at the nape of my neck, and kissing me breathless.

As my oxygen ran low, I thought vaguely that I never needed to breathe again as long as I could have this from him.

When we parted, he kept me close and ran his hands through my hair before bringing his knuckles to my cheek for a soft caress.

"How is my siren and *mon petit choux*?" he asked me quietly.

My belly warmed at his pet name for our baby, his little cabbage.

"We are both blissfully happy," I told him as I had told him every day since we were married.

I'd been lucky that my morning sickness had been tolerable and hadn't lasted beyond the third month. Now, I felt fantastic, and I was beyond proud of the swelling baby bump under my dress.

Sinclair placed his palm flat against my belly and spread his fingers out, his eyes on his hand as he did so. I struggled to absorb the enormity of love and awe in his electric blue eyes. How was it possible that after all I'd done, I deserved such a man?

"I'm still upset that you didn't wait to reschedule the appointment at the doctor until I could attend," he said as he led me to my seat and settled me with a kiss to the forehead before he retook his chair.

"Even you agreed that it was best I didn't miss any appointments after what Christopher did to me," I reminded him softly even though I hated saying that name.

Sin pressed his lips into a flat line and reached across the table with his palm up, demanding my hand. I gave it to him, watching as he gently clasped it between his fingers and began to play with my wedding rings. It was a habit he'd quickly developed, one that I knew brought him comfort. My Frenchman liked to reassure himself often of our connection, and in public, when he couldn't take me or sit with his hand pressed intimately to my belly over our growing child, he settled for touching the rings that legally made me his.

"We are celebrating our one-month anniversary today, not speaking of that man. Let me change the subject. How did the interview with Jerry Saltz go?"

I beamed at him as I thought back on my interview with the art critic from the *New York* mag. He'd written one of the best reviews after my gallery showing and demanded Rossi give him my phone number so he could get an exclusive interview with the woman "who dared to be deviant."

"It went beautifully. He's an incredibly interesting man. I still can't believe he's so interested in my work," I admitted.

A server arrived at our table with a bottle of sparkling apple juice that, after a chin tip from Sinclair, he proceeded to open the way one would a bottle of champagne.

"Fancy," I joked, but Sin's face was set with sobriety.

"Jerry is one of the best in his field, Elle, so it is, in fact, not at all surprisingly that he would champion your work given that it is remarkable."

I stared into his eyes and realized for the millionth time that Sinclair would never rest until I understood my own potential and loved myself at least half as much as he loved me.

I squeezed his hand gently and said softly, "*D'accord.*"

He nodded curtly, which made me bite back a smile.

"Caprice has prepared a special meal for you, if she may?" the server asked.

Sinclair nodded but kept his eyes on me as the other man swept away. He cocked his head slightly, narrowing his eyes at me.

"What is it, my love?"

I sucked in a deep breath and straightened my shoulders to steel myself against the possibility of disappointment.

"I, I found out the sex of the baby today," I admitted.

Sinclair's eyes flashed and crackled like lightning. "Tell me."

"Sin..."

"Elle, tell me now," he demanded, leaning forward with an intensity that vibrated the air around us.

I swallowed thickly but managed to look into his heartbreakingly beautiful face.

Maintaining the contact, I slid the brown paper-wrapped present I'd plucked from my purse across the table toward him.

He stared at me for a moment before opening the present efficiently with one hand so that he could keep his other laced with mine. I was staring hard at his face as he unearthed the frame from within. Otherwise, I might have missed the way his breath stuttered and came to a stop in his chest.

I waited for him to recover, but he didn't. He just stared and stared at the silver picture frame that held the first picture of our child. On the top of the frame was written in cheesy but beautiful words, Daddy's Little Girl.

"A daughter," he finally said, his voice so soft I nearly missed it.

"Yes, a daughter. She's going to have your eyes and your laughter and, I hope, your brain," I babbled on because I was nervous about his lack of reaction. "Basically, I hope she is a mini Sinclair."

"No," Sinclair said, his voice whipping through the air to crack against my sensitive skin.

I flinched, then breathed, "No?"

"No," he said, tipping his face up from the frame so I could see the way his eyes burned beneath the lacquer of tears. "She will be exactly as her mother is, and just as I feel for her mother, no one will ever love her more than I will."

I hadn't realized how tense I was until the starch washed out of my skin.

"Sin," I breathed.

"Come here," he ordered.

I went there, folding myself into his lap even though we were in Mama's gorgeous and sophisticated restaurant. People were staring, but I didn't care because my Frenchman had his arms around me, and he was so thrilled about having a daughter, he was even moved to tears.

He captured my face in his hands and stared deep into my eyes to say, "I love you more than any man has ever loved any woman. I don't care if that's arrogant. It's the fucking truth."

"I know," I replied instantly. "Because I feel the same about you."

"We aren't staying for dinner," he told me.

I pulled back with a frown. "But Mama made us a special meal."

"If they can pack it up, we'll take it, but I'm taking you home now. I plan to have you naked and spread out like my own personal buffet within the next twenty minutes. I think that will be enough to satiate my hunger, and Elle, I can promise you I will feed you enough of my cock that you will forget all about food."

I wriggled in his lap as wetness pooled between my thighs. "Yes, sir."

His eyes flashed then darkened, and as the server walked passed, he ordered brusquely, "Bill, please."

"Show me, my siren, how you kneel so prettily for your husband."

Instantly, my body collapsed like wet clay to the ground, ready for his hands and will to mold me into whatever shape would please him best. My hair swished over my shoulders as I bent my head to assume the proper position, and I shivered at even that delicate touch.

"Such a good wife," Sinclair told me even as his foot came out to kick slightly between my thighs. "Now, spread those creamy thighs nice and wide, and show me how wet I make your pretty pussy."

I whimpered as my clit throbbed to the beat of his words even as I obeyed him. Cool air wafted over my molten core as I spread my legs to the point of pain, desperate to show him how much I needed him.

"Mmm," Sin hummed as he gracefully fell into a crouch before me. I gasped softly when he reached out with two fingers to open my pussy up further so he could run his thumb through the silky wetness at my entrance and over my pulsing clit.

I writhed under his ministrations and begged softly, "Please, sir."

"Tell me what you need."

"More, sir."

The blue of his eyes flashed frozen as he coolly reminded me, "Use your words."

"I need your cock," I panted as his fingers circled my entrance and dipped just barely inside me.

I knew better than to grind down on his hand, but my hips twitched in protest, my cunt clenching against the emptiness.

"Better," my husband praised, then rewarded me by sinking three thick fingers deep into my wet heat.

I tipped my head back, eyes still on his as I groaned. He thrust deeper, lifting me into the air by my pussy so that I was balanced precariously, entirely dependent on his hold to keep me aloft.

My legs shook as my wetness coated his fingers and began to slide down my inner thighs. Somehow still keeping me raised, he pumped his fingers and rubbed against the knot of sensation on my front wall while his thumb skirted delicate figure eights over my clit.

He had been touching me for two minutes, and I was ready to come.

"Keep yourself spread for me, Elle," my Frenchman ordered.

I whimpered, desperate to rub my legs together, to grind down on his talented fingers. Instead, I held myself still as a marble statue. Only my pussy moved, grasping at him as he pistoned in and out.

"Such a greedy cunt you have, Elle," Sinclair said conversationally.

He reached out to pull the cups of my bra under my breasts so that they were indecently plumped up. I watched dazedly as he brought his free hand to his firm mouth, and his tongue flicked out to wet the pads of two digits. Quick as a lightning strike and just as painful, he lashed out to twist and pull one of my nipples.

I gasped loudly, hips bucking against his fingers as the pain burned through my chest and turned into radiating pleasure.

He did it again with the other nipple. I grounded down shamelessly on the steady, slowly pumping fingers in my pussy.

The burn of the pinch contrasted against the cool his wet fingers had left on my skin. It was so delicious, I almost couldn't stand it.

"Please, sir," I cried out softly.

He ignored me, which ratcheted my arousal up another dangerous decibel. Instead, he lazily reached out to give my pebbled nipple a hard flick.

I sucked in a breath between my teeth and rode his fingers hard, my pussy rippling over them.

When my husband spoke, his voice was ice cold, but I could see the deep heat burning in his eyes. Another contrast that twisted me into delectable knots.

"Diamond hard for me," he said, flicking the other nipple. "Should I clamp these pretty red nipples?"

"If it would please you, sir," I managed to breathe.

It was the right response.

Sinclair dropped to his knees, drove a hand into the hair at the nape of my neck, and tugged hard so that my throat was exposed and he was glaring down at me. His face was stern with desire, his jaw a hard cliff's edge, his mouth pressed into a firm line that acted as a dam to his baser instincts. He wanted to let go, ravage me until I was boneless and taken beyond all rational thought. But first, he would dismantle me, thought by thought, until nothing was left in my head but him. His name strumming with each pulse of my heart as it beat strongly through every inch of my body.

"Sinclair," I rasped as it began.

"You please me," he bit out, violent with passion. "Your pussy on my hand, your juices leaking down my wrist, each rebellious twitch of those lush hips."

Impossibly, he added a fourth finger to my heat and drove deeper inside me, bringing me further up on my straining knees so that I was merely an inch from his mouth.

"It pleases me to know that I own this pussy, that you beg to take my cock in your sweet ass, that you love the feel of my cum on your skin because you know you've earned it."

"Yes," I hissed, nearly drooling with want and growing rabid with the need to orgasm.

"Please."

"Such a beautiful word coming from these lips." Sin dipped down to run his tongue along my pouting bottom lip before he swept it through my open mouth, catching my tongue in a wet dance as he sealed his lips over mine.

It was one of the most erotic kisses of my life, and I'd had a lot, given that I was married to Sinclair.

When he pulled away, I tried to follow, but the hand curled through my hair held me fast.

"How much can you take, my siren? If I wanted to plug your ass while I fuck your pussy so hard the chains on your nipple clamps dance, what would you say to your Dom?"

"Please. I want you to do whatever you want to me. I want to please you," I told him, infusing my voice with the potent mix of desire and love he'd cultivated in me.

Immediately, his hands left me. I whimpered at the loss of his fingers and had to clench my thigh muscles tight in order not to fall out of position as I settled back on my calves.

Sinclair strode to the walnut-paneled corner and began to pull out the toys. I shivered as I watched him move with the economy and grace of a large hunter readying for the hunt.

Only, he'd already caught me, shot me through the heart with an arrow dipped in love, and trapped me in a cage built with bars of loyalty and love.

I jolted from my thoughts when he returned. My arms were lax as he lifted them over my head, shackled them in soft leather and fur cuffs, and then affixed them to a bar hanging down from the ceiling that hadn't been there minutes ago.

"Adjustable." Sin's voice came as a whisper against my neck. "So I can take my siren any way I want."

A soft whir sounded as he raised the bar so that I was once again perched slightly uncomfortable on my wide-spread knees.

"Too much?" he asked.

"No, sir." And it wasn't. I loved the burning stretch that bracketed my aching sex.

I felt him move into position behind me and shivered when he wrapped his arms around my torso to pinch my nipples hard. He pulled and released them like taffy until they were as hard, red, and burning as cinnamon candies. Only then did he produce the delicate metal chain that linked together to clamps in the shape of clamshells.

I couldn't help the soft laughter that escaped me at the little reference to my nickname, siren.

Sinclair smiled against the side of my neck, then simultaneously bit firmly into the junction of my neck and shoulder as he clamped one nipple. I shuddered against him. He moved my hair from one shoulder to the other and repeated the same bite/clamping movement.

"Tip your ass for me." When I did as he ordered, his hands came out to smooth over the dramatic curves before one lifted and smacked down hard on my left cheek.

I groaned as the heat radiated through me.

He smacked the other cheek, then spread them so he could run the edge of his thumbs over my puckered entrance. I shivered as one hand left me, and I heard the unmistakable sound of the lube being opened.

"I hardly need to use this to prepare you," Sin said huskily. "Your pussy is dripping onto the floor."

God, that was hot. I loved being that turned on for him.

His thumb returned, wet with lube, and circled my entrance in increasingly firm strokes until I pushed back against it impatiently, and it drove inside.

I hummed my approval even as Sinclair spanked me again.

"Greedy," he chastised, but I knew he loved it.

"Please, sir, I need your cock," I begged.

"If I don't prepare you, it may hurt," he warned.

"Please."

He made a low, rough sound deep in his throat that sent a flurry of fireworks off in my groin. I felt the tip of his hot cock slide through my wetness, then notch at my entrance just as the tip of the butt plug nudged at my ass.

"You'll take what I give you," Sinclair ordered, banding one arm across my hips, ready to rip me apart at the seams.

"Always," I promised.

A second later, I screamed as his thick cock and the smaller plug thrust ruthlessly inside me. Painfully stretched and loving it, I thrust my hips back against both invasions and begged for more.

Sin rewarded me by sliding his cock nearly all the way out and then jamming it back home, grinding his hips against mine so that I could feel him at the very end of me. He kept up that merciless pace for a few minutes until I was sweaty and writhing against him.

"Keep those legs spread for me," he ordered, and a moment later, the plug inside my ass came to life with powerful vibrations that thumped like the beat of a drum against Sin's cock as it pistoned in and out of my sloppy wet pussy.

"Oh my God, oh my God," I chanted unconsciously.

"Take more."

He wrapped his hand around one hip and slammed me back down against him. With his other hand, he dived between my lewdly spread legs and played his fingers in the pool of wetness he found there. I gasped when his fingers slid farther back and cupped my mound, fingers splayed around his cock as it churned inside me.

"This cunt is mine."

"Yes, sir."

"My wife has the prettiest pussy, the greediest ass, and they are both all mine," he growled.

Yes, the savage was coming out to claim me, and I loved it.

"Yes, sir."

"Do you want to come, my siren?" he asked.

"Yes, yes, God, yes," I panted, on edge for so long that I felt stretched thin and ready to shatter at the barest impact.

"Then come for your husband," he commanded as he slid a finger inside my pussy beside his pumping dick and pressed his thumb hard to my swollen clit.

Instantly, I imploded. My womb clenched like a fist, so tight I thrummed with it, and then, just when blackness crept into the edges of my vision, the tension broke, and I melted into a pulsing mass of sex-drenched flesh.

"That's it," Sinclair urged. Then as if that wasn't enough, he quickly undid the nipple clamps, and the blood rushed painfully back into my breasts.

I screamed and screamed until my voice was hoarse as my orgasm continued, wringing every sensation out of every atom until I was disassembled, no longer human but vibrating atoms kept together by Sinclair's cock in my cunt, his hands cupped over my aching breasts, and his mouth clamped gently over the junction of my neck and shoulder.

Vaguely, I heard him groan, long and low and triumphant as he filled me with his cum.

I rested heavily on my shackles as he held me while we came down. His calloused fingers ran tenderly through my sweat-dampened hair, pulling it over one shoulder so he could trail a line of kisses behind my ear to the end of my shoulder. I melted further into him when he slowly pulled out of my aching sex and retrieved the no-longer-vibrating toy from my ass.

I startled slightly when his fingers spread my swollen sex and dived in to play with his cum. I turned my head to watch him watching my pussy as his seed slid from me and slicked my inner thighs.

"I love seeing my cum on you," he told me without taking his eyes off the sight.

I shuddered violently as an aftershock rippled through me.

"I love knowing it made the baby you carry for us," he said even more gently.

"Sin," I whispered, tears tightening my throat.

He looked up at me then with burning eyes that branded me with his everlasting love. "Thank you for giving that to me, my love."

I knew he meant more than my body just then, more even than the baby we'd made. He meant to thank me for our ongoing happily ever after, for giving him a life filled with color and a family worth fighting for.

"I love giving that to you," I told him honestly. "It's the best thing I'll ever do."

Love so fierce it contorted his face for a moment before he controlled it and made quick work of my shackles.

Before I could get cold, he wrapped my body in his arms and cuddled me onto his lap.

I closed my eyes to absorb the loving touch trailing over my cheeks, lips, and breasts, as they trailed down to my swollen stomach and both hands pressed there to frame the bump.

"Mon amour pour toi et notre bebe est plus grand que le monde," he said into my hair.

My love for you and our baby is bigger than the world.

# *Extended Epilogue*

*Sinclair*

We hadn't seen Elena in years.

I knew Giselle was nervous by the way she kept fidgeting, tugging the short hem of her lavender dress as far down her thighs as she could force it, no doubt wondering if her critical older sister would make some disparaging comment about a mother not showing too much skin. I palmed Elle's thigh in one hand and squeezed, relishing the way she instantly stilled, then softened into my touch.

Years later, and the magic of our love still fucking wowed me.

"Papa," Genny called from her high chair where she was coloring on a page the restaurant had given her when we sat down. "What does tante Elena look like? Does she have red hair like Mama and me or black like oncle Seb and tante Cosi?"

I tugged on one of my daughter's curls, staring at the way the sun hit the strands and broke them into multitudes of copper and orange threads.

"Red like you, *ma petit choux*," I told her over her little giggle as I tugged at another spiral curl. "In fact, you look a lot like your aunt."

Her big blue eyes, my eyes, widened almost comically, and her pink mouth made a little 'o' of excited shock. "That's good. I like it when we all look like family. Even baby Theo has red hair!"

I smiled at her because she was so fucking adorable I couldn't even believe she was real sometimes. Still, I noticed Giselle squirm again from the corner of my eye and knew she wondered if Elena would act like family when she showed up. It had been five years since I'd left her for Elle. Five years, a marriage, and two children for us, and countless, often dangerous milestones for Elena in her career as a criminal lawyer and her role as a mafioso's paramour.

Who would have thought all those years ago that Elena would end up with one of the most notorious criminals on the planet? Staid, conservative, socially hyperaware Elena had turned her back on everything she knew.

All for the sake of love.

If she wasn't over her hatred of Elle and myself by now, I resolved that this would be the last time we saw her. I wasn't as nervous as my sensitive wife, though. Though we hadn't seen her in ages, our last interactions with the eldest Lombardi sibling had been largely positive.

Not to mention the time she'd saved my wife from Christopher.

"Where is she?" Genny asked, finishing her drawing with a flourish so she could hold it up in one hand and flap it around like a flag for us to admire. "I made her a drawing!"

Elle finally laughed, caught up in our daughter's constant enthusiasm and habit of exclaiming at everything she found exciting or beautiful, which was most things in life. She had gotten her mother's love of art and beauty, and my desire to be heard.

"It's beautiful, little beauty."

Giselle and I both froze for a fraction of a second as the smooth voice sounded over our shoulders. It was the same tone of voice I'd once heard every day for four years, but the intonation was completely different, smooth and rolling with the lyricism of her native Italy. It suited her high, lyrical voice, but not the woman who had forced herself to speak accent-less as long as I'd known her.

I adjusted Theo's sleeping body against my chest with one arm so that I could turn slightly to see the woman I'd once foolishly thought myself in love with.

And not for the first time in my life, I was grateful for my culti-vated poker face.

Elena was almost a stranger to me then, and I knew by the gasp that fell from my wife's lips that she felt the very same sense of disas-sociation.

Oh, Elena was still elegant as hell, her posture straight as a balle-rina's, her long, tapered fingers tipped red, her dress obviously expensive.

But that was it.

She wore her hair long now, down past her breasts in a messy length of waves that immediately brought to mind the way Elle's hair looked after I'd mussed it in the bedroom. Where she'd always kept meticulously out of the sun to stave off wrinkles and age spots, she was caramelized and baring more skin than I'd ever seen her expose in public before though she was a long way from being indecent.

But it was the expression on her face that rendered her completely altered than the woman I'd once claimed to know.

She was smiling.

A soft curve of her red painted lips warmed her dark gray eyes like sunlit storm clouds and creased her cheeks in a way that brought out a faint dimple I'd never noticed in her left side.

Her eyes were fixed on Genny as she leaned forward toward our daughter and raised a hand to smooth out the drawing she had made for her. She studied it seriously, the way an art critic measured one of Elle's now-famous sensual paintings.

Genny bounced in her seat, her lips rolled between her teeth, her eyes wide as she took in her aunt and waited for her judgment.

"*Bellisima*," Elena declared after a moment before pressing a sweet kiss to Genny's plump cheek. "May I keep it?"

My daughter nodded mutely, a little awestruck by the pretty aunt she hardly remembered. She watched as Elena carefully folded the paper and slipped it into her big leather purse.

"I'll put it on my fridge so I can always see it," Elena told her with a little wink.

I blinked.

The woman I'd dated hadn't even allowed magnets on our fridge.

"I'm sorry we're late," Elena said, finally adjusting her stance to address Giselle and me. Her little smile didn't fall. "You wouldn't believe what it's like trying to corral these two."

"Oh?" Giselle asked, a wealth of questions in the soft sound.

I squeezed her thigh again just to feel her beneath my hand and let her know I was just as shocked as she was.

"They're impossible. I decided not to wait at the front for them to follow because knowing them, it will take them another ten minutes to wade in from the car." Elena rolled her eyes as she moved toward Elle, surprising us both by leaning down in a familiar cloud of Chanel Number 5 perfume to press a kiss on each of her sister's cheeks. Giselle accepted the intimacy with a choked little gasp, her eyes wide as twin silver coins as they caught mine.

When Elena turned to me, she did so with a little frown before extending a hand to me. The many thin gold bracelets on her wrists clinked together as I shook it.

"It's good to see you both," she said, her voice quiet but sincere. "You look well."

"We are," I agreed, instinctively rocking Theo a little as he fussed in his sleep.

"Dio mio," she whispered, catching sight of his little face under his bucket hat. Without hesitation, she leaned close to me so she could trail a finger down his cheek. "I can't believe I haven't met this handsome little man yet. Mama told me his name is Theodore?"

"Theo," Giselle said, her uncertainty drowned in maternal pride. She beamed as she leaned over to adjust his hat. "He's had a long day, and he fell asleep on the way here, but when he wakes up, you'll be able to see just how sweet he is."

"He's my baby brother," Genny informed her aunt solemnly. "If you want, I'll let you hold him when he wakes up."

Elena bit off the edge of her smile and nodded gracefully. "That would be very nice of you. Thank you, Genevieve."

And Genny, who hated going by her full name, didn't even correct her aunt. She was that infatuated.

Giselle made big eyes at me as Elena finally rounded the table to take a seat. I shrugged a shoulder at her.

It shouldn't have surprised us, not really, to see Elena so content and loose with satisfaction. She might not have achieved the dreams she'd always assumed she wanted, but she was successful and in love.

If Giselle and I could evolve in just a week of loving each other on vacation in Mexico, it was only fitting Elena could change vastly after years of loving the right man.

As if summoned by my thoughts, there was a commotion at the doors to the patio behind us, and a second later, Dante Salvatore strutted out into the sunlight.

I'd forgotten how large he was, head and shoulders above the host who was trying unsuccessfully to escort him to the table because he couldn't keep up with the man's long strides. His broad, deeply tanned face was creased at the eyes and beside the mouth, reminding me he was older than my thirty-seven by four years. He wore all black, from his shoes to the sunglasses perched in his ink dark hair. It lent him a villainous presence as he crossed the stone patio, every diner's eyes immediately tracking him across the space.

I looked at Elena, stunned to see the easy, open smile on her face, the beaming contentment I was familiar with from staring at my own face in the mirror every morning when I shaved.

Fuck me, Elena Lombardi in love was a stunning thing to behold.

And it might have been selfish, but it settled something in me I hadn't known still needed tending to. The guilt I'd held on to for years wilted and died at that moment, as the huge mafioso ate over the pavement in his haste to get to his woman.

He ignored us as he bent to cage her against the back of her chair, staring into her eyes for a long moment.

"*Mia lottatore*," he growled almost too low to hear. "Your daughter is impossible."

Elena's laughter was a high, bell-like toll. I'd never known her to enjoy teasing, but she responded easily to his jibe. "Like father, like daughter." She peered over his shoulder at Giselle and grinned. "Am I right?"

Elle nodded, her hand creeping over to my thigh to pinch it. I chuckled a little under my breath at her incredulity, but only because I was feeling it too.

Who the hell was this woman?

"Give me a kiss," Dante demanded next, still not addressing us.

"I don't feel like it," Elena said with a lazy wave of her hand before inspecting her nails as if she had something better to do.

There was another growl from Dante, and then he was lifting her up, up, out of her chair, prompting a little screech of outrage from Elena, before he sat down in the seat and settled her in his lap. Once secured, he roped her hair around one ham-like fist and pinned her still to stamp a rough kiss on her lips.

When he pulled back, he raised an eyebrow. "You should know by now, if you want to play in public, I am only too happy to oblige."

Elena only smiled a small, secret little smile and wiped at the red lipstick transferred on his mouth with her thumb.

When she finished, Dante looked over at us, speaking as if we were mid-conversation. "I don't have to tell you two she's a fucking handful."

Giselle blinked, then burst out laughing, the warm sound flowing over me like sunshine. It made me grin too, looking at the tension leech from her shoulders as she recovered from her giggles and leaned toward them with a genuine smile.

"Honestly, I'm not sure how you handle it," she teased back.

I kept an eye on Elena, ready to scalp her if she snapped at my wife for being friendly.

Instead, Elena only laughed and stroked her hand through the back of Dante's hair as he said with a roguish wink, "A lot of practice."

"Ew, are you guys talking about sex again?" Another voice, this one young and belonging to a preteen girl with long light brown hair nearly the same color as her tanned skin. She strolled the rest of the way across the patio on slow, almost lazy strides until she reached Elena and Dante. "You know I'm already scarred for life, right?"

Dante's huge hand lashed out so suddenly, for a split second, I thought he meant to do her violence, and I tensed to interfere. Instead, he tugged her close so he could plant a kiss on her forehead that she accepted with faux reluctance.

"Giselle, Sinclair," Elena said, her voice bursting with pride as she laced her hand with the girl's. "This is our daughter, Aurora."

Cosima, Caprice, and Seb had all mentioned Aurora at some point or another the past couple of years, but this was our first time meeting Elena's adopted daughter. It was strange to see Elena in her even though they didn't share any blood. Aurora had the same regal bearing, a familiar resting expression of haughty elegance.

"You're family so you can call me Rora," she offered graciously as she tugged an empty chair closer to her parents so she could sit down and keep Elena's hand in hers.

"You can call me Genny," my daughter offered in the same tone, extending a red crayon to her cousin. "And you can color with me too."

"Cool," Rora accepted easily, angling her chair so she could lean over Genny's high chair.

Instantly, the two girls started chattering away in low voices as they worked together on a new piece of paper.

Beside me, Giselle sniffed.

When I turned to look at her, there were big, crystalline tears in those gorgeous grays.

"Hey, my siren," I murmured to her, tugging her chair closer with one hand so I could wrap my free arm around her. "What's going on here?"

"I'm sorry," she said, waving her hand around to excuse her behavior when it didn't need to be excused. "It's just... it's so nice to see you all."

"Thank you for agreeing to meet a little early," Elena said, leaning forward in Dante's lap to reach across the table for Elle's hand. My wife extended hers tentatively. "I just wanted the opportunity to say I'm sorry for everything that has happened between us over the years. I'm not going to say I'm wholly at fault, but I am going to own my part in our broken relationship. I...I had a lot to work through, and it took me years, too many years, to heal enough to realize my own mistakes. We had so many things working against us since we were just kids who didn't know better. It's been so long, but I know now it's never too late to fix a relationship, and I'd like to fix ours. No pressure. I'm not saying I expect us to be best friends, but I'd like us to try to know each other better." She paused, her eyes sweeping to Theo in my arms, then Genny and Rora, who were still coloring and whispering together. "For us, and also for our family."

Giselle blinked at her big sister, then stared down at their hands, the matching tone of olive skin, one with freckles and the other without. When she looked back up at Elena, her eyes were clear and determined behind the lacquer of her tears.

"I can take ownership for my part in it," she agreed easily. "I'm sorry for everything, and I always will, but I am so happy that you've found someone who makes you as happy as Sin makes me."

I wasn't sure how she would react to that, but Elena continued her streak of confounding me, and she grinned widely, her eyes creased at the edges with genuine happiness.

"You can thank him for teaching me that I didn't have to be the villain of my own story."

Dante leaned forward to place a kiss at the curve of her neck and shoulder in silent support. He caught my eye from across the table, and I felt the most bizarre emotion bubble up in my throat.

It was gratitude.

I was grateful for the man who had brought Elena to life as surely as Giselle had done with me. Even though we had never loved each other properly, I'd cared for this woman, known her and lived with her for years. It eased some masculine sense of worry in my chest to know she was cared for by a man who could protect her, even from her most villainous self.

I jerked my chin up him in the universal male equivalent of a back-slapping hug, and Dante? The man the media had dubbed the 'Mafia Lord' and the 'Devil of NYC'?

He fucking laughed.

He laughed because he knew we were the luckiest goddamn men on the planet to have the love of a Lombardi woman.

And I agreed with him wholeheartedly.

So I laughed too.

*Giselle*

 *even years later*

.  .  .

"*It's* raining like a cow pisses," Sinclair muttered in his mother tongue as we held the wide-brimmed umbrella over our heads in the deluge of water spilling from quilted gray clouds.

Genevieve screwed up her little nose as she translated the rather crude expression, tugging on her father's hand in shock as she declared, "Papa, that was rude!"

Sin chuckled lightly, pulled her closer into the fold of his black cashmere peacoat. "The French are never rude, *ma chérie*. We are blunt. There is a subtle but very profound difference."

I shook my head at my husband, biting off the edge of the smile that threatened to curve my lips. He was incorrigible, but even after seven years of marriage and parenthood, he still made me feel like the nerdy kid in school with a crush on the quarterback. There was magic to every moment I spent with him, even the most mundane of them, like standing in the rain at Charles de Galle airport waiting for our Town Car to arrive.

He caught my eye and gave me a faint, curling grin that spoke of wickedness and want.

This was why we were having a vacation in our favorite city in the world, Paris, because the past year had been pure, delightful chaos. Sinclair had been featured in Forbes Richest Entrepreneurs Under Forty for his success with Faire Developments, and I'd been working around the clock on my largest exhibition yet, a series of erotic paintings done of physically disabled and disfigured people to showcase their unique form of beauty. It had been an unequivocal success. Even the kids were busy. Genny had exhibited an affinity and talent for ballet that had prompted her indulgent father to enroll her in the best dance academy in the city with one of the best instructors money could buy. She was only eight years old, but ballet was her life. Unsurprisingly perhaps, with parents like us, both our children were incredibly driven and passionate about art.

Theo hadn't settled on any one thing like his twin sister. Instead, every few months he cycled to another discipline. At first, he loved any sport with a ball, then he loved music and demanded lessons in piano from his Uncle Cage, then violin and guitar. By six, he discovered painting one day when I forced him to wait in my studio, and now, nearly a year later, he often voluntarily joined me there to experiment with oils, watercolors, the printing press, and clay sculpture.

Overachievers, Sebastian often joked. It ran in the Lombardi blood and had only been amplified by Sinclair's.

After a massive meltdown a few weeks ago, when Genny burst into tears after twisting her ankle and Theo yelled at his teacher because she didn't understand how impossible it was for a young boy with ADHD to stay still, Sinclair had decided a vacation was the only remedy.

As usual, he was right.

Even after hours on a red-eye flight from New York, a contentment blanketed our little family, a stillness I hadn't felt in months.

The car pulled up to the curb with a rippling splash of collected rainwater in the gutters, prompting the kids to laugh as murky droplets splattered their rainboots. Sin organized the suitcases with the driver while I ushered our babies into the car.

I closed my eyes, leaning my head back to absorb the soothing sound of my husband speaking in the rolling, lyrical French of the south where he'd been born.

"I'm happy we're home," Theo murmured from where he sat with his nose pressed to the window, staring out at the dreary, unattractive parking lot as if it was a Monet painting.

I laughed softly, love swollen in my chest. "Me too, *bambino*."

"Will I really get to meet Pasha Morozov?" Genny asked, immediately cuddling into me because my girl loved physical contact. Her wide blue eyes were the same shade as her father's and brother's, that electric blue I could never replicate with paint and brush no matter how hard I tried.

I kissed her soft crown of auburn hair. "Yes, I believe he runs in your *oncle* Cage's circle."

Which meant Pasha Morozov, the new diamond of the Paris

Ballet, was a rouge and probably a sensualist. I didn't exactly want my impressionable daughter to meet a man like that whom she already idolized, but Sinclair had reminded me it was hypocritical to judge a man by his sexual proclivities.

My mind wandered as Sinclair and the driver got into the car, and we took off into the lightening dawn of our first day in Paris.

The last time Sinclair and I had been able to have a proper scene was months ago. Yet another reason—one that went unspoken but was implicitly understood—for our vacation in Paris.

I was dying to bloom open under his control again. The itch of submission fizzled under my skin like champagne as I imagined the many ways my Dominant might bend me to his will.

"Ma sirene?" Sinclair's warm, humor-filled voice wafted to me in the back seat, dissolving my fantasy.

I flushed as he grinned at me knowingly.

"How would you kids like to spend tonight with your uncle Cage?" Sin suggested casually.

Immediately, Genny and Theo erupted in excited affirmation. They loved their world-famous uncle even though they often disliked the random women he dragged to our family affairs. To them, he was the pinnacle of success, much more glamorous than their own parents.

My kids were happy and, from the cast of Sin's familiar wicked grin, I knew I soon would be too.

*I* wore silk the color of the inside of an oyster, the color of skin under candlelight, so every inch of me seemed indecently exposed, glowing with some inner light. My hair was brushed and curled into a long curtain of burnished red that rasped over the thin fabric at my breasts just enough to peak my nipples into diamond points.

I knew this was what I'd looked like under my Burberry trench coat when I'd left the hotel with Sinclair thirty minutes prior.

But I did not know how I looked now, kneeling on a small stage in the home of our local friend and BDSM community patron, Madame Claire.

My eyes were concealed by the very same shade of silk corseting my torso and barely covering my sex. The world around me was lost to my sight but heightened in my other senses. I could feel the warm touch of air swirling over me as people moved by, admiring me in faint whispers but never touching.

So sweet, they said in French, the language spilling like satin ribbons, smooth and seductive.

To whom does she belong? one man queried with obvious interest.

To Sinclair, I wanted to respond but didn't.

I wore the collar of pearls around my throat that said more than I ever could in the language of domination and submission about the fact that I was intractably taken.

It was exactly this ownership that grounded me while strangers admired my body. I would never have felt comfortable or open to their appreciation if it wasn't for Sinclair's influence, his voice in my ear telling me I was so beautiful, so worthy of worship.

As if summoned by my thoughts, a light touch trailed from the top of my head down the back of my hair, where a hand slowly twisted my long hair into a rope. Using it as leverage, my head was canted back, my mouth parting instinctively as warm lips sealed over it.

I hummed as Sinclair's velvet tongue slid between my teeth and claimed my own.

By the time he pulled back, I was panting.

"*Salute, ma sirène*," Sin murmured into my air, his hot breath fanning over my exposed neck.

I shivered violently, prompting a dark chuckle from my lover.

"You kneel so prettily for me," he praised, stroking his hand firmly down my hair now. I arched into his stroking like a cat. "So eager to be seen as the perfect submissive for me."

"Yes, sir," I breathed, desperately wanting to squirm as my core started to throb with anticipation, but I knew Sin wouldn't like that.

"Should we put on a show for these lucky people, then?" he practically purred.

"Yes, please, sir."

"Mmm," he hummed as I sensed him stand at his full height again and move away.

There was a soft click of a clasp unlocking that I knew was his bag of toys and implements parting under his questing hands.

A moment later, the cool slide of silk across the curve of my neck and shoulder sent a shiver rippling down my spine. The audience around us hummed with anticipation as Sin sensuously moved the ribbon over my flesh until I broke out in goose bumps.

"I'm going to bind your beautiful breasts," he murmured to me, his hot breath stirring my hair as he bent to trail the scarf around my belly before sliding it up under the crease of my heavy chest. "I want them swollen and pink for me."

I hummed my approval, lost to reasonable sense as I sank deeper into sub space. He was careful only to touch me with the silk tie as he secured it under my boobs, then up over my back and down through the first band so that my breasts were separated and plumped up by the pressure of the bindings. I could feel the dull, warm thud of my pulse in each, my nipple aching for relief as they furled into hard points.

"I know." He hushed me as my breath came faster. "You're so

eager already, but we have so much farther to go before I let you come for me."

He ignored my whimper as he finished binding me, and his hand wrapped around me from behind to pluck hard at my nipples. I arched into his punishing grip, gasping at the ceiling, wondering dazedly how I might appear to the partygoers, wantonly displayed for my Dom.

"Gorgeous," Sinclair praised as one hand trailed down the middle of my breasts to the inside of my left thigh.

I gasped as he delivered a sharp slap there and ordered, "Spread yourself wider for me."

I adjusted instantly, so eager to please that I splayed myself open until my thighs ached from the strain.

"Yes," he hissed softly as his fingers trailed along the delicate skin on the inside of my thighs, making passes back and forth but never deigning to touch my throbbing core.

I was shaking after a few minutes of this mindless sensation play, my head lolling back on my loose neck, my mouth open for my panting breath.

"My siren loves to be on display and admired like the work of art you are," he finally murmured as his fingers trail lightly, too lightly, up the seam of my drenched sex.

On cue, another pair of hands landed on my body, jerking me into sudden alertness until I heard the crooning French tones of Cage.

"It's just me, cherie," he murmured lowly as he moved his big calloused hands over my arms up into my hair so he could hold it away from my neck as Sinclair dipped to puncture kisses down the length of it.

"Cage is here as a prop," Sinclair explained in that cold, exacting voice that made me shiver. "He is here to remind you that I am in charge of your body. That I will always give you what you need, even if you don't know how to voice it. He is here to ground you because, Elle? I am going to fuck you so hard you go flying."

"Oh my God." The words rushed from my mouth like air from a

punctured balloon as my hips rolled and wetness leaked down my thighs.

Why was this so hot?

Years of play, and I never grew used to the heady knowledge that I was Sinclair's. His to do with what he pleased, what would inevitably please me because he knew me better than I knew myself sometimes.

And I'd needed this.

This worship.

This admiration.

I was a mother to two young, busy, and gifted kids. It was a round-the-clock job that owned most of my life and a considerable amount of my identity, especially in the past six months of my hectic life.

Somehow, Sinclair had read my soul as he'd been able to do since the very beginning on that plane to Mexico.

He'd known I needed a night to be nothing but flesh and bone.

Nothing but sex and sin.

Nothing but my womanliness.

Nothing but his.

"How does that sound, hmm?" Sinclair asked huskily against my neck before sinking his teeth into the column in a way that had me moaning.

He knew I wanted it, but he always loved the sound of my voice soaked in lust.

"Yes, please, sir," I said, loud enough for the voyeurs to hear. "I want to be held down and fucked hard."

He made a sexy noise in his throat halfway between a groan and a growl before he was suddenly standing up, leaving my back exposed to the cool air.

"Cage, take my spot," he ordered implacably.

They switched, Cage sitting behind me, his arms banded over my lower stomach to hold me in place, his strong torso a chair for me to lean on. It was an oddly comforting and asexual hold that only heightened the eroticism of the act. He was just a prop, another means to bend me to Sin's will, and I loved it.

Meanwhile, Sin moved in front of me. I didn't know exactly what he was doing behind the blindfold until suddenly his hands were on my thighs, dragging me closer to his open mouth beneath me. I shuddered violently as his lips sealed over my soaking pussy, unerringly finding my throbbing clit.

My hips tried to churn, pressing down harder for more friction because I was already *this close* to coming, but Cage held me intractably still. I made a keening noise I might have been embarrassed about if I wasn't under the entrancing domination of my Frenchman.

"Please, sir," I begged as I tried to thrash in Cage's hold.

Sinclair ignored me.

Instead, he feasted like a starved man on my sex, sucking on my folds, tongue fucking my clasping entrance, flicking his tongue deliciously over my sensitive clit.

"Please, please," I started to chant just under my breath.

He didn't tell me to be quiet. He just listened to my increasingly loud pleas until I was almost sobbing with the need to come.

"You look beautiful obeying him like this," Cage whispered in my ear, and his praise of my submission just sent me higher.

"Sir, please!" My shouted words punctured the air as I arched as deeply as I could into Sin's magic mouth.

He pulled away just enough to say like a commander in the Navy, "Come for me, siren."

A moment later, his teeth were sinking into the tender flesh at the inside of my thigh, his fingers pinched my clit and then abruptly released, and I was coming.

Orgasming so hard I lost my breath as every single one of my muscles contracted almost painfully around the explosion of pleasure at my center.

"Such a good wife." Sinclair's voice found me in the fog as my orgasm receded, and I was vaguely aware of Cage moving away from me, and Sinclair turning me with strong, sure hands to better face the audience as he moved behind me.

It was only when I felt the hot head of his cock notch at my center that I clued back into reality. Instantly, I tried to thrust down on him.

His cruel, smoky chuckle wound around me like extra bondage.

"No, no, hold yourself still for me while I wedge the head of my cock in this tight little pussy and make you come all down my cock. If you come all over me, I may reward you with a nice hard fucking after," he promised.

My thighs quivered as I held myself poised high enough to take just the very tip of his dick inside myself, but the urge to take him to the hilt made me moan and whine without shame.

"Hush, siren," he ordered as one hand went to my swollen breasts, alternating between pinching and twisting each nipple while the other arrowed straight to my weeping, swollen sex where he gently drew tight little circles over my clit.

"Oh my god," I panted again and again, my hips jerking slightly as I fought the insatiable urge to seat myself to the hilt on his gorgeous shaft. "Oh my god, Sin, please."

"Are you going to show all these lucky people how gorgeous you are when you obey me?" He continued to speak to me as he played me like a maestro, plucking, pulling, and coaxing music from my sucking wet pussy, from my taxed lungs and my panting mouth. "Are you going to show them how hard you come for me when I play with you like this? How sweet your pussy looks leaking all over my length?"

"Yes, sir," I almost shouted, the last syllable fading into a ragged groan.

Sweat beaded over every inch of my body.

My mind was empty of words except those, the "yes, sir" a muscle memory, a submissive reflex more than conscious thought.

Everything I was other than his had faded away into the blackness, and the only light I could see was the beauty of his love and possession over me.

"So fucking beautiful," he moaned into my ear. "Kiss me when you come for me. I want to eat those sweet moans off your tongue. They might get to see you come all over me, but only I get to feel it."

His words triggered the release as a climax shot through me like a bullet from a gun, tearing down my center as I fractured open under the pressure. Vaguely, I was aware of the wet sloshing noise as Sinclair clamped his hands over my hips and ruthlessly thrust me down to the hilt on his cock.

I screamed as my release spiraled higher, as he started to fuck up into me savagely, his punishing grip giving me nowhere to run. I accepted his rough fucking the way I accepted harsh criticism as an artist, knowing it made me better, wanting to be driven farther, harder.

I gasped and groaned and yelled Sinclair's name like it was the only word I'd ever known.

And when his voice rose to call my name to the heavens a moment later, the sound of them together, Sinclair and his Elle, settled something in my soul I hadn't known needed ironing out.

Even though we'd been busy, with little time for intimacy, even though we'd been together for ten years and had two kids, this was the truth of our lives.

The truth of us.

Sinclair and Elle.

Our love for each other was bigger than anything that might come at us, try to separate us, test us.

And as I came down from that physical high, Sinclair read my mind again as he held my damp, lax body close and brushed a tender kiss over my throbbing pulse before whispering, "*Mon amour pour toi est plus grand que le monde.*"

"Forever," I murmured back, knowing in a way I didn't think I ever could have comprehended before that our love was the backbone of our lives, and nothing and no one would ever change that.


*Le Fin.*
The End.

## Enthralled, (The Enslaved Duet, #1)
## Excerpt

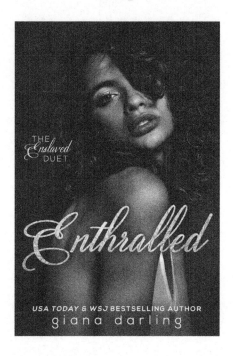

**From Amazon top 40 best selling author Giana Darling comes a dark, twisted tale of an Italian woman sold into slavery to a cold, calculating British modern day Earl with his own dark agenda...**

It was the biggest day of my life.

I know most people say that about something joyous; a graduation, a wedding ceremony, the birth of their first child. My situation was a little different.

Sure, it was my eighteenth birthday, but it was also the day that I was sold.

Sold to a man with hair like a crown of gold and eyes blacker than the darkest pits of Hell.

He bought me to own me, to control me, and to use me as a means to an end.

I was his tool and his weapon.

And through it all, somehow, I also became his salvation.

# Enthralled: Chapter One Preview

*I*t was the biggest day of my life.

I know most people say that about something joyous; a graduation, a wedding ceremony, the birth of their first child.

My situation was a little different.

Sure, it was my eighteenth birthday, but it was also the day I was sold.

And I don't mean sold metaphorically. As far as I was concerned, my soul was still intact although my father might have been selling his in return for the thousands of dollars he would receive for my body. He wasn't that worried about it. And honestly, neither was I. If Seamus Moore had a soul at one time, it had long ago dissolved into cinders and ash.

You're probably wondering why I went along with it. Even as I sat in the beaten-up red Fiat my twin brother, Sebastian, had just fixed for the fortieth time beside my potentially soulless father who was singing along to Umberto Tozzi as if it was a normal day, I was wondering the same thing. My eldest sister Elena was taking a free online ethics course, and even she didn't know the moral answer to the question my life had been reduced to—was exchanging one body worth the price of multiple persons' happiness?

I didn't really care that she didn't have a response. To me, it was worth it.

"You remember what I told you, *carina*?" my father asked over the tinny swell of sound from the car speakers.

"*Si.*"

"In English," he reprimanded gently with a crooked smile in my direction. It was as if I was just being a silly child and teasing him with my mini rebellion. I wanted to tease his skin with the edge of a cold blade, but I held my tongue between my teeth and bit down hard until the fantasy dissolved in pain.

"Tell me," he continued.

"No."

His hand found my slim thigh, and his steely fingers wound around it in a rough squeeze. I was used to his physicality, and it did not intimidate me, not now when I faced a potentially much more dangerous future. But I indulged him anyway.

"I am not to look his eyes—"

"*In* his eyes," he corrected.

"*In* his eyes. Or speak unless I am directly spoken to. I will obey him in all things and keep him in comfort. I understand, *papa*, it is like Italian marriage, but with a contract instead of vows." I was fluent in the language, but stress ate at my erudite mind like termites.

He grunted, unamused with my droll comparison. Even though Seamus was not Italian—his Irish accent, deep red hair, and ruddy complexion would always betray him as otherwise—he had assimilated himself into every facet of the culture until being Italian had become a kind of religion to him. And my father's version of a priest? Let's just say, you'd never want to meet Rocco Abruzzi, the man who ran a large gambling operation for the current Neapolitan *capo*, Salvatore Vitale. He was unassuming enough with flaccid features and brows that sagged over wet black eyes, but he had unusually large hands and he liked to use them to deal cards, diddle women, and pound in the faces of those who reneged on debts, those like my father.

Seamus drew a hand over the lingering bruises on the right side of his jaw with fingers that were scabby and missing their nails. There was only one reason, in his mind, that I was being sold. And that was to pay off his incredible debt to the underground leaders of Napoli. For years, I wished that they would just finish him off, slice him up and drop him into an alley somewhere for someone to find and kick at, too afraid to report the murder to the police. A few times, when he had been missing for long enough, I thought my fantasy had come true only for him to show up the next day, bright eyed and bushy tailed as if he had been at the spa, and not on the run from men with wet eyes and bloody hands.

"You must speak English with him, *carina*, in case he does not speak Italian."

I straightened at the information, not because I was uncomfortable speaking English. Seamus had made sure that all of us could speak it to some extent and I had studied rigorously for the past two years with Sebastian. If we were going to get out, English was going to be a thread in our lifeline. No, what had startled me was my own father's lack of knowledge about who was waiting for us in a villa inside Rome.

"You don't know who is buying me?" My grinding teeth made my words gravelly, but I knew he could still understand me.

My heart was in my stomach, and that was in my throat. I felt like one of Picasso's strange imaginings, my body twisted up with tension and fear so that I couldn't even recognize myself as human anymore. I was trying to focus on anything but the great and terrifying unknown of my future—the dust motes in our dirty car, the smell of alcohol leaking from my father's pores, or the way the hot southern Italian sun burned through the windows like flames.

"I hope you aren't going to question your new..." He paused. "... guardian like that, Cosima. Remember, respect. Have I taught you nothing?"

"Yes. You've taught me to distrust men, never blindly obey anyone, and to curse God for giving you the capacity to father children," I said blandly.

I could focus on the hatred of my father that blazed like a dying star in my belly instead of that awful fear threatening to overwhelm me.

Hatred was more powerful than fear. One was a shield and an armament I could utilize while the other could only be weaponised against me.

"Be grateful someone is willing to pay for you."

"How much?" I had refrained from asking so far, but my pride wouldn't allow me to go on unknowing. How much was I worth? How much money could be found in the flare of my hip and the divot of my collarbone, in the meat of my tits and the folds of my sex?

It was his turn to grind his teeth, but I wasn't surprised that he didn't answer me. Honestly, I didn't think even he knew. It was a perverted friend of a perverted friend of my father who had set up the interaction, some human trafficker that Seamus had played cards with one time when he was drunk enough to admit he needed money and give away the secret of his beautiful daughter, the virgin. His trump card, as he often, tenderly, referred to me as.

The news had gotten back to the Camorra, and the rest was history.

"For how long?" I asked, and it wasn't the first time I'd done so. "He can't possibly own me for the rest of my natural born life?"

"No," he conceded. "A period of five years was promised... with the possibility of renewing the contract again for double the price."

"And how much of this dirty money will Mama and my siblings see?" I demanded even as my mind whirred.

Five years.

*Five.*

I'd be twenty-three when all was said and done. If I was off the modelling track for that long, I would be too old to continue to any kind of fame and fortune. I could have done without both, but I wanted to be able to provide for my family until the end of their days.

If I were a twenty-three-year-old washed-up model without any education to speak of, I wouldn't be able to do that.

So, some of the windfall from my sale *had* to go to my family.

There wasn't any other option.

"Enough to cover my debts," he admitted, adjusting his sweaty hands on wheel. "Nothing more."

I closed my eyes and rested my forehead against the windowpane, bringing up the sepia toned snapshot of my childhood home in my mind's eye. A box of concrete pasted together by crumbling mortar and bandaged with planks of brittle wood my brother had cut himself. It was a small home on the outskirts of Naples in a part of town the tourists could never reach even if they became lost. My city was a place of dangers and illusions; webs cast between buildings and at the end of roads, catching you in their sticky fibers just as you reached for a promise behind the netting. No one could escape it, yet tourists came, and people stayed.

I didn't want my family to be condemned to those depths forever. There was no way I was going to sell my life away for anything less than security for my family.

Seamus shot me a concerned look. "I can feel you thinking, Cosi. Put a stop to it right now. You are in no position to ask for anything more."

"And you are in no position to tell me what to do or think," I retorted.

Just when I thought I had a lock on the anger, he had to do something to break those chains. I hated the taste of fury in my throat, and the metallic bite of it on my tongue. I wasn't a senseless, angry woman. I was passionate, but to a point.

Elena had taught me from a young age that if you could understand something, its motivation or context, you held power over it and over your reaction to it.

I tried to channel that now as I sat in a car with my father on the way to my new master with little to no assurances for the people I was even doing this for.

As the car pulled farther away from the spidery tendrils, I could feel the throbbing pulse of the city recede at my back. It wasn't beautiful like the rest of the country, though it rested on the ocean. The harbor was industrial, and though it was only an hour away from Roma, unemployment plagued Neapolitans like the Black Death, and it showed in the dirty faces of adolescent pickpockets and garbage strewn across the walkways in place of pretty flower boxes. People were tired in my hometown, and it showed. But I wondered how people couldn't find a certain beauty in that?

I didn't want to leave. It wasn't my choice, yet I had accepted the pain of its inevitability easily, my body absorbing the shock without consequence. My love for crumbling, beautiful Napoli was a drop in the bucket compared to my love for my crumbling, beautiful family. I was doing this, selling my body and maybe my soul, for them. I'd get them some of the money they were due or else the sale was dead in the water. The mafia would kill my father; we would still be haunted by the looming shadow of their influence, and we might never get out of that godforsaken city alive, but at least we'd be together.

I drew up their beloved faces in my mind's eyes, etching them into the black screens of my lids so that every time I blinked, I would be reminded of the reason for my sacrifice.

I knew all too well the realities of our situation. If Sebastian didn't leave soon, no matter our economic status, he would be forced into the Camorra, who had been nipping none too gently at his tender heels for the past two years. He was now eighteen, old for recruitment when the average age of youth inducement into the mafia was as young as eleven.

I squeezed my eyes shut to distort the vivid image of my male self with a gun in one hand, blood on the other, and money, stacks of it, in his mouth. Sebastian was smart and able, afflicted with a beauty so striking it often brought him unwanted attention. I hoped that he would use some of the money to leave, maybe for Roma, and use his beauty to pull himself out of the stinking hole of poverty we had been born into. Even though I knew he wouldn't—couldn't—bring himself to leave our sisters and mother alone, I chose to believe my fantasy.

Just as I hoped that the money would continue to go toward the education of my prodigal younger sister, Giselle, so gifted with a pencil or brush that she could render whole people on a page with their emotions and blood trapped beneath the surface of her painted strokes. I'd been practically living in Milano and Roma for the past year working any gig I could get in order to send back money for Giselle's education at *L'École des Beaux-Arts* in Paris. She was too talented to be held back by our poverty, and too pretty and soft at heart to deal with the shark-infested waters of Napoli. I knew last year when Elena's older boyfriend began to take undue notice of our shy sister that she had to leave. Her education was funded on my ability to provide for it with my modelling, and now that I was being sold, I needed to assure she would have the means to continue without me.

Ideally, funds would be left over for my smartest sibling, Elena, so she could attend a real school and earn a real degree. For Mama, a new home with a kitchen well equipped to deal with her delicious fare. And for my father—the man who just then was driving me towards my future as a bought woman? Well, for Seamus Moore, I could only wish for the best his soul would buy him in this life. A quick death.

# Thanks etc.

I cannot believe we have reached the end of The Evolution of Sin Trilogy! I first conceived of Sinclair and Giselle's romance when I was sixteen years old and I wrote it down in a notebook only to discover it years later. I loved the idea of pitting loyalty and blood against passion and true love. Sometimes, people are too obsessed with what is right and wrong instead of what is best for them. I admire both of these characters for having the chutzpah to face the consequences of their love and their actions; I hope you do too.

I have so many people to extend my heartfelt thanks to for encouraging me throughout writing this series and throughout my first year as a published author. I have to start with Kiki and Amber at The Next Step PR; they supported me through rookie questions, family emergencies and three release blitzes. They are my writer's guardian angels and I love them endlessly for going above and beyond for me!

Najla Qamber from Najla Qamber Designs is a graphic genius. I loved everything she created for this series; no one could have more perfectly captured my vision.

Patricia, my feisty editor and friend, has been a constant cheerleader and keen eye. She is the type of person I have met through writing that makes me so proud and grateful to be an author. You have here to thank for the lack of typos in all my manuscripts!

Also, thank you to Jenny Sims from Editing 4 Indies for giving this book new life.

My beta readers, Mela, Angela Plumlee, Eliza and Belle, thank you so much for reading my rough and tough first/second drafts! You ladies provide me with invaluable feed back <3

I wouldn't be a writer at all without the love of my best friends. They have encouraged me my entire life to follow my dreams, however unrealistic and potentially dirty they may be! I would be half a woman without you two.

Even though it hurts, I have to thank the love of my life, H, for teaching me how to love, how to worship and how to let go even when it hurts. You are the context behind my romanticism and certainly behind my eroticism.

And finally, my readers! Thank you, thank you, THANK YOU for being so patient as I dealt with all that life had to deal out to me this past year. You waited so long and so beautifully for Sinclair and Elle's happily ever after, I hope I didn't let you down. Stay tuned, darlings, and thank you again from the bottom of my heart!

# About Giana Darling

Giana Darling is a *USA Today*, *Wall Street Journal*, Top 40 Best Selling Canadian romance writer who specializes in the taboo and angsty side of love and romance. She currently lives in beautiful British Columbia where she spends time riding on the back of her man's bike, baking pies, and reading snuggled up with her cat, Persephone, and dog, Romeo.

Join my Reader's Group
Subscribe to my Newsletter
Follow me on IG
Like me on Facebook
Follow me on Goodreads
Follow me on BookBub
Follow me on Pinterest

# Other Books by Giana Darling

## The Evolution of Sin Trilogy

*Giselle Moore is running away from her past in France for a new life in America, but before she moves to New York City, she takes a holiday on the beaches of Mexico and meets a sinful, enigmatic French businessman, Sinclair, who awakens submissive desires and changes her life forever.*

*The Affair*

*The Secret*

*The Consequence*

*The Evolution Of Sin Trilogy Boxset*

## The Fallen Men Series

*The Fallen Men are a series of interconnected, standalone, erotic MC romances that each feature age gap love stories between dirty-talking, Alpha males and the strong, sassy women who win their hearts.*

*Lessons in Corruption*

*Welcome to the Dark Side*

*Good Gone Bad*

*After the Fall*

*Inked in Lies*

*Dead Man Walking*

*A Fallen Men Companion Book of Poetry:*
King of Iron Hearts

The Enslaved Duet

*The Enslaved Duet is a dark romance duology about an eighteen-year old Italian fashion model, Cosima Lombardi, who is sold by her indebted father to a British Earl who's nefarious plans for her include more than just sexual slavery... Their epic tale spans across Italy, England, Scotland, and the USA across a five-year period that sees them endure murder, separation, and a web of infinite lies.*

*Enthralled (The Enslaved Duet #1)*

*Enamoured (The Enslaved Duet, #2)*

The Elite Seven Series

*Sloth (The Elite Seven Series, #7)*

Coming Soon

Fallen King (A Fallen Men Short Story)

*When Heroes Fall (Anti-Heroes in Love, #1)*

*When Villains Rise (Anti-Heroes in Love, #2)*

Printed in Great Britain
by Amazon

45728441R00215

HERBS

OILS

NUTRITION

Marie D. Jones

# Natural Health

## Your Complete Guide to Natural Remedies and Mindful Well-Being

MEDITATION

SUPPLEMENTS

EXERCISE

# MORE VISIBLE INK PRESS BOOKS
## BY MARIE D. JONES

*Celebrity Ghosts and Notorious Hauntings; Demons, the Devil, and Fallen Angels*
ISBN: 978-1-57859-689-8

*Demons, the Devil, and Fallen Angels*
ISBN: 978-1-57859-613-3

*The Disaster Survival Guide: How to Prepare for and Survive Floods, Fires, Earthquakes and More*
ISBN: 978-1-57859-673-7

*Disinformation and You: Identify Propaganda and Manipulation*
ISBN: 978-1-57859-740-6

*Earth Magic: Your Complete Guide to Natural Spells, Potions, Plants, Herbs, Witchcraft, and More*
ISBN: 978-1-57859-697-3

*The New Witch: Your Guide to Modern Witchcraft, Wicca, Spells, Potions, Magic, and More*
ISBN: 978-1-57859-716-1

*Toxin Nation: The Poisoning of Our Air, Water, Food, and Bodies*
ISBN: 978-1-57859-765-9

# ALSO FROM VISIBLE INK PRESS

*The American Women's Almanac: 500 Years of Making History*
by Deborah G. Felder
ISBN: 978-1-57859-636-2

*The Big Book of Facts*
by Terri Schlichenmeyer
ISBN: 978-1-57859-720-8

*The Handy American Government Answer Book: How Washington, Politics and Elections Work*
by Gina Misiroglu
ISBN: 978-1-57859-639-3

*The Handy Anatomy Answer Book*, 2nd edition
by Patricia Barnes-Svarney and Thomas E. Svarney
ISBN: 978-1-57859-542-6

*The Handy Answer Book for Kids (and Parents)*, 2nd edition
by Gina Misiroglu
ISBN: 978-1-57859-219-7

*The Handy Biology Answer Book*, 2nd edition
by Patricia Barnes-Svarney and Thomas E. Svarney
ISBN: 978-1-57859-490-0

*The Handy Chemistry Answer Book*
by Ian C. Stewart and Justin P. Lomont
ISBN: 978-1-57859-374-3

*The Handy Diabetes Answer Book*
by Patricia Barnes-Svarney and Thomas E. Svarney
ISBN: 978-1-57859-597-6